WANTING RITA

A Novel

Elyse Douglas

Broadback Books

Copyright © 2012-2024 Elyse Douglas

All rights reserved

The characters and events portrayed in this book are fictitious. Any similarity to real persons, living or dead, is coincidental and not intended by the author.

No part of this book may be reproduced, or stored in a retrieval system, or transmitted in any form or by any means, electronic, mechanical, photocopying, recording, or otherwise, without express written permission of the publisher.

ISBN: 9781484958117

Cover design by: Ken Kenyon
Library of Congress Control Number: 2018675309
Printed in the United States of America

For Lana

*Flare up like a flame
and make big shadows I can move in.
Let everything happen to you: beauty and terror.
Just keep going. No feeling is final.
Don't let yourself lose me.*

                                              RAINER MARIA RILKE

Part One
Now and Then

CHAPTER ONE

"She'll be there, Alan," Mrs. Fitzgerald said, in a quiet, hopeful voice. "She'll be at Jack's Diner. She's been working there for a month now. It...well, it would just be a good thing...a nice thing if you could..." Her voice trailed off, then grew weak and brittle. "You're the only person she's asked about. But... you must be so busy. I mean, I know doctors are always busy. Of course, you're busy, but... Well, if you could just go and see her..."

Then there was desperation. "I'm sorry to call you at your office, but I just thought...well, if she saw some old friends. She needs to...get out and..."

I'd heard that voice frequently working in the ER during my residency. A voice stripped of pride by a mounting panic.

"She'll be so glad to see you again, Alan. I just know it. She was always so fond of you, you know."

Just as I was about to end the conversation, she broke down, repeating the story of Rita's tragedy in deep sighs and choking sobs. I waited, impatiently. She rambled and paused, hoping for a response. I didn't offer any, so she continued on with a weepy intensity, with anger, remorse, and an occasional hacking cough. I listened coolly, aloof, frequently checking my watch. I was already behind. Patients were complaining to reception. I had mountains of paperwork to do and I hadn't eaten lunch.

Mrs. Fitzgerald persisted, with surging emotion. Her pace became a desperate sprint to the finish line, jumping from self-pity to scorn, to cursing, to rage. She trampled on all my efforts to cut her off. So I waited for the end of emotion; for the end of her confessions; for the shattered voice that finally fell into a withering and feeble "Oh, God... please go see Rita... Please..."

I wasn't moved in that hollow silence. My heart contracted with an icy chill—with the rush of unwanted memories. I wasn't even moved when she timidly called my name to see if I was still there.

"Yes... I'm here, Mrs. Fitzgerald, but I have to go now. Thank you for calling."

I hung up, abruptly, without another word. I wanted to erase her—erase the entire population of Hartsfield, Pennsylvania—from my mind.

I'd already heard the story. My sister, Judy, had called eight months before, stunned, teary and grateful to share. Two hours later, an old friend from high school, whom I hadn't heard from in six years, called me stammering, shocked, and depressed. Then my father had called, using cold, sharp words. "They were trash. Didn't you date that girl a couple of times? What was her name... Rita?"

It had briefly hit the national news, I was told, although I didn't see it because I was in Barbados on vacation when it happened. Of course it upset me. It would upset anyone, but I had never been particularly fond of Mrs. Fitzgerald when I was a kid. And when I was a kid living in Hartsfield, she'd never been particularly fond of me. But then, with few exceptions, nobody was. Except Rita. Rita, at least for a fleeting miraculous time, had been fond of me. Perhaps, she had even loved me. And I, without a doubt—any doubt—had loved her.

Mrs. Fitzgerald's phone call had surprised me. I hadn't seen her in five or six years, since spending the Christmas holidays with my parents in Hartsfield. We had passed in the drugstore. As she approached, her eyes had flickered down and away, hoping to avoid me. But I didn't let her. I was in medical school and an imposter of maturity.

"Merry Christmas," I'd said, friskily.

She scarcely paused, her eyes still not meeting mine. "Home to see the folks?" she'd asked, meekly.

"Yep."

"Nice."

"How's Rita?"

She struggled for a bright tone. "Good. Still living in Oklahoma."

"Good."

"Still in school?" she asked.

"Yeah... still at it. Takes a long time to be a doctor."

She hurried away; then, after a quick backward glance of sorrow, she exited the store.

I hadn't thought of her since. But I had thought

of Rita. Rita was hard to forget. She was one of the most exciting things that had ever happened to me growing up in Hartsfield. Rita Fitzgerald, "The Blond Blaze of Hartsfield, P.A.," the local paper had once described her. Rita Fitzgerald, who had gone from ugly duckling in elementary and junior high schools, to a dazzling beauty in high school. Rita Fitzgerald, who had won the local beauty pageant two years in a row, and had sky-rocketed to local stardom. In her senior year, Rita was eighteen when most of us were still seventeen. Because of illness, she'd lost most of a year and had had to repeat a grade. Rita Fitzgerald was my first love.

On Saturday morning, two days after Mrs. Fitzgerald's phone call, I drove the 212 miles from Manhattan to Hartsfield. The night before, I told my wife, Nicole, that I had to do something with that damned house.

"If it wasn't so far away, we could rent it out during the year and use it as a summer home," she said.

I cringed at the thought. "No way. The quicker it's gone, the better."

I entered the town limits, seeing it with familiar eyes and old memories, hands sweaty on the steering wheel from humidity and a touch of nerves. I did want to see Rita again, and I had a tabloid curiosity about the tragedy's aftermath and the town's current psychological reaction to it. And my ego had purred when Mrs. Fitzgerald mentioned that Rita had asked about me, although secretly I'd doubted it. I certainly didn't want to return to Hartsfield. I was not, nor had I ever been, particularly comfortable growing up there. But I had been putting off a trip. Six months before, my father had suffered a stroke, and Judy and I had moved him to Florida to live with her and her family. Judy was also managing some real estate that Dad had purchased in Florida in the mid 1990's, so it was agreed that it was my duty to sell the Hartsfield Queen Anne Victorian house, with its ten acres, and most of its contents.

After seeking advice and doing some of my own research, I'd decided to have an estate auction. My father vehemently opposed it. "That house has been in the family for generations," he protested, in his now trembling voice.

But I didn't want to live in Hartsfield, and Judy's life was with her husband and their children in Florida. Mom had died two years before of cancer, and none of her family wanted the house. Dad's family had moved away years before, expressing no interest in returning to or purchasing the house.

The physical and fiscal responsibility of maintaining the place, from over two hundred miles away, was not practical and, frankly, I just wanted to be free of it.

So it was May, and I was returning to Hartsfield for what I thought would be one of my final pilgrimages. After the house sold, I had no intention of returning and every intention of trying to erase even the faintest memories of the place.

But I did want to see Rita; if only from a distance; if only for a few minutes.

Hartsfield had been a factory town, producing thermal underwear, t-shirts, pajamas and other apparel. The wages were modest, but most workers lived within their means and considered the simple way of life a good one. Nearly everyone worked for a factory or in some vigorous support of them. The factories had been the temples of commerce, employment and ambition. They nurtured gossip, friendship and the occasional stirring romance.

The long red brick factories helped to define the culture, the attitudes and the political debate. They supported community pride and ethical works. They were the throb and pulse of Hartsfield. They were the hearts.

After graduating from high school, people went to work for the factories, expecting to reap an equitable retirement. It was a good and decent middle-class life. Up through the 1960s, workers could expect a yearly raise, lessening the gap between rich and poor. The great equalizer was the sense of purpose: the gift of having a job that enriched the worker, the family, the community and the world.

The roads to and from the factories carried workers past sweeping hills, arching trees and scattered lakes, to modest neighborhood homes, churches, schools, shops and cozy bars. They passed the baseball diamond and the once new mall, tattered now, a silent testament to hard times. The main road continued across a covered bridge, dipped and meandered out to the peaceful hills and quiescent groves, where deferential oaks and elms stirred lazily over graveyards. Here, generations of Hartsfield's best and worst lay side by side; their joys and sufferings, their ambitions and family failures proudly remembered and shared by the living.

But everything had changed several years ago. One by one, the factories closed. The hearts stopped. The companies moved away or outsourced to Honduras and China. The factory buildings, with smokeless chimneys, became cold shells, empty of consciousness, where restless birds darted from shattered windows, and newspapers sailed the parking lots with old frantic headlines shouting out for attention; shouting out for relief from pain. *How Can We Compete with 55 Cents an Hour*!? they asked.

I'd read about it in the *New York Times* and, before his stroke, my father had kept me informed, not that he was ever impacted in any way. He'd been a financial advisor and owned an accounting business, with wealthy clients as far away as Pittsburgh, Philadelphia and Chicago. He'd never lacked for work. We were considered rich, although I'd never really thought of it that way. I had believed that no one who was truly wealthy would ever live in Hartsfield.

The young were moving away. The old were being retrained to work elsewhere or nowhere, but it gave them something to do. It gave their minds something to cogitate on. Middle-aged men, with low chins and sloping shoulders, now padded the empty streets, bracing themselves with memories of the days when they worked 60 or 70 hours a week, on weekends and holidays—whenever they were needed. Now, they wandered like old dogs, sniffing about, looking for distraction, pushing down anger and depression, realizing that Hartsfield would soon be a ghost town.

Many women had graduated from high school and marched to the factories in triumph. They raised families. They missed little league games, bake sales and picnics, but that was fine because the factories needed them, and the factories were the hearts. They were the trust; the saving grace. They were the promise and security in old age.

But globalization called. It was business. The global people were calling. Eager, strong hands demanded work. A higher profit for factory and shareholders beckoned; a better life for foreign workers. The workers there worked for less—but over there, less was good. There, the factories were becoming temples of commerce; the trust; the saving grace. There, Hartsfields were being born.

I didn't think about it so much then. I didn't think about the people and their monumental struggles. That would come later. After I saw Rita again.

It was raining. Slanting steel-gray arrows pocked

the streets and the maroon Saab, sounding like little pebbles. I drove through a quieter town than I had recalled, passing red-brick Victorian store fronts, cast-iron street lamps, and weathered row houses with their missing shingles; they reminded me of the old and the toothless.

City streets had buckled under the punishing winter, unrepaired, a clear indication that money and spirits were low. Sidewalks were broken and warped in sections, twisting and rising like the unexpected track of a rollercoaster. I swerved to miss chug holes and damned up pools around blocked drains.

I turned left on Poplar Street and drove past the tall oaks, maples and elms which skirted the road. They were nearly fully leaved and moving in bursts of wind. I was suddenly lifted by their abundance, because I'd forgotten that. I'd forgotten how beautiful the trees were. I slowed down and took in their sturdy trunks, remembering that Rita and I had roamed them once, hand in hand. She'd stopped, abruptly, and thrown her head back, skyward, raking strands of golden hair from her eyes. The quick autumn wind had tossed it in luminous waves and I'd wanted to grab handfuls of it. I wanted to tackle her, wrestle her and love her. But I didn't. I stood planted, like an oak, looking as bleak as a winter day, because that was my style.

She'd shaded her eyes with the flat of her elegant hand and shouted, "Hello trees! I bet you're even smarter than Alan James!" Then she bowed to them, like a princess at court, while I looked on, perplexed and rigid.

"You are SOoooo damn stiff, Alan James," she'd said. "Bow to the trees. They're always bowing to you."

But I was obstinate. I didn't bow. I was a certified nerd, with black framed glasses, short, stiff black hair and a wiry build. I was a rebel. Most of the other guys had long hair and, if they needed them, wore wire rimmed glasses or contacts. Not me.

"Why do you keep calling me Alan James, Rita? My name's Alan." Then after a temperamental pause, I said, "Nobody calls me Alan James."

She grinned, mischievously, and tossed her blond hair from her eyes. "Yes, Alan James, but we know why I call you Alan James, don't we?"

I drove on, nosing forward, peering into the gray haze at the ghostly red glow of neon lights looming ahead. JACK'S DINER. It was still there. The old hangout. Rita was in there, working. I felt the need to take a breath. My forehead was damp.

The parking lot wasn't full and that surprised me. This was the breakfast rush after all. Years ago, it would have been bloated with cars, with a line of restless customers waiting at the door. I found a parking space, shut down the engine and eased back, listening to the pecks and pings of rain, staring as the water washed and blurred the world, impressionistic.

Jack's Diner was a facade of two old, converted

Baltimore & Ohio dining cars, expanded and enhanced with old red brick, wrought-iron railings and a little red caboose. The diner had veins of red and yellow neon lights running along the edge of the roof and down the sides, which lit it up like a giant juke box. In the old days, you could smell hamburgers grilling for at least a quarter mile away, and when the music was high and driving, the place seemed to pulse with it.

Jack's had once been *the* place for private parties or win-or-lose late night football or basketball celebrations. It was a date stop before or after a movie. It was a cool-down stop after making out under the quiet pines and elms by the dirt road that threaded Crystal Lake. It had been there for at least 30 years, and it was something of a landmark. Rita and I had finished our third and final date there, I being sullen and seething, she, flirting with Dusty Palmer, the man she eventually married.

In the last two years of high school, Rita had blazed with a beauty and magnetism that burned through a crowd like wildfire. She possessed a kind of languid rapture and soft exotic glow that I compared to the starlets of the 1940's and 50's; that mysterious mixture of fire and ice that arrested the eyes and heart in a breathless expectation. She was art, with her refined aristocratic nose, long chiseled neck, and voice like pure unraveling silk. Her lips were red, full, and often parted, as if in want of a kiss, though there was no pretension in this. At least, I never thought so.

She was full-figured and statuesque, with honey blond hair that fell in waves over thin ivory shoulders, in a longing, really—in a natural invitation to touch and caress. And she moved in an easy rhythm, as if hearing distant pagan music, with a gentle sway of her hips that sent ripples of fervent pleasure through any gathering of guys, and a humid jealousy through any crowd of gals.

Rita had been the town treasure. The prom queen. The beauty queen. The trophy. Men with cigars on the Courthouse steps jerked nods of agreement that Hartsfield could produce more than just thermal underwear. They produced Rita Fitzgerald: beauty, talent and personality. She'd go somewhere, New York, LA, and become somebody, and they'd be the proud town fathers who had supported her, nurtured her and helped her along. She could sing and dance, and she wrote poems and short stories that were published in the local paper. She was even going to write a novel about Hartsfield. For weeks after this fact was published in the Sunday paper, I observed that teachers, neighbors and town folk all had broader smiles, softer dispositions and kind words, where few had been offered before.

Whenever she had shined her large sea-blue eyes on me, I saw tenderness, wonder and intelligence; and when she took me into them, fully, and held me for a time, I felt primitive and exalted. During those rare moments when Rita and I had been close and I felt her soft breath on my cheek or in my ear, and whenever she leaned into me and I smelled the spring scent of her and looked into her blue eyes, wide with magic, I saw them break into prisms of fire so magnificent that I often went dumb and silent with desire for her. She thought it was a morbid seriousness. That's what she'd called it.

"Alan James! You are always so serious. I wrote about it in my last short story. I described the character as having a morbid seriousness."

That had been our connection: Ms. Lyendecker's English class. We both wrote short stories, then exchanged and critiqued them. Ms. Lyendecker encouraged us and challenged us. Once when I said that I liked non-fiction better than fiction, because it was true and not a pack of lies, Ms. Lyendecker said, "If fiction is true, then it is non-fiction from the first word."

Ms. Lyendecker went to Columbia University, and taught at a college in Massachusetts for many years, returning to Hartsfield when her mother became terminally ill. Upon her mother's death, Ms. Lyendecker stayed in town, teaching English at Hartsfield High.

Technically, Rita and I only dated three times. But there were moments in the past fifteen years, when I could still feel and taste that "authentic" Rita kiss; and if I closed my eyes, I could transcend the hectic moment, the boredom of a meeting or the aching loneliness of a sleepless night and feel something like peace and fulfillment, as if the long search for home had finally come to an end.

But not everyone in town had been enamored with Rita—"taken in" were the words used by a small feverish group of teachers, parents and church brethren. These were the more pious and ethical folk, who were disturbed by Rita's dangerous femininity and meteoric rise to small town fame, as well as the potentially bad example she provided to the young and impressionable. They were also shaken in some profound way—driven to a blistering criticism of her and the entire youth culture of sex, drugs and rock and roll. Rita stirred the loins and prurient imaginations, as well as the hearts of Hartsfield. She was a living testimony to enlightenment or to perdition, depending on your particular lens on the world. Rita Fitzgerald was an old, old story that was continuously being revised in raptures of anxiety, pleasure and desire.

Four months after graduation, Rita married Dusty Palmer, the Viking Quarterback who looked like a Viking—the guy who had blazed right alongside of Rita the last six months of high school. The guy who never missed a mirror, glass or reflection. The guy who had always smiled at me—and it had seemed genuine—but I'd never smiled back. An easy, likeable guy, whom everyone seemed to have a good word for, including my father. When the Hartsfield Vikings football team won the division championship he'd said, "Dusty Palmer's got talent. No doubt about it." That really upset me. Dusty definitely wasn't a nerd. He'd even volunteered at the hospital as an orderly, the act of a sucker, I'd thought: working for nothing. I was certain he was only doing it for show, barnstorming his charitable works for Rita's delight and the nodding approval of the town.

Together, Rita and Dusty had celebrity wattage and star power. They turned heads and seized attention. They fired up old, withered hearts in Hartsfield, and beyond, when they announced they were going to go to Hollywood to be in the movies. Surely if anyone could make it on TV or in the movies, they could.

But they never made it to Hollywood. Dusty went to Penn State on a football scholarship, but blew his knee out his freshman year. Dispirited, and a poor student, he'd dropped out and moved back to Hartsfield to work at the factory. Rita enrolled at the community college at Riverton to get a teaching degree. After a year or so, Dusty got restless, so he and Rita left Hartsfield, probably to save face, as my mother said. They moved to Oklahoma, where Dusty went to work with his father in the family construction business.

When Rita's and Dusty's daughter was born, Dad sent me a clipping from the local Hartsfield paper.

> *Darla Hayworth Palmer has the fortunate beauty and blond hair of her mother and the gentle spirit of her father, it was reported by a family friend. 'She's just the most*

> *beautiful thing I have ever seen,'* Rita's mother, Betty Fitzgerald, was quoted as saying.

I sighed, angling a look at Jack's, reconsidering my decision to go inside, pondering whether I should skip breakfast altogether and just drive to the house. I had plenty to do. I had an appointment to meet the real estate agent and auctioneer that afternoon. Dad had waited much too long to sell the place. The real estate market had been bludgeoned and I was sure the house would bring much less than it was worth a few years earlier, despite the added baths, antiques, extensions to the bedrooms, and remodeled kitchen. But the auctioneer had been upbeat and positive, of course.

For a man with an inborn practicality and gift for numbers, Dad also had a great fear of change. He'd become sentimental and melancholy at the thought of vacating his family home, because of a vow he'd made to his father many years ago, and because he simply liked living in Hartsfield.

"I'd be like a damned retreating general," he once said. "No sir. I will not retreat. This is where I'll die. This house was built in 1870 and, God willing, it will be here until 2870." He said this only a month before the stroke buckled him to his knees, causing him to spill his coffee and drop his hardback copy of *The Autobiography of Benjamin Franklin.*

Dad had had to retreat after all, and during my last visit, I saw the disgrace of his retreat written on his gaunt, narrow face, as he sat on Judy's living room couch, diminutive and shaky.

As I stared vacantly ahead at the garish neon lights of Jack's Diner, I felt the rise of apprehension and dread. Surely Rita had changed. Had the tragedy blunted her beauty and zest for life? Did I really want to see her defeated and small, working as a waitress at Jack's Diner? Did she really want to see me?

I reached for my umbrella, zipped up my brown leather jacket and hesitated once more before pushing out. Retreat suddenly sounded good.

But I wanted to know, first hand, and not from gossip, newspapers or TV, why Dusty Palmer, the guy with that easy smile and gentle nature, entered their living room on that chilly September Sunday morning with a .45 caliber colt handgun.

In the past few days, I'd reread several accounts of the incident and had produced a movie in my head about the terrible sequence of events.

From the living room, Dusty walked deliberately into the kitchen, where he found his daughter, Darla, and his wife, Rita. His full head of hair had rapidly thinned and he was nearly bald. The Viking body had morphed into a chubby softness.

Darla, 12-years old, blond and glowing with grace, was seated at the kitchen table eating breakfast. As she turned toward him to say, "Good morning, Daddy," as she often did, he raised the gun and fired twice into her head. She died instantly.

The shots jolted Rita with a savage horror, but her brain locked up and froze her rigid. It took minutes, it seemed, before the yellow plate of pancakes slipped from her grasp and shattered on the floor. With its impact, her heart seemed to explode. She burst into a wild, agonizing scream.

Dusty was five feet away. He leveled the gun at Rita's head. His thick arm was steady, his hand still, his pool-blue eyes serene. Rita lost her voice. The sight of her lifeless daughter sent a knifing pain that washed her face to whiteness. Death eclipsed the fire in her eyes. Her screams fell into a near silent anguish, a low, terrifying moan.

Dusty was motionless. He did not seem to see. His eyes seemed to see nothing at all. Rita shut her wet eyes tightly, waiting for the slam and shock of the bullet's impact. Welcoming it. Praying for it. When she heard the shot, she screamed and kept screaming until she lost her voice. Until the next door neighbor rushed over.

Rita's eyes opened. Through tears and a stabbing shock, she saw Dusty sprawled on the floor. He'd blown the back of his head off.

CHAPTER TWO

I entered Jack's Diner. It seemed smaller and grimier than I had remembered, and it was immediately obvious that it had long lost its novelty and shine. The yellow plastic upholstered booths were sagging and patched with black masking tape, looking deflated and wounded. The almond tiled floors had worn, shiny gray patches around the cashier station and at the sloping entrances to the bathrooms. Faded yellow walls held old high school football, baseball and basketball team photos, where players stood or crouched in poses of strength, staring with the bold, proud eyes of conquerors. There was also the random oil painting of old trains, steaming through canyons and tunnels and across towering trestles, probably an art class project from many years ago.

Memories flooded back to me. The smell of coffee, bacon and eggs reminded me of early mornings, and that low dragging energy I felt after an unsuccessful night hunting for elusive excitement—or any girl who would stoop to talk to me. And for a brief moment, I had the gift of time travel to the past. I heard the toasts, the cheers and the shouting matches, the recaps after the games. I saw the proud glossy faces of old classmates roaming the booths, girlfriends in tow, slapping shoulders and smoking cigarettes, while Bon Jovi sang *Livin' On A Prayer* from the scratchy overhead speakers. I saw adults with bright eyes, straight backs and open grins, enjoying the show, remembering their day and believing that the cycle would go on like this forever.

That morning, Jack's wasn't busy. Four booths were vacant, as were two swivel chairs at the counter. There was no music from the speakers, and other than the occasional rattle of dishes and the dull ring of the order-up bell, there was an eerie pall, like a museum past closing time. Chins rested in hands over coffee, and sleepy eyes stared indifferently, avoiding the windows and the persistent rain, weakly acknowledging the plates of food when delivered. I plunged my dripping umbrella into the bucket along with others, stuffed my hands into my back jean pockets and lowered my head.

Waitresses in blue nylon dresses, with white ruffles at the hems, covered the floor in a lazy shuffle. I quickly examined their faces. I did not see Rita and I was grateful. I wanted to get settled first. Then it occurred to me that I may have seen her but didn't recognize her. After all, she could have changed, drastically.

I advanced to the counter, eyes down, shoulders up. I swung into the swivel chair, folded my hands on the sandy Formica countertop and waited, uneasily, feeling like that nerdy kid again, feeling my face tightening in defense and superiority. Did Rita know I was coming? Had her mother told her? Perhaps Rita had seen me and slipped away. Perhaps she hadn't come into work at all.

During one of Mrs. Fitzgerald's fiery stream of consciousness moments on the phone, she'd mentioned that Rita was writing again. "Real nice stories. Pretty stories." According to her mother, this was Rita's therapy now—a technique that had been suggested by her therapist to help point her mind away from the past, toward releasing pain creatively. After the tragedy, Rita had slipped away into a debilitating depression and had attempted suicide, by swallowing sleeping pills. Her mother had quietly and swiftly admitted her to a hospital near Philadelphia.

A waitress approached. I straightened, noticing mostly crooked teeth, short dyed red hair and the blank eyes of the bored. She wasn't familiar. She was older than I by about five or six years.

"Coffee?"

"Yes, thank you," I said.

She splashed it in. "Do you know what you want or do you need a menu?" she asked, with a powerful indifference.

"Oatmeal and a banana."

"Bowl? Cup?"

"Bowl."

Without acknowledgment, she slouched away.

I sipped carefully. The coffee tasted good. The men next to me spoke in a low monotone. Something about the Pittsburg Pirates. The pitching was a problem. They spoke about the rain. More this year than last. I looked over. They wore ball caps and denim jackets, and weren't familiar.

I suddenly became aware that I was hot and perspiring. Blood had rushed to my face. I slipped out of my jacket and draped it over the back of the chair. The drumming pulse in my neck was the further sign and symptom of "Rita Unease", or so I used to call it. The Rita Fever. The Rita Syndrome. I'd had many names for it. But I wasn't a kid anymore. I'd just turned 33.

I fixed my gaze on the dull yellow ceiling for a time, then followed the lazy turn of the ceiling fan, until my eyes traveled down the walls to a faraway place outside the rain spotted windows. Rita had always done this to me. She scared the hell out of me with all her beauty and wild spontaneity. She knocked me so far off balance that it often had taken me a full day and night to recover. Whenever she left me, I was in a perfect storm of instability and obsession and needed a compass to know where the hell I was and how to find my way home.

She unlocked and unfolded me, exposing burlesque emotions, astonishing potential and a terror so acute that it set my heart and mind reeling, like a biplane spinning out of control. But I was a kid then: a nerdy kid, skilled in the evasive arts of hiding behind books, severe eye narrowing, and a starched expression.

"I'm never playing poker with you, Alan James," Rita had once said. "I'd never win. I never know what's going on behind those dark gray eyes of yours. You're like a big reptile on a rock in the sun, Alan James. Staring without movement, awareness or ambition, and yet seeing everything and everybody. Then I can just imagine the tip of your sharp tongue flicking out at me, like a jet flame, darting its long pink mass into the deep portions of my cavernous mouth. Taking me in like a poor old helpless thing."

"You're reading too much Tennessee Williams," I shot back. "You sound like you're imitating Maggie in *Cat on a Hot Tin Roof*."

She went into her lazy southern accent. "And what if I am? I'm gonna play that role some day, Alan James." Then she playfully kicked one foot back and upward. "Ba-Boom!" she'd added, grinning.

I called it our first date, but in reality it was a simple meeting of Rita and me in Jack's, nervously exchanging our short stories over a soda, a hamburger and a large order of fries. Of course, I knew why she'd agreed to this little "date." I'd calculated it down to the exact minute, location and homework assignment. I had discovered Rita's weakness and I used it to my swift advantage.

I was unquestioningly the brightest kid in school and there was no doubt, whatsoever, that I would be valedictorian. It was my one bit of notoriety. Without it, I would have been just another unknown slob at Hartsfield High. But I had my distinction, and I owned it and guarded it like a miser guards his gold. I would be valedictorian, that was a given. I had been working on my speech for months, writing it on my Apple Power Mac computer. I excelled in academics the way Dusty excelled in sports, and everyone knew it.

Rita was intelligent—I knew that—but I also knew, from careful scrutiny, that she lacked a certain confidence in herself academically. It was the way she gently coughed before answering a question—stammering out the first few words before hitting her stride of logic. If she had a question, she'd raise her hand, not fully, and then she'd flash a quick coquettish smile that held more secrets than assurance. But it fertilized the barren atmosphere of the room, as well as the egghead of any adoring male teacher, producing effusive and desirous communication.

I'd delighted in studying every detail of her long regal neck, how it flushed red whenever she'd been given a break, an obvious favoritism, when, for instance, after a Herculean struggle with a calculus problem, Mr. Burkett, our math teacher, had offered her a possible solution which, of course, *was* the solution. Rita consistently lowered her head in defeat, eyes dull with disappointment in herself, even though Burkett always made it seem that she had answered correctly, and regularly praised her.

Despite a towering command and influence over all things male, over all people of authority and influence, male and female, I had observed, with sweet relish, that Rita Fitzgerald did not believe in herself. What a happy day that was! What a stupendous observation! What a brilliant and fortunate opportunity! Rita did not believe she was intelligent. For all of her astounding beauty and above-average intelligence, she had an inferiority complex. I skipped through the woods in delight and soared with geese that were flying south for the winter. I was ecstatic! This would be my doorway to paradise—the golden doorway that would lead me to the heart of Rita Fitzgerald!

I caught up with Rita in the hallway, after English class one Tuesday. I'd pumped myself up with repetitive thoughts and images of power and courage. I stared into the mirror and told myself that I could do this because I was the best student in the entire school, and Rita surely knew it and respected me for it. So I approached her, with my chest out, head up. I knew I couldn't look directly at her or I'd fail the mission. Her soft, glowing blue eyes would strike me like lasers and kill my courage. I'd blur my words, and my beady eyes would become an icy glare of defense and she'd hurry away in fear and loathing, like other girls had done. So, I fixed my gaze on a little dark speck on the wall, just over her right shoulder. I fixed it there and kept it there.

"Hey, Rita," I said, with many hours of practiced indifference. "If you'll read my story and give me some constructive criticism, I'll read yours." My speech gained speed and force. "We could do it at Jack's, if you want. No big thing. I feel pretty good about mine, anyway. Ms. Lyendecker thinks students should work together so I thought we should just maybe, if you want to, work together."

Once the words were released, my heart ached in pounding hope. We were standing by a long row of faded green lockers, outside Mr. Burkett's math class. It seemed to me that Rita waited an entire hour before answering. "I'm surprised, Alan."

"Oh, yeah?" I said, barely squeezing the words from my clenched teeth, feeling an astounding weakness in my legs.

"You always study alone. You never show your stuff to anybody. You don't really seem to like anybody."

I kept my bulging eyes glued to that speck. I shrugged and swallowed away a massive lump. A hot coal of fright. What if she said no? I knew I'd faint dead away and my valedictorian speech would lose all of its potency and impact, because the entire senior class would be snickering through every clever turn of phrase, philosophical concept and inspiring idea. I could just hear them.

"Alan Lincoln is such a weak little jerk-off," they'd say. "Passed out in the hallway like an idiot."

"Smart, but a skinny fart with no heart," the girls would say, and often did.

"I bet he said something to Rita—something really, like dirty, and she punched his ass out," Barry Barker would say.

"It's the quiet little shits you have to watch,"

Ellen Tucker would undoubtedly say.

The stakes couldn't have been higher.

Rita's alto voice rose an octave. "I'd love it, Alan. A great idea. Let's do it. Let's meet after school. Today."

"Today?" I said, stunned, needing some time to recover.

"Sure. Why wait. I'll meet you after school. My story's not that good, but I'd love to read yours. I mean, you're so smart."

I stared in wonder at her flowering opulence and swallowed hard.

And so we met at Jack's, on a sparkling autumn afternoon, seated in one of those gleaming yellow booths, two of only five people in the entire place—a rarity at Jack's and a good omen, I'd thought. I wanted to slap myself to see if I was asleep and dreaming. I, Alan Lincoln, was sitting alone with Rita Fitzgerald on a little deserted island in Jack's sea of booths.

Outside, the leaves were a blast of colors, falling, sailing and spinning in the cool wind and sharp Pennsylvania sunlight. The world, for the first time that I could remember, looked like a wonderland and I was a hero.

Rita wore a pink v-neck woolen sweater and designer jeans; I wore my usual loose jeans and black shirt. We said little at first, and I struggled to decipher her mood, to probe behind the quiet blue eyes to see what lay hidden, but all I sensed was a low anxiety. Then she presented me her story, with some hesitation, and asked for mine. We exchanged them, warily, like ransomed goods.

While Rita read, I settled into the soft cushion and took her in, like a first long breath of life. I drifted into hypnotic daydreams of idyllic future days of lovemaking, marriage and family. I unlocked the cages of the irrational, flung wide the gates, and released my wild shimmering dreams. Rita and I passed through the entire cycle of life, from courtship, marriage and children, to retirement on a high white bluff overlooking the emerald Florida sea. We were madly in love from the very beginning —from the time she'd read my short story in Jack's Diner entitled *Left To Live*. We'd tell the story about that meeting—this very meeting—until the day we died.

The vision shattered when Rita's face fell into darkness. Her troubled eyes closed, opened, then returned to the page, widening, swimming over the words.

Now, my eyes scarcely rested on her as she read, for I became keenly aware that even the slightest disapproval from her could cause permanent emotional scaring. It became painfully obvious that I had no real power over Rita whatsoever. She held it all. She was the Queen of the Earth, and she held the power of life and death over me with a simple arch of her eyebrow, the turn of her hand, or the subtle readjustment of her body.

I watched anxiously as her slender fingers gently twisted the pure golden strands of her hair; I struggled to relax as her peculiar radiance put me in a state of restlessness. I knew my story was good. I knew a lot of S.A.T. words and had used as many as possible. But none of that would matter unless she actually liked the story.

Then Rita shifted. I heard the squeak of plastic and my eyes opened. She made a little grunt of displeasure and lifted her gaze to meet mine, preoccupied. She was silent, needing time to adjust to the change of reality, as she pondered my story. "Aren't you going to read mine?" she asked, pointedly.

I stiffened and sat forward. "Yeah, sure…"

My eyes snapped to the pages before me and I began reading her story. By the second paragraph, I realized that it was not only good, it was remarkable. It flowed effortlessly, like the quiet meandering of a river, unraveling the plot and ideas in a natural, sensitive style. It was quality, mature writing.

It was about a woman who fell in love with a large oak tree that had spread itself generously over a little dirt road, at the foot of a sloping hill.

The tree told the stories of the people who had passed and paused, using its trunk and shade for rest; it told of the families and the events it had witnessed, of conversations it had heard, and of advice it had given during its long, good life.

The idea seemed a little odd to me at first, but the writing was compelling.

When the tree saw the girl come into view, it instantly fell in love with her, and vowed that it would always love and protect the girl from any harm for as long as it lived. The girl said that she loved the tree more than anything else because she thought it the most beautiful and magnificent thing she'd ever seen. She lived and slept in its broad, sturdy branches and learned many practical and inspiring lessons from the tree.

By the sixth page of the story, I was impressed and humbled. I paused long enough to pass Rita an admiring glance. She sensed my gaze and looked at me over the pages of my story.

"What do you think? she asked, uneasily.

"I'm almost finished," I said.

Meanwhile, a crowd of the curious was collecting in booths and at the counter; they whispered and passed us sideways glances. Rita didn't seem to care or notice. I swelled with happy conceit, adjusting my proud shoulders. I wanted to shout, "Hey, losers, I'm with Rita Fitzgerald. You're all just pathetic jerk-offs."

I finished Rita's story about the same time she finished mine, because she'd re-read particular paragraphs. She was silent and contemplative, so I spoke up.

"Why does the tree die at the end?" I said.

Rita quickly scratched some notes in her spiral notebook, laid her pen aside and folded her hands, twisting them gently. "Because the girl had to leave."

"A little pun?" I asked, trying for a bad joke.

Her forehead wrinkled, not getting it.

"You know, leave... Tree. Leaves."

The forehead smoothed in recognition. She chuckled, a low throaty sound that struck me someplace deep in the chest.

"No pun, intended, Alan," she said, smiling. "No, it's just that it was a road. The tree lived on a road…"

"Okay…" I said, still not getting it, but nodding my head.

"You know, roads and movement."

A vague idea struck. "You mean like the road of life or something."

Rita lit up. "Yes! Yes, Alan. You got it! I didn't know if anyone would get that!"

I didn't really, but I didn't want her to know that. Her perfume entranced me. I grabbed a french fry and chewed vigorously.

"You see," she continued, "life is always moving. Things are always passing, people coming and going, like on a road."

It was almost too poetic for me. "What's the tree stand for then?"

"Protection. Safety, I think."

I nodded. "Yeah, but you were in love. I mean, the girl in the story was in love with the tree. Why didn't you stay with the tree? Stay and be protected?"

"Because the tree also means life—you know, the tree of life. But it has to die, too. I mean, everything dies. Just look outside at the trees. All the leaves are falling. Some of the trees have died since last fall. Birth and death right outside Jack's Diner. So, the girl realized, I think, I mean, I'm still working on it with Ms. Lyendecker but… the girl realized, at some point, she'd have to go off down the road anyway."

"You mean, like living her own life? Growing up?"

Rita licked her lips, thoughtfully. "Yeah...I think so." Then more firmly, grabbing the idea. "Yeah. You've got to grow up. That's it, Alan James. That's good!"

"But she left before the tree died," I said. "I mean, I just don't get that. The tree died, I think, because the girl left him."

Rita's eyes clouded over. "Yeah... I'm not really sure about that. Maybe it just sounded good. Maybe she left before the tree died. Maybe she couldn't stand to see the tree die. It would hurt too much. So, she left."

That struck me as tragic and I'd never thought of Rita as being tragic. But I was still greatly impressed with Rita's story and explanation and I wasn't going to risk being offensive. "Oh, yeah, well, it's good. The writing is great. I mean, better than good."

Rita fumbled for her pen. "You really like it?"

"Yeah. It's really good, Rita."

Her faced opened into pure pleasure. "Thanks, Alan. If you like it, then I'll keep working on it."

Seconds later, her mood changed. Her mouth puckered in indecision and she slumped and faced the window, squinting into the sunlight.

"What's the matter?" I asked.

She stared down at my story as if there was a big ugly bug crawling across it. "Alan," she said, with quiet authority. "Everybody in your story is so angry."

My heart jumped. I shrugged, in obvious agreement. "Well, yeah. I know. That's kind of my style."

Rita was silent.

"You didn't like it?" I asked, masking a tepid anxiety.

She squirmed. "It's not that I didn't like it... Well, I mean, what's it really about?"

I shrank a little. My voice lost its vigor. "You know, it's kind of a play on the phrase, 'Left To Die.'"

Rita nodded. "Okay... Yes. And so this guy, Pete, is angry because people don't really understand him?"

I got defensive. "Well, it's not just that. Pete believes that people and nature are basically destructive, but despite that, he has to fight on. He's actually a hero."

"I don't think all people are destructive or bad," Rita said.

"Oh come on, Rita, you're just naïve. Nature is constantly eating itself. People are stealing, killing and fighting wars all over the world."

Her voice gained strength and conviction. "I'm not naïve, Alan! What is your middle name?"

That disarmed me and I stammered. "Whaa, why?"

"What is it?"

I hesitated. "It's James. Alan James."

"Alan James," she repeated, reflectively. "I like it."

"What's that got to do with anything?"

"I feel you'd be less pessimistic if you used both names. Alan. James. Alan James. It adds strength and optimism. I'm going to start calling you that."

"That doesn't make any sense, Rita. A name doesn't…"

She cut me off. "I'm going to show you how fun the world can be, Alan James. I'm going to show you how to be Alan James, not just boring and brooding Alan." She leaned forward and narrowed her eyes, for emphasis. "I'm going to rehabilitate you."

"Rehabilitate…?"

"Yes."

I blinked rapidly, tingling from head to toe. "Okay…" It sounded delicious and daunting, but her treatment had already begun to take effect. I felt absolutely euphoric.

My oatmeal arrived, steaming. The banana came sliced, overripe and piled in a little mountain on a separate blue chipped dish, but it smelled good. The waitress refilled the coffee and withdrew, wordless. I added sugar and some milk to the oats, and spooned a couple of bites, chewing slowly and stealing sporadic glances, looking for Rita.

A moment later, I felt a tap on my shoulder. Startled, I turned.

She was heavy, with a fleshy round face and short brown hair. Her smile was uncomfortable. "Hi, Alan."

I swallowed the bite. "…Hi."

"You don't remember me, do you?"

I came up blank and she giggled. "Oh, my, well it's been fifteen years or more and you didn't come to the tenth or fifteenth high school reunions. Picture me about seventy pounds lighter, with long auburn hair."

The giggle jarred my memory. "Ellen Tucker..."

I stood when she spread her fat hands and grinned, as if she was about to perform. "That's me! I recognized you as soon as you came in."

I stood awkwardly, laying my paper napkin on the counter. "Well...how are you?"

"Just fine, well, you know, as fine as one can be these days with everything that's going on. Things changing so fast, you don't know which way to point your head."

"Yeah, big changes."

She looked me over. "Well, look at you, Alan. You've gone and got yourself handsome."

"You always were a charmer, Ellen," I said, lying.

She giggled again. "We both know that ain't true, Alan. And I haven't changed any except that I'm fat. But you have. You're all filled out and your hair's long and as thick as a brush. You're never going to go bald."

"Good hair genes," I said.

"You even look taller."

"Still 5'10". So how are you? What are you doing?"

"Training to be a nurse. I'm going to be working at the county hospital. Thank God I'm still young enough. A lot of the older folks are just standing in place. Don't know what to do with themselves. Just watched their retirement vanish. So sad."

"Town seems quieter…"

"Lots of people moved away, especially after the factories shut down and …" Her voice trailed away and she shook off a sorrowful thought. She swiftly changed the subject. "And you're a doctor, I hear."

"Yes…"

"Living in New York City?"

"Yes."

"Married?"

"Almost three years."

Her face was alive with interest. "Three years. Why you've just started. Keith and I have been married twelve years now. You remember Keith Parry?"

"No, I don't believe…"

She cut me off. "He was a year behind us." She batted her eyes, playfully. "I married a younger man. We have two boys, both little terrors. Do you have any children?"

Under her scrutiny, I shifted my uncomfortable gaze away from her. "No… no children."

"Well, you have lots of time. I bet your wife is one of those career women, isn't she?"

Her questions were beginning to irritate me. "Well…she's an attorney. She stays pretty busy. We both stay really busy," I said, a little defensively.

"Well, Hartsfield is proud of you. Sure are. We knew you'd do well. Just knew it. I heard your father had a stroke and moved away."

"Yeah. That's why I'm here. To sell the house."

"That was one of the prettiest homes in town. Still is."

I pocketed my hands, nodding. "Yeah…"

We'd pushed the small talk to its limit, and had arrived at the respectable moment to speak about Rita. I'd seen the constraint in Ellen's eyes during our brief catch up and heard the forced gaiety in her still little-girl voice. But she trembled, just a bit, as she spoke, and her eyes lacked luster.

I was straining to appear cool and blank as marble, while my head was a tangle of unexpected questions and unanticipated emotions. My brow was wet. I fought the urge to reach for the napkin and mop it. I'd been in Jack's long enough to feel that grief and loss had crept into every corner and crack of the place; had seeped into the walls and yellowed the photos; had smothered the old triumphant breaths and soaring cheers that had once crackled in the air; had transformed the life of this popular teenage beauty, with all the vitality and joy of spring, into a wizened old crone.

Ellen's voice dropped to a whisper. "I guess you heard about poor Rita and Dusty?"

"Yes…"

"What a tragedy. What a horrible and terrible thing. Darla was such a pretty little thing, just like her mother. So smart, so sweet." Then with a quiet ferocious agony, she said. "God in heaven." Her eyes filled with tears. She recovered, with effort. "This town…after all we've been through with our job losses. Lord, Alan, we are all still so devastated for her. Have you seen her?"

I felt a bead of sweat race down my cheek. My voice cracked. "No…no. I haven't seen Rita in fifteen years."

Ellen quickly scanned the room. Suspicious eyes were now watching us.

"She works here, you know."

I lifted an exaggerated eyebrow. "Oh, really?"

"Yes. You wouldn't know her. She's…well, she's…" Tears returned and glistened. "She's in the back somewhere. Sometimes she has to stop and rest, but I heard that her doctor said she should work, and Jack's son, Dean, God love him, runs the place now. Jack O'Brian retired to Florida. Well, anyway, Dean gave her a job. I think it was real nice of him, don't you think so?"

I nodded, looking hesitantly toward the closed kitchen door. I felt the slow crawl of a shiver.

"Are you going to see her?" Ellen asked, dabbing her eyes with a tissue.

My attention snapped back to her face. "Yeah, I guess so."

Ellen touched my arm, squeezing it gently. "You won't know her."

"Have you talked to her?" My voice sounded urgent, despite a struggle for calm.

She gave a quick shake of her head. "Rita doesn't talk to anybody. I mean, she'll take your order, you know things like that, but no real conversation to speak of. She lives with her mother, you know, the same house over on Marion Street. Never goes out. The damned reporters were over the house for the longest time. Betty Fitzgerald said they nearly drove them crazy. She tore the phone out of the wall finally. Just couldn't take it anymore."

I saw the scene clearly. The boiling, frantic energy around that broken down house, the invasion across the driveway and scrap of lawn, the greedy, taunting calls for a picture, a word, a statement. I'd never even given it a thought. "Are the reporters finally leaving them alone?"

"Pretty much. It's old news now, but they squeezed every last bit of life out of it and Rita. Rita just went inside of herself and I don't know if she'll ever come back to us. I've gone over to see her so many times but she won't talk to me. Just won't talk about nothing."

I shifted my weight and passed another glance toward the kitchen door. It swung open. My heart kicked, forcing a sudden breath. But it wasn't Rita. It was my waitress.

Ellen continued. "Rita just stays by herself in her room when she's not working, her mother says. Sleeps, reads, writes. She comes to work three or four days a week and goes to her therapist once, sometimes twice a week, over in Eden Grove. I've said hello to her so many times right here at Jack's, but she barely even lifts her head to me. Acts like she doesn't know me now."

I let out a slow exhalation through my nose and scratched my head. "Maybe I shouldn't see her.

Maybe it would be best for her if I didn't."

Ellen's face softened. "She really liked you, Alan. She did."

I reached for the napkin and mopped my forehead. "Long time ago."

"You know what she told me once? We were out by Crystal Lake, both of us smoking, eating potato chips and drinking beer. It was one of those perfect days with so much sun and brightness. It was late autumn. She hadn't dated Dusty yet. We were so relaxed and happy, so sure our lives would be all lightness and adventure, you know, just like all kids who think life is going to be wine and roses or whatever that expression is. Anyway, I sometimes think about that day and cry."

I waited, with some impatience, wanting her to continue.

"Anyway, Rita said she wanted to marry you."

I felt as if I'd just fallen into an icy pond.

CHAPTER THREE

After Ellen Tucker left and I'd finished my third cup of coffee, I sat with my elbows propped on the counter, playing back her words. I was startled by their lingering impact. Fifteen years of experience, including school, work, relationships, travel and a marriage, had all suddenly receded to some deep part of my consciousness. It was as if I'd hastily bundled them up in an old sack, dropped them into a deep well and walked away without regret or reflection. Rita's words "wanted to marry you" aroused me—brought a new longing to see her again. I looked for her, expectantly, feeling a strange sense of loss and yearning. Then I suddenly remembered my wife, Nicole, with unease.

I pictured her spread out on the soft brown Italian leather couch, an elegant long stemmed glass filled with OJ in her small hand; a trial folder on the floor, next to the scattered sections of the Saturday *New York Times*. It was her oval hazel eyes I saw first, then her smooth olive skin and brown hair wet from a recent shower and combed tight to her head. Most likely, she wore the thin blue satin robe I'd bought her on her last birthday, naked underneath, because she was always naked on Saturday mornings; and her fingernails and toenails were an electric red after a Friday afternoon visit to The Nail Boutique on 2nd and 62nd.

Though petite at 5' 2", and weighing a mere 105 pounds, Nicole's skillful intelligence, half-French blood, and refined, resolute features gave her stature. She was seldom intimidated by anyone—including prosecutors, judges or colleagues.

"What time are you leaving?" she had asked, the night before I left for Hartsfield. We were having dinner at our neighborhood French Bistro.

"Early in the morning. God, I hate getting up early on Saturdays."

I was eating the striped bass and she the lamb shank, with boulanger potatoes. I sipped a glass of Condrieu and, she, a glass of Cahors. We sat wrapped in aloof solitude, eating with a sheen of sophistication. Nicole wore a black spaghetti strap blouse and designer jeans. I had dressed in brown khakis and a salmon cotton shirt. The room was dimly lit and cozy, with brown wood-cut tables and red leather banquettes.

"Are you sure you want to sell that place?" Nicole asked, her eyes distracted by a passing fire truck. "It's valuable real estate."

"I'm sure. I'm beyond sure. I want to close the door on that house and on that town forever."

"Maybe the town should buy it," Nicole said. "They could turn it into a historical tourist thing or something."

I leveled my doubtful eyes on her. "They don't

have the money and anyway nobody would ever go there. It's off the main highway and Hartsfield's practically a ghost town."

"Well it's up to you," she said, indifferently.

"The money could go toward a place in the Hamptons. Maybe we should go away next weekend," I said. "Shelter Island or someplace and look around?"

"Maybe," she said, half-heartedly.

And then after a long silence, I said, "Want to see a movie tonight?"

Nicole took a long thoughtful sip of wine. "I always forget how full-bodied this is. We should get a case of it." Then as an afterthought. "I don't think so. I'm going to do some work tonight."

"Come on, Nicole, it's Friday night. We should do something. Do something together."

She looked at me, with discontented eyes. "Yes, we should...What's playing?"

"I don't know. We can find something." I took out my phone and began to search.

She sighed a little. "It'll be so crowded... I hate fighting for a seat. Maybe we should just go home and find something on HBO. Why did we cancel Netflix?"

I sighed, heavily, glancing up. "I always chose the movie and you never liked it."

"Not never."

"We haven't watched a movie together in weeks."

"I'm sure we have."

"We haven't."

Nicole nudge her plate forward. "Okay, just choose any damn movie and let's go!" she said, irritated. "I'll probably fall asleep in the middle of it anyway. I mean, it's not a big deal."

I snatched my wine and drank generously. "No, Nicole, it's not a big deal."

"Let's just not make every thing a problem, okay?"

"Whatever."

"We've both been busy, Alan. That's what happens when people grow up and have careers. They have responsibilities and they get busy."

"I'm sure that's true," I said, refusing to look at her, eyes unfocused.

For the rest of the dinner, we spoke in a monotonous agitation.

We took a cab to the Lincoln Plaza Cinemas. Our first choice was sold out. We stood in a long line for the second; in silence; in a snappy wind. Nicole was bored and indifferent. I was feeling the calcification of thought, as if I hadn't had an easy thought—an inspired thought—in months. How had we come to this? I thought back to our wedding.

Nicole was a gorgeous, sexy bride. A storybook princess in her white cake-like frosting wedding dress, garlanded with lace; delicious to look at, ecstatic to make love to; and we did make love at the hotel before the reception: her in that cream puff dress and sheer veil, enticing me on with puckered lips, and me in my tux, tie still on, pants gathered at my knees. We fell into each other, mad with love, our bodies soggy with sweat when we finally sank after that glorious frenzy.

Everyone said we were in love—they could feel it—see it in the photos. I saw Nicole's tenderness in those photographs—a vulnerability that did occasionally emerge and blossom. I saw me—a little reserved—but eyes fixed on her, grinning.

On our wedding night, as we sipped Champagne, naked in a king-sized bed, Nicole turned to me, shining with love, "Alan," she said, "I want to be there when you grow your first gray hair. I want to be there to pull it out."

"Of course you'll be there. But don't stop there. Pull the others out too."

"I will. Just as soon as they pop out of your head."

"You'll be the gray hair police. If they pop out, you pull 'em!"

"Even on your chest?" she asked, yanking a black hair from my chest.

"Ouch! That hurt!"

"Love hurts, baby doll," she teased, grabbing for my pubic hair.

I broke free and sprinted away—she pursuing—cackling like a demented witch.

By the time Nicole and I reached the ticket window, the movie was sold out. Nicole lashed out at the ticket person, a wizened woman with blank eyes. "Why don't you people know how many tickets you have? You can see the line. We've been waiting for ten minutes."

Nicole stormed away from the ticket window, striding uptown. I followed. We went home and blamed the whole event on the woman in the ticket window.

Nicole had once said, "I want our life to be a romantic comedy. Then after we have two or three kids, we'll switch from romantic comedy to family comedy."

I'd made an ugly face. "Too wholesome. Too hokey. When have you ever seen a really good family comedy? They're all forced or silly. I want to see the hard reality of family life," I said. "Family drama!"

"Oh, like you had such a rough childhood," Nicole said, shoving me gently.

"Well, it was definitely family drama and not family comedy."

I suddenly remembered one particular family drama that had concerned Rita, and I privately grinned at the thought.

"Are you going out with Rita Fitzgerald, tonight?" Mom asked, casually.

We were seated at the oak dining table, under a gleaming chandelier, my father and mother at opposite ends with me in the middle. I was cutting into a baked green pepper, stuffed with hamburger, onion and peas. Our black cook and housekeeper, Delores, had cooked one of my favorite dinners. But it wasn't Dad's favorite. He thought it too humble, although the word he often used was "noncommittal."

I watched as he dissected and examined the pepper, squinting in toward it, as if doing exploratory surgery. He finally lifted his fork and knife in mild exasperation, looking up at my mother. "I don't know, Catherine, didn't we ask Delores to try to be more adventurous?"

"She tried a new recipe today and it failed," Mom said. "So, she fell back on what she knew and is comfortable with."

Dad sighed. He would never fire Delores nor even consider it. She'd been part of the family for over twenty years and he loved her, although he never said so. He loved her jokes, her honesty and her hard work. He also loved her applesauce cake. So he sat properly erect, resigned to his fate, and made the best of the pepper, chewing in a slow, deliberate rhythm, swallowing only when the food had been ground to fine paste.

His charcoal eyes became focused on the TV in the living room, where the evening news flickered. The sound was muted, a compromise my parents had made some years back. Mom wanted dinner to be on the table at 6:30. Dad wanted to watch the national news. So after various debates and hard stares, it was finally agreed that dinner would begin at 6:45, allowing Dad fifteen minutes of news in the living room with sound, and fifteen minutes in the dining room, without.

"So, are you?" Mom asked me, more forcefully.

"What?" I asked, playing dumb.
"Going out with Rita Fitzgerald?"
"Yeah..." I answered, head down.
"How many times have you been out together?"
I took a bite and swallowed. "We meet at Jack's sometimes."
"Where are you going?"
I shrugged.
"Alan, you must know where you're taking her."
Mom was attractive, petite, and prim, with long burnished auburn hair and deep brown glittering eyes. She walked briskly, spoke fast, and laughed at things no one else thought was funny and didn't laugh at jokes or stories when everyone else did.

Her father had been a doctor on Long Island; she went to the best schools and the best country club dances. Her passion now was the flower and vegetable gardens that surrounded the house and the pond. She collared Judy and me on late autumn mornings to help plant crocus and daffodil bulbs and yanked us out of bed on early spring mornings to hoe, plant seeds and pull weeds. Dad built the rose trestles and designed the rock gardens by the pond. We all pruned the blackberries and raspberries, and then picked them in August. Dad grumbled away from his newspapers and biographies of Washington, Hamilton and Lincoln to help plant string beans, cucumbers, radishes and tomatoes, and he never missed an opportunity to say, "Catherine, we can hire people to do this, you know."

She never responded. She just kept on working.

There was no secret that Mom disliked Hartsfield and wanted to move closer to New York. It was no secret that the gardens were her therapy and she let everyone know it. "How did I wind up in Hartsfield" was one of her monthly mantras, when the weather was dreadful, when she was bored or when she and my father had jousted over shopping, vacations or politics. It was effective ammunition that consistently sent my father into a frustrating silence.

Dad was efficient, deliberate and suave, looking like one of those actor doctors on TV, advertising insurance or antacid, giving off a distinguished calm and trustworthy comfort. He had married late and was 16 years older than Mom. He had a broad face, steady dark eyes and brush strokes of gray above the ears and at the temples. He never hurried, seldom raised his voice and always held himself proudly erect and appropriately serious, as if he was one of America's founding fathers who had to keep up appearances for all of posterity, forever and ever. Amen. He was what was known as a "stuffed shirt." He was 58 years old. Mom was 42.

He had inherited the house, some real estate and the family accounting business, as well as a substantial amount of money from his petulantly stern father, with the proviso that he live in Hartsfield and in that house. So that's how it was. Mom died in Hartsfield but was buried in Bayshore, Long Island, because that was her wish.

"So where are you taking Rita, Alan?" Mom asked.

"We're just going to drive around, I guess."

"Drive around," she repeated, distastefully. "Alan, you must have some goal in mind. Some specific planned destination."

I raised my impatient eyes to hers. Mom always dressed expensively and impeccably. She wore a blue silk blouse, pearl earrings and black woolen pants with heels. She firmly believed that women should always wear heels. I never, not once, saw her in sneakers or flat shoes. I reasoned it was probably because she was 5' 1". Even when she worked in the gardens, she wore a stylish shoe with a slight heel.

"Maybe we'll go to a movie."

My father mumbled something at the TV.

"Alan," Mom continued. "Rita is a very pretty girl, and I'm hearing that she dates a lot of boys."

"Yeah... I know."

Mom looked at Dad, who was fixed on the TV. "Richard."

He pulled his face toward her with difficulty, and with some irritation. "Yes, Catherine."

"Judy called last night. She's dating a nice boy, a minister's son, and he's also majoring in accounting."

"Yes, I talked to her. She wants to bring him for Thanksgiving. Her tuition has gone up ten percent over last year. Can you believe that!? Ten percent!" The sudden remembrance assaulted him anew. The TV suddenly took a subordinate position. He wanted to expand his indignation.

Mom wasn't having any of it. After a sip of her wine, she continued. "Well, anyway, Judy told me that Rita's father has been in prison. Is that true?"

Seeing he'd lost, Dad's beady eyes went back to the TV. He cleared his voice. "Yes. But you won't read about it in the local paper, because they won't print it. Not now anyway, with Rita Fitzgerald becoming the darling of the town. No one has seen him in two years or more."

"I'm not dating her father," I said.

"Don't be a smart-aleck," Dad said. "Your mother has a right to be concerned, Alan. This town always gets caught up in some kind of new distraction. Rita Fitzgerald wins a local beauty contest and the next thing you know, the town's all caught up. Caught-up." Then, some urgent thought turned Dad's head toward me. He stared strangely, as if he'd just realized that 2 + 2 actually equaled 3. He took off his horn-rimmed glasses. "Alan...why is Rita dating you?"

Mom slammed down her fork. "What does that mean, Richard? That Alan is not good enough for Rita Fitzgerald? Pahleesse."

Dad recovered brilliantly, with a couple of slow blinks and a thoughtful sip of the Bordeaux, carefully chosen from the basement wine cellar. The mahogany wine racks, that were a full 13½ inches deep and finished in a rich oil stain, occupied a lot of Dad's free time and contemplation. Dad spent most Saturday mornings studying *Wine Spectator* magazine, planning future purchases, or carefully examining the cooling unit, insuring the display was at twenty degrees and steep enough to keep the wine from touching part of the cork. With the eye of a detective, he scrutinized the racks for any signs of decay and mildew. The wine cellar: Dad's escape from it all.

Dad took another taste of the wine, as he considered his response. "Catherine... I only meant that Alan hasn't dated much."

"One date," I clarified. "Edna Thomas. But we went out twice." My father seized on the idea. "Yes, Edna Thomas. Edna is a nice girl, but hardly a beauty."

"She has a nice body," I said.

Mom gave me a disapproving glare. "Nice body? Come on, Alan. You're intelligent enough to find more respectful words when describing a woman."

"Okay, she's nice. Her body speaks of Venus and Aphrodite."

"Very funny," Mom said, not amused.

"And she's the best debater on the team," I added. "But, Rita Fitzgerald, she isn't."

"There's nothing wrong with having good looks, Catherine," my father said, with a quick, playful wink. "Nothing at all."

"Good looks are only part of it, for God's sake!" Mom said, sharply. "Edna is a wonderful girl who has a very bright future ahead of her. Doesn't that count for something? Are good looks the only criteria for whether a woman is a worthy topic of conversation, whether she should be dated, or whether she has any real worth at all in this male-driven, male-dominated, male-drenched testosterone world!? Give me a break, Richard!"

"Of course not, Catherine," Dad said, lowering his voice to cool the atmosphere. "Of course Edna has worth. She's a fine girl, and her family has a wonderful college fund for both her and her brother, Bert. I only meant, well…" Dad sought words. "I was only saying that Alan is careful about who he spends time with. Rita Fitzgerald doesn't seem to be the intellectual or scientific type."

Mom said, "Well, I'd never even heard of the girl until last year. Her father, yes, although I didn't know the details."

I took a long drink of milk. Mom was waiting for me to give an explanation, so I did. "I heard she was kind of ugly until her sophomore year. Then, I don't know, something just happened. She just turned gorgeous."

"What you're really implying is that you boys finally grew up," Dad said, with authority and proud wisdom, as if he'd just cracked the genetic code.

"Rita's smart and she's a great writer," I said. "And, hey, she's like the prettiest girl I've ever seen."

"Her beauty will come and go like pride before a fall," Dad said, going back to his wine and the TV.

I thought that cruel, but Mom didn't respond. She seemed disgusted with us both. She shook her head and turned toward the lace curtains, as if to summon patience. I followed her gaze, past the curtains, where darkness had already descended and the distant comforting orange glow of the streetlights was visible.

"So that's why you're dating Rita, Alan?" Mom asked, quietly.

Dad's ear was cocked my way.

"Yeah. Because she's gorgeous, she's smart and she said she'd go out with me. Hey, I think all of those are really good reasons."

Mom was circumspect, but satisfied. "Okay, fine. You're 17. You're old enough to make your own decisions."

We went back to our solemn dinner for a few minutes. The TV flickered with images of the racing IPO market, and then something about a stock market bubble. It annoyed my father.

"Blast it!" he said. "I told you, Catherine. I told you that this whole internet thing, with its IPO's popping up everywhere, is just a disaster waiting to happen. Mark my words, Catherine! I've been telling my clients this for weeks now!"

My mother ignored him. "Alan," my mother said, staring at me with renewed intensity. "Sometimes girls date boys for a variety of reasons. Sometimes, mistakes can happen."

I knew exactly what Mom was getting at, but I played dumb. It didn't matter why Rita had said she'd go out with me: because I was rich or smart, or because of my family name. The fact was, she'd said she would go out with me. The most popular and beautiful girl in town, or most probably in the entire state, had said she'd go out with me.

Mom looked at me, affectionately, with a parent's concern. "Boys can make mistakes, too, just as easily as girls. It is so easy to make the biggest mistake of your life, Alan. A mistake that can literally ruin your life. So, needless to say, stay away from drugs, alcohol and anything else that you know is morally and ethically wrong."

Mom gave Dad a knowing glare. "One mistake, a decision made in haste, an act that may only last a few minutes, can completely alter your life and cause you to regret it for the rest of your life. Remember that when you're with Rita tonight, Alan. She is a very pretty girl."

CHAPTER FOUR

An hour later, I was at Rita's door. It swept open and Mrs. Fitzgerald appeared. Time had passed heavily upon her. Her untidy mop of gray hair and long bony face lent a harshness; her stooped shoulders suggested burdens and worries and a sense that life had the daily habit of victimizing her in a variety of creative ways. When she spoke, her voice was thin; she clipped her words, as if flinging them out like little darts.

"Rita will be down soon," she said curtly. She did not ask me in, so I stood on the porch like a delivery boy, waiting for a tip.

She tried to ignore me, pitching her gaze over me, around me and back into the house, where I heard the blurring voice of the TV. She stuffed her hands into her pale, blousy, blue-patterned dress pockets. I did not understand how such a beauty had come from such remarkable homeliness.

I stepped back, hearing the soft creaking wood beneath my feet, struggling not to notice the cracked and peeling paint; the streaming rust stains from a faulty gutter. The night wind was damp and smelled of burned leaves.

"Why are you going out with Rita?" Mrs.

Fitzgerald asked, pointedly, in a low even voice that nearly fell into a course whisper.

The question jarred me. "Why?"

I thought, why is everybody asking me the same damned question? It seemed so obvious. "Why am I going out with Rita?"

"Yes."

"...I... like her."

"Do you?" It wasn't a question. It was a challenge.

"Yes."

I adjusted the collar of my denim jacket, hoping the conversation would shift to another subject.

"Have you always gotten what you wanted?" she asked. Her voice took on a grinding quality that unnerved me.

I couldn't think of a response. "I like her stories," finally emerged, as I glanced expectantly toward the pale second floor window, wishing Rita would hurry. "I like her."

In the uneasy moment, I heard the agitated raspy bark of the dog next door. He didn't seem to like me either.

"Rita dates a lot," her mother continued, in a supercilious tone. "Many boys. *Handsome* boys."

"Yeah... I bet."

"A photographer from a Philadelphia magazine is coming to take a whole bunch of pictures and she's going to model a new line of clothes for Clayton Stores all over Pennsylvania. On television."

"That's great," I said, rocking on my heels. "Nice."

"She'll be in the state pageant, too."

"Yeah, I heard that."

She still wasn't looking at me. Her tone turned ugly. "Why is Rita going out with you?"

This time, the question really irritated me and my voice rose with emotion. "How the hell should I know!? Ask her!"

"Don't talk to me like that!" she snapped.

"Well, why don't you ask your daughter, Mrs. Fitzgerald? Ask her. Not me!"

"I don't need to ask her!" She yanked her bony hands from her pockets. They clenched into fists. "You and your family…so much money. Your mother so snobby, your father, so special with his expensive suits and gold watch. Walking around like they own the town. Walking around looking down their noses at us. Now you want Rita. Rita… my daughter. My daughter! You think just because your parents have all that money that you can have anything you want, don't you?!"

Her face was raw with accusation.

There were many things I wanted to spit out, but I kept quiet. I drew a hot breath, just as I heard Rita's quick footsteps clicking down the wood stairs. When she stepped onto the porch, trading glances with us, Mrs. Fitzgerald suddenly expanded with importance, gaining two inches in height. She moved aside adroitly, allowing Rita to pass under the amber glow of the porch lamp. Studying her daughter, Mrs. Fitzgerald was suddenly transformed into near attractiveness. For a brief moment, I saw her drowning in glory, like a woman having a religious experience. The transformation was startling. She crossed her thin arms and viewed her statuesque enameled girl, dressed in a taut ruby-red blouse, dark pants, and two-inch matching red heels. Her hair, lush and shimmering, was twisted up and artfully tied with a golden silk scarf. Giving off perfume, Rita presented her face to me and smiled warmly. I shuddered with a man's desire.

"Hello, Alan James."

My mouth was parched. "Hello, Rita. You look great."

I heard the stir of the elm tree near the wrought iron gate, heard the gentle rocking of the porch swing and the howl of a train. I felt Mrs. Fitzgerald's eyes on me. When I glanced at her, her dark eyes glazed over with a new bitterness and she fell back to homeliness.

Rita viewed us both, curiously. "Why didn't you wait for me inside?" she asked.

I shrugged.

"Alan didn't want to come in, Rita," she said sweetly. "He said he wanted to be out in the night air. He said the autumn air is so relaxing." Rita gave her mother a doubtful, dismissive glance. "Don't wait up for us, mother."

Her mother's voice took on an edge. "Don't come back here late, Rita Fitzgerald! Don't you do it!"

Rita ignored her, took my hand and led me out to the curb and the awaiting 1994 blue Dodge Intrepid. We drove away in victory and splendor; at least, that's how I remember it.

Over the previous four weeks, Rita and I had met five times at Jack's, reading and discussing our stories; arguing, laughing and sharing french fries. We became comfortable and trusting. We became friends. We became loose and flirtatious. We met with Ms. Lyendecker after school and discussed passages from short stores by Sherwood Anderson, O'Henry and Eudora Welty. Ms. Lyendecker read us poems and critiqued our stories. She was more critical and uncompromising with Rita's work than with mine. Rita's trust in her teacher bordered on devout worship, and she never wilted or blanched under Ms. Lyendecker's judgment.

I grew in confidence, became more cordial to my classmates and was told, by my mother, that I had developed a kind of "punkish" swagger. I was elated!

During our fifth meeting at Jack's, while french fries, sodas and story plots merged, I screwed up the courage to ask Rita out on a "real date."

"Your stories aren't so angry now, Alan James," Rita said. "Especially the last story. I like the part about the wheelchair-bound boy whose arm was so strong he could throw a baseball all the way across the state of Pennsylvania. I liked it that he wanted to become a doctor someday so he could heal people."

"Yeah, it's not bad," I said, pleased. "I loved your story about the girl who fell in the lake and couldn't swim. I loved the way you described how she sank to the bottom 'like something heavy with fatuous love.'"

"Did you get the symbolism?"

"You mean that she could breathe under water because she breathed with her whole heart and not just with her lungs?"

"Yes! I don't believe it, Alan James! You really got it!"

"Because you said so in the story, Rita."

Rita frowned. "I did?"

"Yeah...at the end, on page seven."

"Dammit. I thought I took that out. Ms. Lyendecker suggested it. She said I was telling too much, not showing."

"But I liked it, Rita. I mean, it's so unlike anything I could ever write. I just don't think like that."

Rita glowed. "So the rehabilitation is working, Alan James."

"What do you mean?"

"You're not so moody and brooding," Rita said. "Your stories are happier. More positive."

I stared at her boldly. "Really? So...do you think you're good for me?"

We dropped into a silent, exciting intimacy. She touched my hand. The sun poured in from the window and drenched her in gold. I seized the moment. "Go out with me this Saturday night, Rita."

She tilted her head toward the window, watching Dusty Palmer emerge from his 1992 red Mustang. "I'm dating other people," she said.

I shrugged. "I know. So...date me too."

She waited, considering my offer, and I was sure

she was going to say no. "Where will you take me?"

"I don't know. A movie? Pizza?"

She frowned. "How about I take you somewhere special," she said. "You're going to hate it."

I laughed, nervously. "Why will I hate it?"

"Because I'm going to make you do something with me."

I felt a flush of desire. "Then I won't hate it."

Happy to be free of Rita's mother, Rita and I drove recklessly down Highway 59 on our official second date. I felt like a wild puppy. I drove fast, squeezing around tight curves, edging past the baseball field, out and beyond the cemeteries and thick dark forests. I was following Rita's instructions and she sat relaxed, angled toward me, discussing an idea for her next short story.

Twenty minutes later, she shouted, pointing right. "There! Turn right!"

I hit the brakes and swerved toward a narrow road, mostly hidden by trees. We left the highway, tires screeching, and entered the forest, skidding onto a dirt road, fishtailing, hearing the tires pop across loose stones. I felt the rush of a towering sexual energy: helplessly roguish and delightful. I gunned the engine and we shot off past black trees, the headlights frantically sweeping thick trunks and jutting rocks. We plunged deeper into the forest, ramping and bouncing, the car straining for balance, like a boat in a wild storm. Rita gripped the edge of the bucket seat, at first surprised, then tense.

"What are you doing?"

I ignored her. She locked her eyes ahead, ignoring my frequent glances to see if she was impressed and frightened. I wanted to frighten her. I wanted her subservient and meek. I wanted to show her my courage and power. I wanted her to see that I was as manly as all the others she dated: the high school jocks, the twenty something tall, dignified attorney from Boston; the local D. J., Jeremy Peels, who dressed in black leather, smoked cigars and talked about Rita on his radio program.

Rita grew noticeably peevish. "I'm not impressed, Alan James," she said, struggling to steady her voice.

"By what?" I said, innocently.

"You know."

"I don't."

"You do."

"Don't think so."

"Tennis conversation, Alan James. Back and forth. Who will win?"

"I will," I said.

The radio blasted out John Fogerty's *Rock and Roll Girls*.

"Will not."

"Yep."

"Nope."

"Bet?"

"No."

"I'm gonna win!" I said, forcefully, almost desperate.

"Gonna lose," Rita said, hands on the dashboard,

bracing herself.

"No way."

"Yes way. Slow down, dammit!"

I punched the accelerator. Our heads whipped backwards. I fought the steering wheel, almost losing control. The car careened toward a bank of trees.

"Stop. Alan James. Stop!"

I muscled the car into a hard left turn. We grazed low branches. They slapped and scraped the side of the car as we charged ahead.

"Alan!"

"I win." I said, fighting the twisting road, terrified, but determined.

"Okay. You win. Stop."

"You mean it?"

"YES. Stop!"

I punched the brakes. We came to an abrupt stop that pitched us forward, then snapped us back, hard, against the seat. Our hearts raced in the dizzying silence. I slowly exhaled, relaxing my grip on the steering wheel, rolling my tight shoulders, feeling a nervous twitch in my right foot. I felt drunk and wonderfully sexual.

Rita sat rigid, her hands still on the dash, the steady rise and fall of her breasts suddenly prominent in the vague moonlight. She angrily switched off the radio and faced me with scolding eyes. "To be so smart, that was dumb, Alan James. Really fucking dumb."

I sat with a cold dignity. "I'll take that as a

compliment. I've never been called dumb in my entire life."

Her lips formed a beautiful petulant pout. I nearly reached a finger to touch them. I grinned instead. "You are SOooo serious looking, Rita Fitzgerald."

"Shut up!" she snapped, composing herself. "You're a little scary, you know that? I never thought of you as being reckless and scary."

"So are you."

"I am not!"

"Here we go again. Tennis conversation."

She twisted away from me. "What's with you, Alan James?"

The question pleased me. It made me seem mysterious and special. She wouldn't forget me. She would never forget the wild, reckless ride with Alan James. "I don't know."

She faced me again, blinked slowly, sizing me up in a new way, and then, surprisingly, she smiled as she adjusted herself in the seat. "Well… it wasn't so bad, Alan James. Not so bad."

She gave a happy little laugh and touched my cheek with a single soft finger. I felt electric and conquered. She'd won, with a simple touch.

"How much further?" I asked.

"Just ahead."

We started again. I squinted into the shafts of headlights. "I don't see anything."

"There's a clearing ahead. You'll see the lake. Moon Lake. At least that's what the fishermen call it.

Everybody goes to Crystal Lake because they don't know about this place."

I drove slowly. The moon was nearly full, sliding in and out of purple clouds, swimming through the black lace of trees. I slanted a look as the forest gradually fell away, and then as through an invisible door, we entered a clearing and viewed the gorgeous domed sky swarming with stars. I drove across a carpet of leaves to the edge of a high bluff, staring in wonder at the panoramic vista of the world, a moon-sprinkled lake and the distant silhouette of rolling hills.

"This is incredible," I said. "I didn't know this was here."

Rita's head lolled back, relaxed. "Not many people do. I used to come here on my bike when I was fifteen. I came here to escape the house, school… everything. I'm glad you like it."

"You thought I wouldn't like this?"

"No… there's more. But that can wait. Let's just sit here for a while."

I silenced the engine and we sat in an intimate stillness. Finally, I turned to her. "Where did you learn to write so well, Rita?"

"It's sweet that you think so, Alan James. Really sweet."

"You do, Rita, you know you write well."

"My father."

"He wrote?"

"He read. He was always bringing me books and making me read them, especially when I was sick and couldn't go out."

"Really?"

"Yeah. He loved books."

"What books?"

"Jane Austen, Steinbeck, C. S. Lewis, D. H. Lawrence. Most nights, when he was around, which wasn't often, he'd put me to bed and then read to me awhile. Then he'd ask me to tell him a story. I was too embarrassed at first. Nothing came, just bits and pieces of things I'd read, but he made me keep trying. Sometimes he'd help get me started. He'd start it off:

"'In a silky black sky, where the round yellow moon drifted through moving dark clouds, a young golden-haired girl emerged from her sleep, crept to the window and peered out, hopeful and wanting. Someone below called to her.'"

"Wow, you remember all that, word for word?" I asked.

"Yes, because he started every story that way, for like, weeks, and then he'd ask me to continue on and finish it. So I started mixing things up, and stringing together lies and half-truths of my own life; my dreams and things I'd read. I started looking forward to it, those nights. Scratching out those little "lies" in my diary, and reading them to Daddy when he got home after a week or a month."

She turned reflective and averted my gaze. Her voice was low and soft. "They were for him. The stories. I wrote everything for him, then. He'd say, write me something, Rita girl. Write. When I'm home, you can read them to me. So I did."

I waited a moment. "Where is your father, Rita?"

Without answering, she pushed the door open. "It's time, Alan James. Turn on the radio and join me."

The radio came alive when I turned on the engine. It was playing Billy Joel's *Honesty*. I left the car, stretching in the cool autumn wind, and went to Rita. She was at the edge of the bluff, peering down at the thirty-foot drop-off to the lake below, ticking off little rocks with her shoes.

"Be careful," I said.

"I always am, Alan James."

As I approached, she turned with an arresting gaze that plunged me into silence. The moon hung just over her left shoulder, riding through puffs of wispy clouds, spilling its light upon the lake and on her fine artistic hairdo. She reached up and released the scarf, allowing it to fall to the ground. The lush waves and curls bounced to her shoulders and she gave a little shake of her head to loosen them. She unbuttoned the top button of her tight-fitted blouse, already strained and pinched. The tops of her breasts were visible and fetching.

"Have to set the mood," she said, breathily.

I heard the gentle lap of waves below. I swallowed. "Okay."

"We're going to dance, Alan James."

I shifted, uneasily. "I don't dance, Rita."

"I know. I read your story about the boy who hated music and thought dancing a bore."

"Yeah...I don't really like music all that much.

I mean some rock stuff, you know...but I don't dance...or anything."

"Music is one of the most uplifting things in this world, Alan James. You need to start listening to good music. Now, relax, Alan James. Just relax and let dancing happen. Give me your hand."

Our hands almost touched. But when I heard him, that voice coming from the car radio, I froze. It was the whiny voice of Jeremy Peels. Our local D. J.

"Okay all you rascals and rascalettes out there. Listen up. It's 8:30 on the dot, and the beautiful and sexy Rita Fitzgerald is out there somewhere with another man, you gorgeous two-timer you. Anyway, she has requested this song by the great Bette Midler to be played at precisely 8:30. You're breaking my heart, Rita. Who is the lucky guy, boys and girls? Who is that rascal? Well, anyway, here goes. Anything for you, gorgeous."

The song began.

"Do you wanna dance and hold my hand..."

I felt violated and nauseous. My face surely revealed it.

"What's the matter, Alan James? Let's dance. Come on." She reached for me.

I backed off. "I hate that guy."

"What guy?"

"You know what guy. Jeremy Peels. He's an asshole. A big pain in the ass asshole."

"He is not."

"He is."

"You don't even know him, Alan James."

"I know him alright."

"No, you don't."

"I do."

"No way."

"Yes way."

Rita threw her fists to her hips. "Not this again."

"Yes, this again."

"You don't even know him, Alan James."

"And I don't want to!"

"Are you going to dance with me?"

"No. I hate that song."

Rita stiffened. "You little shit."

She stormed off to the car, yanked open the door and snatched her red leather handbag from her seat. She took out a pack of cigarettes, shook one out and placed it between her lips. Turning from the quick wind, she flicked her bright green lighter. It flared and she lit the cigarette, blowing the smoke skyward.

I approached, incredulous. "What the hell is this? You don't smoke."

"Really?" she asked, sarcastically. "Because you've never seen me?"

"I hate cigarettes."

Her full lips broke into a mirthless grin. "Smoking is Sooo terrible, isn't it?"

"Yes! It's a dirty, filthy habit."

"It's one of the worst things anyone can ever do in this world, isn't it, Alan James," she said, mocking me. "One of the very, VERY worst."

"Yes, it is!" I said, with self-righteous force.

"What would everybody say if they saw you smoking?"

She took a long drag and let the smoke curl from her lips. "Oh, they'd probably say something like, let's see..." She posed, cigarette dangling provocatively from her mouth. 'Rita Fitzgerald. Smoking!? No way. She shouldn't. She wouldn't. She couldn't!"

She inhaled, took the cigarette from her mouth, and blew the smoke at me. "They'd scowl and wring their hands. My God, not Rita. Please let it not be Rita. But then, they'd suddenly realize the truth behind this awful and atrocious deed. They'd realize that I, Saint Rita of Hartsfield, was led to this despicable and desperate act, by none other than..." She advanced aggressively toward me, jabbing an accusing finger. "...YOU, Alan James! YOU are the real guilty party here. Not little ole Rita."

I threw up my hands in irritation and tried to speak, but she threw up a hand to silence me. She stood hipshot, head back, lips wet; her half-hooded eyes set in a lusty invitation. "...YOU, Alan James, tempted and enticed and forced me to do it." She threw a dramatic hand over her overwrought face. "I didn't want to, ladies and gentlemen of the jury. Please, please, understand the whole truth and nothing but the truth. It is such a dirty and filthy habit and one for which I should surely be sent to the stake, smoking all the way. But, and I say, but, with all humility. But!" She shouted with a firm, loud intensity, pausing to take a long drag. "...Alan James made me do it. He did. I swear. He was so seductive with his, 'Ah, come on, you little bitch, you'll love it. Just one little sexy puff. You'll love it, absolutely love it.'"

Her voice lowered to a throaty earthiness. "And I, in turn, will love you, Rita Fitzgerald, like you have never been loved before. I, Alan James, a rascal, and a whisky drinker, will show you how a real woman should be treated. How a real woman should be held and loved! I can guarantee that you will leave my strong arms breathless, satisfied, and forever and ever more grateful."

I stood belittled and angry. "Go to hell!"

She laughed wildly. "Alan James, you are a little stuck up, rich, snobby, tight- assed shit!"

I burned past her, jerked the door open and slid in behind the wheel. I switched off the radio, crossed my arms and fumed.

Rita ignored me. She sauntered toward the lake and finished her cigarette. I watched her irritably, heart pounding, veins throbbing, and then turned away. For a deliciously revengeful moment I thought of driving off and leaving her. The longer I sat, tense and beaten, the greater the temptation. That would show her! The whole town would know. They'd know that Rita was a low-life bitch! Just as I slammed the door and found the gear, I heard the passenger door open. Too late.

Rita got in and closed the door. I faced her with anger. She gave me a soft appealing look. "Hey, there, Alan James, were you going to leave me?"

I ignored her.

"Turn off the engine," she said, at a whisper.

I remained inert.

Her voice dropped into a rich tone of desire. "Turn it off, Alan. Please…"

Reluctantly, helpless now, I did.

She leaned toward me and sought my eyes. "Look at me."

I felt like a little boy, but I did, with a stony stare that soon melted. I was struck by a quiet vulnerability in her eyes—by her long, curled eyelashes, by her long lazy and sensual gaze. I felt myself unravel as she took my hand and squeezed it. "Come on, Alan…Let's go outside."

Outside, we went to a place where fallen leaves made a carpet, near the edge of the cliff.

"Let's dance."

I crept close, took first her left hand, holding it loosely at my side, then her right, raising it to shoulder level. We stood eye to eye; Rita was 5'10" in her heels. We danced to silent music, keeping four inches between us. The power of her enveloped me with a strange pleasure, so I turned away, avoiding her gaze, embarrassed and rigid.

"Not so bad, Alan James. Not so very bad for a concrete man."

The chilly wind shifted direction and a shower of leaves fell around us. I was vaguely aware of the waves on the lake below brushing the shoreline. Rita nestled close and placed her head gently on my shoulder. I tensed up.

"Relax concrete man," Rita joked. "Relax."

I don't remember how long we danced before Rita took off her heels, knelt, reached up and drew me down to her, keeping her steady eyes locked on mine. We faced each other, close. I tried to keep my face as blank as possible. I was petrified.

"It's not so complicated, Alan James."

"...What?"

"...I like you. Simple. I like you very much."

I couldn't speak. Rita took me in for a moment, searchingly, and smiled. When she kissed me, her lips damp and soft, I shivered. My heart throbbed with the first wildness of true love, and suddenly and unexpectedly, I cried. All my defenses were breached and my senses were stung by a sweet and wicked bliss. My eyes were fully open and Rita saw the tears. She touched them in wonder and surprise, and kissed them, as the shadows danced around us. Feeling hopeless and ashamed, I looked away.

"Hey...don't turn away from me, Alan James. No, no, don't turn away. No one has ever cried for me before. Ever. No one." She took my head in her soft hands and looked deeply into my eyes. "It's okay. It's okay to want me. Wanting me is okay."

I reached for her with a new surprise, with a man's strength, and pressed her lips against mine. They were moist and yielding. I quivered. The wind scattered her scented hair, and as it brushed my face, my erection pressed and ached.

She helped me when I fumbled with the buttons of her blouse, but she didn't rush; she kept her deliberate eyes on me. She released her bra, but allowed me the gift of peeling it from her breasts. I did so slowly, overcome, and breathless. The leaves were wet with moonlight, and that same moonshine flooded her. As she tilted her head and gently lifted her torso, proudly, I released a labored breath. Her breasts were large, firm and straight, her waist naturally slim; her nipples erect. I touched them, held them, and felt the assault of love.

It was a moment without thoughts, a moment of turmoil and excruciating desire. When she removed my glasses and flung away my shirt, she stared for a time, grinning. I shivered in the snappy wind. "It's not the worst thing, Alan James. Not the worst."

Her nakedness exposed my own inner nakedness, breaking open something inside that began to pulsate and rise. She seemed to sense it and she coaxed it on with her wide, dreamy eyes. "Come on, Alan James. Come on, baby."

In a blur, our remaining clothes were tugged off and whipped away. She reached for my erection. Her touch sent me into spasms. She squeezed and pressed, without force. She came against me, allowing the full thrill, the ripeness of her body and spirit to have its mesmerizing effect.

She nudged me backwards, and then lay down on top of me. Her breasts were warm and heavy on my chest. I was hot and cold, kissing her neck and hair.

We tangled and played and rolled across the rough leaves and heard distant thunder that made the moment seem destined and primordial; an acknowledgment by the gods that this extraordinary moment was blessed, sacred and inescapable. When she straddled me, I was surprised. I panted, hotly, unsure, confused, seeing a hunger in her eyes.

She handled and guided me, slithered down the length of me, with a shutter and a gentle cry. I faltered, as if struck. We remained motionless for a time as she waited, eyes shut tightly. I pulsed.

Then something deep gathered into a force—a rage of startling passion—and it compelled me to action, a steady drive for satisfaction. Rita was stirred by it, meeting me with a cry of pleasure, drawing me to her, with a poetry of touch and kisses. It became simple then. We kept finding each other, by abandoning, discovering, and sharing. Our eyes met with a shock of pleasure, our march to gratification steadily escalating.

I felt the start of a tremor, the swelling of desire —of loss, of grace, of death. I saw the taut muscles in her neck, saw the growing strain and urgency on her face. I slid in and out of madness, helpless now under the currents of a savage sensation.

When she cried out into the sky, a rocking agitation found a sharp release. The end of longing, fantasy and passion poured into Rita with a driving desperation—with a prayer that my seed would fill her, impregnate her, and mark her, for all time, as my lover. I drove as fast and as deep as I could, prayerful, until I fell into a damp exhaustion.

Thunder rolled across the sky. The strobe of lightning caught us. Rita began to unfold in a slow crumbling descent, coming to rest on my trembling body. I wanted to stay inside her, warm and blessed. I wanted to breathe only her breaths; hear only her words; make love only to her with a man's raw strength, love, and lust.

Her face fell into peace, and I held her, feeling the heat of her waning desire.

"Rita…" I whispered. "I love you…"

A coffee cup shattered on the floor. I was jarred back to the present. One of Jack's customers had dropped it. Coffee lay in splattered geometric designs on the floor behind me. The diner was quiet now. The two men next to me had left. The booths had mostly emptied; there remained only an elderly couple eating oatmeal, and a family of four sharing eggs and pancakes, not talking. A teenage busboy mopped up the spill, while my waitress wiped the counter, refilled my cup, and then stopped to take me in, as if for the first time.

"Anything else?"

"No. Check please."

I was already buzzed from too much coffee. I reached for my wallet, convinced that Rita had gone home or had every intention of ignoring me. It was just as well. I felt slightly irritated at myself for reliving those memories, and surprised by the power of them to leave me strangely sad and wanting.

When the waitress dropped the check, I stood, releasing a little sigh of disappointment and relief. Instinctively, I passed another glance toward the kitchen door, and for a second or two, I thought I heard someone call my name, at a whisper. I quickly scanned the room. Nothing. No one.

As I pivoted away from the counter, the kitchen door opened and Rita slowly emerged. I stood in a strained formality, heart racing. She made a tentative entrance, like an actress on opening night, unsure of her character or lines. Her appearance startled the doctor in me to rigidity and alarm. For the boy of 17, who remembered the goddess, there arose a swift agony. I waited. All eyes were on her, rapt. The room became a tableau. I sensed that she felt my presence before she saw me.

She turned slowly, finding my eyes. All that luxurious long hair was gone, replaced by a mercilessly short style, spiked with gel, and lusterless. Thin and bony, her body lacked shape under the loose blue nylon dress; and the damned dress cheapened her; demeaned her.

It was the ravaged body of a starved animal, the pallid color of an old rag, and the hollow, deep set eyes of someone who had just emerged from a tomb. I met her gaze, seeing the once brilliant fireworks had vanished, replaced by a cold, vacant darkness.

Her vibrancy and inner light, once so palpable and contagious, were smothered. She stood like a woman so damaged by tragedy, so spirit-killed, that it was painfully clear that somewhere, behind those swollen dull blue eyes, she believed that not even death itself offered an escape.

She stared at me with an expression of reproach and pain, and without a movement or word, she held my gaze for the longest time. I was still. I could not find a voice to say "Hello." An excruciatingly long moment later, her miserable gaze slid to the floor, and in a slow, awkward turn, as if being careful not to shatter, she exited through the door to the kitchen.

CHAPTER FIVE

I arrived at the house a little after ten, turned into the driveway and stopped. The morning rain had passed, but fog remained. It hugged the elms and maples and draped the beautiful salmon-stoned Victorian house, with its grand porch, soaring gables and large bay windows, in a thin cotton blanket, giving it the peculiar ghostly appearance of hovering between worlds. In that pearl light, it seemed a place where the past could easily and naturally return to life in a splendor of reenactments, as if from a play. My mother would enter, stage right, emerge from around the house on Saturday morning, dressed for gardening with those little heels, of course, snipping the shrubs, examining the petunias, snap dragons, and pansies, pursing her lips in contempt because I hadn't cut the dewy lawn.

"Alan…" she'd call, from the bottom of the stairs, minutes later. "Why do I always have to get mad and cross before you'll cut the lawn?"

And from the dining room, where he lingered over coffee, a donut and a book, my father would almost always add, "For Pete's sake, Alan. Listen to your mother!"

My bedroom was at the top of the stairs and sound carried terrifically and annoyingly. "I'm studying," was my response, knowing it would buy me more time in bed. Though no one was fooled, it always worked. Studying was such a sacred word to my father, that to oppose or question it was tantamount to being damned for all eternity. To Mom, it meant that I'd gotten the message. There was no more to be said.

Even then, the lawn was professionally landscaped, but Dad left a half-acre, untouched, just for me. Tending that little plot of sloping earth, Dad believed, was good sound character building and exercise, necessary for a boy of privilege and promise. And he knew it pleased my mother that I was helping out in the yard.

"You've got to get out of your head now and then, Alan," Dad would say, although *he* seldom did. He abhorred exercise, unless going to get coffee and donuts was involved. "Get out there and breathe that good, healthy Pennsylvania air, son."

I'd finally get up and drift downstairs. Mr. Dog, our old German Shepard in residence, would be languishing in his L.L. Bean Scottish colored bed next to the masonry fireplace, his brown eyes lazy, his pointed ears as still and tall as church spires. I'd pet him and pull him up, and we'd slump off toward the dreaded chores of the day, like slothful, apathetic soldiers.

Outside we'd find Mom, sealed tightly against any intrusion, assiduously at work. Dad would soon be retreating to his wine cellar, and I to the rider mower. Mr. Dog, inspired by scents and sounds, would trudge off toward the trees, with a happy swinging tongue and a passionate nose, vacuuming the grass.

I shut off the engine and lingered a moment longer, until the images faded. They were swiftly replaced by Rita's devastated image that stuck to my eyes, like an overlay. I got out, pausing to take in the ten acres of landscaped grass, trees and shrubs. For the last three months, I'd received bills for the landscaping and other needed house repairs. I'd paid for them. It allowed me to feel that I was helping Dad, and it helped assuage my guilt for not visiting him regularly. Dad and I were never the typical father and son, nor was our affection for each other ever expressed except in a handshake, a pleasant formal word, or the rare pat on the back. Dad kept me at a distance, and most of the time, that had been fine with me. There was something about him that made me a little uncomfortable and, I suspect, he felt the same about me.

My sister, Judy, on the other hand, was his joy. She was adoring, extroverted and perky: all the qualities he and I lacked. Though not typically "pretty," Judy was earnest, resourceful and religious. The Presbyterian Church was her second home and had been from an early age. She married the son of a Presbyterian minister and they became true and stalwart "soldiers for God" in a large church in

Florida.

Judy was popular at school, was a talented administrator, and, like me, had a great gift for numbers and facts. She became an accountant and works part time to help supplement her husband's already handsome income as a dentist.

If Dad and Mom were not "soldiers for God" then they were, at least, supporters of the battle from a comfortable distance. They tithed, were socially involved and had an appreciation for the pedagogical foundation the church offered. "Leaning toward the light" helped sustain the family nucleus, in a corrupting age where sex, drugs and rock and roll proliferated, weakening and destroying the delicate fabric of home, town and country.

Mom took me to church, insisting that I wear a suit and tie, insisting that I sing at least one hymn, insisting that we "gently" debate the sermon on the way home. Judy was never comfortable with this and Dad just stayed out of it by saying, "Let's not get all carried away about this."

Judy and I had passed through various states of closeness over the years, but grew especially close during Mom's illness and death. Judy's religious faith deepened during that time but mine, which was always tenuous and tied to my deep love for Mom, nearly breathed its last when she did. Hers was not an easy death and, for a woman who possessed the finest of hearts and the best of faiths, her painful suffering death at sixty seemed a personal insult.

I crossed the walk, pulling my suitcase, and climbed the front stairs heavily, dreading the calls to the real estate auctioneer and the antique dealer. I turned off the alarm system, opened the door and entered. I closed the heavy oak door, and leaned back against it, standing in the broad foyer, facing the two-story chestnut winding staircase. In that ringing silence, I felt straining tears. I hadn't cried since Mom's funeral, but I couldn't get Rita out of my head. I felt a storm of emotions.

It seemed to me that fate, or God, or whatever, had thrust a knife through Rita's soul's heart. And if, as my sister says, suffering brings wisdom, then the human race, for all of its suffering, remains supremely stupid.

I wandered the rooms, aimlessly: the dining room, with violet walls, Chippendale dining set and a massive, gilded brass chandelier. Two pink French vases still emitted the rose and vanilla floral scent of Mom's favorite potpourri. "I want this room to be spring-like all year long," Mom had said. I heard the echo of her voice.

My father was truly religious when it came to the house: it was the heaven that had been secured for him by his great grandfather's force, money and holy prestige, and Dad worshipped it with an undying devotion.

I stepped across the threshold of the living room. It hovered in a lively silence and solemn dignity.

The mauve-colored walls ricocheted back to me my parents' arguments about its color.

"Catherine...Catherine," my father pleaded, "That color... well, it just reminds me of a house of ill repute. That's all I'm saying."

Mom glared, hands on her hips. "And how would you know that, Richard Lincoln?"

Poor Dad blustered and stammered. "Catherine...that...that is not worthy of a response and I'm disappointed in you for saying it. Now let's just go with it and forget the whole thing."

Mom had the last word. "That's right! Forget the whole thing!"

The generous stone fireplace contained remnants of cozy talk on cold December nights about Christmas parties and school concerts. The plush Victorian couch, loveseat and side chairs, all red velvet and beechwood, reverberated with low gossip and sips of tea from Mom's weekly bridge games.

There were two five-foot stained-glass windows, depicting nymphs, shepherds and fat little cupids, wings fluttering, bows cocked, arrows in flight toward the heart. Twice a week, Dad paused on his way to the library to take them in, with a satisfied nod, as if he were checking the accuracy of a grandfather clock.

The formal parlor had been redone in a Rocco Style, with rich blues and whites and a black marble fireplace. Dad's wealthier clients, the minister and the mayor had all walked through it, impressed and assured.

I climbed the stairs, lethargically, feeling the weight of time, hearing old sounds. My mother's hairdryer. Dad's electric shaver. Mom's flat singing voice. Judy's enthralled voice, describing her new boyfriend to Dad. I heard Dad's bathroom radio announcing the morning business report.

I drifted into my parents' upstairs bedroom. Mom had chosen a Greek Revival theme, with salmon, rose and reds. Dad never liked it much, either.

"I feel like a man possessed," he'd once said of it.

"And you are," Mom had thrown back, with a chuckle.

My room was Early American, complete with antiques, including a four poster bed. I sat on it for a moment, gently bouncing, staring, remembering the nights I lay thinking of Rita and imagining her lying next to me. I saw my writing desk and recalled the arduous hours spent on my valedictorian speech. I'd stalked the room, like a mad poet, gazing out the windows and cursing Rita. After our break-up, I had to completely rewrite it, changing the themes from "Optimism and Hope" to "Challenges and Strength."

"If a door slams in your face, find another and open it wide!" I'd written.

I smiled at the memory, and then stood, ready to complete my re-acquaintance of the house.

There were hidden cupboards, deep closets, a back spiral staircase, and a wonderful attic packed with old letters, paintings, furniture and photographs that dated back to the 1890's. It smelled old and, for America, it was old.

I finished downstairs, in Dad's library. There was a museum quality and stillness about it. Without Dad's presence, it seemed sad. I felt like an intruder.

It was gothic, with arches and a vaulted ceiling. It was a wise and lofty room, lighted by tall windows and surrounded by window seats with green cushions that looked out on rolling hills, our little pond and Mom's flower gardens. It had built-in floor-to-ceiling mahogany bookshelves, mostly empty now, once stacked with hardback first editions of Hemmingway, Steinbeck and Faulkner, as well as a stunning variety of 18th and 19th century novels. Biographies of Jefferson, Washington and Franklin occupied space with Shakespeare, Pope and Ruskin. In an adjoining bookshelf, he kept the latest books and periodicals on the tax code, Pennsylvania tax law and various revised editions of the Bible and its commentaries. He had a massive collection of records and various turn tables (he had an aversion to CDs) and when the three B's, Brubeck, Bach or Beethoven were "ON", the house throbbed. My mother would have to complain and ask for "Restraint, for God's sake, Richard! Turn it down!" She would swiftly march to her room, slam the door and the competition would begin. Within seconds, The Beach Boys or Credence Clearwater Revival would thunder out in a sweet retaliation.

Dad preferred leather furniture, and it was all

a rich chocolate brown from couch to chairs. His desk was an old-fashioned American antique roll top, bought from the editor of the Hartsfield Press over forty years ago, and Dad executed all of his correspondence there with great pride and alacrity, feeling, as he'd once said, "Like a man infused with the practical and independent spirit of Jefferson and Franklin." I was going to ship it to him in Florida. It would certainly lift his dark mood.

I settled into a deep leather chair and suppressed a sigh. I stared at the majestic trees, the foggy pond and a narrow winding path that led to it. As the fog lifted, my memories returned.

Mom had found me here the night I'd made love to Rita. She switched on the overhead light and adjusted the dimmer. "Why are you still up? It's after one o'clock."

I peered up at her. "I could ask you the same question."

I suddenly noticed that she was pretty. It had seldom occurred to me: she was just Mom, and like most of the young, I was self-absorbed. But after making love to Rita, I seemed to have brand new eyes. I saw my mother in a different light. Her lips were ruby red, her cheek bones were high, her long glossy auburn hair was slightly tangled and askew. Her makeup and lipstick were smudged. She had a stately, refined stature and lovely formed hands. She stood before me flushed, youthful and dreamy-eyed.

Standing in her full-length cream-colored silk

robe and high-heeled slippers, I felt great love and affection for her. I swiftly recalled my parents' private little winks and covert touching when they thought Judy and I weren't looking; recalled the glimmer of something both tender and racy in my mother's prissy little smile and playful eyes. I saw my father's ready acknowledgement and anticipation: that the night would bring a lucky rapture.

It was obvious then that they'd just shared such a rapture. She averted my eyes in gentle embarrassment, suddenly aware that I was studying her in a curious way. She spoke at a whisper, as if the walls had ears. "Your father...I mean, his snoring. Well, you know, it keeps me awake sometimes."

I gave her a knowing side-long stare. "Why don't you just move in to the spare bedroom?"

She flicked an impatient hand at me. "No way. A husband and wife should never sleep in separate beds. That's something for you to remember when you get married." She began finger-placing the loose strands. "Why are you sitting down here? Are you all right?"

I was feeling slightly melancholy and restless, struggling to sort out my chaotic feelings. Making love to Rita had shaken me. I mentally wandered from bliss and sexual excitement, to fear and confusion.

Only a few months back, I had been to a Pittsburgh strip club, with an older cousin. I saw exposed breasts and round bare asses, bouncing and grinding under strobe lights. One glorious redhead, with pouty lips, had even swooped down, whipped her massive breasts in my face, and set the silver tassels spinning in perfect symmetry. Yes! I was ready for her. But she threw me a sassy kiss and strutted away in her red glittering stiletto heels, to a much more handsome guy. I had fantasies about her for a week.

I'd kissed two girls in my life, and I had seen my fair share of porn magazines and movies. I understood attraction and lust and I liked them. But I did not fully understand the naked, tumultuous, and emotional effect that Rita had had on me. What did I mean when I told her I loved her? When she didn't respond, what did that mean? I'd felt foolish, exposed, and small. I felt like a boy, not a man.

My mind flooded with the sight and smell of her. Violets! My emotions were in riot, remembering our second love making, in the backseat of the Dodge Intrepid later that night after inhaling a medium pizza.

When I entered Rita the second time, I felt like a prince, a pirate, a hero. It was a playful and bewildering experience; the pleasure scintillating and elaborate; my emotions volatile. The hard rain striking the car gave us the furtive intimacy to explore. We finally arched in a perfect cadence and drifted to rest, legs and arms tangled, hair tousled, mouths open, gasping air.

Afterwards, Rita was silent. I could feel her rapid pulse and soft breath on my neck and I said, "I love you, Rita. ... I do."

But when Rita remained silent, seemingly unmoved, there came the inevitable thought: Why me? Why did Rita go out with me? Make love to me? Am I good enough for her? Is this skinny, nerdy kid good enough?

My mother was watching me with keen interest. "How was your date with Rita?"

I was guarded. I did not want any expression or gesture to reveal the slightest emotion. I shrugged. "You know, fine."

"Just fine?" she asked, with a gentle lift of her chin and a dubious gaze.

"We had a good time."

"What did you do?"

"You know...movie. Pizza."

"What movie?"

I was prepared. "*A Time to Kill*...with Sandra Bullock. It was good."

I looked away.

"Did Rita like the movie?

"Sure."

"Does she like you?"

I grew uncomfortable. "I guess."

"Did you kiss her?"

"Come on..." I protested, turning aside.

"Did you make another date with her?"

"We'll meet at Jack's... On Wednesday."

I admired my own self-command. When I'd dropped Rita at her door, I'd asked her out for next

Friday night. She gave me a carefree, innocent smile. "I don't know, Alan James. Let's meet at Jack's on Wednesday. I have a story I'm working on I want you to read."

Then she left me in a light rain. Her mother had watched us, silhouetted from behind the screen door. I pictured her stern and somber face and accusing eyes, because Rita's hair was long, frizzy and sexy. Obviously, Rita had let it down for me.

On the drive back to the house, as the wipers slapped the windshield, I played back the events of the evening. An unpleasant thought appeared. I wondered if Rita had planned the entire night. She was so very theatrical and erratic. Maybe she had simply been acting—playing one of her roles; the role of beauty queen, seducing the poor, homely nerd. Maybe it was research for one of her stories? Maybe she'd tell others: that asshole D. J. Jeremy Peels; the Boston lawyer; her girlfriends!

I hated the thought and it sickened me. I felt the rise of cold rage and, with it, came the beginning of a dark plan. I decided to be icy and indifferent to Rita at our next meeting on Wednesday. I'd even tell her that I hated her story, whether I did or not. She'd be confused and off balance by my behavior, but I'd just let her dangle and fret.

"You seem a little upset, Alan," Mom said.

"No...not at all. Just sleepy."

"Go to bed then."

I nodded, looking at her again, with slow probing eyes. "You know what? You got all the good looks in the family."

Mom smiled, modestly. "There's nothing wrong with your looks, Alan. Nothing at all. You have your father's coal black eyes and strong chin. I find those very attractive." She winked at me. "I bet Rita Fitzgerald does, too." She started for the door. "Good night, Alan."

At school on Monday, I was cool toward Rita and she was remote. That confused and unnerved me. We met at her locker as she gathered books for her next class. She wore a peach-colored sweater and designer jeans. We stood near the tall window where a shaft of sunlight framed her, and she seemed to glitter.

"You didn't call yesterday," Rita said.

"Your mother hates me."

Rita shrugged. "So?"

"So, I don't like her. She's a bitch."

Rita shot me a disapproving glance. "Don't call her that!"

"Okay, fine. Whatever. She's a wonderful woman," I said, sarcastically.

"What's the matter with you?"

"Nothing."

With a little shake of her head, she slammed her locker and walked away, leaving me there, humiliated. Students passed, whispering, snickering, turning to watch Rita's hasty retreating steps, and then commenting. Dusty Palmer strode by, with good looks and confidence all about him like a blessing.

"Hey, Alan. How's it going, man?"

I ignored him.

He stopped abruptly, left the two beefy guys he was with, and wandered over. My postured improved, as I tried to gain height. Dusty was 6' 2".

He shoved his hands into his pockets and looked me over curiously. "You dating Rita?"

I dropped my voice, aware that mine was already naturally lower than his. "Yeah. I am," I answered, proudly.

But he already knew that. He'd seen us at Jack's and everyone at school knew what Rita was doing and who she was dating.

"I dropped math," Dusty said, scratching his long sandy hair. "Just not good at it. Did okay in geometry. Algebra knocked the shit out of me, you know. But calculus, hey no way, man, no way. Mr. Burkett said I'd still graduate if I dropped it. That did it, man, I dropped it quick…like fast and quick, man. Fast and quick."

I waited, observing his broad handsome face working on another question. "So, Alan…" He said, standing awkwardly, "You're good in history, right?"

"Yeah…and math, too. I'm excellent in math," I said, watching him squirm and enjoying it.

"Yeah, well, I was kind of wondering if you could, you know, maybe give me some help…you know, pointers or something with history. I'm… well, I can't drop it. I've already dropped math. I can't drop history too and graduate, and I figured that history has got to be easier to pass than math. You know what I'm saying, man?"

I nodded, silent.

"I'm not stupid or anything... I just don't... I don't like it, Alan. It's so damn boring, man. I mean dates and names and all those places. Shit, man, I don't get the need for it. Nobody out in the world cares whether I know where some damn revolutionary battle was fought or what Andrew Jackson did in the Civil War."

"Andrew Jackson didn't fight in the Civil War," I said, with a haughty little sniff.

"Okay, Alan," he said, brightly, as if to hammer in his point. "Okay, you see, I need some help with this shit. So can you, you know, tutor me a little? I mean, I'll pay you. I don't expect nothing free. I just need to pass a couple of tests and then I don't give a shit. I'll pass the course with a C or D and that's okay with me, man, because I'll graduate. What do you say?"

I couldn't believe my good fortune. I was dating Rita Fitzgerald, and now, Dusty Palmer, the All Star Quarterback, who was said to have the eye of a couple of pro team scouts, was asking me to tutor him.

I made a long sad face. "I'm sorry, Dusty. I just don't have the time. I get so many people asking me to help them all the time and, if I helped all of them, I'd never have the time to study myself."

Dusty blushed from the roots of his hair, meek and wounded. It surprised me. I'd expected anger or hard, sneering words. I had braced for them and even had a retort. I was going to say "Hey, buddy, what can I do? It's a time thing. No hard feelings."

But Dusty softened into vulnerability. "Hey, yeah, man. Hey sure, I can dig that. You've got your own shit to get together. Okay…Yeah and I'm gonna just bend my head around that shit, Alan. I'm gonna just do it. Hey, maybe this is what I really needed… somebody to kick me in the ass a little."

He held up a hand to high five me. I hated doing it, but I did. We slapped hands and he lumbered away, head down, shoulders hunched.

The hall had emptied of students, but it echoed with muffled voices, filtering through open classroom doors. I heard the shuffle of books, the shrill ringing late bell and the final slam of a locker. I was late to math, but I didn't care. I'd already completed the week's assignment. Mr. Burkett, as always, would be impressed. The students jealous. I swaggered off, feeling a little nauseous. The nausea intensified as I thought about the conversation with Dusty. I grew so nauseous that I skipped lunch.

CHAPTER SIX

On Wednesday afternoon, Rita and I sat in Jack's Diner, avoiding each other's eyes, as well as the mound of overcooked french fries. Rita was wrapped in an elegant gloom and had said little since we'd arrived. The diner was quiet. Don McClean sang an old song, *Starry, Starry Night*. Outside, winter dropped in with a harsh wind and a light dusting of snow that sugar-coated the world and augmented my bad mood. The low gray clouds and snow mocked that thrilling autumn night—only four days ago—when Rita and I had made love in moonlight. My first time. My first love. The lover introduced to love by a Goddess.

Now, with the damned cold weather, the whole episode seemed to have been an elaborate fantasy: something oddly imagined or witnessed, but not experienced. Rita and I were further away, not closer, and I didn't understand why. The longer I searched for reasons, the further from her I felt. I was desperate to return to the magic.

The wind rattled the windows. Rita finally lowered her eyes on my story. Rita's story lay before me, like a bad omen. Neither of us wanted to read, but we did, because we'd lost the thread of a dismal topic of conversation and couldn't think of anything else to say.

"It's kind of an essay/short story," Rita said, raising her chin slightly with uneasy pride. "It's kind of an experiment. Ms. Lyendecker made some suggestions when she read it yesterday."

I noticed her perfect posture, her brooding, insecure eyes.

I began Rita's story.

Riding The Fence
by
Rita Fitzgerald

She never liked making choices, because every choice she'd ever made led her to the realization that the "Yes" or "No" of any choice always led basically to the same place: to the experience of something utterly regretful or astonishing. Therefore, she stopped making choices some time ago. Now she observed that love or rejection never boomeranged back on her in either disappointment or satisfaction, because she simply rejected the idea of making a choice.

It seemed an absurdity to make any choice at all when everyone led to a basic unknown anyway. What was the point? To grow? Then, surely, any choice would accommodate. Or no choice would also do. The weights and balances of the heart would decide, or not decide. A balance of experience would supersede the "This and That."

And so it was that when she met Oliver, she did not kiss him on the first date, not because it was a conscious choice, but because she was deft at reading boys' intentions the way an astrologer reads the movement of planets or the truly inspired minister interprets the Bible.

So she did not kiss Oliver, but it was not a choice to not kiss him. No. She knew that, with that first kiss, he would demand another, and finally another, until the long humid evening would climax in a slapped face and a disagreeable departure. That would happen. It was a fact. It was a natural outgrowth of the friction of two "hot" people in one space. And yet, she wanted Oliver to kiss her. Another complexity. A contradiction of choice.

But she would turn away from

Oliver, indifferent, smoke and brood. She would strike a balance between the "ify" choice of this and the firm choice of that. She would, simply, wait and just BE. Let the choice of BEING and NOT BEING grind together in a friction of possibility, so that she could truly be born into a LIFE of BEINGNESS, and not be a slave and a whore to choice.

I tossed the story down in frustration. "I don't know what the hell you're talking about here, Rita. It's too damned abstract." As soon as the words left my mouth, I wanted to retrieve them.

Rita lifted her eyes from the page, surprisingly pleased by my comment.

That encouraged me, so I went on. "I mean, … well, she didn't kiss him. Okay. But no matter how you look at it, it was still a choice not to kiss him, whether she wanted to or not."

"No it wasn't."

"It was."

"No. She knew the outcome."

I felt the temptation of argument rise, giving strength to my voice. "Okay, fine. She knew the outcome. Big deal. It was still a choice. I mean, this is a world of dual things. Physics tells us that: The law of cause and effect. For every action there is a reaction. You didn't kiss him, because, I don't know, because you knew he'd like try to have sex with you or something. Okay, fine, but that was a choice."

Rita shook her head. "No. The choice never happened," Rita argued. "She did not choose."

"By not choosing, she chose, Rita. There's no way around it."

"No. By rejecting both choices, she went beyond choice to a 'happening'."

"Come on, Rita. So the point is to become a victim and just let fate make all your choices? I just don't get that."

"You're missing the point."

"No. It's pointless. It's way too abstract for the reader. And this whole comparison of the astrologer and preacher. Any preacher I know thinks astrology is the devil's work."

"It gives tension, Alan James. It gets your attention. It provokes."

"It's too damned abstract."

"Okay, it's too abstract. Good."

I leaned forward. "Rita, all this character did was make a choice based on a feeling or an experience. But it was still a choice. There's no way around it. And what does 'grind together in a friction of possibility, so she could truly be born into a LIFE of BEINGNESS' mean?"

Rita's face became flushed, animated. "Freedom. The struggle for freedom to live without the fear of making a bad choice."

"That's how we learn, Rita. You make a bad choice, you learn not to make that choice again."

"No way!" Rita protested. "If you'd finished the

story, you'd see that it's about the freedom to truly be what you are. The freedom to cut a path through water, leaving no foot prints."

"And what if you can't walk on water, because you can't, and the water's too damned deep and you drown?" I asked.

"Then so be it. Better to die free and true to yourself than to be scared and a slave."

I threw up my hands. "I don't know, Rita. You've been reading too much Thoreau or something."

She went into her recitation pose and I waited for a quote from Thoreau. 'What I am I am, and say not. Being is the great explainer.'"

"Thoreau was an airhead," I said.

"Okay, what about Blake?"

"More than an airhead. He was whacked out. Who can even understand what the hell he's saying half the time."

Rita's expression turned philosophical, and I braced for a Blake quote. 'I must create a system or be enslaved by another man's. I will not reason and compare. My business is to create.'"

I blew out a frustrated sigh. "I still say your story is illogical and idealistic, and don't get mad at me or anything, but it's just…just… idiotic!"

She looked at me with amused tolerance. "Thank you, Alan James. Coming from you, the hardheaded pragmatist, the brainy kid who would be king, that's a compliment."

I didn't know whether to be angry because I'd been insulted, or laugh because she was so clever.

But I didn't really care if she'd insulted me. The somber mood had been broken and I swiftly made my move. I took off my glasses and narrowed my hopeful eyes on her. "So, what if I pick you up at 7 o'clock on Friday night?"

She rested her alluring eyes on me. "Where are you taking me?"

"Back to the lake?" I asked, hopefully.

She shook her head slowly. "Nooooo... Never repeat, Alan James. Be original and inventive. Otherwise, life becomes flat. Boring. Let's go to a movie."

I shrank back, disappointed. "A movie!? How ordinary and boring is that? A movie!?"

"Yes, Alan James. Your choice. Then, afterwards, we'll improvise."

I liked the sound of "we'll improvise."

She picked up my story. "Now, let me read your story. Let's see what the young Mr. Einstein has written for us," she said, playfully flitting her eyebrows.

I grabbed three french fries, salted them generously, and pushed them into my mouth.

Extraordinary
by
Alan Lincoln

Harry Pine awoke one morning and, to his utter astonishment, he felt EXTRAordinary. He'd never really felt extraordinary before. Not in his entire life. It had never even occurred to him that it was even possible to feel extraordinary. The

word itself had never even been part of his vocabulary; had never occupied any space within his vast universe, nor in the quantum field of the subatomic particles of bosons, leptons, and quarks. But there it was. He couldn't deny the obvious. The remarkable! The incarnate! As he looked into the mirror, he saw on his face, written clearly and boldly, the word E X T R A ordinary.

Harry had fallen in love with Lizzy McAlpin, a girl who had startled the best and the worst in him; caressed him into disorder with her white willowy arms and sent him off into that extraordinary world of delightful pain.

All would not be well. Nay, never again. Harry Pine would never again play the electric guitar with those sharp Hendrix riffs, or wind-mill through chords like Springsteen, or scream out hoarsely like Zepplin. No, he was in the world of the extraordinary now and he was doomed to a world of tripping and stumbling through Dylan-esque words and phrases, on the fruitless search for the true meaning of that word: E X T R A ordinary.

Rita laid the pages aside, nibbling the tip of the blue striped straw, taking the occasional thoughtful sip of her soda. When the glass was drained, the straw scraped the bottom in little staccato hisses and crackles. I waited, peeved, by her deliberation and obvious stalling. When she finally turned to me, her eyes had filled with a firm conviction. "Okay, Alan James...Okay. Only a couple of things."
"No way," I said, defensively.
"I don't like the girl's name, Lizzy McAlpin."
"Big deal."
"And" she stressed with a raised finger. "And...I skimmed ahead and read the middle and end of the story. Harry only talks about himself. HE felt. HE this, HE that."
"It's his story." I protested.
"It's a selfish story, Alan James."
"Bullshit."
"I want to know more about Lizzy. You don't even describe her. Not once. We only hear about Harry. Harry this and Harry that. It's selfish, Alan James. Pure and simple."
"Rita, it's a story about Harry."
"No, Alan James. It's really a story about what

happened to Harry after he met Lizzie. It's their story. Maybe more her story than his."

"It's from Harry's point of view, Rita!"

"Just tell me this. Would there be a story without Lizzy?"

I squirmed. "No, but..."

"Okay then."

"Okay, nothing. You're missing the whole point."

"Which is?" Rita asked.

"Harry has been utterly changed. Transformed. Because of Lizzie. I'm focusing on him!"

"Yes, and I say it's selfish. I want to know who Lizzy is. What she looks like. Why Harry likes her. What was it about her that changed him? You've got none of that in your story. It's Harry, Harry, Harry!"

"It's a short story, not a damned novel."

Rita reached for a french fry. "That's just an excuse, Alan James."

Frustrated, I sat back. "You are wrong," I said, with a jerk of my chin, just like my father, when he wanted the last word.

Rita grinned. "And you, Alan James, need to rework your story because it is selfish."

I spent the next two days living on the edge of exhilaration and irritability. Every emotion was heightened, every brief conversation with Rita examined for some potential treachery, or indication that our sexual intimacy and literary relationship had fueled a solid foundation of love and trust, although I had neither. At school, Rita talked to other boys. Laughed with them. Touched them. They hovered, delighted to be on the outer ring of her resplendent Planet Rita. The jocks struggled for smooth words; the others, "the rabble" I called them, hungrily grabbed the scraps of her comments—of any comments—as they nudged forward with slanting eager eyes.

"Yes…tomorrow I have a photo shoot for *Pennsylvania Getaways* Magazine," she said. And "Of course I'm trying out for *Picnic*. William Inge is one of my favorite playwrights." Or, and this made me want to vomit, "No, I'm not going to tell you who I was with Saturday night when Jeremy played *Do You Want to Dance*."

"Was it Alan Lincoln?" Dusty asked, so close to her that their arms nearly touched. What a striking couple they were. They were natural, like sky and sea. They rang true and any idiot could see that. It was devastating.

Rita didn't flinch. She drew closer. "That's nobody's business, Dusty," she said not meeting his eyes, but I could see that Dusty's near touch had had an effect on her. She grew a little restless and self-conscious.

"He told me, Rita. Alan told me himself," Dusty continued.

Rita shrugged.

"Alan's a dick," somebody said. Dave Webster, I think.

"A smart dick with a good head," Kenny Hill said.

They all chuckled. Not Rita.

That was the cleverest thing I'd ever heard Kenny say. He'd be lucky to graduate from high school and yet his insult of me was nearly worthy of Shakespeare.

I kept a safe distance from "the ring". A "Rita Distance," she'd called it. "I need space, Alan James," she'd said only the day before. "I'm not comfortable holding hands in the hallways or meeting for lunch and sitting together all the time like we're little lost fluttering doves in love. I hate that."

So from a Rita distance, I watched Dusty take in the elixir of her presence. His devotional eyes found her lips, her breasts, her neck; when he breathed, he expanded and was transformed from boy to man. I hated him. I hated myself and I hated Rita.

Rita did not come to school on Friday. She had her photo shoot. Friday night, I was in the bathroom splashing on my father's Brut Aftershave, when the telephone rang. I expected the worst, and I wasn't disappointed.

"It's Rita Fitzgerald," my father called from the living room.

That pissed me off. He could have just said "Rita." I would have known. Why did he always have to be so proper and exacting? So damned uptight!?

I stared into the mirror, seeing the bottled-up contradiction on my face. I hated Rita with a love that overpowered me, that debased me. I took some quick breaths and went to the hall phone. I answered sharply.

"Yeah!"

"Alan James?" Rita's voice was tense.

"Yes…"

"Something's come up."

Dusty, I thought bitterly. "Yeah…"

"My father's here."

"Your father?" I asked, surprised. I hadn't expected that. A lie? The truth? I couldn't think.

"Alan James?"

"Yes…Yeah… When?"

"An hour ago. I haven't seen him in almost 2 years." Her voice suddenly sounded strange. Tentative. "I can't make it tonight."

I looked toward the ceiling, the walls, the floor. I switched the phone to my left ear.

"Alan James?"

"I'm here."

"I have to be with him. Him and Mom."

"Have to? Where's all that freedom? I must create a system or…"

She cut me off. "…Don't be a prick!"

"Then don't lie to me!"

"I'm not lying! You think I'd lie about this!? Do you, Alan James!?"

"What do I know?"

"You are a shit, you know that!?"

"Yeah, I am, especially when I know you're lying to me."

Her voice dropped an octave, in a challenge. "Okay, Alan James, come by tomorrow and meet him."

That unsettled me. "What…What do you

mean?"

"Alan James," she said with contempt. "You told me you have a near photographic memory and an I.Q. of at least 142, right?"

"Yeah."

"So, don't play stupid with me. You called me a liar. Okay, I'm asking you to come by tomorrow and meet my father so I can prove to you that I'm not a liar. Afterwards, we can go to the movie. Is that very clear, Mr. Smart Ass? Can your brilliant little mind grasp all of that or do I need to repeat it fifty times or put it into some mathematical equation or draw you a very clear and precise picture?"

I cleared my throat, shrinking in height.

"Are you there, Alan James?"

"Yes."

"Are you afraid to meet my father?"

I was. "No, of course not."

"So...?"

"Yeah. I got it. What time's good?"

"Seven."

She hung up.

After I hung up, I moped down to the kitchen, utterly depressed. Before she'd left for the movies with her girlfriend from church, Mom had prepared a plate of left-overs for me: meatloaf, mashed potatoes, brussel sprouts and apple sauce. I ate alone, picking and shoving food from one side of the plate to the other. I built a little mashed potato hut, and then destroyed it with a single violent slap of my fork.

Dad wandered in, dressed in his black cardigan sweater, white shirt and blue perfectly creased pants. He held a book entitled *Masks of the Universe*, by Edward Harrison. It was my book, written by a physicist about man's search for meaning in the universe.

"I didn't know you liked reading that stuff," I said.

"Physics has always interested me. The dance of atoms and waves." Dad opened the bookmarked page and began to read.

> "'We cannot predict actualities, only their probabilities, and an element of chance is thus involved. And yet the phantom world of becoming itself is deterministic and free of all caprice.'"

Dad closed the book. "I don't understand all of it, but I find it stimulating. It's an interesting change from reading about Thomas Jefferson's demons in *A Portrait of a Restless Mind*. Jefferson would have loved the new universe theories, I think."

Dad could see I was preoccupied. "Did Rita Fitzgerald stand you up?" he asked.

"No," I said, snappily. "Something came up."

"Came up, eh? Well, I'm sure she can find lots to come up with."

I angrily pushed my plate aside. Dad was pleased with his clever joke. I would have stormed out, but I had a question—a burning question to which I knew he'd have the answer. One of the natural "perks" of managing money for the poor and rich alike was the "necessary and professional" gossip about the neighbors next door.

"Dad.... What do you know about Rita's father?"

He turned the question over in his mind. "Not much. Sent to prison for armed robbery and forgery, I think I read somewhere, or heard from a client."

"Held up a bank?"

His right bushy eyebrow lifted, like Spock's on *Star Trek*. "Yes... a bank, maybe more than one bank."

"Have you ever seen him?"

Dad took off his glasses, pulled a handkerchief from his back pocket and polished the lenses. "Oh yes, years ago. Nice looking and very personable, as I recall. Used to work in one of the factories. Layton's Factory, if memory serves. Carl Layton Sr. had been a client then. Anyway, I'd see Frank Fitzgerald sometimes. But that's been, oh, at least fifteen or sixteen years ago."

"Why would you remember him out of all the others?"

"Yes, why? Good question, Alan. Because infamy stimulates memory." Dad took on his look of the solid expert, as if everything he was about to say was to be held in the strictest of confidence and was of vital importance. He was a financial man—and all his clients expected this confident authority of manner, his carefully selected words and the austere gleam in those very dark eyes. He eased down in the chair next to me, an earnest statue with a professorial delivery.

"He played softball for the factory team. He was quite good. A star player. He was a big man and a homerun hitter. Sometimes, on a nice summer night, your mother and I would get a baby-sitter for you and Judy and we'd go out to the softball game. It was good business to be seen by the owners and the factory workers in those days—to be supporting their team, even though I didn't give a damn who won or lost. I hated the game, and still do, but it had to be done. Our business was expanding. Then it was just my brother, Robert, my first cousin, Ed, and I. We took turns. I was so happy when we lost that account."

"Why did you lose it?"

"Well...in those days, there was a son, I won't mention names, but a vice president of the company, who was using the company funds as his own personal piggy bank. I found the discrepancy and discretely brought it to the attention of Mr. Layton Sr. and to the chief financial officer."

"They didn't know?"

My father lowered his lids to half-mast. "Let's just say they were in the process of searching for a solution and had tried to cook the books so I wouldn't find the problem. But I did. Of course I did. It was a matter of pride and ethics. Well, they thanked me, politely, for my earnest and conscientious work and said they'd be in touch. That evening they called and discharged us."

"Discharged you! Why!?"

Dad chuckled. "But that was fine with us, Alan. Just fine. We understood perfectly. We had even expected it."

"Well, I don't get that," I said, leaning toward him.

"That's how business works, son. The following week, they called to advise us that they had recommended our firm to a rather large retail company in Pittsburg. The son was eventually sent away. Because of that referral, we were paid handsomely for our discretion. You see, son, that retail company is now one of our largest clients, and they're expanding to Europe and the Far East. We actually made more from them than we ever would have made from that little factory."

"How does this tie in with Rita's father?"

His brow knitted as he slipped his glasses back on. "Yes, Rita's father. Well, Mr. Frank Fitzgerald was very good friends with the greedy son. It seems that they were, as they say, thick as thieves. When the son left town, so did Frank. I surmise that Frank was paid off by Mr. Layton Sr. to keep quiet about his knowledge of Junior's many indiscretions and misdemeanors. So Frank vanished. A couple of years later, Frank was sent to prison for bank robbery. One would assume that he got used to the good life or, perhaps, he wasn't quite as clever as his friend; or perhaps he had been set up in some way. I don't know. I never had the inclination to follow-up with it."

"What happened to the son?"

"The son... He seems to be involved in a number of shady deals, but manages not to get caught. He is clever. As I said, perhaps Frank is not so clever."

Dad stood. "After Frank left, the factory team had a string of disappointing seasons. Frank Fitzgerald, it seems, was both an inspiration and a driving force."

My father started to leave, but I had a final question. "What about Rita's mother?"

He didn't turn to face me. "A poor soul, Alan. A very unfortunate and poor soul. She kept her job at the factory when Frank left, but struggled because of some kind of illness. She finally had to quit. Thanks to Rita's sudden rise to small town fame, her mother got that job at the drugstore as cashier, and I believe she makes out pretty well."

Dad waited, lowering his head, as if remembering more. He faced me. "The woman's sister has money and I believe that's how they've kept going all these years, keeping up the payments on the house and the little bit of land. Otherwise, God only knows what would have happened to them. I understand that Rita is making some good money now, modeling. I hope she saves it. Bad times are always chasing good. That money should come in handy for them now. Very handy indeed. Maybe you should suggest she make an appointment to come and see me. It couldn't hurt. It couldn't hurt at all."

CHAPTER SEVEN

I drove in an uneasy darkness toward Marion Street, where Rita and her family were waiting for me. Or were they? Maybe they'd fled. I hoped so. Surely her father had more interesting things to do than hang around the house and wait for me. He must have old friends to see and old stories to tell. Knowing Rita, she probably hadn't even mentioned me to him. Maybe I'd pull up to the curb and she'd break from the house, slip into the car and tell me that the whole thing was a joke.

That morning, I was sure Rita would call with an excuse, and I'd hung around the house most of the day in case she did. But the call never came, and so I prepared for the date with a fidgety fussiness that finally irritated me. I'd combed my hair six different ways before deciding to return to my usual and most effective style: stiff and sturdy, like thousands of little black soldiers standing at attention. I showered twice, once in the morning with Dad's sandalwood soap, and once in late afternoon with Mom's oatmeal soap. I trimmed my nose hairs, already becoming a problem and a curiosity, and clipped my jagged toenails, the natural predators of my socks.

I dressed in tight black denim pants, a pale blue

shirt and black cowboy boots: they added an inch to my height. I selected the lightweight and stylish black cotton and rayon jacket that conferred on me the appearance of someone who meant business, like Stallone in the movie *Cobra*. It was tight at the waist and full in the shoulders.

By the time I'd pulled out of our driveway, I realized that I'd splashed on too much of Dad's potent aftershave and I began a steady regimen of sneezing and sniffing. I rolled down my window and drove for a time with most of my head poked out the window, hoping to dissipate the smell. Unfortunately, as I approached the lights of town, Wally Sherman, a trumpet player in the band, passed in his black 1991 Dodge Charger, with his girlfriend, Angela Daysberry, who was glued to his side. They were obviously on their way to the "big" football game, and they were late. If the Hartsfield Vikings won tonight, they'd go to the playoffs in Ohio, and I could have cared less.

Wally laughed, pointed and shouted. "Hey Alan, stick your tongue out, pant a few times and give me a couple of barks. I'll submit your name to Letterman's Stupid Pet Tricks!"

I waited until they were well past before I hollered back, "Eat a big one, Wally! You moron!"

At ten minutes to seven, I parked across the street from Rita's humble, narrow three-story house, where naked trees stood like somber inky shadows. The pitiful porch light flickered erratically from bright to dim, like a code, a warning. To stall for time, I counted the contrast of light to dark: how many long "brights" to short, muted dims and vice versa. There was no particular mathematical pattern, except that I did ascertain that the swells of brightness lasted longer than the "fades" to near darkness.

At exactly seven, I left the car and started for the house, walking into the face of a sturdy wind. I climbed the few steps to the creaking porch and ignored the recessed doorbell, thinking it probably didn't work anyway, and knocked lightly on the door. I heard approaching footsteps. I found a strong stance, feet apart, shoulders back.

The door opened. Rita appeared. "Hello, Alan James." She was cool but genial. It was difficult to read her face in the eccentric porch light.

"Hello," I said, much too brightly. My voice cracked.

She stood aside, invited me in to the close hallway, and shut the door behind me. Her long brushed hair was drenched yellow under the overhead light; a shimmer of blazing summer sun on rippling yellow fields. She wore a gold cashmere cardigan sweater, blue silk blouse, chocolate brown corduroy pants and short dark brown heels with studs. Conservative dress for Rita, but whatever she wore she improved and enhanced.

"Did you model that?" I asked, stiffly.

She was distracted and edgy, glancing over her shoulder. "No...No, not this." She made a vague gesture toward the living room. "Let's get this thing over with. They're waiting."

I gently lifted my shoulders, released the tension, and followed her across the threadbare hall carpet into the square unprosperous living room. I saw heavy brown curtains and worn 60's style furniture, with swirling patterns of orange and tan. I intuitively felt that despair and cheerlessness had seeped into the very icy blue walls. The light above was lurid; revealing, with unapologetic candor, every crack, scrape and flaw of the room.

The humidity instantly shot up. Damp smudges formed on my back, underarms and forehead. My clothes were heavy from it. My aftershave filled the room like an insult and I saw Rita wipe her nose and sniff.

There they sat, Mr. and Mrs. Fitzgerald. She with the cold stare of an enemy, and he with the friendly but cunning, shifty eyes of a salesman. Mrs. Fitzgerald wore a royal blue dress and makeup, neither of which helped to thaw her severity. Her hair had a sculptured beauty shop look—as if it had been poured into a mold and baked into a hard gray crust. It accentuated her thin wrinkled neck and her sagging left eye.

Frank Fitzgerald was not what I had expected. He appeared younger than his wife, more vital and certainly more handsome than she was pretty. I didn't see the match, and the disparity was so stark I stared at them much too long. What in the world had brought them together? He seemed bold and magnetic, a bit sinister; she, worn and frosty, filling a disturbing space.

Frank rose from the frayed brown recliner and seemed to keep rising. He was tall—a least 6' 2"—but probably more, and most likely in his middle 40's. The face was angular, a bit hard, though the blueberry twinkling eyes softened it. He had clipped blond hair, thinning, a short ginger beard and a strong chin. He was lean, with an obvious love for weightlifting. Under the black T-shirt were a broad chest, pinched waist and powerful shoulders. They were not only impressive, but intimidating. A four inch tattoo of a threatening saber, on his right thick beam of a forearm, suggested a formidable foe. He wore tight jeans and stood firmly, anchored by large feet in polished black boots.

He offered his hand: strong, skillful hand of a craftsman. I took it reluctantly, expecting a good punishing crush. He hardly squeezed. "So, you're Mr. Lincoln," he said, in a smooth baritone.

"Yeah...Alan. I mean, you can call me Alan."

"Alan James," Rita said, standing rigidly, as if expecting a confrontation.

"Okay, Mr. Lincoln," he said, finally releasing my hand. "I'm Frank." He indicated toward the squashy looking couch. "Have a seat, Mr. Lincoln, and tell me a little about yourself. Rita hasn't told us much about you."

I sat, noticing the mantel above the obvious non-working fireplace, where oval and square framed photographs displayed Rita, young and old. The one that caught my eye was a recent photo of her in a canary yellow bikini, wearing a broad-rimmed red hat, striking a sexy pose against a deep blue sky. Her smile welcomed, her alluring eyes beckoned.

Another photo grabbed my eyes: it sat next to me on the rickety-looking end table. It was a 5 x 7 color photograph framed in gold of a young Frank in a baseball uniform, with his arm around a very young attractive woman. It took seconds for me to realize, with surprise, that it was Mrs. Fitzgerald! What do you know? She *had* been attractive, once! There was a touch of Rita in the cheek bones, in her elegant long neck and in that timid smile. Her raven black hair was long and shimmering. There was none of the present hardness on her face or in her sultry dark eyes. On the contrary, she looked into the camera with friendliness.

Frank turned his severe eyes to Rita. "You gonna sit?"

"I'll just stand."

"Sit!" he commanded. "We're going to be a while."

Grudgingly, blinking rapidly, Rita eased down next to me, folding her arms. I could still feel the heat of Mrs. Fitzgerald's disapproving stare. I tried to ignore it.

Frank did not sit. He remained on his feet, taking thorough possession of the moment and the room, pacing and appraising Rita and me with a calculated practiced control. He was loose and uninhibited. The room seemed too small for him; perhaps he required a stage for a one-man show. Though he appeared affable, I sensed a covertness and a quiet discontent.

"Rita says you're smart," he said.

"I guess so."

"Where are you going to college?"

"Harvard."

"Ah, yes, of course, Hahvahd," he said, in an exaggerated Boston accent. "I bet you have connections there, don't you Mr. Lincoln?"

"My uncle knows people there."

He grinned, but it held secrets. "It's good to know people, Mr. Lincoln. Why are you going to Hartsfield High School?"

"Why?"

"Yes. With your smarts and your father's money and connections, why aren't you attending a private school?"

I folded my hands, humbly, and then shrugged.

Frank stopped, smiling indulgently. "Doesn't make sense. Bright kid like you going to a public school."

I felt Rita's eyes on me.

"My father is a traditionalist," I said, hoping that would be the end of it. But it wasn't.

Mrs. Fitzgerald spoke up. "But you did attend a private school for a while, didn't you? I'm sure I heard that."

Sweat rolled down my back. I was going to take off my jacket, but I didn't want to lose my Cobra edgy look. "Yeah, for a few years. I went to the Hiller Academy in Massachusetts. I transferred to Hartsfield High in the second half of my sophomore year."

Frank looked at his daughter. "Did you know that?"

"No. Look, Dad, maybe Alan James doesn't want to talk about this."

"Sure he does, don't you, Mr. Lincoln?" he said, then concluded with an encouraging smile that lacked any warmth. "What brought you back home?"

I gave him a slightly offended look. "My mother was ill."

"Ill...? As in sick?" he said, with a mocking tone.

"Yes, she was sick. My father thought it would help her recovery if I came home and went to school here at Hartsfield High."

"What was the matter with her?"

"Dad! That's enough!" Rita protested.

"He doesn't mind, do you, Mr. Lincoln?"

I sat in a miserable silence.

"Okay, so Mr. Lincoln does mind."

"You can call me Alan," I said, with some irritation.

"Are you related to *the* Mr. Lincoln?" he continued.

"Not that I know of."

Frank wandered to the fireplace and leaned against the mantel, examining his daughter's photographs. "So what do you think of our Rita, Mr. Lincoln?"

I heard Rita sigh.

"...I like Rita."

He chuckled. "Yeah…She's become a real beauty, hasn't she?"

I felt myself sinking deeper into the quicksand of the mushy couch. "Yes."

Rita stood, glancing at her new gold watch. "Okay, we need to get going. The movie starts soon."

"Sit down!" Frank barked.

Rita glared at him.

"I'm your father and as long as you live in this house, what I say, goes. Okay, Rita girl? I know you're all famous now and grown up, but you're still under this roof. My roof."

Rita eased down, ignoring him.

He swung his attention back to me. "So what are you going to major in at Harvard, Mr. Lincoln?"

"Pre-Med."

"Pre-Med," he repeated distinctively, as if he were reciting Shakespeare. "So you're going to be a doctor."

"I hope to."

"What kind of doctor? What specialty?"

"Not sure. Maybe a surgeon."

"Good money in that. Is that why you want to be a surgeon, Mr. Lincoln? For the money?"

"Nothing wrong with money," I said.

There was a noticeable shift from insipidness to bright recognition. He straightened. "You are correct, Mr. Lincoln! So very correct about that! Without money, you're a damned castaway—an outcast. A sucker. The rich know that Mr. Lincoln. The rich know all about money and power, and that's why I always made it one of my goals to meet and greet the rich and the powerful. But, unfortunately, as it turned out, that was a mistake."

He paused, for effect, as if waiting for his close up. At least I knew now where Rita had gotten her dramatic sense. "You know, of course, that I was in prison?"

I averted his eyes, looking at Rita. She lit up with embarrassment. Mrs. Fitzgerald shifted for the first time, patting her mound of hard hair.

"I heard that, yes."

"Do you know why?"

"…No…"

"Come on, Mr. Lincoln, a smart boy like you? Surely you've heard about the evils of Frank Fitzgerald. This is, after all, Hartsfield, the town of big mouths and ugly gossip."

"Dad…" Rita said, plaintively. "Don't do this."

"Hey, Mr. Lincoln told me about his life. I think it's only fair that I should tell him about mine. Right, Mr. Lincoln?"

I stole an extra breath. "Sure. Why not?"

"So, you did hear about me, didn't you?"

I scratched my head. "I heard some things."

"Some things. Good! Real good! Some things. Well, let me tell you the simple truth: I got shafted, Mr. Lincoln. That's it. I got to know people. Rich people. Well-off people. Made friends with them, trusted them and, you know what? They shafted me. So I went to prison and they hit the road, free and easy. You see, they had money for lawyers. I had no money. I got the worst fucking lawyer you can imagine. A real loser.

"You got to be careful who you trust in this world, Mr. Lincoln. Or is it whom you trust? Anyway, be real careful about that. Especially when it comes to money. Be extra careful when there's money involved. I bet your old Papa knows about that. Most certainly he knows all about that, doesn't he, Mr. Lincoln?"

I nodded. "Yeah, I suppose so."

"You see, Mr. Lincoln, your father has money—was born into money and had all those wonderful opportunities that money can buy: nice clothes, good food and wine, meeting all the right folks—and that's so damn important, isn't it—networking I think they call it today. So along with meeting the right people, your father went and got himself a fine education and now he makes good, honest money. Good for him! I applaud him."

Rita sat somber, in a hopeless resignation. Mrs. Fitzgerald was on the edge of her seat, thrilled by her husband's performance.

"And you know what else, Mr. Lincoln? With all that money your father could buy any book he wanted to buy. Any book. Hardcover books, creamy paper, the finest sturdy bindings. First editions." Frank shook his head in wonder, his eyes bright and bold. "Can you imagine, Mr. Lincoln, how truly wonderful that is?"

"Yes sir. I like books."

"I just bet you do, young man. I have heard about

your father's fine library. It is a fine library, isn't it, Mr. Lincoln?"

"Yes sir."

"Why I bet he has books on pretty much everything—from wine making to politics to horticulture—I mean there's got to be a vast collection of horticultural books from the look of the flowers and gardens all around that house."

"Yes, sir, my mother loves flowers and gardens."

"And good God love her for it, young man! God love her for that! And your good father must have one of the finest wine cellars for hundreds of miles."

"I suppose so, sir. I don't know much about it."

He threw an accusing finger at me. "Well you should, Mr. Lincoln! Don't go off to Harvard until you have learned about your father's wine cellar. That's disrespectful."

"Yes, sir," I said, looking toward the front door.

He started pacing again, lost in thought. "Did you know, Mr. Lincoln, that when I was growing up —right in the same town as your father—my parents did not have the money to buy books? Did you know that?"

"No sir."

"It's true. We barely had enough for food. That's a fact. And I really loved books, Mr. Lincoln. I surely did. You see, I figured that if I read enough books, I'd become a somebody. Maybe not a somebody with a capital S, like your father, but a small s somebody." He narrowed his eyes on me. "Can you understand that?"

"Yes, sir, I can."

He paused, twisting up his lips, letting the uncomfortable silence expand. "My father got sick. I had to work. My mother got sick. I had to work. I had to help them. I had to put food on the table, Mr. Lincoln, because that's the way it was. That was life. Those were the cards given me. You understand?"

"Yes sir."

"And so I did it. I worked in the factories, sweeping and cleaning toilets; I worked in the hot fields harvesting soybeans and corn; I worked at Monty Baker's used car lot washing his cars for one dollar an hour and I put food on the table, Mr. Lincoln, and I paid the doctor bills and I even washed your father's beautiful silver 1992 Cadillac Eldorado. Yes sir, I did that and I put food on the table." He nodded, rapidly, his face flushed, eyes cold. "I did that, yes, but I couldn't put myself through college. No. I had to keep working at the factory and take care of my sick mother. That was my duty and I did that."

He glared at me. "I did that, Mr. Lincoln. And you know what else I did. I bought books. They were paperbacks, but they were the best damn books I could find—the classics—and I read them any chance I got because I was not going to be damned to hell as a low life white trash ignorant boy from Pennsylvania who didn't know Herman Melville, John Steinbeck or Sinclair Lewis. No sir. I read them all and I started my own library. No way I was just going to borrow books from the Public Library. No sir. I was going to own them. Hold them. Read them as many times as I wanted, when I wanted. I even read Jane Austen. You ever read Jane Austen?"

"No sir."

"You should. Got to read Jane Austen. Rita can tell you all about Jane Austen. She's read them all," he said proudly. "All the great ones and all the classics."

He shifted his gaze toward his daughter. His eyelids twitched. His voice grew flat and unemotional. "No, not just poor stupid folk who worked the factories. Educated folks. Self-educated, maybe, but educated by the blessings of books. Right Rita girl?"

I saw a quiet turbulence spread across Rita's discontented face. "Yes... Dad." She seemed to pitch the labored words to the upper air, like a plea to the gods for mercy.

Frank wiped his glossy forehead, and took a long deep breath. He let the air out slowly, through his nose.

"In the end though, Mr. Lincoln, it gets down to money." He rubbed his thumb and fingers together, menacingly. "Money, Mr. Lincoln. Money. If I had the cash, I would have finished college. Hey, maybe I would have been a doctor or a lawyer. A teacher maybe. I would have been a good teacher. Inspiring."

"But I needed a car, Mr. Lincoln. I needed to make house payments. I needed to pay doctors! I needed to buy baby clothes and cribs and food and keep my wife, my sickly wife, Mr. Lincoln, my sickly wife who caught Lyme's Disease but it wasn't diagnosed right away, because we didn't have enough money, Mr. Lincoln, to go to the best doctors."

He licked his lips and returned to the recliner. He sank down, his hard jaw and good looks accented. He spread his hands and lowered his voice, now a little weary from his performance. "So, Mr. Lincoln, you understand, I'm sure. I am guilty as charged for all my transgressions against society. I am penitent and sick at heart for all that I've done." He leaned toward me, with a pinched, angry face. "I am SOooo sorry."

He grinned, darkly. "But now, thanks to Rita, we are in favor in this town. Rita has made the Fitzgerald name respectable. Well, at least Rita and my wife are respectable. And Rita is making money and, if she's smart, she'll save it; maybe go to New York or L. A. and really hit the big time. Really make some money. Be one of those top models who goes on to be a big movie star. Wouldn't that be something, Mr. Lincoln?"

"Yes, sir," I said, squirming.

He sighed deeply and shook his head a little, as if shaking off a disturbing dream. He eased back and sighed again and his chin lowered to his impressive chest. "You kids go on now. We've had our little get-to-know each other talk. We've had a good long talk, didn't we, Mr. Lincoln?"

"Yes sir."

"Go to your movie now."

Frank looked at his daughter. "And you, Rita girl, look ravishing."

Rita turned away, in a frown of discontent.

CHAPTER EIGHT

My father's library suddenly filled with sunlight, but by the time I stood, stretched, and blinked away the old images of Frank and Betty Fitzgerald, the sunlight had vanished again. I stepped to the window and watched as the sun played hide and seek with chunky gray clouds. Pushing open the back door, I stepped down onto the red brick patio, took a deep breath and felt a humid breeze. I shaded my eyes, peering at the slivers of sunlight that cast the distant pond in an artificial metallic sphere.

I glanced at my watch. It was nearly 12:45. The estate auction agent was due at two o'clock. Back inside, I went to the kitchen, searching the maple cabinets for anything to snack on, shuffling through coffee filters, bags of nuts, packages of chocolate chip cookies (Dad's favorite) and cans of soups. Finally, I found an old Clif Bar—Crunchy Peanut Butter. I tore it open and munched it while I made more coffee. I felt groggy and lethargic. From Rita's reproving glare back at Jack's Diner, it was clear that she didn't want to see me again. For those few excruciatingly long seconds, she seemed to burrow into me with her probing, wounded eyes, as if working some magic to banish me forever from her world, past and present. But then, what the hell should I care anyway? I had always existed on the periphery of her life, always an afterthought, maybe a distraction, while she slithered through shimmering currents of seduction; the siren, the mermaid, seeking her true hulking beachcombing mate: Dusty Palmer.

Why had I gone to Jack's anyway? I should have known better. I'd had a grueling week of thirteen hour days, with little sleep, and the last thing I needed was to resurrect antique emotions that should have been exorcized years ago.

But it was seeing Rita again "that way" that cut me sharply—that ripped away the stitches, exposing the old, buried adolescent sores. You think you've outgrown it. "Hey, I'm grown, dammit! I've got the years, the degrees, a marriage to prove it! I've grown way beyond all that stuff." I heard the dialogue in my head, like a script from a bad TV movie.

"She was just a girl I dated three times in high school when I was barely eighteen years old! I'm thirty-three now, a respected doctor that people rely on, who makes careful but rapid decisions, who takes control and urges others to do the same. I help heal people."

My emotions are balanced and mature, my passions "commingled," as *Hamlet* said.

> 'And blessed are those whose blood and judgment are so well commingled that they are not a pipe

for fortune's finger to sound what stop she please. Give me that man who is not passion's slave and I will wear him in my heart's core.'"

I poured coffee into my favorite old mug: the big red one. Printed on it were the words "I Don't Like Nobody Who Likes Me." I grinned, reflectively. Rita was right. I had been a little shit.

I stared out the windows at the scattering sky, studying the blue patches, the gauze of gray and white clouds, the soaring diving birds, which skimmed the tops of swaying oaks and elms.

There I stood, leaning back against the kitchen island, looking out through the same windows I'd looked out of when I was seventeen: the library windows, the kitchen windows, my bedroom windows. Had I ever really left this house?

With the smallest amount of effort—no, not effort—ease—with frightening ease, I could feel that old emotion, reborn, now crying out for attention, gasping for air, desiring, with a vengeance, Rita Fitzgerald. How was it possible that the anger and hurt—the teenage despair and frustrated desire—had never dissolved or grown a callous? How was that possible?

My third date with Rita began in silence, rose to a heightened madness, and then fell into disaster.

We hurried away from her house, from her fearsome father and her ice queen mother. I drove the speed limit, glancing quietly at her. Rita sat erect and smoked, trying not to show that she was shaken. She didn't turn on the radio. She didn't speak or move, except to inhale and blow the smoke toward the windshield, as if to test me. A rolling fog gathered, but I didn't roll my window down. I wanted her to know that I was an ally, because I was. Besides, there was no doubt in my mind that she was spoiling for a fight and I wanted no part of it. Her energy was prickly and defensive. Her gaze fixed. She was trembling.

After we had passed through town on our way to the interstate, Rita rolled down her window and flicked the cigarette away. She presented her face to the rushing wind and closed her eyes. Her hair snapped and played across her face. The cigarette smoke fled the interior, like a retreating ghost.

I had turned onto the interstate en route to the theatre when Rita finally turned her fierce eyes on me. "Fuck the movie!"

I lowered my voice, the way my father did. "Okay...Where to?"

"Who cares?"

I was quiet.

"Why do you always drive so damned slow?"

"I don't always."

She turned away. "Take exit 19."

"Okay. Where are we going?"

"Holiday Inn."

I drove without talking. When I saw the exit and the brilliantly lit billboard ad for the Holiday Inn, I slowed down. "This it?"

Rita lit another cigarette. She nodded.

Minutes later, I pulled into the lot and parked near the entrance. I cut the engine and waited until she finished her cigarette.

"I have a credit card," I said.

She laughed, but it was bitter and then loud. "Of course you have a credit card, little Alan James. Your daddy and mommy wouldn't let you out of the house without a big old credit card now, would they? No, no, no!" Her voice turned acerbic. "You won't need it. I know the night manager." She shoved open the door and got out.

She walked briskly toward the entrance, not waiting for me. I got out and followed, concerned and anxious. She was already inside, talking to a pudgy night clerk with a bushy black mustache, when I came up to the blond lobby desk.

"Alan James, this is Robbie Styles. Robbie Styles, Alan James."

I nodded sheepishly and he grunted something, allowing his shifting eyes to ignore most of me and land instead, with pleasure, on Rita. She blossomed with coquettish charm and a forced cheery voice. It was a bad performance, but ole Robbie sure liked it.

"So Robbie, here's what I need," Rita said, blithely. "A bottle of vodka, some OJ and a key to get into that beautiful heated indoor swimming pool of yours."

Robbie's white, round floppy face dropped into alarm. He sank and whispered. "I can't do that, Rita. Well, I mean, not the vodka. Come on...you know that. The pool...?" He looked at his watch, working on a solution. "In about fifteen minutes, when it closes to the guests, I'll let you in, but you've got to be quiet." He passed me a disparaging glance. "... And no messing around? I mean none, Rita."

Rita leaned in close. "Robbie..." she nodded to me. "Alan James has money." She turned to me. "How much cash do you have, Alan James?"

I shrugged.

Rita held me in her domineering gaze. "Come on, Alan James, how much?"

I stammered. "About eighty."

Rita smiled triumphantly. "Okay. Good. Robbie, Alan James is going to give you about eighty dollars for that bottle of vodka and OJ. Now I think that's a damn good deal."

Robbie raked a puffy hand through his thinning forty something salt and pepper hair. "Rita... I... I mean."

"Come on, Robbie. You know me. Have I ever trashed this place? Have I ever caused you any trouble?"

"No, but you..." he stopped, throwing me a nervous glance. "You were with somebody older. Somebody of age. Of legal age."

She laughed. "Robbie. Alan James, here, is wise beyond his years. He may be only seventeen, but he's actually more like forty. I mean, it's kind of like dog years with Alan James. He's so conservative, worried and uptight that he just gets all older and wiser the more you get to know him. And he barks and yaps and fusses...And he follows me around, sniffing and whining and wanting. Well, anyway, you get the picture."

I felt myself blush red with humiliation.

Rita batted her eyelashes playfully. "So...Robbie, do we get the booze or not?"

He considered it, then shook his head. "I can't do it, Rita."

Rita's face actually became ugly with rage, as if she'd quickly put on an evil mask. "Listen, Robbie," she said, low and threateningly. "Get me the damn vodka! I'm in no mood to argue. Just get it. Okay? GET IT! I know the owner of this shit house and believe me, I'll call him right now and tell him you just tried to rape me. You got me, you fat chicken shit?"

Robbie's face passed through a range of expressions: shock, anger, disgrace, and finally, resentful consent. "All right, Rita." His voice broke. "Okay, if that's what you want." His eyes glowed with shame. "You two wait in the car for about fifteen minutes, then come around to the pool. I'll have the... bottle for you."

Rita regained her beauty and curtsied. "I take it all back, Sir Robbie, sacred knight of the Holiday Inn. You are not a chicken shit at all, sire, you are a gentleman, and a Don Quixote de La Mancha, who has just rescued his dear, wayward and undeserving Dulcinea."

Robbie lowered his eyes and turned away from her, busying himself with the row of mail slots, but not really accomplishing anything. He finally stopped moving at all and just stood there, head bowed, as if in prayer.

Rita gave a peculiar smile and turned to me. In the blue mirror of her eyes I saw a profound sorrow and defeat. "Shall we away to the car, old Alan James?"

In the car, we waited in silence. Rita smoked, distracted, and agitated. I stared, hard into the middle distance. I wanted to say something—I wanted to tell her what a bitch she had been, heartless and unfeeling. I wanted to hold her, comfort her, but her harsh words had frightened me and I was still recuperating from their sting. I turned and looked at her fully. She faced me, only briefly, with contemptuous eyes. I saw a layer of impenetrable hardness and fear—the stare of a trapped animal.

"We could run away, Rita," I finally said. "You'd never have to see your father again."

Then she surprised me. While trembling, she broke into a lavish smile that glorified the atmosphere. "Oh, my shimmering knight, Alan James Lincoln…"

Fifteen minutes later we approached the glass enclosed pool and found Robbie waiting nervously by the door. None of us spoke. He inserted the key, swung open the door and nodded for us to enter.

"The vodka bottle and orange juice are under a towel near the diving board."

Rita avoided his eyes. "Thanks, Robbie."

I reached for my wallet.

"I don't want your damn money," he said, bitterly.

Robbie ignored Rita, closed the door behind us and shambled away.

The emerald water shimmered under dim overhead lights. The silence intruded, seemed accusing. The smell of chlorine reminded me of childhood vacations in Florida and the west, where in route, motel swimming pools were oases from long hours of driving.

Rita slowly circled the rectangular pool, arms laced behind her back, taking in the little corner palm garden, the white ribbed pool chairs, the tables, and diving board. There, she stopped. Pausing, she raked a strand of fallen hair from her left eye, bent forward and lifted the lush royal blue towel. She took the bottle of vodka and tucked it under her right arm. With her free hand, she managed the quart container of orange juice and some clear plastic cups. She stepped to a nearby table, placed them there, and twisted off the top of the vodka with a little wince. I stood twenty feet away watching her.

"He forgot ice, Alan James. Would you go get some?"

I spotted a gray metallic ice machine near a portable bar. I filled a plastic container and took it to her. She mixed a screwdriver and handed it to me. I took it. She mixed another for herself. With her glass raised, she touched mine. "To Don Quixotes and

Dulcineas." She threw back half of it. I sipped.

"Alan James, you really should go easy on that aftershave. When used sparingly, it's seductive, when abused, it's a weapon."

"I could say the same about your good looks."

She shot me a heated glance. "What does that mean?"

"You know what I mean."

"Oh, here we go again," she said, making a grand sweeping gesture. "Once again, the great and perfect Alan James disapproves of Rita."

"Rita... It's just that..."

"Oh shut up."

Rita whirled from me. She drained her glass and violently slammed down the cup. Ice exploded into the air, landing and scattering poolside like thrown dice. She whipped off her sweater and tossed it. She kicked off her heels and quickly stripped to her bra and panties, while I watched, wishing I'd kept my self-righteous mouth shut.

She mounted the diving board, rushed to the edge, bounced twice, rose, arched and plunged into a clean head-first dive that scarcely wrinkled the water. I saw silvery bubbles. Her hair rose like grass. When she popped to the surface, she wiped her face and glared at me. "Alan James, instead of becoming a doctor, maybe you should go to the seminary. Then you could just preach away, day and night, to everyone and everybody about whatever. Blah, blah, blah all day and night. And you'd get paid to be a high and mighty fucking pain in the ass!"

She dropped to the bottom, kicked hard and swam, deeply, the length of the pool. On the far side, she broke the surface, pushed from the wall and began a back and forth crawl, applying gentle arching strokes, as her feet chopped up white bursts. She had perfect form: her head was down, her feet up without kicking hard, without struggling. She kicked down with the opposite foot from her arm pull, gliding along, turning her head slightly, without lifting at the forehead. I'd learned those techniques at the Hiller Academy. I wondered where Rita had learned them.

She maintained a rigorous pace for about fifteen minutes, while I sat in a dark mood, swallowing more of the screwdriver than I'd intended, feeling a smooth, hazy buzz. Finally, her stroke began to fall apart. Her body wavered, her arms slapped clumsily, her feet lost rhythm, became dilatory. Still, she pressed on. I poured more vodka, watching her drag herself across the water, like a thirsty man on a desert, clawing his way toward a distant oasis.

"Hey, Rita. Enough. You're tired."

She kept going.

"Rita! All right, already!"

She struggled on. When exhaustion struck, she was halfway across, and in deep water. She coughed and shuddered, went limp and sank. Alarmed, I shouted. No response. I shot to my feet, yelling. I slung off my jacket, shed my glasses and shoes. In a running dive, I hit the water. It was a drenching blue, and sharp with chlorine. I saw Rita, rippling in the azure currents, bubbles rushing from her mouth like pearls. My clothes were heavy and binding, dragging on me. I pulled toward her and wrapped her waist with my arms. I felt the cool living weight of her. I planted my feet on the bottom, crouched and sprang off. We rocketed up, breaking the surface, near the left edge of the pool. I sucked in air. With my right hand securely around her waist, I drew her to the edge, gasping. My clothes ballooned and swam around me. My heart thundered. I panted.

Suddenly, Rita reached and grabbed the concrete ridge. Her eyes popped open, wide, lustrous and wonderful. "Hello, Alan James."

"Are you okay?" I asked, nearly frantic, wiping my face.

Rita let out a naughty laugh. "I'm great, Alan James. Just great!"

I must have looked confused. She giggled and shoved away toward the center of the pool, dog paddling, her laughter echoing off the glass walls. "I knew that was the only way I'd get you in this water, Alan James. If I hadn't tricked you, you wouldn't have taken off your jacket and shoes and swum with me, now would you?"

I slapped the water with the flat of my hand, instantly feeling the sting! "Damn it, Rita. That's not funny!"

She blew me a kiss. "Yes it is, Alan James. It's funny. Look at you. Your face is all proud and heroic. Your little bristling dark hair is all shiny. Your clothes all wet. Yes, it is funny. Very funny." She laughed wildly.

I charged after her. Startled, she turned, kicked, and made a desperate rush for the opposite end. We chopped and raced, splashing geysers. She reached the corner stairs and escaped just as I lunged for her ankle, missing it by inches. Rita darted away, her breasts bouncing, water flying from her hair and shoulders. I scrambled out and started after her, my clothes squishy and gushing, my socks slapping across the rubbery surface.

"Now, Alan James," Rita said, playfully frightened. "A sense of humor is very attractive to a girl."

I was pissed off. I lumbered ahead, head down, eyes fixed and darkly determined. Rita scooted off, rounding the diving board, snatching the towel, and skipping away. I marched forward, lengthening my stride.

"Alan James, you're scaring me, now. It was just a joke. That's all."

I kept coming and she kept running. Finally, I broke into a mushy jog.

"Alan James! What are you going to do?" Rita asked, fleeing. Her voice rose to a squeal. "Alan James!"

I was closing the distance. I saw the amused panic on her face. I growled. "I'm coming. I'm coming." I growled louder, hanging my arms like an angry grizzly bear. "God have mercy on your soul, Rita Fitzgerald, The Blond Blaze of Hartsfield."

Rita screamed.

We rounded the pool twice before Rita, deeply winded, stopped and stood firmly, her breasts rising and falling. She focused her narrowing eyes on me, now standing her ground, her back to the pool, only inches from the edge. In a Mae West voice she said, "Okay, big boy. Come on and get me!"

I growled, ran and pounced. She screamed. We tumbled backwards and hit the water heavily, making a terrific splash. Underwater, I grabbed her by the hair and pulled her lips toward me. We kissed, tongues exploring, bubbles tickling and dribbling from our noses and mouths. I found her breasts squeezed and played. She reached for my hard penis and played. We tangled, circled, broke away, and got caught again in an underwater embrace. When my lungs burned for air, I finally released her and drove to the surface. I came up first, coughing and spitting water. Rita followed, gulping air, laughing, and pulling wet strands from her face.

"Oh, my God, Alan James. That was great. So great."

We were in the deep end, both dogpaddling, sucking in air. "So much fun." she continued. She seized me and pressed her cool lips hard against mine. "You are the biggest nut case I've ever known, Alan James."

Twenty minutes later we sat under a clay potted palm, relaxed, high and quiet, sipping refreshed screwdrivers. Rita had dried off, dressed and turbaned her hair with the blue towel. I was damp, sticky, and miserable in my clothes.

"You should take them off and sit in your underwear, Alan James."

"Yeah, and if somebody walks in? Or looks in from outside? No way."

Rita chuckled. "What am I going to do with you?"

"Yeah, well you're the one who got me all wet like this."

"No, Alan James. You were already wet like that."

"Well, aren't you clever? Very funny."

Rita drank generously, and leaned back luxuriously. "So tell me something about physics, Alan James."

I was on my way to being good and drunk. "Physics!? Who cares about physics at a time like this?!"

"Well, you're the only person I know who likes physics. So tell me something about it. Anything."

My mind was a cluttered muddle. I stared at Rita with hungry eyes, feeling rock hard for her. I struggled to focus. "I don't know, Rita. Physics is so… so unphysical."

She laughed deeply. Her laughter was contagious, so I joined her and we laughed much too hard.

"Come on, now, Alan James. Give me something here. Physics! I want physics! I want physics!" She began to chant.

"All right, okay. Let me think for a minute. I'm like…drunk, Rita. I can't think straight. I've only been kinda drunk like this once."

She grabbed the vodka bottle, clutching it dramatically to her chest. "Then no more for you, Alan James! Who knows what you might do to me, a poor helpless girl, alone with the great physicist and drunkard, Alan James Lincoln. And don't try to change the subject! Give me physics! Come on, honey baby, give it to me! Give it all to me! Don't hold back any of it, Alan James."

"Okay, dammit! Wait a minute!" I sat up and shook my head, struggling for a centered thought. "Okay...here's something. ...Here it is. Quantum physics basically says that there is no underlying reason for reality."

Rita sat up, groggy eyed. "What the hell does that mean?"

"It means there's no natural explanation for this reality—the reality we live in. Atoms, that make up mostly everything, or, I guess, everything, are nothing but mostly space."

"Just empty space?" She asked, waving her hand through the air, as if trying to catch atoms.

"Yeah... and yet things appear to be solid things, even though they're mostly not. And they're always shifting around. An atom that helped make up the moon last week might be inside you tonight."

Her face contorted with thought. She shook her head. "I like that... but I don't understand."

"Neither does anyone else, Rita."

"Then what good is it?"

I looked at her, dreamily. "I don't know. All I

know, Rita, is that your atoms are the most beautiful arrangement of atoms and subatomic particles that I have ever seen or will ever want to see in my whole, big, stupid life."

Her face melted into a soft pleasure and admiration. She straightened. "Now see, Alan James, when you're like this, I just want to eat you up. You're so human."

"I'm always human!" I protested.

She shook her head. "Nope. Not always. But you are now. And you made physics, so… wonderfully physical."

We shattered into laughter, hooting, screaming, and slapping our knees. Finally, we exhausted the humor and fell into a dull silence. Rita leaned back again and, suddenly, there was a sharp memory of pain on her face, impossible to ignore.

"What's the matter?" I asked.

She turned from me. "Nothing. I think I'm just drunk."

"What were you thinking?"

She shook her head impatiently. "Nothing. Nothing at all." Then brightly. "Hey, there's a football game tonight!"

"Yeah, so?"

She stood, abruptly, unraveling the towel and dropping it on her chair. "So, it should be almost over by now. Let's go to Jack's."

"Jack's?"

"Yeah. It'll be fun."

"We're having fun here."

"Don't be boring, Alan James. Let's go."

"No way. It'll be loud and filled with assholes."

She seized my hand and tugged on me until I got up. "Come on, antisocial, stiff old man, Alan James."

I pouted. "I'm way too drunk to drive right now."

"Then I'll help you."

"Yeah, right, like you're sober."

"So we'll get some coffee."

"Rita, that doesn't help. Alcohol has to work its way through your system. Everybody knows that."

She mocked my voice. "Everybody knows that. You go outside and stick your stubborn, elitist face into the cool wind. That will sober you up."

"Where are you going?"

"I have to take care of something."

I looked at her suspiciously. "Yeah…like what?"

She shook out her hair. "Never mind. Just go."

I looked at the half empty vodka bottle. "What are you going to do with that?"

"I'm going to dump it. Go, Alan James. I'll meet you out front."

I took an intimate step forward, lowering my eyes on her. "Can't we go back to the lake?"

She looked at the pool, avoiding my eyes. "No, Alan James. Not tonight."

Outside, the night breeze burst over tops of trees in little ripples, flinging leaves into dips and spirals. Wind assaulted my damp clothes, bringing shivers and chattering teeth. I was on my way to the car and some heat, when curiosity struck. I stopped, spun about, and crept back toward the hotel entrance, slapping my shoulders for warmth. There was a finely manicured 5-foot hedgerow that bordered the great lobby window. It would give good cover. I ducked behind the hedgerow and used my head like a periscope, rising and falling, stealing looks at Robbie Styles at work behind the desk.

From a side hallway, Rita strolled purposefully across the sea green carpet, without the vodka bottle, and approached the glossy lobby desk. She stopped and faced Robbie, head on. His head was lowered over pink papers. Rita waited, hands folded, head bowed, contrite. He ignored her, and, when she tapped the little service bell and it "dinged", he turned from her and searched for busy work with little scratches of his head and a squaring of his sloping shoulders.

Rita said something, but I couldn't understand the words. She waited, patiently, for a response, but Robbie was unmoved.

Finally, I watched in utter disbelief as Rita took two steps backward and, slowly, descended to her knees. She spoke again. Robbie's head curved around and down until he found her. His face registered shock and embarrassment.

While Rita spoke, she made prayer hands. Robbie's quick moving eyes were nervous. He shook his head in firm disapproval and swung out from behind the desk, rushing toward her, glaring down and firing a scolding shaking forefinger. She took his rebuke humbly, without the slightest movement, without any defense. Robbie yelled something loud. It was a demand like "Get up, Rita!"

She didn't move. She gently reached for his hand. He stiffened and faced away again, absorbed in a vehement denial of her. Rita's arm remained extended, continuing to offer him the elegance of her hand in sacrifice. He shouted again, and I heard it and read his lips when the words were muffled.

"Son of a bitch, Rita! You didn't have any cause to talk to me like that! I've taken so much shit from that guy! That shithead! I always treated you good, didn't I? Never said anything! Always respectful to you and that damned D. J. jerk! You can't just walk over me like that! I've been good to you and your friends. I've got feelings, dammit! I'm not just some fat nobody!" He spun away from my view. "Dammit! What the hell are you trying to prove! Get up!"

Rita stayed down, head bent close to the carpet until damp strands of hair brushed the floor. She held the strained posture, like a sorrowful whipped dog, still reaching for her master's hand.

Robbie turned, face red and pinched. He focused on her gradually. "Didn't I do you favors? Never asked for nothing? Hey, you know…what goes around comes around, Rita. You be nice to somebody and they'll be nice to you."

Rita nodded.

"Then why did you talk to me like that?"

I couldn't hear what she said, but it seemed to soften him. His shoulders relaxed. "Get up! Rita. For God's sake, get up!"

She was motionless.

Seeing her resolve and fearing a customer might wander in, Robbie reluctantly, and with agitation, finally gave her his left hand. She took it, held it preciously for a time, and then brought it to her lips. She kissed it. To complete the penitent ritual, and to be absolved from her sin, she pressed the hand lightly to her forehead.

Robbie shuddered.

A long moment later, Rita released his hand and rose. Both stood in an embarrassed silence, eyes near-missing the other, until, finally, Rita turned and started toward the front entrance.

I scampered away out of the light.

CHAPTER NINE

"Have you been dating Robbie Styles, too?" I asked, gravely, weaving out of the Holiday Inn parking lot, fishing for words in a murky pool of inebriated emotions.

She looked at me with impersonal eyes. "I thought you were in the car."

"I wasn't. I watched."

"Don't be a jerk, Alan James. Robbie's a friend." She made a vague gesture. "Well, was…a friend."

I drove clumsily, under the speed limit. We both leaned gratefully toward the vents, feeling the warm breath of the heat rush over us.

"Alan James, you must be drunk. The car's moving all over the road. You're over the yellow line!"

"I am not!"

"Why do you always say you're not doing something, when it's obvious that you are? It's one of your weirdest qualities."

I ignored her, slapped myself across the face and pointed my crazy eyes on the meandering road. I felt dizzy and lazy, my mouth was numb. I was terrified that a cop was going to pull us over and, conversely, I wanted to speed and crash into the ludicrous night with mad ravings of love and hate and demonic laughter. I somehow restrained myself.

It seemed hours before we arrived at the Hartsfield exit. Rita had fallen into another one of her strange silences. I glanced at her, at one point, and saw her eyes shifting about, anxiously, as if she were seeking help from one of her guardian angels.

Approaching Jack's from Sawmill Road, we saw a soft amber glow hovering low in the night sky, as if a house were on fire. I turned left and, through the dark trees, Jack's seem to drift slowly toward us, bright and strange, like a phantom ship on a black sea. It was evident that Jack's was having a stellar night. I wanted to turn back, but Rita was suddenly on the edge of the seat, alert, eyes wide, picking up the busy neon lights. We began to hear the dull blare of horns and we instantly knew that the Hartsfield Vikings had won the game.

"We won, Alan James! We won!" Rita shouted.

"Well, whoop di-doo," I said, flatly. "Those blockheads are actually going to the playoffs."

Jack's parking lot was a bright and giddy chaos. Cars flooded the place, circling the lot, parking where they met obstacles and clogging the entrance and exits. Headlights flashed high beams, feisty girls swung wild from the open doors of cars and cheered. A firecracker rocketed high, screamed and exploded into red, glassy diamonds. More cheers and blasting horns. Boys barked like hound dogs chasing squirrels, as another singing firecracker roared skyward and broke into a fist of thunder, raining green sequins over Jack's roof.

A paunchy security guard darted about like a duck in a rage, bellowing orders, but was playfully bounced from car to car, like the ball in a pinball machine.

I parked the car opposite Jack's, in a weeded area, next to five others. A red and black NO TRESPASSING sign was clearly posted. It had always been ignored.

Rita pushed out of the car and was hurrying across the two-lane road before I'd come to a complete stop. I caught up to her in Jack's parking lot, where bedlam had taken hold: kids walked across cars, sat on cars, drummed on cars, smoked on cars and danced to The Bee Gees', *You Win Again*, between cars.

Most of Jack's patrons had spilled out of the diner and had joined in, including Jack O'Brian himself, a ruddy-faced man with a bald dome, stubby arms and a coarse pirate-like voice. With a fat stogie clamped between his loose lips, he danced down the stairs to the parking lot, doing hip shots and head wobbles. It wasn't pretty, but the crowd loved it, erupting into piercing whistles and screams. "More, big Jack! Go big Jack. Get em' Jack!"

Jack bowed politely. He hopped high, dropping lightly down, snapping to attention, raking the crowd with his bulging eyes, as if to say, "Don't nobody turn away." Then, like a little cherub, he broke into an amazing Irish jig. The crowd crushed forward in a collective "Whhaaattt!?" They gaped, clapped, and cheered him on as he fluttered and bounced playfully, arching his stumpy arms above his head, circling his space with quick, agile feet, puffing aggressively on his cigar. A heavy woman joined him, skipping, twirling and kicking. The crowd parted to give them all the room they needed to dance through the rowdy night.

Moments later, a chorus of girls and guys joined them, swinging careless arms and rubbery legs, finishing the dance with a clumsy Rockefeller Center Rockettes' style kicking chorus that left them winded, wild and thirsty.

And then, every boy became a quarterback—cocking a tense arm, heaving a can of beer through the air to be tracked, reached for, and snatched—just missing the windshield, the girlfriend's head, the hood of the car. Tabs popped loudly, heads snapped back and beer sprayed the world in ejaculations of victory.

Rita was on the periphery, getting all the news about the game from Ellen Tucker and her boyfriend, Tom Mullen, the senior class vice president, a cleaned and pressed manikin with startled eyes. "We're going to the playoffs in Ohio!" Tom shouted over the celebration. "We won in the last thirty seconds with a twenty yard pass. Dusty was brilliant. Just brilliant! I can't believe you weren't there!"

"Family stuff," Rita said, flatly. "Just couldn't make it."

It was nearly impossible not to feel the almighty joy of it all. I began tapping my foot to the music and bobbing my head, like a real participant. And even though I tried my sarcastic teenage best not to feel pride in our football team and high school, I was secretly delighted that the Hartsfield Vikings had won and were going to Ohio to "kick some ass."

"We did it, Alan!" Rupert Tugs screamed, grabbing my shoulders, and shaking me about, like I was a rag doll. His eyes flamed with a mad ecstasy. "We fucking beat them, Alan!" He was blocky and square, like a Maytag refrigerator. He'd always loathed me, even before I'd left for private school. He beat me up in the third grade and again in the fifth. "We kicked their asses. We kicked their fucking asses!"

The spirited night was so heightened that guys who had hated my guts for years grinned at me and slapped my back. I glanced around, astounded to see that there were no enemies, no evils, and no limitations. Camaraderie and merriment reigned.

I nodded firmly to them all as I was propelled into the swaying masses. Although I called for Rita, she melted into the dancing crowds, shouting, laughing and drifting out of sight. So I threw myself forward into the mad foam of beer and conquest, slapping backs and saying things like, "We're going to kick some Ohio ass!" or "Now those assholes will know Hartsfield!"

The feeling was a rare one—that fine sense of belonging; to have a common cause that lifted me high into the lower and minor consciousness of popular value; to find the right pitch of the night, and sing out like all the other bulls, a howling mating call that drew the girls, the sharp nods of approval, and a cold crinkly can of illegal beer. I drank it all in, with gulps of pleasure.

When Terry Gardner, aka "Blade Man," surely a Hell's Angel in training, wrapped my shoulders with the wide sweep of his massive arm and shouted, "We're number one, Alan! We're number one, man!" I glowed. Then I pumped a fist of defiance into the night sky, made the terrible face of a nerd to be reckoned with, and shouted back in a raw and savage voice right in the center of Blade Man's red stormy face, "YEAH!"

I finally found Rita in the back lot. As my father would say, she was all "caught up," and for the next fifteen minutes, I dragged along behind her, like a poor soul, as she covered the remaining real estate, researching and discussing every detail of the game, listening to the same stories in tireless variation from overheated girls and raucous hot-breathing guys. She was animated and thrilled with each telling and, unfortunately, she was also looking for Dusty. I sensed and smelled it. I knew the look.

"He'll be here soon," somebody said.

"He's with Amber," another shouted.

Amber Conrad was pretty—even sexy—but next to Rita, she was plain ole ordinary, which meant that I was growing more edgy by the minute. When Rita took my hand, squeezing it, intimately, it was an easy lie to believe that she was still with me. The booze tickled and taunted my emotions and helped to support that lie. I was a man child, firmly anchored next to the goddess and, by some fortunate whim of the gods, I had become sanctified.

Rita introduced me to her friends with pride, and they, shockingly, returned favorable expressions and scrutinized me anew. Surely if Rita was with me, there was something there, in "that Alan," that they had missed. There was perhaps some shining jewel of quality that had been buried deep inside me that Rita had brought forth from the hard rock of my personality.

And so it was, from that night on to graduation, the other students and I, once sworn enemies, became, at least, dubious friends.

"I'm starving, Alan James," Rita said, after she'd exhausted the stories and her voice was hoarse, low and sexy. "Let's go inside and get something to eat."

We found a narrow booth that had just been vacated, with a clear view of the entrance. We had already ordered cheeseburgers and sodas when, from outside, a boisterous cheer from the lot drew our attention to the windows. Rita stood, expectantly, and faced the entrance. I lowered my head and drank ice water.

Dusty entered Jack's, looking every bit the conqueror that he was, with a bright grin and the flush of lingering exhilaration on his fatigued face. His hair, still damp from a shower, was combed back smoothly from his broad forehead. He wore jeans, a robin egg blue shirt, and a black leather jacket that gave him the look of a good-natured punk. His eyes glowed like a brand new day, with all the promise of eternal blue skies and wide open vistas. He took in the standing ovation with a series of slow rapturous blinks. I studied Rita and saw a suppressed thrill pass across her face. Amber noticed it too, and she scowled at Rita, drawing Dusty close.

When Rita left for the bathroom, and she went out of her way to pass Dusty, I knew it was over between us. Perhaps she had slipped him a note or maybe they'd spoken earlier by phone. Maybe it was just a recognition—an intuitive understanding that they were meant for each other: their attraction was unmistakable and terrible.

The food arrived just as Rita returned, but I'd lost my appetite. So had Rita. The room vibrated with energy and praise, as Dusty and Amber drifted to an awaiting booth and sat. Amber's dewy worshipping eyes, famous sharp breasts and frosted long brown hair did all they could to hold Dusty's attention, but the pull to Rita was a magnetic miracle. Dusty had sat strategically so that Rita had access to his gaze. They stole a couple of knowing, guilty glances, and everybody saw it. Amber and I began to brood.

Surprisingly, I wasn't angry. Not then anyway. I'd known it all along. Known that Rita would move on. Why would she stay with me? It was an impossible thought and it always had been. So I began a slow retreat from her, and from all those splendid memories and emotions, when, with a great effort, she pulled her eyes from Dusty and returned to me. The turbulence would come later. I knew that. I knew that much about myself. When hurt came, I always had a delayed reaction to it. Now, I just felt isolated and small.

A moment later, Rita took my hand and looked at me sadly. A light glimmered from her eyes, gloomy, reflective, and I strained to grasp the process of her thoughts. "Alan James," she said, softly, just barely audible. "I like you very much…"

I slid my eyes away from her, toward the windows. The parking lot party was still a thing of manic furor. I saw the red sweeping dome light of a police car.

"Alan James. Look at me."

I didn't.

She made a frustrated gesture. "Alan James… you know how much I like you…You know that." She leaned in close and whispered. "Alan James… I showed you that, didn't I? Do you think I do that with everybody?"

I seized the opportunity to strike. "Of course you do."

She threw her head back, insulted, and all that wonderful hair bounced, instantly, bringing back the night of love, and with it, a torment of desire. "Alan James!"

I shrugged. "What do I know?"

"Stop it!"

I felt unexpected and unwanted tears. I fought them.

"Alan James, please look at me."

I didn't.

"You knew about Dusty, didn't you?"

I ignored her.

"Alan James...I need to explain something to you so you'll understand."

"I understand," I said, evenly.

"No, you don't. Look...I've got to..."

I cut her off. "I don't want to hear it, Rita. I mean, I don't even know who the hell you are. You could date me, too, you know! It doesn't just have to be Dusty..."

"Okay, fine with me. Fine I will. But can you accept that?"

"Hell no."

"I knew you'd say that. You're just so damned uptight about everything.

"I'm sick and tired of hearing you say that."

"Okay, be flexible."

"Not with Dusty. And I guarantee that within a week you'll be going steady with him. You won't be dating anybody else. Not even the asshole D. J. what's his name."

Rita fumed. "So that's your choice then?"

I shook my head, vigorously. "Yeah, right. My choice. I'm supposed to sit around on Friday or Saturday nights while you go out with Dusty? No way. No damned way, Rita. Anyway, you're just kidding yourself."

Rita tried another approach. "Alan James... Don't complicate it."

"You're complicating it. I say simple, like you and me. Simple. Go steady with me. Simple."

She looked past me toward Dusty and I knew the answer.

"... You'll always be my best friend, Alan James."

"Oh, bullshit. Just bullshit, Rita. You're like, I don't know, so full of yourself. I thought you were more than that, but you're not. You're just another airhead blond bimbo."

She drew back, not angry, but wounded. She slumped. "... Okay... okay."

I jumped up and went to the cashier. I asked for the check and paid it. It seemed to take forever. When I returned to the booth, I didn't sit. "I'll take you home," I said, feeling a debilitating melancholy.

She averted my eyes, slid out of the booth and stood. I walked ahead of her with a dignified restraint, out of Jack's, across the parking lot, picking my way through swaying, delirious crowds, across the road, where the weary security guard was now directing traffic.

The drive to Rita's home was short and quiet. Rita asked one question. "Can we still meet to discuss our writing?"

"No! I'm tired of writing. I'm tired of reading. I'm tired of the whole damned thing."

I found a parking space two doors down from her house. I didn't turn off the engine. I didn't get out.

"Alan James... I want you to know the truth." She drew a breath. "Dusty and I went out last night.

He called late. My father had left to meet some old friends with my mother. So…we went out."

I stared ahead.

"He's breaking up with Amber."

It was a punch in my aching heart. So I attacked. "Did you take him out to the lake?"

"Don't say that, Alan James. Please don't. I've never taken anyone else out there but you. Never… Don't hurt me like that."

"Hurt you!! Yeah, right."

"It's true, Alan James."

"Fine, so it's true."

"Alan James, listen to me…"

I interrupted, refusing to face her. "Just get out, Rita! Just get out of the car."

She sighed deeply. She left me, closing the door softly, walking wearily toward the house. My foot came down heavy on the gas and I shot away, tires squealing. But I didn't go far. I drove around the block and parked a short distance up the street. I waited. I waited an hour. At 11:36, Dusty's Mustang came purring down the street and stopped. Rita appeared from the shadows and entered the car. They drove away. I followed them as far as Crystal Lake, then turned around and began the endless ride home.

Four days later, in the cafeteria, I overheard Dusty telling some friends that his two right tires had been punctured by, what appeared to be, an ice pick. He was furious and was blaming it on Amber. I grinned darkly. I'd figured he'd think so and I also figured that Amber, delighted by the accusation, but disappointed that she hadn't thought of it, wouldn't deny it. She soon spun out an entire short story around the savage act and, for the rest of the year, she became a person of influence, trust and secret confidences for many girls in the junior and senior classes. I don't even think Rita suspected me. Maybe. But I don't think so.

I artfully avoided Rita for the rest of the year. She and Dusty became a steady thing, just as I had predicted. I caught her eyes twice during my valedictorian speech, saw pride for me in them, but I quickly looked away, over her head, over everyone's head, just as I had been instructed to do by Ms. Lyendecker.

I saw Rita one last time before I left for college. It was late August, right after a heat wave and a pounding rain the night before. The air was fresh and cool, the sun brilliant. I spotted Dusty's car and followed it out to Crystal Lake. I followed them as they left the car and took a stroll in the woods. At some point, Rita separated from him and I trailed her.

I hid behind a thick oak and, with tense fingers creeping along the ridges and canals of rough bark, I stealthily angled my head to watch her. On the worn path, sloping down toward the lake, she wandered, subdued and unhurried. She brushed a patch of sunflowers and lingered under stirring elms. Cicadas scratched at the air, sounding like little maracas. Rita seemed to draw the sun to her face and bare tanned shoulders; seemed to unite all the glorified elements of late summer into a focus of awe and worship. In the yellow strapless sun dress and matching wide brimmed hat, she ambled under trees, through liquid currents of dappled sunlight and shadow, lifting her perfect nose to the softly scented breeze, pausing with closed eyes to merge with fading summer's grace.

The impulse to rush to her was sharp and hurtful. I could beg. I could demand, cajole, pour out my feelings and say, "I know I was just like all the others, but I really am in love with you! I'm different! I'm better! I'm better than Dusty because I'll always love you better than anyone or anything else! Rita, I'm up at night wanting you. I spend my days wanting you. I'll always want you!"

When Dusty came into view, stepping heavily, arms sweeping elegant branches aside, calling for Rita, the magic of the day fled. Birds screeched and scattered. The sun hid behind a cloud and the light paled. Rita's eyes opened, searched and found him. He advanced toward her. She smiled, faintly.

I felt a cruel sadness. I watched them retreat, hand in hand down toward the lake, past a low horizontal limb. They edged around it into shadows and faded from view.

Part Two
Transitions

CHAPTER ONE

Howard Fry was a stout man in his late forties, with a heavy face, sad-looking mustache, and patchy dark hair. His overlapping stomach and reddish face suggested a love of spirits. His dark pants sagged; his green and white cotton sweater, with an embroidered pine tree in the center, was too tight, and not particularly flattering. He didn't inspire confidence. He was the estate auctioneer.

"How do," he said, with a firm hand shake. He entered the house, immediately sweeping the place with his appraising eyes. "Nice… Real nice. Sold one like this up north about, oh… six months ago. Got a damn good price. Everybody was happy."

I closed the door behind him. "How long did you say you've been in business, Mr. Fry?" I asked, as casually as possible.

He nodded, tightening his mouth. "Yep, yep, yep," he said, rapidly. "Yep. Nice place." He gave me a quick, but thorough look, the same look I'd often given elderly patients when they said, "You look too young to be a doctor."

"Like I said on the phone, Dr. Lincoln, we've been doing business since 1937. You said we'd been recommended to you?" he asked, narrowing a keen eye at the antique card table in the living room.

"Yes," I answered. "My wife's father. He said one of his friends sold a home through your company."

"Name?" he asked.

"Martin Long Hanson. Upstate New York."

"Yep, yep, yep. Remember them. Good price on that house. Damn good price. Yep."

He pointed to the card table in the living room and crossed the wine-colored carpet for a better look. "Now that's a beaut… Yep. My partner, Cindy, will be here soon. She's the real expert on antiques. What is it?" he asked running his hand across the smooth satin finish.

"Eighteenth century Anglo Indian satin wood. My mother loved it."

"Yep. See why."

"Mr. Fry…?"

"Howard, Dr. Lincoln," he said, with a brief grin.

"You can call me Alan," I said.

"Yep."

"Howard, once you complete your appraisals, how long will it take to sell the house?"

"Well, shouldn't take long."

"Hartsfield isn't exactly a booming real estate market right now," I said.

He scrunched up his nose, still studying the place with a sharp shiny eye. I could almost hear the calculator clicking in his head. He was gaining my confidence. "We'll find you multiple bidders, Alan. Yep. We have lots of sources and, don't forget, people buy houses for lots of reasons. Now we'll get you multiple competing bidders, Alan, and that always brings higher revenues. No doubt. Yep. Then we'll negotiate with a single buyer. After that, non-contingent contracts and 30-day settlements are required, which means a quick transaction for you. Yep."

When Cindy Purty arrived, I gave them a tour of the house and property. We wandered the grounds under a milky sun. Occasional spears of light shot from hazy broken clouds and bathed the land in a glory of sparkles. The rain had cleaned the world, leaving behind a cool wet wind and a brilliance of light and dark greens. Pink and red tulips flashed. Irises opened. Late daffodils vibrated, shimmered in clusters across the sloping hills, joining daisies down toward the pond.

"My mother planted most of these," I said. "She loved spring."

"It's gorgeous," Cindy said, shading her eyes and taking it all in. Cindy was in her thirties. She had short red hair, dancing brown eyes and an attractive face and heavy figure. She was friendly and enthusiastic. Whenever Howard said "Yep" she'd say "Yeah."

Over coffee in the living room an hour or so later, she raved about the English oak cabinet with its twenty-four compartments and paneled arch cupboard doors. I told her my mother had found it at an auction twelve years back. Cindy said she'd make me an offer for it next week, after she had done some additional research. "It's perfect for my guest bedroom."

Cindy was very straightforward and practical. She spoke clearly and carefully. "I do want to stress," she said, "that I believe, we believe," she said, including Howard with a quick sweep of her warm eyes, "that you'll be pleased with the auction price; however, on auction day, the market will ultimately determine what valuation is acceptable for your property."

"I understand," I said. "Who actually pays the auctioneer fee?"

Howard spoke up. "It's paid via the buyer's premium, which is added to the buyer's final bid."

"And the auction will be held here?"

"We hold most auctions on-site, Alan," Howard said. "On-site, bidders are constantly reminded of the positives, and there are many here. Yep."

"Yeah," said Cindy, brightly.

Howard continued. "Which, in turn, can encourage a higher bid."

I clasped my hands, suddenly sleepy and longing for a nap. "Okay."

"Will your wife come for the auction?" Cindy asked.

I looked down at my hands. "I don't know."

Howard and Cindy left the house, praising the place and reassuring me that I'd be delighted with the results. They were to be in touch next week.

I fell asleep on the couch and dreamt of Rita. The 18-year-old Rita came sauntering toward me along a narrow dirt road, embroidered by tall palms and neon-red exotic flowers. She carried the tanned breeziness of one who has just returned from a full morning at the beach. She was dressed in tight yellow pants, high-heeled sandals, and a cream strapless top, within which her breasts were conspicuous and fetching. A yellow wide-brimmed hat was cocked stylishly to one side. Her arms were swinging easily. Approaching me, she smiled warmly, parted her moist lips and lifted her chin in a playful invitation. She paused for a moment, gave a little sigh, and then removed her hat and flung it away. It sailed, like a Frisbee, into the trees, where a startled butterfly fluttered off toward the lake.

"Hi, Rita," I said, leaning against a tree near the water. "Been a long time."

"Hey, Alan James. How's physics?"

"It's bad, Rita. Real bad. I failed the test."

"No... not you. You've never failed any test."

"Oh, yeah, Rita. I failed the physical test."

"Really? The physics of physicality test?"

"I took so many tests, Rita. So many. You have no idea how many tests I took. I'm a doctor, you know, and I know how to take those tests, Rita. I'm smart that way. I took all those tests."

"And you passed them, didn't you? You always got A's, Alan James. Straight As'."

I shook my head sorrowfully. "No, Rita. Not this time. This time I failed."

She stepped forward and brushed my cheek with her soft caressing hand. "Well, it's alright, Alan James. I love you anyway. I'll always love you anyway."

I turned half around. "No, Rita, you don't understand. I failed every single test. It's over."

She laughed. "Well, you never should have married her in the first place. Why did you, anyway?"

Suddenly, Rita blurred and rippled into a blue nebulous fog, that rapidly morphed into my wife, Nicole, a red formidable giant who swelled up into a towering genie of intimidation. Looking down with folded arms, her dark reproachful eyes finally settled on me, as she grew ten- to-twenty stories high. "Alan, why did you come here?" she hollered.

I cowered behind a rock, petrified.

"You are such a fool! When are you going to learn that you just keep deceiving yourself over and over again?"

I awoke sharply, sat up and threw my legs to the floor. I rubbed my eyes and stood, glancing at my watch. Almost six. I needed a good run. I needed to clear my head of the dream and of the past. I needed to stop thinking for a while.

In my room, I found some old jogging shorts and Reebok running shoes (I hadn't used them in at least five years) and pulled on a yellow T-shirt that had NO TIME LIKE NOW, written across the chest in bold black letters. I had no idea where I'd gotten it. I paused at the mirror to look at myself before leaving. Why had Rita looked at me so reproachfully back at Jack's Diner? What had she seen in my eyes or on my face?

In the mirror, I saw a face that will never be handsome. That nose is too dulled, the skin too pale, the eyes too far apart, the ears flat against the head. There's no sharpness in the jaw line. The dark eyes, though cool and intelligent, have a disheartening force emanating from them that keeps the world at a distance. The mouth is small, lips well formed, but closed tightly with a hint of impatience. Do my patients see that!?

The hair, a thick glossy black, falls stylishly over the forehead. It's a quality feature; the one genetic quality that helps to soften the severity a little. I stepped back to view the body. The shoulders weren't impressive, though the carriage was erect and the chest open in a pride of confidence and correctness. But, quizzically, at the macro viewing, when I looked deeply into that face, I saw some submerged relic of emotion, pacing, molding the body in a contradiction of features and expressions. Who and what art thou, Dr. Lincoln? See how you've let yourself gain weight, not quite thick around the middle, but losing waist definition. Why? To never be called a skinny nerd again. No, give me the serious man of substantial stature, who is skilled at projecting attractive fronts. Yes, the primary care physician who sees patients every fifteen minutes, writes referrals, documents every single bit of minutia of communication, prescribes pills and advice and sometimes bullshit (because I haven't a clue what to say or what medical advice to give).

Despite the attractive fronts, blur of years and stellar achievements, swimming in my veins were aged and unfulfilled adolescent hormones, like a good, aged wine, still waiting to be uncorked and tasted with the "supper" of Rita. Bloodwork couldn't analyze them. They couldn't be detected by MRI or x-ray. They couldn't be heard with a stethoscope, nor rationalized or interpreted by therapy.

I was still searching for fulfillment, for the blush and passion of reunion with the 18 year-old essence of Rita.

I sprang away from the house and jogged sluggishly in the direction of the old railroad station, over a sharp green slope, past a withered vegetable garden now mostly flooded with purple wild flowers. The railroad station was at least two miles away and I remembered a route that would take me along dirt paths and open fields to avoid busy roads.

I should have done some stretching. Every muscle seemed knotted and stiff. I jogged easily, not going for speed, slipping into a cool bank of trees, exiting the other side, near a garrulous brook, and then up a steep dirt path. The flat moan of a train whistle soothed, dissolving my mind's screen of rambling images, calling me to focus on the soft evening light, settling over the land with a prayerful serenity and creeping low shadows.

Further along, the stiffness in my legs and back persisted, but I built speed gradually along an old tar-covered road, where years ago, I'd whirled on my bicycle toward Sawmill Lake and an afternoon of fishing. I soon left the paved road for another dirt path and after a mile or so, when I was winded, I slowed the pace, struggling to balance my inhalation and exhalation. I listened to the comfortable and steady thud of my shoes striking the earth, and for a few seconds, I shut my eyes, enjoying the sound and feel of my feet being gently sucked and released by the soft mud. It felt good being in touch with the earth that way; to have a kind of physical call and response dialogue with it—feet patter—so intimate and distinctive and far from the city. I'd forgotten that—forgotten that Hartsfield had restful paths, quiet fields and protected streams and trees. I glanced skyward and saw geese beating up from a lake, rising over trees, angling, honking into the pink pastel horizon.

Minutes later, I broke from a winding path into an open field, and looked left at teenage boys playing soccer. Their orange and green jerseys and their urgent, jubilant cries pierced the peace, but didn't shatter it. There was comfort in it, like the noise of children during holiday celebrations.

The sun sparked off little puddles and from a wet cement wall in the distance, near the old, boarded-up, red-bricked railroad station. I was well aware of why I'd chosen this spot for my jog. Rita had returned home from the State beauty pageant, by train, in late October, fifteen years ago. Dad had sent me the article my freshman year in college and I'd read it, repeatedly, as I worked on a slow anger.

In the photograph, Rita was standing on the train platform in a low-cut dress, head thrown back, with a killer smile, waving, obviously enjoying the summit of the moment. But she hadn't won. She'd come in third. I thought it impossible. The smoke of irritation and resentment had hovered about me for a week. "It was rigged. It's all politics. They're all blind idiots!" I'd ranted.

But in the photo, I saw no sadness in Rita—no sign of defeat or regret. On the contrary, she projected grace and natural dignity.

My father had written: "I think that's the last we'll hear of the regal Rita Fitzgerald. She had her fifteen minutes. Her star has risen and fallen. Her revels have now ended and she is melted into air... into thin air. She and Dusty Palmer are getting married next month."

My father's quote from *The Tempest* irritated me. I thought his comments were petty. I realized then, with some disappointment, that he had been jealous of Rita. In what form or manner, I didn't know, but it radiated off his scratch pad like the smell of rotten fish, so that the beautifully printed script at the top of the sheet: "From the desk of Richard Alan Lincoln," actually seemed to say, "We, the fortunate and superior, have won again and, God willing, it will always be so."

I ripped up the clipping, and his note, and threw them in a dumpster on my way to Psychology 101. Now, I wished I'd kept them.

I cut through a field of wild flowers, feeling a sudden burst of energy, and sprinted toward the station house just ahead. The porch was broken-backed over the post that had once supported it, and unruly shrubs and weeds were taking "the little red house" over. I circled it twice, imagining Rita descending the train to the platform, into the cheering, welcoming crowds. Dad said there were over 300 people there that day. I hopped and skipped the rails and scaled the squeaky wooden platform, feeling a great solemnity, a guilty sorrow, a great loss. I didn't want to leave Hartsfield until I saw Rita again. I needed to see her one more time.

I ran in place, squinting up at the wooden sign hanging lopsided on the face of the station. Ten years of punishment from sun and rain had left the white and black paint cracked and faded. I could just barely read the letters: HARTSFIELD, PA.

I circled the station once more, dodging broken glass, tall weeds, and old railroad tiles, and then started for home.

Approaching the house from the left side, maintaining a slow even pace across the sturdy grass, I saw a sun-faded gray car in the driveway, parked behind mine. I ran toward it, leaping the two-foot hedge, turning sharply toward the front porch. When I saw her, sitting on the stairs, on the edge of sunlight and shadow, I came to an abrupt stop, winded and damp.

Rita's lowered head lifted with surprise and interest. A rabbit burst from the hedge, struck the ground, leaped, and darted away, finding shadows and then the safety of forsythia and box hedges. Rita didn't seem to notice. She arose slowly, eyes timid, her posture stiff and uncertain. She held a brown manila envelope in her right hand that she shifted to her left as I started toward her. She seemed to have retreated into her loose jeans and large, off-white sweatshirt. The red sneakers were faded and tattered. She wore pink lipstick, but little makeup or eye shadow; there was a small diamond stud glittering in the right side of her nose. She was ruler-thin and pale, with a recessive energy that made it seem as if her heart pumped grudgingly.

I studied her in detail, taking her apart, searching for a clue to her state of mind, struggling to breech the jarring moment with an easy word or careful phrase that would link us back to the past, but keep us cleverly anchored in the present. She descended the three stairs and came to me.

I quickly wiped my sweaty face with the tail of my t-shirt, still catching breaths, anxious. There was a deep stillness around us, as if we stood in the center of a lake at noon.

"Hi," I said, almost at a whisper.

She didn't speak, enlarging the silence.

I tried again. "It's…good to see you, Rita. I'm glad you came by."

She drew herself up to a weak dignity, but didn't talk. She offered me the manila envelope, as the sunlight retreated to the tops of trees and far-away hills, gilding them. I took the envelope.

She swallowed, and seemed to want to speak, but didn't.

"Can I open it?" I asked.

She nodded.

I pinched the two copper pins together until they were vertical, lifted the flap and drew out the paper-clipped typed pages. I examined the first page. It was entitled *The Infinite Letting Go*.

Rita stood in a remote politeness. She looked down at the cement walk.

"So you want me to read it?" I asked.

She nodded again.

"Okay...I'd love to."

She shrugged, delicately, then turned and set off for her car. I went after her. "Rita..."

She stopped, but didn't face me.

"Rita...I really am glad you came by."

She entered her car without a word. I waved as she drove away. Silly, I knew, but I did. I lingered in the yard, moving through retreating shadows. I sat on the porch swing, feet flat, stationary, staring into the distance, until sleepy clouds, flamed by a setting sun, were brushed gold.

I laid the pages on my lap and began to read. There was still enough light.

The Infinite Letting Go

There was a large round boulder that sat, like a wise meditating sage, in her backyard, just beyond where wild roses grew in summer, near a natural brook, whose quiet music crept into her dreams and daydreams; and it lay under the wide protective spread of a very old sycamore tree, where she'd played and slept.

The boulder had been there since the beginning of time, or so the old man had told her, and it had a very important and unique purpose: it anchored the world. If it was ever removed, so the old man had said, the world would simply drift out of orbit, lose its laws of motion and gravity and, like a balloon, float endlessly toward nowhere and no place.

So she watched the boulder from her bedroom window—with wide, alert eyes—and prayed that it would never be taken away.

And so it was that the boulder, so gray and formidable, lay undisturbed for many years, until the day the bulldozers came. That day was known as "Bulldozer Day." A big house was going up and land was needed and had to be cleared. The sycamore tree would have to come down; the wild roses destroyed and burned; and the boulder, scooped up and taken away.

For many, many days the girl watched the bulldozers cough smoke and scour the land, crawling like strange yellow invaders toward the boulder, toward ultimate destruction. Her Daddy drove one of those machines, and he loved leveling and remaking the land. He loved the God in it: the God of creation, who overrules old, wild things.

The old man came by one day. The girl watched him mope and stumble across ruddy earth, rock and broken trees. She watched him shake his bony fist at them and curse them in a brittle cry of rage. But it did not even crack the hard shell of the growl and scrape of the masticating machines.

He stood firmly by the boulder, stooped though he was, and he called down the wrath of any god whose ear was close. He prayed and wailed for many hours, mouthing sacred mantras and incantations, evoking the ancestors, the spirits, straining in a hoarse, pleading voice for some ineffable being to stop the invaders. But the bulldozers approached, like big locusts and, because the old man was old, they waited and they did not remove the boulder that day. The world was safe, for one more day.

The girl visited the boulder that night. She circled it. Touched it. Felt its hard crevices worn smooth by an eternity of sun and rain; felt an old warmth and pulse radiating from it, like a heart; sensed its wisdom at the base where ripe green moss clung pungent and soft. She prayed that the old man would return. She did not want the boulder to go. She did not want to drift away. She did not want to float around in the universe forever, without ever being anchored to anything.

She did not sleep that night. She watched the crimson stain of dawn reveal the creeping gray silhouettes of the men of the new creation, as they climbed their sleeping giants and woke them up. The girl watched, terrified, her nose pressed to the cool window, her heart racing. "Will the boulder cry out? Does it have the magic to stop them? To save itself and the world? If so, would her Daddy survive? It was his bulldozer that lumbered and squeaked over mounds and furrows of earth toward its goal: to drive away the old boulder.

The bulldozer drew up to the boulder and stopped. Threateningly, the yellow monster snarled and belched out black acrid smoke.

The boulder did not move. The heavy shovel struck the ground, hard, and was caught glaring by the blinding spark of sun. The girl shaded her eyes, hearing her tiny, horrified voice call for the old man.

The shovel shot forward and, like a predator with a clever tongue, it scooped up the rock, effortlessly, and snapped it backwards with easy precision, as if swallowing it. It lifted it high, like an offering and a prize, parading the severed head of the old gods, holding it skyward for all the cheering masses to see.

And then it was taken across

the bare, ravaged fields, across the now muddy stream, and casually, routinely, it was dropped off the edge of the world.

The girl waited, breathless, and when it happened, she was not surprised. Her room and all the objects in it began to rise and float. She lost her footing and, like smoke, she drifted. Outside, all the men and their machines began lifting from the earth, rising, hovering for a time and then, finally, evaporating into a lusterless blue sky.

She had but two choices: to let go, to drift, lost, like a cloud, or to find the old man and then, together, search for the boulder. The old anchor. The old comfortable gods.

As she drifted higher, she reached for something—anything—to grab on to, to steady her, to anchor her, but all the vaporous objects that passed were just out of her reach. So she drifted and looked for the old man and for the boulder that had been dropped off the edge of the world.

I sat staring down at the pages until darkness

descended; until the sounds of the crickets and bullfrogs, and a quickening breath, stirred me to my feet. I walked the land, holding the pages of Rita's story, as if they pulsed with life. The night air shifted directions and became silky and cool. I was thrilled by thoughts of Rita; strengthened, eagerly, by the certainty that I'd see her again, because she had made contact. She had left the story with me. She was reaching out! That pleasurable thought expanded into aching, rapturous fantasies that kept me awake until two-thirty in the morning.

CHAPTER TWO

Morning light startled the land. It fell on bright green rippling grass, drenching the trees and lakes with a trembling radiance, like millions of silver butterflies.

I had risen early, pulled on slacks and a green shirt, and made a run to the local Farmers Market for a few groceries. Returning home, I traveled the back roads, driving slowly, searching the unraveling fields for reasons—trying to understand why I'd wound up back in Hartsfield, seeing Rita again. Feeling 18 again. Feeling anxious again.

By the time I returned home and called Nicole, my voice must have sounded pensive and faraway.

"I start the trial tomorrow," she said, with her own tone of detachment.

"Yes, I remember."

"You're not saying much, Alan. You sound kind of out-of-it."

"Oh… I didn't sleep very well. Old ghosts or something."

"You met with the estate auctioning agents?"

"Yes. Things went fine. I don't think it will take long. I'm leaving this afternoon. Should be home by 6 or so."

"Let's eat out tonight," Nicole said. "Something simple."

"Sure… Nicole, I was thinking this morning… we've both been working a lot of hours. Why don't we go to your father's place on Shelter Island the weekend after next? Your trial should be over by then and I can get Megan to cover for me on Monday."

Nicole was quiet.

"Nicole?"

"I don't know."

"…Because?"

Silence again.

"Nicole, we could talk."

"We have talked."

"Don't be difficult."

Her voice took an edge. "Then don't be redundant, Alan. We already know what the choices are. It's time to take some kind of action. I've said that before."

I was pacing the kitchen, gripping my cell phone. "Then let's talk about what action to take. I need that, Nicole. I need for us to be together—away from everything—so we can move on this."

"Okay, fine!" Nicole said, irritated. "So, we'll go and talk. Maybe we'll even get somewhere. Who the hell knows!?"

"Okay then, we could go back to Barbados. We had fun there."

"You know I don't have time for that."

"Do you have a better suggestion?"

"We'll go to Shelter Island. Fine. Let's do it! Let's do it and get it over with! Look, I've got to go. I've got a trial to get ready for."

I slumped in the nearest chair. "I'll see you for dinner then."

While I was making coffee and toast, the doorbell rang. I made a side sweep toward the sound, paused, and left the kitchen to answer it. Rita stood framed under the arch, in sunlight, cool sunglasses perched on the top of her head. Our eyes glinted at each other and she seemed to freeze a little. She held a plate of cookies, covered by clear plastic wrap. I immediately saw that something was different: her hair lay natural and careless, as if dried by the wind. It made her young, seemed to smooth the lines around her eyes and mouth. With light makeup, there was blush in her cheeks, and she looked back with a milder gaze. She wore jeans, a yellow cotton shirt and a light blue cotton jacket that put false meat on her thin bones.

"Good morning..." I said. "Are the cookies for me?"

She nodded, demurely.

She offered me the plate and I took it. "Wow... they look great."

I passed my nose over them and couldn't smell anything. "They smell wonderful. What are they?"

She worked hard to speak, and it was barely above a whisper. "Oatmeal, raisins...nuts."

"I love oatmeal. Want to come in?"

She gave another little nod and I stepped aside as she entered. She looked around with an uneasy awe at the rooms and staircase. There was the hint of a breeze, a spring breath, fleeting, but it stirred the bottom ruffle of the cream sheer curtains in the living room.

"Had breakfast?" I asked.

She swallowed and then spoke, faintly. "Yes…"

It cheered me to hear her voice again. "How about some coffee then? I just made some."

Her eyes said yes.

In the kitchen, she settled on a stool at the island and blinked around at the brightness of the day. I placed the cookies on the almond Formica countertop, and looked at her briskly, suddenly buoyed. And then our eyes played a back-and-forth game of "look and look-away" until I grinned and she broke it off, her fingers moving busily.

I shakily poured coffee and bustled about, looking for cream and sugar. "You take cream and sugar?" I asked quickly, nervously. "I know I've got both, well, I mean, not cream, but milk. Sugar I've got somewhere. I don't use it, but I know I have it. My mother used it. Dad never did." I was vamping, as it were, until I could find a true melody of thought.

I had my head in the refrigerator, looking back over my shoulder. "You know, we never drank coffee together, Rita. That's why I don't know how you take it."

"Cream," she said. "Milk…" she corrected, with a faint smile.

I took out two French cups, slim and elegant, and poured the coffee. I poured milk in a little gold pitcher and laid it and the cup before her. I peeled the plastic from the cookie plate and pushed it close to her reach. "They look fantastic. Going to have one?"

She shrugged her left shoulder.

"Well I'm going to."

I brought my coffee, toast and cup of plain yogurt to the island. Leaning against it, I picked a scrumptious looking cookie and studied it. "I didn't know you baked."

"...Some," she said.

I took a bite. It was soft, rich, but not overly sweet. "Good. Very good. Excellent!"

She folded her hands, pleased.

I drank coffee, chewed and strained for conversation. Rita stared blankly out the windows at the thickly wooded hills, her head resting in her left hand. I'd have to be very careful with my words. I didn't know her now, and one innocent or well-meaning word or phrase could easily detonate a terrible memory or emotion. I'd have to keep the subjects general and light, steering clear of the past, treading softly, like a soldier in a mine field. I was skittish about bringing up her short story, afraid that discussing it might drop her into a dark mood, although I was sure that's why she'd come. I decided on something bold.

"What are you doing today?"

She turned her face up to me, with mild surprise. She opened her mouth to speak but stopped. She shrugged again.

"It's such a beautiful day. Maybe we could go for a drive or something," I said.

She considered it while she tasted the coffee. She looked at me, her face drawn with confused thought; and then I saw a wildness and a calm in the depth of her eyes: two distinct incarnations appeared, one sizing up the other, on an inner battlefield. It startled me. Maybe it was the medication she was taking, but I couldn't help but stare and explore. It was as if she'd been split in two and "those two" were hell-bent on war; frightened; stalking; and measuring the distances.

I felt the professional obligation and surge to reach out and help; the irrational passion of an 18-year-old who wanted to rescue; and the faltering man, caught by reawakened desire, who wanted to take her and run off to some far corner of the world.

She twitched away from me.

"Are you okay, Rita?" I asked, softly.

She recovered slowly.

I dropped my apologetic voice to a whisper. "Did I say something wrong?"

She shook her head, and looked at me again, beseechingly. Her eyes filmed with tears. Laboring, she finally spoke. "It was so long ago. Such a long time, Alan James."

I didn't know exactly what she was referring to, but I had to swallow a couple of times to stop the emotion. "Yes…"

In a long silence, I finished the yogurt and toast

while Rita finished her coffee. We listened to birds and a distant droning lawn mower. Not wanting to risk another possible "episode," I waited for Rita. She finally raised herself up and went to the door that led to the patio. She opened it and stepped outside, slipping on her sunglasses. I reached for another cookie and followed her. She pointed to a patch of glowing flowers, leaning in the soft breeze, and she went to them. When I arrived, she was bending toward tulips. The close damp fragrance of them and the sound of bees seemed to give her energy. Her face relaxed.

"Beautiful…" she said. She lifted a hand for expression, indicating. "This house and the land. It's so beautiful. You were lucky to grow up here."

"Yes, I was lucky. My mother planted so many flowers. She loved her gardens. Dad said she'd never planted anything when they first moved here, but after a year or two she told him that the land just called out to her. So she bought books and took some classes and planted flower and vegetable gardens. She grew huge roses and entered them in some contest: came in second, I think, and was she pissed off! She said the whole thing was rigged. She entered again the following year and came in third. That did it! She never entered again."

Rita took a fresh breath. "I talked to her once."

"My mother? Really. I didn't know that."

"She was very kind to me. And she was so pretty and elegant. It was right after the State beauty pageant. We were in the grocery store. She came up to me and said she was..." Rita paused, running a hand through her hair; her eyes filled with emotion. "She said she was proud of me. I never forgot that. I was so disappointed when I lost. It was such a nice thing for her to say."

The day surrounded us in bright yellow glory. Rita nosed toward another red tulip and sniffed.

"I asked her about you," Rita said.

I straightened a little with bright interest.

"She said you were studying hard."

"Yeah, I did study hard. I was a good little boy."

Rita looked me over, closely, I thought, for the first time. She nodded. "So, you're a doctor now."

"Yes."

"Surgeon?"

"No. Primary care. I got tired...And...well, maybe later."

"You've changed."

"I tried to."

"Your face is quieter, but your eyes are sad."

"I don't know..." I said, leaving a number of unfinished thoughts in the air.

"Yes." She squinted another look. "There's confusion there, too. You've filled out. Longer hair. It looks good. I like it."

"Nicole doesn't like it short."

"Nicole? You're married?"

I toed at the ground. "Yes."

"How long?"

"A little over three years."

"What does she do?"

"Attorney. Medical malpractice. She defends doctors."

"Are you happy, Alan James?" Rita asked, presenting her face to the full flood of sunlight.

I pushed my hands into my pockets. "Sometimes."

Her smile broadened, the years vanished and I breathed her in, feeling the growing pull of her.

She pointed to the little pond. "Let's walk."

"Okay."

We started across the lawn to the narrow salmon pebble path, and ambled along it toward the pond, silently, until we reached it. Rita found a large flat rock and sat down, bringing her knees to her chest and embracing them. Shading our eyes from the glare, we watched water spiders and the gray shadows of fish slithering through shallow water. We followed the capricious and ridiculous flight of a yellow butterfly.

"What's she like? Your wife."

"Smart, attractive, ambitious. Fair."

"Fair?"

I didn't reply.

"Too personal. Sorry," Rita said.

"Don't be."

"Children?"

"No. None."

Rita looked up. "Will you?"

"Children?"

Rita didn't move her steady eyes from mine. She must have seen pain. She looked away toward a green field that slanted up to a line of trees, and then our conversation turned careful. The sun was growing hot on my shoulders.

"Did you ever fish here?" she asked.

"Some, when I was a boy. I usually went over to Sawmill Lake. It's bigger and you can swim there."

Rita's face suddenly enlivened with an idea. "Should we?"

"Go to Sawmill Lake?"

She nodded, more vigorously.

"To swim?" I asked.

"Maybe."

"The water will be cold."

"Okay with me."

I felt a sudden release of hope. "Hey. Why not?"

Rita waited downstairs while I grabbed towels, sunglasses, swimming trunks and a couple pairs of flip flops. We took my car and drove back to the Farmers Market, at Rita's request, and bought cheese, bread and bottled water.

Sawmill Lake was one of the smaller but more picturesque lakes in the county. It was more oval than round and was fed by freshwater streams. The lake itself was stocked with large and small-mouthed bass that had drawn both the local fishermen and the prosperous of the county, who had put up modest summer cottages.

As we turned off the highway onto the asphalt road and traveled beneath quiet white birch, oak and elm, I immediately and sadly saw the evidence of relentless progress. There were new bungalows and cottages, and they were all hefty and invasive. Some were still in progress and the smell of fresh cut lumber mixed with the wind, blowing in through our open windows. There was more traffic than I'd remembered and, in the distance, I heard the wicked snarl of a jet ski.

We drove past old trees and protruding rocks that I remembered passing on my bike so long ago; quiet witnesses to the relentless passing of humans and their many dramas. They made me feel as vulnerable and fragile as the little insect that splattered against the windshield. I had no idea where that thought had come from. A second earlier I'd been ecstatic just being with Rita again. It occurred to me that the thought could have been picked up from Rita—a thread or fragment of her thinking. I'd had that ability in the old days, when we met at Jack's.

I looked at her. She looked back. Her expression was subdued, her eyes clouded and gleaming, like the sun shining through a storm. Again, I wondered what medication she was taking.

"Are you okay?"

She nodded.

"There were more woods fifteen years ago," I said. "None of these damned houses."

"Most are vacation homes," Rita said. "The people aren't from this area."

I turned onto a dirt road and parked 10 feet from the lap of the water's edge. We got out and took in the lake, the surrounding trees and the cloudless blue sky. I saw three rowboats. Two were wide apart and motionless, with fishermen hunched over poles, serene and hallowed in the good sun. Another boat crawled along the far side bank, mostly in shadow, its lone rower striding easy, long strokes.

I heard Rita sigh. She slanted me a look of pleasure and nodded.

"Brings back memories," I said. "Long summer days."

Suddenly, Rita rolled up the cuffs of her pants and started for the lake. A moment later, she unlaced her red sneakers, peeled off her socks and stepped to the water's edge. Slowly, she dipped her right wiggling toes into the water. "Ooohhh…Cold!" she exclaimed, yanking her foot back.

I came up. "I told you. I didn't swim here until late July or August. The mountain streams make it like ice water."

In mock defiance, she heaved her fists to her hips and curled her lip. "Going in…"

"Rita…" I said, in a tone of modest apprehension.

But she marched forward, her face set, not breaking her stride as she entered the still water. She stamped in, splashing, advancing deeper until she was nearly waist high, gasping and trembling. I watched in astonishment.

"I wouldn't go too far, Rita," I called.

"Cold!!!" she yelled and it echoed. "Cold!!"

"Yes…" I said uneasily. "Maybe you should come back."

She started to laugh. A low staccato sound, cramped. It crescendoed, found freedom, and broke through a trapped harshness into a tense stridency. It sounded less like a laugh and more like a call for help. I was alarmed.

"Rita!"

I'd never heard the sound before. It was unsettling, disturbing. A violent shout of agony.

"Cold!!"

"Rita! Come back!"

The sound rose and curled around the lake, bouncing, breaking into a piercing frightening scream. "Cold! Cold!! COLD!!!"

The hair bristled on the back of my neck. The echo reverberated and shattered the peace. Birds burst from trees. Fishermen jolted to attention, jerking toward us.

Rita screamed. "GOD!!! GOD!!!"

"Rita!"

Rita struggled forward, head back, raging at the sky, with clenched fists, screaming out venom at the sky, until the lakebed fell away to deep water and she sank, like a stone, leaving a shocking loud silence.

I whipped off my shirt and charged in after her, knees kicking high, my feet exploding plumes of water. I stumbled, reached, and dived, and met the frigid shock of the lake with rasping breath. When I reached her she had already surfaced. She wailed, racking sobs, slapping the water as she struggled for air, swinging, and fighting invisible demons. I embraced her, steadied her arms and pulled her back into my chest—dragged us toward shallow water and up to safety on the bank. I held her, rocked her, whispered to her, stroked her ice cold brow; picked the hair from her stormy eyes and blurry eye shadow. "It's okay, Rita. It's okay… Okay… everything's okay…"

She shivered violently, as the cool air poured over us. I struggled into my shirt, and scooped her up into my arms—labored until I found the center of her weight—and then staggered back to the car. I set her down, leaning her against the car. I opened the back door wide.

Rita was lost, caught in some frightening reality. Her blue lips quivered, her eyes were vacant. She mumbled. I reached in, snatched the towels, wrapped her shoulders and hastily dried her hair. Holding her chilly shoulders, I guided her toward the open entrance and gingerly eased her down and back, and covered her with a fresh towel. She instantly shut her eyes. Her pulse was throbbing. I closed the door and rushed to the driver's seat. I paused briefly to catch a breath, then got in, rolled up the windows and started the engine. I turned on the heat and blasted it back to her.

As I raced down the road back to the house, I instinctively reached for my cell phone, but realized I didn't know who to call. I didn't know who her doctor was, or what medication she was taking.

Rita fell asleep in the back bedroom, the room next to my father's library. It was almost one o'clock.

By the time I'd helped remove her clothes, given her one of my sister's old flannel night gowns and put her to bed, the emotion had nearly run itself out. I'd taken her blood pressure and pulse just before she'd fallen asleep, as she mumbled how sorry she was. Both were normal.

"I'm a doctor, Rita. I can help."

"I don't want you to be my doctor. I have a doctor," she'd said, stammering. "I also have a shrink."

"Do you want me to call your mother?"

"God, no!"

She turned her head away in shame, grumbled out something else about "heroes and heroines," and fell asleep.

I spent the next hour and a half wandering the house and the back lawn, gazing longingly at the pond, watching the sky fill with a puzzle of white clouds, nervously glancing at my watch. If I didn't leave by three o'clock, I'd never make it to New York for dinner with Nicole.

At 2:35 I was standing in the kitchen, absent and nervous, nibbling on some bread and cheese when Rita drifted in, still in the flannel gown, sleepy-eyed. Her hair had tight springy tangles, her eyes were swollen, energy low.

"Hi," I said. "How do you feel?"

She stopped at the island and gave a long stressed sigh. "... Better." She looked at the gown. "Clothes?"

I pushed away from the counter. "...Oh, I washed

and dried them. Hope that was okay?"

She nodded. "I need to go."

I waited. "Sure." But I didn't move. "Rita…"

She held up a hand to stop me. She scratched her nose. "Some reunion… huh?"

"It's okay… Really."

She shook her head vigorously. "No, no, Alan James. I've been good. So good. I've been well." She tried to explain with her hands. "Just… I don't know what happened out there."

"Memories?" I asked.

She lifted a reluctant shoulder and sank a little.

I started for her, but stopped. I could see—no feel—she didn't want pity.

Then she surprised me by smiling a little. "Glad you didn't think I was faking this time."

It took me a minute to awake to her meaning. "Oh yes, the Holiday Inn. The drowning. Yes, well…"

Then she looked through me and beyond me. I saw the struggle of an idea or question and, when she spoke, her voice was small. "I'm not crazy."

"I know that," I said quickly. "I know you're not." But I knew she wasn't stable either. There was something else she wanted to say; I could feel it, but she asked for her clothes instead.

After she'd showered and dressed, she met me on the porch, where I sat on the porch swing, gently rocking. I stood as she came over. Her shoulders sagged a little, her eyes were evasive. "Alan James. In two weeks. In two weeks, on Saturday…" She stopped, gathering courage. "Birthday…"

"Your birthday?" I asked, then immediately recalled that her birthday was in August.

"No, no. I'm asking, because I do need... help."

I leaned toward her, eagerly. "Yes. Anything, Rita. Anything."

"Dar..." Her lips quivered. "It's my daughter's birthday. Darla."

I pocketed my hands. We stood in a long, painful silence. "Yes, Rita."

"...I would like you to come—and your wife. I'd like to meet her. Just for dinner or something. I want to be with friends. I'd like to be with you on her birthday."

Sudden anxiety pinned me to the porch. Nicole and I were supposed to go to Shelter Island that weekend to talk. We had to get away for the survival of our marriage.

Rita's blue glassy eyes suddenly cleared. They held me for a time, exploring, and then looking away in sorrow. "I understand. I do, really," she said, her voice trailing away.

"No, Rita. It's not that I don't want to come. I do."

She looked at me frankly, without anger. "I will not break down, Alan. I will honor Darla. That's what she would have wanted."

"Rita... It's just that Nicole and I are going out of town that weekend. It would be, well, kind of difficult to postpone it."

Rita smiled, understandingly. "Then you should —must—go and be with her."

I reached for Rita's arm, took her soft, thin hand.

"I'm glad that you asked me. Very honored."

With a last unhurried glance, she turned and walked noiselessly toward her car.

"Rita."

She turned.

"I loved your story. I did."

She gave me a half smile. "It's not much…"

When Rita drove away, with a little "toot" of the horn, my body loosened and I sank into an intoxicated disappointment.

CHAPTER THREE

Nearly two weeks later, on Friday morning, June 3rd, I left the apartment on 84th Street and started up Broadway toward the uptown subway. I looked skyward, seeing a spotted white sky rushing overhead, as if matching the pace below. The humidity was high and I felt its damp breath as I walked.

New York City came alive in small pieces of action. Cab doors opened and slammed shut; keys rattled; sudden footsteps emerged from brownstones and subways, marching to silent drums. Airplanes roared overhead, sounding like the ocean. Feet ran to honking cars and hissing buses. Traffic inched forward in lines of extraordinary stubbornness, cars creeping, straining for advantage; and now and then one would break away, finding the rare loophole and shooting toward the next stop light.

A forceful June sun penetrated the haze and shattered the earth into yellow squares, glinting lines and quivering dots. It flashed off fire escapes and windows, and made shadows stretch across streets.

I passed a wandering beggar with little mumbles

on his thin lips; his smelly clothes leaving a foul, trailing scent. A businessman on crutches, clumsily grasping his briefcase, was curbside hailing a cab. Sleepy faces, shut tight to the world, seemed to drift toward newsstands, diners and delis. Prancing teens with predatory eyes moved off toward Amsterdam Avenue, their jerky bodies in helpless rhythm with their musical hormones.

I entered the bagel shop and ordered a toasted pumpernickel with cream cheese, and a small coffee. While it was prepared and bagged, I glanced through the window at a rotund man taking quick snaps at a cheese Danish. His eyes gleamed with pleasure.

I saw stacks of newspapers being tossed from trucks by little stubby men with massive arms, their voices blatant and loud. I stepped around dogs straining on leashes, and a squared-jawed policeman leaning toward a double-parked car, pen and pad poised to punish.

I watched attractive and freshly buffed women striking miraculously straight paths on spiked wobbly heels, heads cocked in cool confidence. I passed a movie theatre and followed rolling red electric titles across the glittering marquee. Through it all, I thought of Rita and wondered if she'd ever seen any of it and, if she had, if she liked it.

I didn't take a cab. I didn't want to get to the hospital quickly. I took the uptown number 1 subway at 86th and Broadway and stood in an open area at the rear of the car. No one spoke as it went thundering across the tracks. Heads were bowed, eyes fixed on something far away. Newspapers set definite boundaries, headsets piped in tunes, and another soiled man, slumped in the corner seat, slept.

I noticed a young girl, who was about thirteen years old. She was blond and pretty, dressed in pink Capri pants and white tank top that had BROADWAY BABY written across her small breasts in bold black letters. There was a little rose tattoo on her upper right arm just below the shoulder. She was texting.

Tomorrow was Darla's birthday, Saturday, June 4th. I'd counted the days. I'd often stared at the telephone, almost reached for it at least a dozen times, to call Rita, but I hadn't. I had lain awake nights imagining the horror of losing a child—losing a child that way. An unspeakable horror. Unbearable. A wound that would never heal. I could not imagine it. My mind would shut off. How was Rita coping?

I left the subway and walked along 110th Street, turned north on Amsterdam Avenue and headed for St. Luke's Hospital, where I was on the teaching staff. I made rounds with interns in the morning, and in the afternoon, I saw patients in my office across the street.

I wasn't ready to go in, so I crossed the street opposite the emergency room entrance, and stood in the garden at the north edge of the Cathedral of St. John the Divine, sipping my coffee and trying to gather my thoughts. Squirrels crept from trees and bushes and begged, flicking bushy tails. I pinched off a piece of the bagel and tossed it toward them. Their delightful agitation entertained me.

I stared at the emergency room entrance and heard a wailing siren approach from downtown. Again, I thought of Rita. There was a great irony about it all. Rita had lost a child. Nicole and I would, probably, never be able to have a child—not naturally anyway: I was infertile. Not sterile, the difference being that my testicles did produce some sperm. Unfortunately, those sperm, what there was of them, were weak swimmers. They were "dumb" sperm. Very low IQ. They died quickly. I'd often pictured them inside the boat of Nicole's body, like dying fish, hauled from the sea in great sweeping nets, flopping, writhing and gasping for life on the vessel floor, wide-eyed and panicked.

Nicole and I had discussed having children before we were married.

"I don't want any children right away," she'd said. "In a few years, after I've made partner. Then let's have at least two."

Less than a year later, she'd changed her mind and we met the cycles, enthusiastically, adding creative romance and humor. We failed. Then came the tests. My sperm count was less than 20 million per ml, which meant "the patient is infertile" or more correctly, "subfertile." The medical term "OLIGO" means few. Therefore, oligospermia is the presence of fewer than the normal number of sperm in semen.

Reproduction is a normal human function that

is absolutely necessary for the survival of the human species. Therefore, infertility is abnormal and it must have a cause. So I was tested for a pituitary tumor and testicular cancer. The tests came out negative. Then I learned that the most common cause of male infertility is varicocele, a term I'd learned about in medical school, but hadn't thought about since. So I was tested for an abnormal dilation of the pampiniform plexus of the internal spermatic vein, and was informed by my doctor that this condition is frequently a contributing factor in male subfertility. Nicole and I were hopeful. Again, negative. Mine was normal.

The last specialist diagnosed me with nonobstructive azoospermia: lack of sperm. The spermatozoa are absent; there is something wrong with the productive organ that produces them. Dr. Harold R. Long had also gone to Harvard and, although he was fifteen years older than I, we reminisced, joked and discussed the current medical crisis, before getting down to "business."

"Alan," he finally said to me, after a long calculated pause. "I'm sure you know that infertility is a problem for both you and your wife. It's a 'couple' problem. Would you like to wait until Nicole's here to discuss the options?"

I writhed uncomfortably. "No..."

Dr. Long cleared his throat. "Well, Alan, patients with nonobstructive azoospermia can be successfully treated by what is called Intracytoplasmic sperm injection, or ICSI. It is a technique performed as part of an in vitro fertilization cycle. Simply put, it involves the injection of a single sperm into each oocyte, in vitro, during an in vitro fertilization cycle."

I felt my eyes glaze over. His words seemed to bounce off my ears and shoot off into the ether.

I felt the rise of a sickening disgust; the foul stench of failure. I did not want to hear what I already knew. Modern medicine had made the infertility business really rather simple—especially if you had the money—and Nicole and I had the money.

You want a child and you're infertile? No problem. Try artificial insemination. It's a simple procedure that involves injecting a sample of specially treated sperm from the male partner into the female partner's reproductive tract. It's performed with the husband's sperm, unless, of course, the husband's ejaculate has few or no live sperm. In that case, donor sperm insemination is a possibility. (For me that was out of the question and, knowing Nicole as I knew her, she would not consider it either.)

What about Intrauterine insemination (IUI)? Again, no problem. The sperm bypasses the cervix without encountering "hostile" cervical mucus which acts like a barrier to the sperm. Whenever I thought of this, a comical image of Nicole swiftly arose. She is dressed as *Brünnhilde*, from Wagner's opera "Siegfried." She is bedecked in a horned Viking helmet, chain mail and sword, gripping a formidable golden shield. She charges forward, sword and shield thrust high, poised for combat, as the helicopters from *Apocalypse Now* sweep overhead and *Ride of the Valkyries* thunders in my ears.

But then, my little comic opera chimera ends, my head clears and I refocus on the IUI procedure. IUI places the strongest sperm into the female genital tract to increase the odds that one of those charging sperm will fertilize an egg. The procedure is relatively quick and simple. It takes place in the clinic office. It usually causes little discomfort.

If these don't work, then try in vitro fertilization. It's more invasive than IUI, but the advantage is that it allows the physician to evaluate whether or not fertilization has taken place. IV fertilization can be confirmed since it takes place outside the body, in a laboratory.

I knew about these options. I'd discussed them with trusted doctor friends, some of which I'd gone to medical school with.

"It's no big deal, Alan," most said.

However, Marvin Addison, from Topeka, Kansas, who seldom smiled, drew caricatures of his patients and had the bedside manner of an old hound dog, had a different approach. He'd become an OBGYN, with an office on Park Avenue. He'd said, "I've seen this kind of thing fuck up marriages, Alan. Big time. Is Nicole committed? Are you? What happens if nothing works, huh? Then what?"

I left Dr. Long's office coming to grips with the fact that something so basic to life as being able to produce life, was closed to me. I felt like I had failed the course "Man 101."

I brooded for days. Became desperate. I finally swallowed my pride and secretly went to a Chinese doctor in Chinatown, Dr. Wong.

His shop was old, close, dimly lit and filled from the floor to ceiling with wooden file boxes that contained musty herbs and moldy spices. He wore a frumpy brown suit and tie, and often ran a shaky hand over his smooth bald head as he shuffled about the place, mumbling, squinting and nodding.

"Yeah, yeah… Burdock Root for you," he said in broken English. I later learned it was also called Arctium minus. It is an ugly weed that grows profusely on the East Coast and in the Midwest.

Dr. Wong added, "Burdock good for impotence and sterility. Yeah, yeah. I also give you Yohimbe Bark. Good for erection. Good for impotence. Yeah. Use with caution."

"Caution?"

"Yeah!" he coughed out. "Easy. Go easy. Good for impotence, but go easy."

He handed me two folded brown paper bags filled with the stuff. I sniffed at them cautiously. "Have you had success with this?"

"Success yes! Good success. Yes. Good aphrodisiac, also. Start running. Build up body. Get stronger. You'll have kid. Yeah, do it."

It was ineffective. My sperm count did not improve. Nicole did not get pregnant. We put off the discussion of IUI and IVF. They weren't "natural";

they involved time and commitment; they involved a change of consciousness; a recognition and admission of failure.

The word "natural" began slipping into our conversation in surprising ways.

"Disappointment is natural, Alan," Nicole said, staring blankly, one morning at breakfast. "Especially when we're both so healthy and young."

At the ballet one night, I said, "It's just not natural that they can dance that way."

Walking in Riverside Park one Sunday Nicole said, "Nature always finds a way to keep itself going, doesn't it? It just so natural for things to grow and blossom. Nature doesn't need any help from us at all."

At the Farmers Market on Thursdays, near Columbia University, the woman I bought wax beans, strawberries and fresh basil from said, "They're all natural. I don't use pesticides. Natural is best."

Cracks began to form in our relationship: quiet indifferences, and then exaggerated concern when we realized them, and then forced humor, stunning contrivances and wise but cynical conversation.

One week-end at Great Diamond Island, Maine, Nicole and I stayed with friends who were political opposites: Bob, a conservative Republican who taught political science, and, Melinda, a liberal Democrat and gifted photographer.

We sat on their second story deck looking out on the quiet bay, sipping wine and breathing in the freshening air. Bob gave us a brief history of the island, and then waved to some young kids on bikes, who pedaled by on the narrow street below.

There was a lull in the conversation.

"It's all about kids, isn't it?" Nicole said.

Her comment struck like a hammer. We all knew of her flagrant sensitivity on the subject of children. I stared at her, confused. We waited, calculating our responses.

"Kids?" Bob asked, studying the wine bottle. His short hair was graying; his quick intelligent eyes always exploring.

"Yeah. Kids define the culture," Nicole added. "They drive everything, from music and art to clothing styles and politics. We're already too old to influence cultural creativity. We've got our professions and our predictable lifestyles."

"We're not that old," I said, lightly. "I've still got a dance or two left in me."

"No, but it's the kids—the young people—who define a generation. Kids are what keep a couple from getting stodgy and set in their ways. They keep things stirred up and fresh."

"Well, the culture that's coming out of this generation is frighteningly vulgar and low class. And they sure don't vote," he said. "And most of them are painfully illiterate."

"My children will vote," Nicole said, forcefully. "I'll see to that!"

Melinda, a thin blond with bold and beautiful eyes said, "If our government was serious about supporting our educational system, kids would have the knowledge to vote."

Bob bristled. "Give me a break, Melinda. You blame the government for everything, and you want the government to pay for everything! For God's sake, you'd have people like us footing the bill for the lazy and poor until we all went broke."

Melinda stiffened. "I'd rather foot the bill for education and helping the poor, than giving corporations huge tax breaks while they rape the land."

I sought to truncate the argument, but stumbled badly. "Today's kids will be working until they're a hundred to pay off all the national debt." I stood, feeling a little silly, unthinking. "So, I say we should all be making as many kids as possible…" I stopped, realizing the stupidity of my words.

Nicole narrowed her hot angry eyes on me. "That's not funny, Alan."

A deep chilly silence ensued.

Nicole recovered swiftly, presenting a forced smile to the couple. "So, how are you feeling, Melinda? Any morning sickness?"

"A little." She slanted Bob a disparaging glance. "Bob was supposed to keep it a secret… until the end of the first trimester… But we all know that Bob tells everything he knows whenever he knows it."

Bob shot Melinda an angry glance.

Nicole's sad eyes looked out on the bay. "He's excited, Melinda, and why shouldn't he be? He just wants to share it."

Bob twisted awkwardly, studying his glass. "It will happen for you two. I just know it will."

Melinda added quickly. "And there are so many ways now to…" she looked at me. "Well, you know that, Alan. You're a doctor."

Nicole inhaled, smoothing out her cream-colored linen blouse. "Yes, of course. But we had hoped to have a child the natural way."

I sat stiffly, feeling defeated and small. They knew the details of our problem. I was quiet while the conversation shifted precipitously to the dinner menu and the next day's itinerary.

That evening, as we lay in bed, wide awake, I turned to Nicole. Tension pulsed. The window fan hummed and did little to cool the humid room.

"Are you okay?" I asked.

"I wish we could leave without hurting their feelings."

"We can't. Melinda would feel terrible."

She rolled away from me. "In college, it was Melinda who was the feminist. She always said she'd never get married or have kids. She hated the idea. I was the one who tutored 6-year-olds, while she was out protesting some stupid cause. How's that for irony?"

I laced my hands behind my head. "We all change."

"Well I haven't changed."

I kicked the sheet off, wiping sweat from my forehead. "Let's try and get some sleep," I said.

An hour later, I quietly slid out of bed, and went

for a long walk.

In Starbucks on Saturday mornings we often repeated the same comforting phrases. "All marriages have their difficulties and challenges. We'll grow closer and laugh at all this once we have a child," we'd say.

We kept trying to conceive, while polishing our positive spirits and public and private faces.

"We can adopt," I said once, so softly that I wasn't certain Nicole had even heard me.

She didn't look up from the newspaper. "Yes…" she'd said, flatly. I saw a flicker of impatience in her eyes. "…Then we might as well go the donor sperm route."

"I'm not ready for that," I said, sharply.

"And I'm not ready to have my eggs retrieved and stuck in some laboratory dish where there's only a 35% success rate that I'll get pregnant and deliver a baby. I don't have the time or the inclination."

"Okay, fine. We could go back to trying hormone therapies," I said.

"We've been there and done that, Alan. It didn't work. For God's sake, stop bringing that up."

Whenever Nicole and I talked over the options, calmly and intelligently, beating back nerves and depression, the issue remained unresolved. We carried choices within us like dying lab specimens, hoping for some kind of miracle: that my sperm would eventually come through.

I remember the day we stopped discussing it.

We were walking in Riverside Park in early spring. The world had exploded with color and life. Birds soared, bees lumbered in yellow buttery petals and hovered over red and yellow tulips. The sky burned a brilliant blue. Nicole and I passed a playground where children screamed, hopped and scattered with abandon. It was a playful battlefield, as parents struggled to keep up, their sharp protective eyes anticipating a stumble, a slap, a brilliant new discovery.

Nicole turned away from the scene, increasing the pace, aloof and insulted. I caught up with her a few minutes later.

"How about a glass of wine?" I suggested.

"How about a bottle," she said, quietly.

We became busy, flushed with achievement, work and friends. We seldom made love and, when we did, it sputtered—or worse, it left us depressed.

I grew strange and unfamiliar. I laughed more. Nicole noticed and commented, "You're in a good mood these days, Alan."

"Yeah, why not? Life's too short."

I bought a silver gray Mercedes Sports Coupe and drove it to Shelter Island on summer weekends, where Nicole's parents had a house. We sped along back roads, the car moving like a sharp knife through the hot butter of the day, rising and laughing with the unraveling dips and curves, over the Bridgehampton horse fields and out to the Montauk Lighthouse. We stopped by the classic car competition in Bridgehampton with its lineup of the 80 classic cars: Jaguars, Ferraris, Rolls Royces, and Mercedeses, all gleaming in the afternoon sun.

We began regular weekly visits to French restaurants, including Bouley, Le Bernardin, and Jean Georges.

Nicole and I grew further apart, civilly, in refinement and style, in intimate and golden snug décors with fresh yellow roses; at tables, shining with fine crystal and silverware, enjoying sautéed frogs' legs dripping with brown butter and garlic, and pike quenelles in Champagne sauce; sharing bottles of Chateau La Mondotte Saint-Emilion 1996 or Chateau Lafite Rothschild Pauillac 1996.

We drank our wine with a slow, greedy, mirthless pleasure. Our pointless conversation resonated with inflated excitement about the promising future: purchasing a house in Montauk, overlooking the jagged cliffs and panoramic sea; returning to Harvard for a fellowship in cardiology; vacationing in Venice, where Nicole and I had hoped to go on our honeymoon; we wound up in Bermuda instead.

"So a house in Montauk would be perfect," I said, repeating a now familiar phrase, as I stood by the kitchen counter one morning, sipping coffee. We both were already late for work. "We could rent the thing out for $20,000 a month during the season."

Nicole listened with a mechanical interest, like a weary high school guidance counselor after a fatty lunch. She ate a piece of rye toast and reached for a glass of freshly squeezed orange juice. "Sure...why not. I know old Rod Evans would rent it from us. He's always looking for a new place to take his Latino mistress. You should have heard him singing *Row, Row, Row Your Boat*, the other day in the courtroom."

"What was that all about?"

"He's crazy. Judge Waxler denied his Motion For Summary Judgment so he sang as loud as he could, and he was terribly off key."

I belted out an exaggerated laugh. But it was the first time Nicole and I had seen each other in three days. She'd been working on a trial and I had been to a medical seminar in Chicago.

"What did the judge do?"

"They're old friends—probably old lovers. She told him to take singing lessons and to get his overweight ass out of her courtroom."

I laughed again and so did Nicole, but during the entire conversation, our eyes had never met. We had become professionals at circumventing the approaching emotional storm.

I made some calls to doctor friends and got the name of a therapist, a Jungian. I was drinking too much wine and losing too much sleep. I knew I was in trouble. Nicole seemed to improve and become skilled at engaging in brilliant conversation about the insignificant. She didn't enlighten. She didn't provoke. She didn't really say anything at all and yet, she could keep the dialogue going when I failed.

After a few sessions, I asked Nicole to join me, mostly at the therapist's suggestion.

"Too busy right now, Alan," she'd say, breezily,

or in an urgent, preoccupied tone. "I'll come when things settle down some at work. How's it going?"

"...Good, I think."

"Good...real good. You'll work it all out, Alan. You've got that special kind of talent for things like that. All of our friends think you know exactly how to make these kinds of things enlightening."

I had no idea what she meant, but it covered up our problems with the best damned manure a law degree could buy and I envied her for her ability.

I finally stopped asking her and I stopped the therapy. Nicole worked longer hours, and was made a partner.

As it turned out, Rita and I did celebrate Darla's birthday together. It happened because of a party —a party given for Nicole by Walker Towne, the managing partner of Towne, Wilkes and Fried. Of course, I had been invited. It was held at his upper East Side suite, with a "breathtaking view." Walker Towne, Nicole had often told me, "came from old money."

That afternoon, black clouds swept in, lowering the sky, bringing a sharp wind and the promise of a chilly rain. When I left the office at 7:30, the rain was pouring down, filling every crack and crevice. The entire city seemed to have a terrible head cold. You could almost hear the buildings sniff and taxis sneeze as they raced by, their tires spraying water. Rain charged head on, like thin gray arrows, and the wind chopped and punched, as if daring you to swing at it. Dog poop melted on the sidewalks, umbrellas went for the eyes and the subway smelled of new urine and old ammonia.

The subway stalled and went out of service, leaving us poor slobs to search the drenching streets for a taxi. Fifteen minutes later, wet and agitated, I found one.

I stepped out of the cab at East 77th Street and Park Avenue, and looked up at an impressive 25-story building. I started toward the front door, passing a tall, ponderous woman with poodle-like gray hair; she was walking two white prancing poodles, whose eyes were alight with authority and intelligence. A cleaned and pressed doorman in blue and white led me into a palatial lobby of polished brass, marble, gold leaf ceilings and glistening mirrors. Another blue and white uniform asked me for my name and whom I wanted to see.

"I'm here for the Towne party," I answered, smugly.

The doorman directed me to the elevator operator. I was whooshed up to a top floor in seconds and found myself standing in the hallway, inhaling some kind of strange orange disinfectant. I strolled easily across the thick royal blue carpet and, as instructed, found a polished oak door and pressed the doorbell. The bolt slid off and the door opened. A tall, remarkably white man of perhaps sixty looked back at me. He wore a dark suit and tie and smiled thinly. His hair was silver and perfectly placed, eyes detached, stern mouth tight. There was no real friendliness about him and not much of anything else either; an animated mannequin, programmed for aloof service.

"How pretentious," I thought, "hiring a butler for the night." He ushered me into a broad foyer, peeled me out of my wet London Fog and took my dripping umbrella. He handed them off to a cold-looking coat check girl, with copper hair, who sniffed at my coat and then at me and the butler. She had a head cold.

With wet shoes and damp sticky socks, I followed him across the brown swirling pattern of the marble floor to the living room. It was grand and spacious, decorated in blues, greens, whites and burgundy. Guests had arrived and were grouped in twos and threes, lingering near the little oak bar, with its six wooden stools. A bartender, with I-don't-give-a-damn stiff black hair, shook up Martinis, Bellinis and Cosmopolitans.

Designer furniture made of suede, leather and oak looked uncomfortable. Little colored silk pillows looked like big candies. There were modern paintings: water colors, oils, swirls of white, blue stripes and green circles; sculptures in white marble; marble and glass-topped coffee tables and stained glass windows.

The floors were polished hardwood and spotted with an occasional oriental rug. Plants bloomed everywhere, hung from the ceiling, and skirting the French windows that overlooked Park Avenue. A white grand piano in the far corner of the room drew my eyes. Seated behind it was a prim and proper young man in a tux, playing waltzes, show tunes and Chopin. On the gleaming surface of the piano were photos—mostly of Walker, posing with various New York City dignitaries and the Governor of New York.

I found Nicole with Walker near the piano, speaking in confidential mumbles. When they saw me approach, their faces became much too animated with the sheer pleasure of seeing me. Nicole kissed my cheek. Walker pumped my hand aggressively. His Nordic good looks and sharp blue eyes glowed confidence. His wide frame and over six feet height impressed and intimidated, especially if he fell into his deep commanding tone of voice that suggested he was certain that everyone would eventually see things his way in the long run—and, by God, they'd better.

"Proud of your wife, are you, Alan?"

"Sure...of course," I said, witnessing a blush of satisfaction on her face that I hadn't seen in months. In her black suit, pearl white blouse and two inch heels, she looked professional and sexy. She appeared happy, and, although I was happy for her, I felt deflated. I should have thrown the party. I'd sent a dozen roses to her office and given her diamond earrings, but those seemed paltry now, next to the extravagance around me. Nicole eyed me strangely, as though I had just been blown in from a distant planet.

"Congratulations, Nicole," I said.

"I'm glad you could come," she said, formally, as if I were just another guest.

"Well, of course I was going to come. Did you get the flowers?"

"Yes...they were lovely."

I noticed she wasn't wearing the earrings. I decided to leave it alone.

"There's plenty of food, wine and booze, Alan," Walker said. "Enjoy yourself."

I waited for Nicole.

"You go ahead, Alan," she said, breezily. "Walker and I are discussing a new case that came in. I'll find you."

I shoved my hands into my pockets and slinked away toward the bar. I'd never tasted a Cosmopolitan so I ordered one. It went down easily. I ordered an Apple Martini and it too slid down with ease.

The room swelled with guests and my head swelled with a playful buzz. The women wore a lot of black. The men wore sports jackets, blue blazers and suits. Waiters with bow ties and white shirts glided about with trays of hors d'oeuvres. The piano music rose and fell in flourishes of Gershwin's "Swanee" and then Rodgers' and Hart's "Where or When."

I rambled, purposeless, sipping a Chocolate Martini. I bent an intruding ear into conversations on politics, sports and adultery. I talked bungee jumping with a bold stout man of 30, although I knew nothing about it and had never been.

When an attractive redhead drew up alongside of me, tall and authoritative, I squinted at her through blurry eyes and said, "Hi. I'm Alan James, at least that's what an old high school girlfriend used to call me."

That's when I realized I was teetering toward drunkenness.

"I'm Greer Dalson," she said, with some puzzlement. "I work with Nicole."

I narrowed in on her.

"We met at the Christmas Party."

My eyes widened with recognition. "Of course... yes, we did. Yes. How are you?"

Greer was two inches taller than I and she had freckles. "Nicole has quite a future ahead of her."

"She had quite a future behind her," I said, earnestly. "You should have been there."

Greer stepped back, studying me anew. "You're a doctor, aren't you?"

"I am a doctor. I'm a doctor who could use a good doctor."

Greer slid back further, cautious and a little put off. "Well, it was nice seeing you again."

"For me also," I said, feeling a wonderful silliness I hadn't felt in years.

I found the buffet table, with its silver serving sets and plates of chopped vegetables and finger sandwiches and pickles. I focused in on the pickles and bypassed the salmon, the chicken, the turkey, the tofu and the grilled veggies. I reached for the pickles. I ate two large green ones and then went back for three more. I chomped and chewed and grinned with the pleasure of a rebellious child. I washed them down with a Manhattan on the rocks and moved on.

I found pockets of conversation and put in my two cents. "I don't like Republicans or Democrats. I want a damned revolution! I want to overthrow everyone and everything. I want disruption, disarray and...well, maybe a little good will here and there."

After that group scurried away from me, I found two attractive women, who I later learned were married to the partners Wilkes and Fried. They were chic, refined and drinking very dry Grey Goose martinis, (or so they said) in great frosty martini glasses. The green olives glowed with an electric green enormity. I fought the urge to grab for one.

"I don't believe in it," I said.

"In what?" Mrs. Wilkes asked.

"In any of it."

"And what would any of it be referring to?" Mrs. Fried asked, placing a strand of her black hair behind an elegant ear.

"That would be birth, life and death. I just don't believe in it. It all seems rather arbitrary and confusing."

They exchanged quizzical glances.

"Who are you with?" Mrs. Wilkes asked, with a sharp enquiring eye.

"I was with Nicole, but she is now with the honorable Walker Towne, so right now, I am with the both of you...and I'm finding you both charming and utterly fascinating." I bowed to each of them, nearly spilling my refreshing Manhattan.

Their eyebrows lifted. Not knowing what else to do, they laughed.

The party reached its zenith when the food was whisked away and a heavy buxom blond asserted herself toward the piano. After a brief conference with its player, she burst into "The Man That Got Away" in a wobbly strident assault of style, notes and key.

I sat dejectedly on the inflexible oversized couch and waited for Nicole, while I finished off my final Manhattan.

I could have gone to her, of course, but she had pointedly said she would find me. So, as a matter of principle and pride I waited, until the speeches and congratulations were finished, until the sing-alongs grew anemic, when no one remembered the words, and until someone said it was after eleven and it had stopped raining. The guests began to float away.

I rose from the couch, spiritless and drunk. I swayed toward the front door and I saw her: Nicole standing close to the sunny Walker; she a fluttering moth in the glow of his sturdy Nordic flame. She was imparting her goodbyes; so graciously, so effusively, so nauseatingly.

I wandered toward them, weaving a little. I saw the sudden anxiety register on their faces as I gracelessly advanced. I must have looked as drunk as I felt.

I lifted my hands, slapped them together and rubbed aggressively. "Well, what a helluva party!

And to think that all this…all this extraordinary effort was to commemorate and honor Nicole becoming a partner. Do you do this for all the little folk who make partner, podner?" I asked Walker.

He stared with insipid eyes. "I think you'll agree that Nicole is exceedingly special."

"Oh, yeah, I will agree. You betcha. She is that."

I shifted my unsteady gaze toward her, feeling a turbulence of emotion.

She shivered, and her disapproving eyes slid down and away.

I faced Walker. "Mr. Towne, may I thank you for an interesting evening and add that I think you are a supercilious parasite, with a forgettable demeanor and an unforgettable, unctuous personality."

His face darkened. "And you, Dr. Lincoln, are a pathetic drunk."

Unfazed, I looked at Nicole. "Are you coming?"

She glared. "No, Alan. I'll come later."

With a great effort, I lowered my head and nudged myself toward the front door.

Needless to say, after that evening, I never again heard anyone say that I knew "exactly how to make things enlightening." Nicole and I didn't speak for days.

I worked early and late, mostly to avoid her, and slept in the second bedroom on the couch. She spent little time at home and always seemed distracted or annoyed.

And then there was a perceptible change in Nicole. Her emotions were bereft of extremes. I, in turn, responded in kind, and our relationship, though stilted and often a little strained, staggered on for a few more days. Until the inevitable day of reckoning.

I blankly stared at the emergency room entrance and drained the coffee. The facetious squirrels helped me finish the bagel. I entered St. Luke's Hospital and went to work. The morning shot by. The interns were of three categories: the ones who leafed through New York real estate and foreign car magazines, dreaming of the money they'd soon be making; the earnest who wanted to save the world; and, the realists, whose parents were physicians. The latter plodded through the hallways, comfortable with the smells, the blood, the politics, the sudden deaths, the ER tragedies and the voluminous paperwork everyone now required.

The afternoon in my office was steady and mostly predictable. The usual chronic cases: diabetes, heart problems, asthma and obesity. Occasionally, there was one not so serious, like the man in his early 50's who presented with blocked ears. Heavy earwax in both ears. I referred him to an ENT. I'd only flushed out one set of ears in my medical career and my nurse, Mary, was hectically stressed and didn't have the time.

When I entered the examination room and saw a 30s something woman, her face contracted with stress and her tired eyes blood-shot, I closed the door behind us and sat down opposite her. She told me her name was Ellen Collins. She was thin and distracted. She fidgeted with her thin, ginger-blond, oily hair.

"Can you give me some sleeping pills, doctor, please?" she asked, pitifully. "I've been out of work for almost two years, and I'm nearly broke. I can't sleep. My husband left me months ago for another woman. My 9-year-old son has asthma and he isn't doing very well in school. My father had been helping us out when he could, but he's struggling financially himself now. He can't help us anymore." Her voice was high-edged and frightened; tears rolled down her cheeks.

As usual, I felt the pressure of time, and I felt the weight of Amos Bower's 240 pounds as he paced the waiting room, fuming, because he'd been fifteen minutes early and would have to wait at least another fifteen minutes because I was late. He would bark at reception and they, in turn, would surely yap at me.

I drew a breath and hoped I was presenting to Ellen a calm, self-assured expression. I'd been to enough doctors myself, and suffered the humiliation of bearing my worst nightmare to a virtual unknown, to realize how important it was just to be calm and listen. Listening was often the most important skill.

I'd heard similar stories to Ellen's since medical school and I had prescribed sleeping pills, recommended counseling, discussed health insurance policies and options. I had even consulted with other colleagues for advice. I'd scheduled follow-ups, documented the session, signed the referral sheet and wished them well. I'd done this many times.

But that day, I wanted to talk to Ellen. I wanted to hear what she had to say. I wanted and needed to communicate. I wanted to feel something—a connection to another human being. I was desperate for it. I saw Rita in Ellen's eyes. I saw myself, struggling to understand, and I saw Nicole looking back at me, regretfully. And so Ellen and I talked and I lost track of time.

When the receptionist's uptight head poked in, jarring me, I turned to hear her say that Nicole was on the phone. I excused myself, stepped into the hall and got "the look" and "the yap" from reception.

In my office I reached over my desk and took the call. "Nicole…"

Nicole's voice was officious. "Yes, Alan. Look, they didn't settle. We're going to trial."

I struggled to shift my focus. "What? Who…"

"I told you. Haines vs. Gomez. The doctor who should have done the Caesarian and the baby died."

"Oh…yeah, right."

"Anyway, the weekend's off. I've got to get ready for this thing."

I felt nauseous. "Can't you work out there, on Shelter Island? It'll be quiet. Nothing to distract you."

Her voice grew cold. "No. I need to work with Walker on this and we've got to find an expert or we're sunk. Know of any?"

"No…No…"

I knew this was the defining critical moment in our marriage. I knew that if we didn't go to Shelter Island and have it out—lance all the boils—the marriage was over. Maybe it was already over, but I wanted to try one more time. My stomach churned, gnawed. I grabbed it. "Nicole…okay…what about Sunday? Can you come out Sunday?"

"Dammit, Alan, what else do I have to say!? I can't! I can't go! Get out of your own fucking world for a minute and listen to me. I can't go."

I couldn't find any words.

Nicole did. "What difference does it make anyway, for God's sake? Who are we trying to kid?" Her voice changed, became quiet and resigned. "Alan…let's not kid ourselves anymore. Please. Let's just move on. Why are you making this so difficult? I've tried…I've tried to let you know…that it's over."

Her words struck my chest like a thrusting sword. I stood rigid for a moment, and then slowly rounded the desk and sat. I'd heard the disappointment and anger in her words and tone. I'd heard failure, finality. I'd also heard the strong imposing voice of Walker Towne in the background. "Nicole, let's get going."

Walker Towne—divorced with two kids—beautiful kids. Walker Towne, handsome Hollywood good looks. Walker Towne, who, I knew for certain, was sleeping with Nicole.

At the extremity of the moment, I pressed the

button to break the connection. I held it down firmly, pressing hard, imagining my head being shoved and forced violently down into deep water. "Drown, you failing son of a bitch," I whispered.

I struggled for a while. Exhaled, and listened, numbly, to the AUM of the dial tone.

CHAPTER FOUR

"I don't know where she is," Mrs. Fitzgerald said, rather coldly. "She doesn't tell me much. Not much at all."

We were on the phone again. I was surprised by her unfriendly tone. I'd expected the opposite. "How is she?" I asked, tentatively.

"She has her good days and bad. Today...well, this morning...well, she didn't sleep all night."

I was an hour from Hartsfield, driving in medium traffic, a half-eaten turkey sandwich on the seat beside me, still mostly wrapped. Twilight gathered in deep blue shadows in the valleys, grew soft gray over the trees and far hills, and glowed orange and purple on the horizon.

"Is she at work now, Mrs. Fitzgerald?"

"No...she doesn't work on Fridays. She...well, she left early this morning. Didn't say where. That's all I know," she said, curtly.

I gave Mrs. Fitzgerald my cell number and asked her to pass it along to Rita when she returned.

"Tell her I'll be in Hartsfield for the weekend."

It was dark when I arrived at the house, pulled into the driveway and got out. The night sky was close and rich with stars. Crickets sang and frogs belched. Lightning bugs flashed golden flecks. I paused on the lower step of the porch to watch, to listen, to take the pulse of the night.

Before inserting the key into the lock, I glanced back at the low-rising half-moon and stared. Seduced, I strolled to the porch swing and sat down. I rocked, easily, listening to the comfortable squeak of the chain. I had brought nothing with me: no suitcase, clothes or food. I hadn't gone back to the apartment after my conversation with Nicole. I'd finished the day, working on automatic pilot, and at the end of it, I had left without a word to anyone. I wanted to run off—to escape—to the house.

It was an oddity to be comfortable at the house that had never seemed quite like home to me, in a town that had often felt foreign and isolated from the "real world". The world where "it was happening." Where history was being made.

But the isolation was now a boon; the quiet sleeping giant of a house, a secret and welcomed haven from the battles of life. It was a retreat; a place to rest, to try to heal, to forget Nicole's last words.

The house was a time capsule, so hauntingly present in the now, so filled with the apparitions and impressions of the past. I continued to swing and breathe easy, feeling the rise of a lonely and lovely contentment. Much of the anguish of the day was lifting and merging with the intoxicating night songs.

I'd longed to be at the house; how it had lifted my spirits to think of it as I finished out the day, making my way to the parking garage on 83rd Street to retrieve the Mercedes. And I thought of Rita. She was a healing thought—implicating me in a crime of passion: Rita would be in Hartsfield, and I couldn't deny that I was refreshed by the anticipation of seeing her again; of escaping the pain I was feeling.

Let Nicole have her Walker Towne, his two kids, and half of everything we owned together, or more, I didn't care. Truth be told—and I was boiling with it as I drove—I'd never felt emotionally secure with Nicole. When she was serene and quiet, an eruption was imminent. When anger or frustration flared or insecurity struck, she craved attention and domination. Lovemaking became a kind of battle that left me confused, while leaving her aloof and hungry for something more or different. She'd leave the bed, pace, drink wine and gossip with her girlfriends on the phone, ignoring me for hours and sometimes for days. What had I done or not done? I didn't know.

And then, she'd somehow hotwire her head to her heart and lavish me with kisses and gentle love making and presents: new shirts, an iPad, DVDs, a pricy stylish sport coat.

"You were a hot baby the other night," she'd sometimes say. I tried not to look back enigmatically.

I stopped the swing, leaned forward with hunched shoulders and laced my hands. I cared for Nicole. I did. No doubt about that. I loved her.

But three years later, I was not the man she'd married. I had failed us, and this was not self-pity, but a fact. I had become distant and mostly passionless. I was barren, and I had cast that compact shaft of light onto both Nicole and our relationship, revealing every stain and weakness. That light had shown into our hearts, illuminating the startled shadowy figures that had been cowering in corners for years.

In the end, we didn't possess the strength—the mature passion—to face them and grow. As a result, we never truly became one. We held on to ME and I, finally becoming just another "them," whom friends and family mention over cocktails or dinner, with a sad shake of the head or a casual remark in an e-mail. "Nope, they just didn't make it together. So unfortunate. So sad. But that's the way it goes. Have you seen any good movies lately?"

What was Nicole saying to Walker right now, over drinks at the Oak Room or some other trendy restaurant or bar? I could hear her voice clearly, a low scratchy sorrow, with a hint of a French accent, persuasive and wise, after two or three glasses of Chardonnay. "Alan always seemed to be holding something back. I wasn't surprised when he learned he was infertile. It seemed to confirm the obvious to him and to me: he lacks true passion, and I am half French after all. I am, if nothing else, passionate. Well, maybe we had that passion once but…"

Nicole would pause then, perhaps recall an intimate touch or night of love, before our problems had congealed, before our wisdom and love begat emptiness. Because she was raised Catholic, there would be guilt, remorse and tears for years to come.

She would hold the chilled wine glass close to her parted thoughtful lips, but not sip it. No, she would first crown the instant memory of us with thorns, as she set off on the arduous journey through the old broken streets, stumbling past crushed hopes and dreams, arriving, alone and resigned, to climb the barren knoll of the present piteous truth, where our relationship would, at last, meet its end on the cross of retribution.

Nicole would finally lift her opulent brown liquid eyes to Walker, drink some wine and say… "And a passionate woman, if she's honest—and she must be if she is to live with herself—a passionate woman wants a husband who wants her, and she, in turn, wants her own, natural child."

Walker was surely nodding, commiserating, sipping scotch, his gleaming randy eyes anticipating a good night of sex. He would toast her. "I think you've made your case, Nicole. Let's adjourn to my chambers."

And what was I thinking here on the porch swing in the magic of the night? "I wish I had a sturdy defense, Nicole, but I don't and, right now, I don't even have the strength to mount one. The defense simply rests."

But maybe this defenseless and weak resignation was nothing more than the happy recognition that the marriage had been in trouble for a long time and it was finally, and mercifully, over.

I saw it all so keenly now. It was mountain-creek clear: I had seen Rita again and that was my crime of passion. Secretly, guiltily, I was glad to be free of Nicole and free to open my heart again to Rita. I had returned to the past and revisited nescient emotions, more true, more natural than experience. Seeing Rita again had made everything apparent, somehow, like a brilliant flash of light thrown from the heavens onto the Ten Commandments of my passionate soul: "Thou shalt love Rita Fitzgerald with all thy heart, mind and strength! Go forth and rediscover that root of authentic love, Alan James! Go forth with Rita Fitzgerald and save her! Find thyself in her!"

I was aware of the illusion—the mirage of molecules; the elaborate webs of self- deception. Run from thyself Alan James. I could simply remove myself from one place to another, carrying all the heavy baggage; slip from present to past and become miraculously reborn and happy in the future. It was so obvious, trite and alluring: don't face yourself, Alan, run to Rita and let her save *you* by your saving *her*. And saving her suddenly dominated my thoughts and gave me a new purpose, a definite goal, a way to channel my disappointment, anger and failure into a stunning success and achievement.

I began swinging again, staring into the darkness, thankful that the world was hidden around me and that, for now, I was very much alone with my eager, private thoughts. Although I was utterly drained and exhausted, I knew I wouldn't be able to sleep. So I rocked.

"Mr. Lincoln?"

When I heard the deep voice, I jerked with a start, anchored my feet to the porch and twisted abruptly toward it. I saw the silhouette of a big man, below on the lawn, strolling toward me.

I rose, tense, peering at the figure. "Yes…"

"I've scared you…I'm sorry about that." The voice lacked warmth. It was quietly grave.

"Who are you?" I asked.

He continued toward me, stopping at the base of the porch stairs, hands in his pockets. "Yeah…who am I? Well, we met many years ago, Mr. Lincoln."

And then I knew—an instant before he said, "Frank Fitzgerald, Mr. Lincoln. Rita's father."

My voice was instantly formal, withholding. "…Yes…I remember." I didn't move. Neither did he. All the night sounds swelled around us—ringing, scratching.

"My wife said you'd called. Said you were on your way into town."

I didn't speak.

"She said you were asking about Rita."

"Yes."

"I just thought I'd drop over…say hello."

He could have called, I thought. There were more polite ways of saying "hello" than sneaking up on someone in the dark. His voice brought the immediate rush of old emotions and memories of that last date with Rita: the artificial deodorant smell of the house; the poor, stale look of the living room; Mrs. Fitzgerald's sneering face and Frank's subtly battering style of conversation—quietly sarcastic and manipulative, as though he were a clever spider, weaving a web to trap. I had sensed a prodigious intellect, warped by frustration and jealousy, with the driving need to dominate in any insidious way possible. All of these memories converged with the smooth chilly sound of his voice, and I shook off a little shiver of trepidation. I instantly disliked him.

"You don't mind, do you, that I wanted to be a good neighbor and stop by to say hello?"

I was irritated at myself for feeling intimidated by him—for feeling like I was 17 years old again. I decided to twist the conversation into another direction. "Mrs. Fitzgerald didn't say you were in town."

"Well...I come and go. There's no work in this town anymore, so I...come and go. I go other places to work and I come home when I can. And you? Coming and going?"

To gain the advantage, I decided to keep asking questions. After all, that's what doctors do all day long. "When did you arrive this time?"

I heard him chuckle. He was probably on to me. He made himself comfortable, taking a seat on the lower step. "Mr. Lincoln...I..."

I was growing hostile. It was partly fatigue,

partly distrust and mostly the sharp emotions of the day. "Alan!" I said firmly. "Just call me, Alan!"

"Okay, Mr..."

I cut him off, sharply. "Alan, Mr. Fitzgerald! Please...call me Alan. If you want to call me Mr. Lincoln, then I'd prefer, Dr. Lincoln." The force of my tone and overreaction surprised me. Without meaning to, I was certain I had provoked him. The silence was stressful.

"Okay, fine, if you feel you need the title, then Dr. Lincoln it is."

"Why did you come by, Mr. Fitzgerald?"

He uttered a short, stout laugh. "Have you come to town to see Rita, Dr. Lincoln?" He emphasized Doctor, as if to slap me with it.

"...I came to sell the house...and to see Rita."

"Yes... the house...an impressive place. Always was impressive, even in the old days. I used to drive by here sometimes on my way to work, and pull over and look at it. Just take it in, like it was some great monument, like Grant's tomb or something. Well, maybe that's not quite the right comparison. More like Jefferson's Monticello or Mark Twain's home in Hartford, Connecticut."

"It's not as grand as all that, Mr. Fitzgerald. It's just a nice Victorian home."

"Ever been to Mark Twain's house?"

"No..."

"Impressive. You should go. I took the tour. Very impressive. You know, Twain once said, 'There ought to be a room in this house to swear in. It's dangerous to have to repress an emotion like that.'"

Frank chuckled again, but it was artificial. I had the feeling that he was more impressed at himself for memorizing and reciting the quote, than he was delighting in the quote itself. I wished I could see his eyes and read his face. But we were two dark shadows, shadow boxing with innuendo and insinuation.

He continued. "You wouldn't believe Twain's bed. Venetian, intricately carved mantel from a Scottish castle. Impressive. You really should go see it. And his pool table. Now that's something to see. You play pool, Dr. Lincoln?"

There was something in his voice: a hot spice of superiority.

"Once in a while. I'm not very good."

"I'm real good, Dr. Lincoln. I wanted to play on that table. I could have told all my friends that I played pool on Mark Twain's pool table. But, then again, most of my idiot friends probably wouldn't even know who Mark Twain was. You ever read much Mark Twain, Dr. Lincoln?"

"Some."

"I love *Huckleberry Finn*. I bet I've read it, oh… maybe 10 times. A classic. Great dialogue. Great characters. It was one of the first books I gave Rita to read when she got sick—the year she missed so much school and had to make up the grade. She was 14 years old. I'd just been paroled, after ten long years. I read a lot in prison, Dr. Lincoln. They had a damned good library. I read lots and lots of books.

Huckleberry Finn was definitely one of my favorites. You ever read that book?"

"No…"

"Impressive… anyway, I gave Rita a lot of books to read that year. I wanted to give her a real education, not some damned public education where they tell you what and how to think. They stifle your creativity, try to kick you down and press you into some damned mold so you'll be like all the other morons in this country. Hell no, I wanted her to be special—to shine with a unique fire—to use that head to reason and think and grow into the authentic truth of herself. To find the fire inside and to live the life she was meant to live and not some stupid paper cutout life of every other kid.

"No sir! I told her, her sickness was a good thing. Be damned thankful for it. Thank the gods, the angels and the demons. Especially thank the demons. They're the ones who will really get you through this racket of a life. They're the ones who will keep kicking you in the ass until you finally figure out that you may have to start kicking a lot of ass yourself. Don't you agree, Dr. Lincoln?"

I didn't answer.

"Well, anyway, I told her to read the great authors—the classics. That's how you'll get an education. That's how you'll find your way in this cesspool of a world.

"So read she did. She read maybe two or three books a week. Then, after a few months, I told her it was time for her to learn how to write. I mean to really write. So I made her copy paragraphs from this one and that one—some bad some good—and then we'd talk about them. Then I'd say, write it better—not the same—never the same. No! Make it unique. Make it better!

"I made her turn off that idiot box TV and read and write. Oh…she hated me for it at first, but then after a couple of months…well, I didn't have to tell her to turn off the TV. She was caught with wonder and surprise like a kid at Christmas. She was reading everything, and writing stories. I mean writing good stories, Dr. Lincoln. Ooooo weeee! Hell, I had no idea she had that kind of talent. Some of her first short stories were heads above things I was reading in magazines, and I told her. Yes sir. I told her she was good! They were original and inventive. They moved me, Dr. Lincoln. Truly, they did move me.

"Then she started reading plays and acting out all the parts: Tennessee Williams, William Inge, Eugene O'Neil, and even some Shakespeare. Damn, you should have seen her. You should have seen that girl. She was a sight to behold."

I was still standing. My eyes had adjusted to him. I saw him look up and face me. "You ever read any of her stories, Dr. Lincoln?"

"Yes…I have."

"What do you think of them?"

"Good. I liked them."

"Good…" he repeated, with disappointment, as if "good" was very nearly an insult.

"Rita is exceptional, Mr. Fitzgerald," I added. "In

many ways."

He seized on it, shooting to his feet. "Yes!" he said, loudly, pounding his fist on the stairs as he rose. "Hell yes…Rita is exceptional! And like many exceptional people, she's, well, she's high strung. She lives a little close to the edge."

"She has good reasons," I said. "She's been through hell."

"…Maybe, but my wife and I think it's best if Rita stays away from the past. Completely away, if you know what I mean. It can't be good for her. My wife told me that ever since Rita saw you two weeks ago, she hasn't…improved. In fact she's been low and she's regressed some. That's what her therapist said."

"Mrs. Fitzgerald called me two weeks ago and asked me to come and see Rita."

"That was a mistake. We know that now."

I moved toward the top of the porch, looking down at him. "I'd love to talk with Rita's therapist," I said.

"Rita wouldn't want that. We don't want that. You have nothing to do with Rita, Dr. Lincoln. All that was a long time ago. You have your life now and Rita has hers. We want Rita to get better and move on past all the tragedy and anything and everything that might remind her of it."

"So do I."

"Good. Then we all agree. Don't see her again. Let her be. Leave the past where it belongs."

"If that's what Rita wants then…"

"That's what I want!" Frank said, with a hint of a threat. "Rita doesn't know what she wants right now. She's just barely hanging on. Barely!"

"Mr. Fitzgerald, she's not 18 anymore; she's 34. She's a grown woman."

"And she's nearly out of her mind! Don't you get that, Doctor? Leave her alone! Sell your big rich house, go back to New York and leave us all alone!"

"That's up to Rita," I said, evenly but forcefully.

"Don't you fuck with me, Dr. Lincoln! Leave Rita alone!"

I watched him pivot and stride off, aggressively, into the night. I went back to the porch swing and sat, not rocking. I closed my eyes and felt my strong pulse, rebellious and agitated. Minutes later my cell phone rang. I dug it out of my jacket pocket.

"This is Alan."

It was my answering service. A patient had an emergency. Mrs. Rivera was having an adverse reaction to some new medication I'd prescribed. I called her back to let her know that I'd prescribe a milder one. I immediately called it in to her local pharmacy.

I had just stepped inside the house and turned on the hall lights when my phone rang again. "Alan."

"Alan James…"

"Rita!" I said, coming alive. "How are you?"

"Fine…better. Mom said…said you're here in Hartsfield."

"She gave you my number?"

"Yes."

Considering the conversation I'd just had with her father, that confused me, but I didn't care. "Yes, I'm here. If the invitation's still open, I'd love to see you tomorrow."

Rita's voice got stronger. "Yes...Tomorrow. Is your wife with you?"

"...No. You're stuck with me."

She laughed a little. It sounded like music. "Okay."

"What time?" I asked.

"Eleven?"

"Okay. Should I pick you up?"

"No. I'll go there. Alan James..."

"Yes."

"I saw a... psychic. Near Pittsburgh."

I closed the front door behind me. "...Yes..."

"I had to talk to her. I had to hear about Darla."

"Yes, Rita. Of course."

"I'll tell you about it."

I tried to sound enthusiastic. "Sure, Rita. Good."

"I'm glad...glad you're here, Alan James."

"...Me, too."

After I hung up, I wondered if Rita knew her father had returned. I wondered if she'd arrived home and had seen him. I suddenly felt a touch of melodrama. If she called back with trouble, I'd drive over.

CHAPTER FIVE

A dream about Nicole awoke me a little before eight the next morning. After a shower and a half-cup of coffee, the dream still hovered like smog. The internal struggles began. I dreaded the ordeal of a divorce but dreaded even more the thought of returning to our apartment and facing Nicole. I just wanted it all to go away. I finally gathered the nerve to check my cell phone for messages, but there were none—not even from my answering service.

I found a clean shirt, brown khakis and an old pair of sneakers and drove five miles, under frothy clouds, to Big Joe's Truck Stop. It was one place that hadn't changed—not in fifteen years. I ordered sausage, eggs and hash browns, and ate while skimming the local paper.

When I turned into the driveway, a little after ten o'clock, Rita's gray 1998 Cavalier came up behind me and stopped. She emerged, walking toward me with a strained, eager quality. I immediately saw a change in her. She'd gained some weight; a healthy color had returned to her thin face, and her eyes were clear. She wore cream colored Capri pants, one inch heels and a yellow cotton blouse. She'd taken great care with her makeup and hairstyle, the latter being partless, artistically careless and gleaming. Black mascara accented the blue dusk of her eyes; her lipstick was a bold red. Long pearl dangling earrings caught the morning sun. From her meek expression and awkward stance, I sensed she hadn't "dressed up" in a long time.

I stared with increasing pleasure, as the air around us carried the scent of freshly cut grass and the sound of frisky birds. I gave her a deep smile. "Look at you. You look...pretty."

Her eyes fully opened on me. "It's a special day."

"Yes..."

A bird nearby made the jarring sound of a squeaky hinge and Rita looked for it, keeping half her attention on me. I studied her and she knew it. The youthful glamour had gone. The voluptuous, formidable body that had once graced and stunned, like a disturbing revelation, now seemed almost frail. But the face—the leonine face—proud and imperial, had dissolved into a regal maturity and attractiveness that reawakened in me an extraordinary innocence and an immediate desire. I certainly felt more of the blaze of life in her, more of the fighting spirit to live, than at our last meeting.

"I wasn't sure you'd make it," I said. "Your father came by last night."

Her eyes hardened. "He threatens. He needs total control. That's his reason to live. He forgets that I've seen death...been dead for a long time. He forgets that... When he tries to scare me...it just makes me pity him."

"Are you okay?"

"Of course. This will be a wonderful day. It's Darla's day."

We took my car and drove toward Greenspot, a smaller town than Hartsfield, where Rita said Darla often went to church. We traveled a quiet two-lane back road, past open fields and the occasional pond. Rita seemed more inclined to talk, and her speech had an easier flow and rhythm. She told me she hadn't taken any of her medication that morning. She said it fogged her mind and speech and today she wanted both to be clear.

"Children surprise…you," she said. "Darla was religious or spiritual or whatever you want to call it. She even talked about becoming a minister. I don't know where she got it. Dusty went to church once in a while, but never seemed present. I just went along with Darla because she wanted to go. I can't say I ever believed in it, even when Mom took me to the Baptist church when I was a girl."

"And now?"

"And now…" she repeated vaguely, staring at a flowering field. "And now…I pray. I pray every night for her. I pray for the whole world. I pray and curse at the same time. Sometimes I pray for death…not so much anymore…but sometimes. I pray for some illumination…for any scraps of small wisdom. I pray to any God in any faith and listen to my words fall silent and dead in the room. But I pray. It's an act of desperation, I know, but desperate acts of faith have gotten me through some very dark nights of the soul."

She turned to me. "Do you...believe, Alan James?"

"I'm a doubting Thomas, Rita. I haven't much —or maybe no—faith. I see no evidence of a compassionate or benevolent God. If God is love, then we've got to redefine and expand the meaning of love. I used to look to Galileo, Kepler and Newton to help me understand things. They were scientists —mathematical wizards—and they were deeply religious. Kepler once said, 'I think your thoughts, oh God.' But I'm not much inclined to longsuffering and meekness in the face of evil and ignorance in the world. I've seen so much suffering and pain in the ER's and hospitals. I've seen so many people pray... and nothing happens. So, I don't know, what good is it? I mean, what is faith? Just hopeful imagination?"

Rita considered the thought. "Darla used to say: 'It's not just about faith, mother, it's also about experience.' I'd say, what do you mean? She'd say, 'If you experience love then you are experiencing God.' So then I would challenge her. I'd say, what about hate, brutality and violence? Some religions say God is omnipresent, all pervasive, all powerful? If that's so, why does he let these things happen?"

"Darla would say, 'All those things: suffering, hate and violence, give us the experience and understanding to see that love really is the best way to go and, ultimately, the only way to go. So we struggle to move toward it.'"

I looked at Rita, to check her state. Her features were composed, her hands quietly folded on her lap. "She was a smart little girl," I said. "But then, she was your daughter."

She sighed heavily. "Yes... She was always reading about the Christian saints. Where did she get that from? I don't know. She had the best parts of us...Dusty and me. She made us seem better than we were or ever could be. She wasn't a little saint or anything...she could whine better than any child I ever heard... but...how I'd love to hear her whine now. When she turned ten, just after we'd moved back here, I actually joined the church and 'got religion.' I became a believer—a believer in my child, not the church. Darla was so proud of me. She said I was the prettiest woman in the church."

"I'm sure you were," I added.

"I know now why I did it, although I can't say I knew then or, if I did, I don't remember. I just wanted Darla to be protected. I wanted God to protect her."

"Protected?"

"Yes..."

We approached Greenspot, a low drowsy town reminiscent of the 1950's. Rita directed me left, across another two-lane road that snaked and dipped around the town proper. Rising unexpectedly out of green fertile land and a line of cooling trees, I saw the impressive spires of a gothic cathedral.

"Is that it?" I asked, pointing.

"Yes. Episcopalian. Darla loved the pageantry. I suppose she inherited the sense of the dramatic from me."

"It's in the middle of nowhere."

"Ninety years ago it had a thriving congregation. An architect from England helped design and build it."

We drove into the deserted parking lot and drew up near the entrance. Rita took a shallow breath before she got out. I viewed the immense stone walls and small stained glass windows as we approached the cement stairs. We ascended them and walked past the open heavy iron door.

"It's open most days," Rita whispered, as we entered.

We stepped into a murky serenity, under a vaulted ceiling, soaring pillars and arches. Soft light filtered through stained glass and bathed Rita in a spiritual light. We strolled the central isle, the atrium and apse. Our footsteps echoed along dark stone corridors. We paused near the organ, with its decorative organ pipes. We examined the carved leafage on the oak pulpit, with an ornate curved staircase, and finally settled into a pew in the choir, silently taking in the glorious rose window.

Discretely, I examined Rita's face. It was blankly unresponsive, but her eyes clotted with tears. I looked away to let her have her moment. The silence was so profound that my ears rang, my shoulders relaxed and I grew sleepy.

Later, Rita and I sat barefoot and cross-legged on a grassy bank, overlooking a sprawling farm, with red rambling fences and grazing cattle. She held a stick, poking at the ground with it. I watched a little airplane make a slow lazy turn, swing and drift away, dwindling, then return, growing, sputtering.

"I thought if I became good—religious—that somehow God would protect Darla," Rita said, quietly. "But I should have protected her."

I searched for the right words. "Rita…how could you ever have known?"

She stabbed the ground. "I should have known. I should have seen it coming…Dusty was lost and had been for years. Oklahoma helped to beat him down—his drunken father and that damned nothing of a construction business; could have made a go of it if his father hadn't been a damned, rotten, abusive drunk. Dusty was always making excuses for him—even when his father cursed him and threw things at him—even when he tried to get at me one night in his drunken worst. But Dusty always made excuses and promises and said things would get better someday. God, was there ever a man on earth who tried harder to make things get better?!"

She tossed the stick away and crossed her arms, trembling. "I was such a fool! I should have protected Darla from all of that. I should have taken her away from there. What kind of short life was that for her?! That shabby house, dodging tornados and Dusty's dark moods. Damn me for not doing it! Damn me for not getting her out of there!"

I almost reached for her, but I didn't. Her raw feeling, set free, was pouring through her words. "I tried to get Dusty to leave. Let's get the hell out! Let's go, Dusty! There's nothing here but loss, failure and sickness. Let's go! But he wouldn't. He'd say, there's nothing back in Hartsfield, Rita. They all think we've made good here. I can't go back there. Those people will laugh at us."

"Let them laugh, Dusty, I said to him. We're withering away here!"

"I can make a go of this business, Rita. I'll get dad set right. I will. Believe in me, Rita. Just believe in me."

"So I did. I did believe in Dusty. I loved Dusty. He was a good man, Alan James. No brain child, that was for sure, but he was a good, sensitive man." She dropped her head and spoke at a guilty whisper. "What a thing to say…after what he did. What a thing to say."

She looked into the hazy sky and made a little desperate sound. "But Dusty was good until the failures, his father's constant abuse and my…loss of faith in him… God forgive me…the loss of faith in us both."

"When his father died of a heart attack, I thought we were saved. I thanked God for that stupid old man's death. And when Darla prayed for him at the funeral, I cursed his damned wicked soul for all the things he did to Dusty. For nearly killing Dusty… And now I curse him for finally killing us all."

Rita looked directly at me, with all the intensity she'd gathered. "God forgive me, I do curse him —every day—Alan James! Every single day I don't forget to curse him. That is my prayer. I damn him to hell every day!"

Rita straightened, lifting her chin to the breeze, her face flushed, her eyes remote. "By the time we got back to Hartsfield, the town had fallen into failure, too. There was no work for Dusty or for me. Dusty slipped away into depression. The people he thought would look down on him, instead opened their arms and welcomed him. They gave us money. They sent us food. They said we were their friends... their family. It was Hartsfield at its best. For Dusty, that was worse than rejection and ridicule. His pride began to strangle him."

Tears spilled from her eyes and ran down her cheeks. "Good people, Alan James. Hartsfield people are good, fine people."

I gently unfolded my legs and stretched them out, not taking my eyes from her.

"Dusty had started drinking with his father... He thought it would help bond them or something. After his father died, then came the drugs... It got worse after we moved back to Hartsfield. It was the drugs and alcohol that devoured the gentleness in him—that destroyed the very goodness of him and turned him mean and violent. And I watched it happen, and didn't protect Darla, and I didn't take her away and didn't do anything to stop it! Dusty and I fought and argued, yes, but I didn't leave him. I was determined to be the good and faithful wife and mother, even if it killed..." Her voice dropped away and she sank into despair. "So I killed her. I killed my beauty. My baby." Her shoulders rolled in torment as she sobbed and wept for minutes. I let her get it all out, fighting the urge to hold her, kiss her hair and hot cheeks.

She drew a tissue from her purse and dried her eyes. "Through ignorance, or pity or anger or confusion, it doesn't matter. It doesn't. Through faith or loss of faith in God, or in Dusty or in us, none of that matters. I killed Darla, and nothing will ever change that; and no amount of therapy will ever change that, Alan James. I just...let it happen."

"No, Rita. No. Dusty killed her... It was..."

She shook my words away. "'Dusty, when he killed us, in his own stupid and desperate way, was trying to give us all a fresh start. I know that...I know that, in his crazy head, when he pulled that trigger, all the goodness of his twisted soul was trying to set us all free again. Free again, like we were in the beginning, when the world watched us be... special. I know that's what he thought... I know that's why he did it. But he couldn't finish..."

Rita's jaw hardened. "It must have come to him in those last few seconds, when he saw Darla lying there. It must have sunk in, and the clouds of drugs and alcohol must have swept away long enough for him to realize the horror of what he'd done. So he left me walking dead...remembering...that I was the one who had failed. Not him."

She lifted her shoulders and dropped them. She inhaled and blew out a staggered breath. "And so I should be here, today, remembering. It's right that I'm here on my baby's birthday, remembering that I destroyed us all."

"Rita…"

But she turned from me.

A light rain began to fall, thin and gentle. Rita didn't move, so we sat for another ten minutes until it stopped, and the sun returned from behind the dark continent of a cloud and dried our damp clothes.

I took her hand and we stood up, in silence. We started to walk, through vivid green fields, on narrow paths, past and beside little brooks. We held hands, tramping across weed-bordered roads, where chunks of asphalt were missing. She asked me about college, medical school and my work. She finally asked about Nicole. When I was vague, she astutely pointed it out. I finally explained that Nicole and I were having problems and had been for some time. I reluctantly told her I didn't think the marriage would last, but I didn't offer details.

She grew quiet again, her focus going inward. Minutes passed before she asked about the status of the house.

"I've postponed the auction for a while," I said, as we stepped across rough and rocky land on our way back to the car. "I thought that maybe I'd spend weekends there, until Nicole and I make some decisions. I'll go ahead and sell most of the antiques. The agent said she's fairly confident she can get good prices at auction."

I glanced sideways to see Rita's reaction. She turned her head toward me, gazing openly. "I'm glad you'll be coming back, Alan James. I'm sorry about your marriage, I really am, but I'm glad you're not selling the house."

We drove a half an hour to Lipton, another small town, where a spring festival was in full swing, pitched on the campgrounds where the Baptist church often held summer revivals. We parked and joined in.

"I came here with Darla last year," Rita said, not sadly.

There were white and brown tents, flapping in occasional sharp gusts, and rows of parked cars and SUVs tucked behind trees and in open fields. The high-pitched cry of celebration and mumbled excitement rose from bake sale stands, flower stands, food stands and crowds of rambling people. A brass band belched out polkas, as couples whirled and bounced, faces glossy and flushed. Dogs barked, pleaded for scraps, then nosed with frenetic hope and busy tails toward the leaning hand, the slipping sausage, or the fallen hamburger from the child's greasy, neglectful fingers.

There were two impatient lines of people waiting to ride the lazy Ferris wheel, with its intimate red, rocking seats and its breathy, hollow calliope melodies, sounding like the comical honks of a steamboat whistle. When I heard *In The Good Ole' Summertime*, for some reason, I smiled.

Rita and I drifted, sniffing pumpkin spice cakes, banana muffins, pound cakes, fresh bread, apple cider, lemonade, sizzling turkey sausage, potato pancakes and lavishly decorated apple and cherry pies. We ordered and ate a turkey sausage on a freshly baked roll, with slivers of red pepper and onions; drank draft beer and shared a hot potato pancake.

When the band broke into the *Pennsylvania Polka*, I surprised myself and Rita by seizing her hand and dragging her into the circle of hefty, romping dancers. In imitation of others, I placed my hand at Rita's waist, took her right hand high and nudged us into the forming circle. We struggled for rhythm and form, laughing brokenly, as we stuttered along the periphery, trying to avoid a collision with the experts, who ignored us and swung on by, confidently delirious.

Then Rita stopped, abruptly, and backed away, knuckle to her lips, as she studied those fast skipping feet with assiduous concentration. I, too, turned ridiculously serious. This was war. We were from Pennsylvania. By birthright we should, and must, be able to dance the Pennsylvania Polka. No backing away. No excuses.

"We can do this, Alan James!"

I jerked a firm nod.

With renewed passion and conviction, we joined

hands and began again. This time we lifted the high knee in unison, found the precise moment and pitch of motion, and then boldly advanced into the vigorous circle, heads held pompously high, feet springing to life.

In a serendipitous wonder of motion, we abandoned ourselves, rounding the space, flying off in quick breaths past the blurring tents, trees and crowds, caught with elation and grins. Hands were clapping loud and sharp. Voices, nearly riotous with the spirit of it, sang on and off key, as we bounced, arched and swayed.

When the three accordions broke into *The Beer Barrel Polka*, Rita and I drew on reserve strength and danced on, whipping each other about, heads back, kicking across the ground with bright eyes from the sheer fun of it all.

> Roll out the barrel,
> We'll have a barrel of fun.
> Roll out the barrel,
> We've got the blues on the run.
> Zing! Boom! Ta-ra-rel
> Ring out a song of good cheer!
> Now's the time to roll the barrel.
> For the gang's all here.

With an abrupt rowdy cadence, the music died away into an echo. The crowd erupted into cheers and whistles. Rita and I were bent over, panting, laughing, searching for a seat to rest. But all were taken, so we traipsed off to an open field and dropped down into tender grass, damp with sweat, giggling and spent.

"Oh my God," Rita said, hand over her heart. "That was right up there, Alan James. Right up there."

I looked at her with happiness, with that old 17-year-old longing. "I thought I was pretty good out there," I said, jokingly.

Rita struggled for breath. "Alan...James... you dance like a kangaroo."

We howled with laughter.

We waited for over a half hour to ride the Ferris wheel. After we drew the steel safety bar across us and began to lift, watching the people and cars grow smaller and the land spread out wide to the horizons, Rita looked at me and smiled. It was her real smile. Her best smile. "Thanks for being with me today, Alan James."

I didn't want to shatter the perfect moment with a response, so I just looked at her and nodded. It was a truthful thing to do, uncompromising, assured and courageous. With all my best efforts, I revealed my love in that look. No thing hidden. No fear, no expectation or anticipation. Just the truthful surrender that comes when all the defenses have been startled quiet by something extraordinary: like snow falling in the desert.

She saw it, I think, and she didn't stir. She looked deeply into me, and we hung at the summit of the sky, rocking a little, when I leaned close.

I drove away from Lipton, sleepy, privileged and working on private thoughts. Rita had closed her eyes but she didn't seem to be sleeping. She'd already given me directions to our next destination: the cemetery where Darla was buried.

We drifted among old gravestones, broken and leaning, some pocked by cruel winters, broiling heat and driving rains. As we climbed the brief rise of a hill, the late afternoon sun caught Rita's face and bronzed it. Down the other side, we passed the tall tombstones, the ancient towers and obelisks, holding down the once wealthy and influential. They were thick with weeds, enclosed by sinking wrought-iron gates, the names and dates nearly rubbed flat by erosion.

We took a winding path through a quiet sloping meadow, rich with wildflower color and movement, and approached the recent graves. Darla was buried there. Dusty was not. Darla's modest white marker lay in soft grass beneath spreading elms, with a good view of the woods and a far pasture, electric green in sunlight.

Rita knelt with the flowers we'd purchased at the roadside stand near the cemetery: a collection of daisies, gladiolas and asters. She placed them carefully, reverently, and hovered a moment before sitting back on her knees, sphinxlike, hands prayerful, the tips of her fingers brushing her whispering lips.

I stood silently, head bowed.

"Your mother is here, baby," Rita said. "Your mother is here on your birthday."

A robin swept in, landed and froze, his chest puffed, head pitched in translation. He sprinted stiffly, paused, drilled and swallowed. He caught the next updraft and rose, banking left, released.

We had one more stop to make, according to Rita's itinerary: a train trestle. When the Palmers moved back to Hartsfield from Oklahoma, Darla had discovered that when standing on the trestle, as the scheduled train thundered underneath, she got a powerful thrill. Rita said that Darla went there at least once a week and, on her last birthday at her request, she and her mother had shared the experience together.

The sun was lowering when we arrived and parked on a little dirt road under a canopy of trees. We got out and walked briskly along a weedy path toward the sooty wooden trestle; it appeared more rickety and suspect the closer we got. I was sure that a good sturdy wind could blow the thing into a worthless pile of sticks.

Rita glanced nervously at her watch. "We've got to hurry. It's scheduled to come through in five minutes."

"You remember that from last year?" I asked.

"Yes...I wrote it in my diary."

The trestle arched over a fifteen foot plunging rocky ravine down to the railroad tracks, and bridged open pasture land, where a leaning, weathered FOR SALE was clearly visible. The trestle had once provided ready access to an isolated factory that lay still and abandoned now, nearly obscured by trees, looking much like an ancient monastery.

Rita scampered up to the trestle, put hands to hips and appraised the 3-foot walkway. With a nod of her head, she grabbed the wobbly handrail and pulled herself along the wooden planks, stepping gingerly in those clicking heels, until she arrived at the crest, looking triumphant and impressed, like a mountain climber who'd just reached the summit of Everest.

She turned to me, grinning broadly. "Come on, Alan James!"

She gripped the wooden rail, testing its reliability. There was a lot of play in it, but that didn't seem to bother her. Satisfied, she leaned over, looking straight down.

I studied the trestle warily, shaking my head. "Rita, something tells me this thing has taken a huge beating since you were here a year ago."

"Still the cautious man, Alan James?"

"Yes, Rita Fitzgerald. Somebody should put up a sign on this thing that says keep off or something, or at the very least, travel at your own risk."

"There was a sign here last year that said that very thing," Rita said, amused.

"And you probably took it down and threw it away."

"No… We just ignored it."

"Not surprised."

"Come on, Alan James. You're going to miss it."

With some overdramatic emoting, grunting and face twisting, I mounted the walkway and shuffled up the slope to meet Rita.

"See. Nothing to it," she said.

I glanced about but didn't look down. A puff of wind mussed my hair and rippled Rita's yellow blouse. Rita stared intently ahead, checking her watch frequently, as if she were in charge of the whole effect coming off just right and precisely on time.

I held the tenuous railing without putting any weight on it, and gazed out at the straight long stretch of tracks, enclosed on both sides by steep banks and overhanging trees. About a half-mile away, it curved abruptly off to the right and out of our vision. Another mile or two beyond that, the train would have once stopped at the old Hartsfield train station.

"It's late!" Rita said, contemptuously.

"Maybe it doesn't even come this way anymore. There are a lot of weeds growing on the tracks, not that I'm looking down or anything."

"I hope it comes," Rita said, puckering her mouth in disappointment. "It's so much fun, Alan James. It gives you such a power rush."

We waited.

"Alan James…"

"Yes."

"Do you write anymore?"

"No."

"Why?"

"No time…nothing to say."

"I loved reading your stories…talking about them in Jack's. I always looked forward to that. I really missed seeing you and doing that."

"Yeah…I did, too."

"Why did you come back to Hartsfield, Alan James?"

I looked at her. "To sell the house."

"No, I mean when you were in high school."

"High school?"

"When you left that private school in Massachusetts. You said once that your mother was sick and your father thought that if you came home it would help her to recover."

The chilly memory returned; the sinking disappointment of leaving my good friend Chazzy Lynch, the bright kid with a lisp and red mop of unruly hair. "…I didn't find out the truth about that until my mother told me what happened a month or so before she died."

"Don't tell me if you don't want to. It just popped into my head this morning, out of nowhere."

I shifted my weight to my right foot and massaged the bridge of my nose. "I thought my mother got sick because my father had a girlfriend or something. Anyway, that always seemed to be what happened in a lot of families. It happened to my best friend's parents, only it was his mother who had a lover. So Chazzy said, 'Your old daddy is doin' it to some young thang' Alan. No doubt, man.' Well, that's not what it was at all. Looking back now, I realize that my father was too conservative and too much in love with my mother to ever do anything like that.

"It was Mom's sister—twin sister—who had died. She was mentally retarded and physically disabled. Mom kept it a secret from my sister, Judy, and me. I don't know why. Mom said it was just too painful to talk about. Here she was, living a perfectly normal life—a good life with a man who loved her and two wonderful kids—and her sister, Jeannie, I think that was her name, was all twisted up and pretty much dumb to the world.

"So when Jeannie died, Mom just fell into a deep depression. She couldn't get out of bed; wouldn't eat; wouldn't talk. Mom told me all this on one of her last good days. So anyway, Dad got desperate and he said he'd do anything—take her anywhere, give her anything if she'd just get better. Mom said he was on his knees. So… she said, I want Alan home. I want my child home with us."

I shrugged. "So that was it. Home I came."

"Did you like that school?"

"Yeah. I loved it. I wasn't the smartest kid there—close maybe—but not number one, but I had good friends who were more like me or, at least, I thought so then. I guess I thought I had more in common with them."

Rita grew a little uneasy. "God, I hated it when

you came to meet my parents. That whole night was a nightmare."

I heaved out a sigh. "We had some fun at the Holiday Inn pool though."

Rita turned away embarrassed. "I got so drunk."

"You didn't seem that drunk."

"I didn't show it. Never have, but I was blasted. God I was so horrible to poor Robbie Syles."

"What ever happened to him?" I asked.

"Mom said he moved to Georgia about 6 or 7 years ago. He's managing another Holiday Inn down there. He never forgave me for that night, and he shouldn't have."

"Don't be so hard on yourself. It was a bad scene with your parents."

"A nightmare…"

"I couldn't even see the damned road when we drove to Jack's," I said. "The steering wheel felt like it was wandering all over the front seat."

Rita squealed out a laugh. "You were all over the place, and your little eyes were so intense and you kept saying, 'I can see where I'm goin', Rita! Shut up! I know how to drive!'"

We both chuckled, acted out our parts again, laughed wildly, and then gradually, when the memories drifted to the more unpleasant, we turned quiet again. I stared into the afternoon light at the distant zipper-like tracks. "I don't think it's coming, Rita."

She slumped a little. "Oh well…everything changes. Trains go down different tracks just like people."

But we waited, watching dragonflies circle the fields.

"Alan James...after my father got out of prison and came home, things got bad. Worse, I guess you could say. Mom never was a very secure person; always felt inferior to everybody—even at the factory. She's painfully shy. Dad was abusive, even before he left us. He started in again when he got back, after those 10 years, shouting out orders, putting us and everybody else down. I was always so embarrassed when Mom and I visited him in that prison. I hate to say it, but he looked right at home in that damned place."

I faced her. "But you once talked about him so lovingly. He brought you books, you wrote stories for him. You told me that's how you started writing and reading."

"Lies, Alan James. Dad was a bully. He bullied me into reading and writing all the things he liked. He beat me when I didn't do it. I'm surprised I continued when I didn't have to. To his credit, I did learn to love books."

I moved closer. "So you never wrote the stories for him or..."

"Of course not. It sounded pretty and I wanted to impress you. I didn't want to be the stereotypic poor girl from the other side of the tracks who was dating a rich boy. You were smart, came from a wealthy family and I liked you. I certainly wasn't going to tell you that my father knocked my mother around, stole money from people and raped me when I was 16."

Shock froze me rigid.

Rita stared at me deliberately, coolly. "Old stuff, Alan James. I've worked through most of that in therapy in the last few months. The second time Daddy tried to take me, I stabbed him in the shoulder." She gave a firm nod. "He stopped trying."

We got quiet again.

"Pretty stories, aren't they?" She narrowed her eyes on me. "Don't pity me, Alan James. I don't need pity, and I certainly don't need to be saved." She paused a minute. "I always thought you wanted to save me and I hated that. It was one reason I told you to keep a Rita Distance."

I shook my head. "No…well…I don't know. Maybe I did."

"I cared about you, Alan James. I really did." She turned away. "I loved you."

I took a shallow breath. My voice became thick with emotion. "Why….? Why did you go to Dusty then? Why?"

"Alan James…come on. You were never going to marry me. I was a low life."

"You weren't, Rita! Never! You were smart and classy and beautiful!"

"I was pretty and I used it to try to escape from what I was and where I was from. Oh, hell, it's such a trite old story. I mean, could you imagine my family and yours at the wedding? No way. And anyway, you were going off to college. I needed—no, not just needed—I had to get out of that house. When Daddy came home in my senior year, from who knows where, I knew I had to get away from there as fast as I could. I saw that so clearly when you came to meet them. I also needed protection from him. He scared the hell out of me. I knew, sooner or later, that he'd come at me again. I saw it in his eyes. He was sick and cunningly smart. Still is. I knew Dusty was big enough to protect me. I knew that as soon as Dusty and I started going together, Daddy would leave me alone. Sure enough, he did."

She raked her fingers through her hair. "I told Dusty I wanted to get married as soon as we could. He didn't know what hit him. I swarmed him with plans and dreams and love. He wasn't so strong, Alan James, but he was a good father and husband until the last two years."

"But you loved him?"

"Yes. I grew to love him very much, and never regretted marrying him, until... We were good and faithful to each other and we worked hard to make our marriage work." She tended her hair, absently. "We worked so damn hard..."

"Why didn't you have another child?" I asked.

"We did... I lost it in the second month. That was almost eight years ago. Then Dusty wanted to wait until the business grew and he wasn't so busy. That was okay with me because I wanted to go to college and finish my degree anyway. But he didn't want me to. He got weird about it. It made him insecure or something. Made him feel like a failure. He said we didn't have the money for school and that I should just go get a job. We argued about it awhile, then, I don't know, I just got tired of arguing, and so I didn't finish school and I went to work as a cashier at a supermarket. When I look back on it now, I can see that we were already beginning to separate."

Rita peered down at the tracks, and slumped a little. "Well, anyway, we didn't have another child." A moment later she turned to me with a weary acceptance. "The weeds are pretty high on the tracks, aren't they, Alan James?"

I wished the train would come. I prayed for it to come roaring, thundering toward us—puffing black balls of smoke like those hulking iron trains in old westerns. I longed to hear the low growing rumble, the hiss of steam, the blaring, powerful blast of the whistle stunning our ears. I longed to feel the soles of my feet and chest vibrate; feel the entire trestle violently shake us to forgetfulness; feel the victory, the driving charge of the train's approach and the explosion of gusting wind whipping us ecstatic, as it passed, scattering leaves, weeds and the old dust of our lives to some fresh plot of ground. I wished hard for it to come.

I hung my head over the railing. "Yeah, Rita, the weeds are real high. Trains don't come this way anymore."

CHAPTER SIX

We left the trestle disappointed and quiet. I thought it might cheer us if we returned to the lake where we'd first made love, although those weren't the words I used with Rita.

"Remember that beautiful lake we went to on our second date, when you tried to get me to dance? Moon Lake?"

"You remembered the name," she said, brightly.

"Of course I remember."

"I wrote all about it in my diary that night."

"Really? What did you say?"

"Oh, something like, Alan James is a terrible dancer, has a snotty, pompous personality and I wish we could run off together, become writers and live happily ever after."

"I wish we had," I said, reflectively.

She worked on a slow thought as she turned to me. Her face softened. "Me, too, Alan James."

I turned off the main highway onto what was once an old dirt road, now smoothly paved and called "Spinnaker Drive." Rita said I wouldn't know the place, and she was right. Summer homes spotted the entire area, along with a wide variety of NO TRESPASSING and PRIVATE PROPERTY signs. When

Rita directed me toward the turnoff that led to the magical view of the lake, I immediately saw the yellow DEAD END sign and the imposing two-story house and two-car garage, that now rested precisely on the spot where I had lost my virginity. We pulled up and stopped, craning our necks to view just a sliver of the lake.

The owners owned that spectacular view of the lake now, which included the vague outline of bungalows and cottages on the opposite shore. They owned the sounds of migrating birds, the creeks splashing down from high cliffs, and the lazy lap of the lake below. They owned that soaring vaulted piece of sky, the cool fresh air and the dawn and sunset. But I comforted myself with the thought that I owned, and would always own, the memories of that wonderful night with Rita.

While I gazed, I recalled a poem I'd memorized for freshman English class. I settled into the seat while I played it back in my mind. It was by Rainer Maria Rilke:

> *Flare up like a flame*
> *and make big shadows I can move in.*
> *Let everything happen to you: beauty*
> *and terror.*
> *Just keep going. No feeling is final.*
> *Don't let yourself lose me.*
> *Nearby is the country they call life.*
> *You will know it by its seriousness.*
> *Give me your hand.*

We returned to the house around six. Before leaving the car, Rita touched my arm. She wanted to take me to dinner, she said, and she wanted to pay. I finally agreed, seeing the determination in her eyes. She gave me the address of the restaurant. I was to meet her there at 7:30. She said she'd make the reservation.

After she drove away, I went inside, turned on my cell phone and checked messages. There was one from the office that I followed-up on. There was nothing from Nicole. She seemed thousands of miles away. I showered and rummaged up an old blue blazer, blue striped shirt and a tight fitting pair of gray slacks.

Nicole was a convenient comparison, now, to Rita and me—one that I could hold up in the mirror, as I dried and brushed my hair, and say "See, we couldn't have really loved each other—no, not truly, because the relationship didn't last. It wasn't a love like the love I had, and now have again, with Rita—a constant love that can take any blow and withstand any deep cutting wound."

Hadn't I always known that—even at seventeen? Wasn't it always a strong certainty? I just simply knew, without a shadow of doubt, that Rita was "my" true love. Seeing her again only confirmed it. My love for Rita, incessant and true, had once again been awakened from its long sleep. As I stared into the mirror at my expectant face, I saw that love—and it was as stark, inexplicable and uneraseable as the red flame of a birth mark.

Nicole was already becoming a kind of fiction to me. Our entire relationship was fast becoming a story I'd once read or written, where entire episodes of our marriage were becoming half-read, half-remembered paragraphs and chapters. Who could remember what the whole thing was about, anyway? We were minor characters, not so important now, except that we had helped to shine pure light on the main plot: the real story of Rita and me, and the future.

I parked in The Ashford Inn parking lot and got out. It was 7:20. It had clouded up, and cooled down; it looked as though it could rain at any moment. The Inn was quaint, a colonial style building with a sloping roof, burgundy shudders and ubiquitous white Christmas lights adorning the surrounding trees and shrubs. There was a little white sign near the entrance, announcing that Ben Franklin had actually eaten there, once, on his way to New York.

In the foyer, I waited for Rita, taking in the pastoral landscape paintings by Philadelphia-area artists. Rita finally appeared at 7:43, flushed and anxious, in a powder blue dress, 2-inch heels and gold hoop earrings. Her perfume drew me toward her.

"Are you okay?" I asked, concerned.

She nodded, but I could see trouble in her eyes. "...Sorry I'm late. Let's sit down."

The main dining room was cozy and sedate, with muted lighting, cream-colored walls and white linen table cloths. It was only half filled. We were seated at a table a short distance from the fireplace, with a clear view of a male guitarist. He was on a platform, seated on a stool under a blue pin spot, plucking a combination of light classical music and jazz.

The menus were dropped, our little table candle lit, and the water poured.

"Your father?" I finally asked.

She nodded. "He'll be gone soon. He never stays long." Rita worked to brighten her mood as she perused the menu. "The duck looks good... and the crab cakes."

I forced a little enthusiasm, feeling threatened by Frank Fitzgerald's all too near presence. "Duck with gingered raspberry-Amaretto glaze and almond cous cous sound awfully good."

Rita glowed warmly in the soft candlelight. "The crab cakes come with cottage fries and cabbage slaw in a remoulade sauce," she added.

"You've sold me," I said.

Rita looked up. "On which one?"

"All of them."

Rita laughed.

I ordered the crab cakes and Rita the duck. Rita let me order the wine, while she left to freshen up. I was sure she needed the time to recover from the argument with her father. Despite the crab cakes, I chose a Cabernet Sauvignon. I thought it would be better with the duck, and white wine reminded me of Nicole: she seldom drank red.

By the time Rita returned, all smiles, the bread was served and wine poured in elegant crystal glasses. We toasted to "reunions" as the guitarist played *It Might As Well Be Spring*.

We talked in generalities for a while, carefully evading any uncomfortable subjects. She brought me up-to-date on the town, classmates and teachers. According to Ellen Tucker, Ms. Lyendecker was living alone in a small town about twenty-five miles from Hartsfield. We both thought it would be fun to drop by and see her. I suggested tomorrow and Rita brightened.

When the food arrived, we ate with an aggressiveness that surprised us. Rita said she hadn't been that hungry in months. I was driven by mild nerves and a mounting sense of stress, aware that there was serious conversation to come. I wanted to propose something to Rita and I was hoping she'd agree.

The wine and music gently intoxicated us, gradually slowing our pace and lulling us in a comfortable trance. After the table was cleared, Rita leaned forward on her elbows, folding her hands and resting her chin on them. Her eyes had a dreamy, relaxed quality, a youthful playfulness I hadn't seen in fifteen years.

"Alan James…"

"Yes…"

"I'm a little drunk."

"So am I."

"I haven't had alcohol in a long time."

"We'll go slow."

"But we didn't, and the wine is almost gone."

"Okay, so we'll pretend we went slow."

"I haven't taken any medication today. None. I feel better. I talk better."

"Good. But you probably shouldn't drop it cold turkey. Maybe you should talk it over with your doctor."

She shrugged. "Yes, Doctor."

Over coffee, Rita asked me more about my life; more details about college and medical school; about my parents and sister and what it was like being a doctor. We talked easily and long. Still emboldened by the wine, she finally asked again about Nicole. I told her how we met, where we lived and explained, again, without going into any specifics, that we'd gradually lost our love for each other.

When there was a pause, I gave a quick glance around, deciding the moment was right to share with Rita what I'd been thinking.

"Rita."

"Yes, Dr. Alan James. Does anyone else call you Dr. Alan James?"

"No. Rita...Listen, I want to propose something to you."

"I'd love to, Alan James."

"You don't know what it is."

"I don't care. I'd still love to."

"Rita... I want you to move into the house."

Her eyelids fluttered. She lowered her hands and lifted her head. "Your house?"

"Yes."

She unclasped her hands and picked at the tablecloth. "Why?"

"You'll be away from your father and I'll have someone to look after the place when I'm not there. And...I thought I could come and visit you on weekends."

For a moment, Rita fidgeted with her left hoop earring. I couldn't read her thoughts. I looked into her wavering, uncertain eyes. "Rita?"

She groped for words. "Alan James...When I saw the psychic ...You remember I told you about that."

"Yes..."

"She went into this kind of trance and she said that... Darla was happy. She said she was in a very pretty place and that she was happy."

"I'm sure she is. I hope she is."

"But you don't believe in heaven and all of that stuff, do you?"

"I don't know, Rita."

"I talked to her...to Darla." Rita's voice became soft and reminiscent. "Darla said she was happy and that I shouldn't worry about her. She said...she said..." Rita faltered, sudden tears forming, and her eyes shined in the candlelight. "She said...she didn't feel anything when she died. She said angels were waiting for her—beautiful angels—and a girlfriend who had died only the year before, of leukemia. Darla said, the girl was there waiting for her. They're good friends there, Darla said. She said they are happy together and that I shouldn't worry and grieve about her anymore."

Rita wiped her eyes.

I sat still, hearing rain strike the nearby windows.

"I believed it all, Alan James. I did. I believed every damned lying word of it, and I felt better for a few hours. I might even go back and listen to the same lies all over again. Maybe I'll go to another psychic and believe her lies too. Hell, maybe I'll start giving séances myself."

I took her hand. "Rita... I want to help you through this. I want to go through it with you. I think if you stay at the house—away from your father, your past... away from..." I had a sudden thought. "You could work in the gardens! Plant flowers, vegetables, take walks. You could do whatever you want. You could write! Whatever. Wouldn't you like to work in the gardens?"

Her mood seemed to fall as she considered my offer. I was just about to despair when she smiled a little. I sat up a little straighter when I saw that old girlish invitation in her eyes. There was nothing like it. It was an allure that brought heat and pleasure, swelling desire.

She leaned intimately close. "Alan James...I love being with you...talking with you. I always have."

I didn't respond, but she surely saw my desire for her.

There was a little wine left. She poured her glass half full and tasted it, swallowing it thoughtfully, as she studied me long and hard. Finally, she lowered her voice, almost to a whisper, into an exciting intimacy. "Alan James...I want to feel alive again. But I am so scared."

I squeezed her hand. "Don't be scared, Rita. I'll help you. I'll be with you no matter what happens. You know that."

She trembled. "I've been scared for so long, Alan James. Scared of waking up and facing another day; scared of people; scared of killing myself."

"Stay at the house. Please, Rita. Just try it for a while. If it doesn't work out, then you leave, that's all."

Rita considered the offer, with shifting eyes.

The waiting seconds became unbearably long.

"Can we?" she asked, in a small voice.

"What, Rita? Can we what?"

"Can we start again...?"

I leaned toward her. "Yes, Rita. I believe it. I believe in us. Yes."

She lowered her head. "I'm sorry your marriage didn't work out," she continued. "I am...but ever since Mom called you—and I did ask her to call you... I know I should have called you myself, but I didn't have the courage. So, I begged her. I begged her until she finally agreed. It was one of the hardest things she ever did and, when she broke down like that, I was sure I'd never see you again.

"Alan James... I want us. I want the life we missed. I want to try to get better."

I heard Rita's words, and I took them in with excruciating pain and pleasure. She looked at me strangely and, for a moment, because I didn't answer, she retreated a little, surely afraid that she had said too much.

"Then come home, Rita. Come home with me."

CHAPTER SEVEN

In the living room that same night, Rita and I lay naked on a thick burgundy comforter spread on the floor, touching and kissing in the meager yellow light. A growing fire washed the walls with trembling shadows and enveloped the room with the scent of pine. Rain ticked at the windows, and the antique grandfather's clock ticked relentlessly, like a reminder that I'd already lost fifteen years of life with Rita.

Nothing was rushed or forced in those moments before joining, when Rita's long lashes opened, revealing dewy eyes, filled with longing and anticipation. I found her lips parted and waiting, and I took them, believing in us, believing in the power of my body as I found the moist deepness of her. I moved us. When she grew eager, I steadied us, remembering all the days and nights I'd waited for her. I wanted the forever of our love; the "now" of love that buffets intrusion. So I found new places to kiss her neck, breasts and stomach.

But she was fervent and wanting. When emotion overwhelmed, I went with her, believing, driving us forward into the future, with all my gentle and forceful love. I drew myself away and back to her, high-edged and strong, watching her face in shadow, waxy and intense, loving her with breath, strength and spirit.

Wild rain and wind lashed at the house, as we rocked toward the burning core of love, helpless in intoxication, silent and loud, echoing rapture, arching and bracing for climax. I kept believing, kept praying, kept building my passion—feeling the hardness lengthen, the hot pool swell to a boil. When the moment came and I let go, her body seized me, grasped and milked the exploding seeds of love. She worked and twisted and drew it all from me, in frantic rhythms and cries, until we both fell away into exhaustion.

Dawn came quietly, with pale light and singing birds. The storm had passed. Our love-making peaked in silence; in worship of ourselves; in gratitude and wonder. When Rita fell into a deep sleep, bundled within the comforter, I sat crossed-legged and watched her until sunlight streamed in through the stained glass. In the fireplace was a bed of white ash. I closed my eyes and prayed for us, to any God who might be listening.

When I brought her breakfast on a tray, with a newly picked rose, she awoke with a marvelously sleepy face, slitted eyes and unruly hair. We drank orange juice, ate Total and sipped coffee.

With an unexpected self-consciousness, she covered herself with the comforter and screwed up her lips. "I know I'm skinny, Alan James, but in a month, I'm going to be the sexiest woman you've ever seen."

I drained my coffee and smiled. That's when I should have told Rita the truth. It would have been so easy. Simple. I should have said, "Rita, I'm infertile, but there are options. Easy options. Medical science has it all down to a science."

But I didn't tell her. I told myself that it could wait. Why spoil the mood. Why risk a setback if Rita took the news hard. No, it could wait. Meanwhile, I decided to see another doctor—a referral—a doctor friend had told me about some months back. I called for an appointment as soon as I got back to New York.

The next day, on Sunday, I helped Rita move into the house. We chose a time when her father and mother were gone. She packed quickly, only taking essentials: toiletries, two suitcases of clothing and a few books. Rita wrote a note and left it on the kitchen table.

> Dear Mom:
> I have moved in with Alan James. I'll call you tomorrow.
> Love, Rita.

* * * *

Throughout the summer, Rita lived in the house and I came down every Friday night, staying until early Monday morning. I took a week's vacation in

July and Rita and I worked the gardens, pruning roses and repairing trestles. We went swimming and fishing; walked the hills and made love. She continued to work four days a week at Jack's, at her insistence; she cleaned the house and paid for all the groceries. She also worked with Cindy Purty, who brought buyers for the antiques. Meanwhile, Rita expanded her knowledge of antiquing from books and the internet, and she and Cindy became good friends.

Back in New York, I walked the streets nervous and shamed, avoiding faces, as if they all knew that I had failed and that Nicole had left me for a real man. I didn't return friends' curious and sorrowful phone calls and I didn't return Nicole's repeated requests to call her to discuss divorce proceedings.

"Alan, will you please call me back. I want to get on with this, just as I'm sure you want to. Call me."

I didn't.

She called the office. I told reception to tell her I was out.

I did make an appointment to see Dr. William Keffer on Park Avenue at 55th Street. He had extensive experience with male infertility evaluations, as well as contemporary sperm retrieval techniques.

He was an earnest man, with quiet dark eyes, short white hair and a thin athletic build. With his black-rimmed glasses and quiet reedy voice, he reminded me of one of those concerned scientists from a 1950's sci fi movie, in which the deadly invaders from outer space were fast approaching, but he possessed the calm assurance that modern science could repel the bastards, come what may.

I sat opposite him in his brightly lit, cheerful office, where floor plants bloomed little white flowers and abstract oil paintings of white and pink filled two walls.

Seated behind his desk, with small hands folded, he directed his pleasant gaze on me. I blinked rapidly and sat stiffly in his burgundy upholstered chair. I related, in a halting voice, the inevitable divorce, largely because of my infertility, and my pressing need to correct the problem so that I could have a child—if the situation presented itself—with another woman.

"I received your medical records from Dr. Long," Dr. Keffer said. "However, I'd like us to start over. I want a complete medical history—the full range of tests—including childhood illnesses, medical illnesses, surgical and sexual history."

I felt a nervous dread. Most of the tests I'd already had. The thought of repeating them nauseated me.

Dr. Keffer continued. "I also firmly believe in genetic testing. Genetic abnormalities are a well-recognized cause of male infertility."

I sighed audibly. Dr. Keffer smiled. "I know it sounds like a lot, Alan, but I'm sure that as we proceed, step by step, we will find a satisfactory solution and a successful remedy for this problem."

My hands had formed tight little fists.

"Finally, Alan, do you exercise regularly?"

"I sometimes jog."

"Do it more often—or perform some other regular workout."

I left his office, feeling every city sound beat at my nerves: the taxi horns, the jack hammers, the low rumbling subway beneath my feet. I couldn't wait to get back to Rita and the quiet of Hartsfield.

I joined Rita in an exercise routine of jogging three miles four times a week. I ran with her on weekends and ran alone in Riverside Park when I was in the City. Rita ate generously, gained 10 pounds by the middle of July and became tantalizingly voluptuous again, more so, I thought, than when she was 18. She developed a golden tan working in the gardens; her hair grew thick and long, and there was a new flame of life in her. She laughed easily, cooked us delicious and creative food, and with the aid of her doctor, (whose identity she kept secret) she gradually reduced her medication. She told me she had begun several short stories, but she didn't show them to me.

Rita's father, Frank, did leave town, just as Rita had said he would, and her mother found a job at the hospital, filing medical records, answering the phone and processing insurance forms. It comforted Rita that her mother was working again, and she met her twice a week for lunch. Rita told me that her mother was pleased we were living together, but she thought we should leave Hartsfield. Frank Fitzgerald was out of town, but he would surely return and her mother wanted to avoid provoking him.

The thought of Frank coming to the house when I wasn't there alarmed me. One afternoon, I finally sat Rita down and delicately stated my concern. I mentioned to her that Dad had a .38 caliber pistol that he'd kept in the house for protection and that I should show her where it was and how to shoot it.

Rita grew edgy and frightened. "No..." she said, sharply. "No guns. I hate guns! No." She stood abruptly, folding her arms, head turned away from me. "He won't bother me here, Alan James."

"How do you know that, Rita?" I asked, forcefully. "The man's a psycho. How do you know?"

"Because I know him! And anyway, he may never come back."

"You said he always comes back."

"I never said that."

"Look, let me just show you where the gun is, just in..."

"No, Alan James. A gun killed my little girl! No!"

She fled the room. I found her minutes later, working in the vegetable garden.

Rita continued to suffer from nightmares. She dreamt of the tragedy or some variation of it. She dreamt of Darla and jerked awake sobbing, searching the house, nearly out of her mind, trying to find her. Once she dreamed that Dusty was chasing her through the house with a shotgun, screaming that it was her fault that he'd killed Darla. I held her and talked softly to her until she relaxed and drifted into uneasy sleep.

Sometimes after similar dreams, we'd slip downstairs to my father's wine cellar and choose a bottle of wine. We'd sit in the kitchen, or out on the front porch, and sip and talk until the dark emotions passed; until the stillness, the chat and the wine loosened the knots of fear and stress. Then we'd return to bed, light-headed and jolly. Those were the best nights—the easy talk about books and philosophy; reminiscences of high school and our dates; words that soared with ideas and promise for the future.

I always drank the wine stingily and uneasily, conscious of the fact that alcohol does affect the reproductive system. By mid-July, I had completed most of the tests that Dr. Keffer had prescribed and I was taking an experimental medication that hadn't been fully tested, but one I was willing to try and one Dr. Keffer sanctioned.

I felt strong and optimistic about my chances to get Rita pregnant. And I wanted her pregnant. I wanted to prove it to myself, to Nicole, and to the world that the waste and extravagant failures of the last two years were far behind me. The thought and image of Rita carrying our baby began to consume me.

On a warm summer night, as we lingered on the porch swing, sipping wine, nibbling cheese and discussing plans to paint the house in the fall, Rita turned her serious eyes on me, staring as if she had a new idea.

"What?" I asked.

"Alan James. I'm very fertile."

My throat tightened.

"I've tried not to think about it," she added, playing with the curls of her hair.

"About what?"

"Having your child."

"Having our child," I corrected.

Pleased, she smiled. "Have you thought about it?"

"...Yes."

"I'm still so damn scared. What happens if I get pregnant and something happens again? Something awful."

"Nothing awful is going to happen."

"But it could, Alan James. You know how unpredictable and terrible the world can be."

"Rita," I consoled, soothingly, "the world can also be beautiful. The world also contains happiness. Just look at the moon and stars. Look at us now. Aren't you happy right now?"

She smiled. "Yes, Alan James. I am very happy."

"Okay then. There's no need to be scared or create a problem where there is none."

"Maybe I'm not ready yet to get pregnant. Maybe I'll never be ready. Maybe God is punishing me."

"Don't say that, Rita. Nobody is punishing you."

The dim porch light caught the side of her face, and she fixed her eyes on me solemnly. "Do you want a child, Alan James? Did you and your wife want a child?"

I considered all the possible responses. I considered lying and continuing to withhold the truth. I closed my eyes and tried to anticipate her response, her expressions, her actions. Would she crack apart if I told her of my failure; if I revealed my darkest secret? How would I feel? Would the truth set us free or destroy us?

"Rita...," I faltered.

"You don't want a child, do you?" she asked, her voice sad and flat. "That's why you didn't have children."

"No, no...it's not that. I do. Of course I do. Especially with you."

She sat up straight. Her eyes brightened. "God, Alan James. God, I love you for saying that."

I swallowed hard. "Rita..."

She brought her face close to mine. "Why so serious? You are always so serious, Alan James, and after all my hard work." She tried to lighten the mood.

"Rita...I have to tell you something. I should have told you, but I...well, I couldn't."

Her expression registered sudden fear. "You're not going through with the divorce, are you? You're not going to divorce your wife?"

"Of course I am. No, it's just that... Rita..." I released the imprisoned demons of failure, with a deep stuttering sigh. "Nicole and I didn't have kids... because there was a fertility problem... It was me. I was infertile. It broke us apart." Something in my chest, near my heart, ached. I paused to take a breath. "Something else would have broken us apart, anyway, but it was the infertility that finally did it. Nicole couldn't handle it. Hell, I couldn't handle it. There were so many alternatives we could have explored; so many other possibilities but...we couldn't do it."

My pulse quickened. I rose and stepped to the banister. I spoke in a contrite, nervous manner. "I was going to tell you but...I couldn't. I just felt so damn bad about everything. My marriage, my life... And I was afraid I'd lose you. I couldn't risk that. I can't lose you again."

I turned to gauge her reaction. Her eyes filled with questions.

"...But I'm taking a new medication and I'm exercising. I feel strong and healthy. I know things will be different with us. I feel it."

I waited for her swift disappointment and wrath. I waited, peering out into the warm darkness, feeling a mustache of perspiration form. I wiped it away.

When I finally faced her again, heart racing, Rita's eyes were uncertain, moving. Then she was calm, contemplating my words with disbelief, with a struggle to understand and even, perhaps, to forgive. But slowly, a vague compassion gleamed in her eyes that soon gave way to a bright illumination. She folded her hands; moved her thumbs and tipped her head in thought.

"She didn't love you enough, Alan James."

My eyes must have conveyed confusion.

"Don't you see? It won't be a problem for us, because I love you enough to make it happen. You'll help me and I'll help you. We love each other enough to have as many babies as we want, Alan James. Now, I'll stop talking and thinking about the past and you stop thinking about the past too. We're only going to think happy thoughts about the future. Happy and positive thoughts. Okay?"

I felt too much emotion to speak. I stared at her as the wind blew warm and soft across my face. I sat next to her, quiet and relieved.

Rita gave a little silent smile and I felt her head, sweetly heavy on my shoulder. "You know, Alan James, it was so smart of you to become a doctor. Think of the doctor bills we'll save."

I leaned and kissed her, feeling her gentle breath. That old Rita fever had returned.

Our lovemaking that night was patient and tender. A gentle wind ruffled the curtains as a smoky moon slid from purple clouds, crept across our window and dropped soft light across the floor. The bedroom was a sanctuary of peace.

CHAPTER EIGHT

Over the weeks, Rita's sleeping improved while my nights grew shorter and more restless. I dreaded leaving her every Monday morning to return to New York.

In June, I had rented a one-bedroom apartment on Riverside Drive, near Columbia University, but I spent very little time there. The weekdays were painfully slow and stubbornly demanding. The nights were lonely. I called Rita and invited her to visit, but she said she wasn't ready. She still needed the peace of the house and the support of Hartsfield.

I finally felt strong enough to meet with Nicole, at her request. We met for lunch in a Greek diner on West 68th Street on one of the hottest days of the summer. Heat shimmered off the streets and taxis, as weary citizens puffed along the sidewalks, wilted and damp. Stale cigarette smoke and exhaust lingered, cooked in the pot of steamy air, assailing the nose and eyes.

I waited for Nicole in a booth, on red plastic vinyl, sighing into a cold glass of water in an atmosphere of welcomed air-conditioning.

She arrived late and irritable from the weather. She flopped down into the seat and blew out a heavy, exhaustive groan, blotting her hot forehead with a tissue. "God, I hate this weather. Should have been in the Hamptons. Damned trial. I thought they were going to settle."

It was the weather that offered us a grateful common ground of conversation, allowing our racing pulses and anxious gazes to settle.

"Yeah, I never much liked summer," I said, "unless I was at the beach."

"Fall is your favorite season, isn't it?"

"Yeah…and yours is spring?"

"Yes…"

Nicole looked stunning, as though she'd just left the spa and the boutique, wearing a pale gray suit, blue blouse and pearl earrings. Her short hair was stylishly cut, her skin a deep golden brown.

I wore shorts and a T-shirt, having changed at the office before coming.

She looked at me vaguely, and then evasively, finally allowing her eyes to rest on her water glass. "I wish you would have returned my calls."

"I should have."

I folded my hands on the table and tried for calm, though I was repressing a towering anxiety. Seeing her again had accomplished everything I thought it would: it reawakened every raw and tender nerve.

She noticed my clothes for the first time. "Aren't you working today?"

"Yes. I changed. It's too hot to wear long pants. I have to be back by 2 o'clock."

"God, isn't it too hot?"

She ordered a tuna fish on rye and an egg cream. I ordered egg salad and a coke.

"Still the egg salad," she said.

"Yes... I know. You don't trust the egg salad to be fresh."

She glanced about. "Well, maybe they have a lot of turnover here. For your sake I hope so."

"Why did you want to meet in person, Nicole?" I blurted out, not wanting to prolong the ordeal. "Our lawyers can do all of this. We're not going to fight over money, the flat screen TV, the iPhones, the DVDs or the books..."

She cut me off. "...Because our last conversation was dreadful. I didn't want you thinking I was a heartless bitch."

"I didn't think that. I don't think that."

"It was a terrible day."

"It was."

"I've been so damned angry and confused. I've been confused for a long time."

"Me too."

"And when I played back all of the conversations of the last three or four months, I realized I sounded...well, like a horrible bitch."

"And I, a bastard... Is that the equivalent to bitch?"

"Son of a bitch, I think, although I loved your mother and wouldn't call you that, although I think I did a few times," Nicole said. "I wanted to be like her. I was sorry I only knew her for a year or so."

I watched the waiters scramble about, trying

to keep up with the lunch crowd. "Nicole... Look. Things just, I don't know, didn't work out."

"But I wanted them to, Alan! I wanted us to work out."

"So did I."

She twisted up her emotional mouth. "Dammit...I just...well. I didn't... I don't want you to hate me."

"I don't hate you. I hate what happened to us, but I don't hate you."

"Well, all our friends are siding with you. They're all saying that I was such a selfish bitch because I couldn't..."

I interrupted. "Then they're not friends, Nicole! Most of our 'so called' friends are losers anyway."

Her full brown eyes opened on me. "I tried, Alan. I tried as hard as I could... But I wanted our child. Does that make me a terrible person!? Can I help it if that's what I feel?"

"It was more than that, Nicole. You know it was."

"More?"

"You know it was. On some basic level, we never, I don't know, connected."

She seemed hurt by my words.

"Don't you think?" I added.

She pulled back. "No...No, I don't think that at all." She turned defensive. "I really don't agree with that. That's just...I don't..." she left her thought in the air.

I suddenly felt Rita's absence, and I shifted my weight.

"How didn't we connect?" she persisted.

I looked away, crossing my arms tightly across my chest. "I don't know."

"No, Alan, I want to hear this. It's important."

"It's over, Nicole. What does it matter?"

"It matters to me."

I shut my eyes and took a breath. "...Nicole...we should have been able to get through all of that stuff." I opened my eyes and narrowed them on her. "We should have. We should have been strong enough. Couples who really love each other and are committed should be able to find support in each other."

She flicked my words away with her hand. "I hate this 'should' bullshit. And you're still evading my question."

"I'm not on trial."

"Okay, just forget it then," she said, curtly. "I mean, we did the best we could...I know I did. I did everything I could and then some. Sometimes, things just don't work out and it's nobody's fault!"

I nodded, grateful for her response. "Yes...sometimes..."

We sat in a tense silence as our food was delivered and we took fretful bites.

Finally, I pushed my half-eaten sandwich aside. "You have a new life now. You're a partner...you have a new relationship."

Her eyes darted up at me, with surprise. "What relationship?"

"Come on, Nicole...I'm not an idiot. I know

you're with Walker. I knew you were with Walker back in April. Maybe even sooner."

She pushed her sandwich aside. "All right, look, it just happened, okay," she said defensively. "I didn't plan it. I didn't want it to happen like it happened… It just did."

"Okay…fine."

"I always hate it when you say 'fine' like that. 'Fine' doesn't mean anything."

"It means, get on with your life, Nicole. We're finished."

She fumbled for her purse; on edge and despondent. "I just wanted to meet…I didn't want to leave it like I left it." Her eyes filled with tears, as she looked at me. "We had so many wonderful times, Alan. We really did."

I reached for my coke, beating back emotion. "Yes…we did."

She examined me, closely. "I heard that you're seeing your old high school girlfriend. The one whose daughter was killed."

"Yes…"

"Have you been seeing her for a long time?"

"Not while you and I were trying to work things out."

She seemed relieved. She stood, staring into the floor. "Whenever you talked about her, your eyes would brighten. Did you know that? I was jealous of that."

I remained silent.

"I hope it works out for you, Alan. I really do."

I nodded, avoiding her eyes. "You too."

"Okay…Alright then. I really need to go."

I developed insomnia and spent hours pacing my room or reading old paperback mysteries, purchased from sidewalk book vendors. What would I do if I lost Rita again? What if she didn't get pregnant, regardless of our persistent love? So I prescribed myself a non-controlled substance to help me sleep. Silenor had worked in the past and its only side effect for me was constipation.

I continued my exercise routine, in New York and in Hartsfield.

I was deliriously happy and, at the same time, utterly terrified. I felt like a man on the run, dodging the inevitable bullet, hoping and praying that the medication, exercise, and positive thinking—all of my serious attention and discipline—would result in Rita becoming pregnant.

Rita was always waiting for me on Friday nights, wearing something naughty or sexy. I brought her necklaces and earrings from Tiffany's, perfume from Saks Fifth Avenue. I stunned and delighted her with a Cartier tricolor interlocking diamond ring, set in 18Karat gold. She wept when I slipped it on her finger.

Rita's body, ripened with love, invited love, glowed with a hunger to be filled with love; and so our love-making deepened, occasionally becoming a giddy madness or a high-spirited adventure when she created a saucy role or a playful new position.

She found new scents for her neck and hair, new lipstick, new sexy bras and panties. She cooked gourmet dinners, bought me shirts and underwear, and reawakened the house with her light spirit and flowers from the garden. She often escorted me on tours of the gardens where swelling tomatoes ripened, cucumbers lengthened and snapdragons and petunias blossomed. "Everything will ripen soon, Alan James. Very soon. Don't worry." She winked at me, knowingly. "I'm getting stronger and healthier."

We discussed marriage and agreed that as soon as the divorce came through, we'd have a simple, private ceremony at the Episcopal church Darla had attended. Rita felt comfortable with the minister, and I didn't want another lavish spectacle of a wedding, as my first had been.

Summer expanded us; freckled us; made us reckless with hope; frightened us and made the world incongruous. We braced ourselves against the heat, skipped through the lawn sprinklers in our underwear and fled from the thunderstorms and hard rain that swelled the pond and nearly flooded the cellar.

One Sunday morning, in late August, Rita awoke with a start. "Alan James..."

I stirred, wiping my eyes. "What?"

"I'm pregnant."

I got up to my elbows, startled. "What?"

She felt her stomach, flushed with joy. "I am. I know it. I feel it!" She grabbed my arm, holding it. "I am, Alan James! I'm pregnant! I told you we would. I told you it would happen, didn't I?"

"...Yes..."

"God, I feel it, Alan James!"

I swallowed anxiety. "Are you sure?"

"Of course I'm sure! I know my body. A woman knows when she's pregnant, Alan James. At least this woman does."

Rita bounced out of bed and hurried to the mirror. She was naked, breasts firm and round, body full and superbly majestic. She turned sideways to view her stomach in profile, rubbing it with her hand. "Just think, Alan James, in a few months, your woman's gonna be fat and beautiful."

She came to me in a rush, wrapping her arms around my neck, kissing me hard and long. "Alan James, another reason I love you so much is because I know you'll always love me, even when I'm old, wrinkled and stupid."

I reached for much-needed humor. "When you're old, yes. Stupid, yes. Wrinkled...never."

She playfully slapped my face. I grabbed her, pulled her down and kissed her. If Rita truly was pregnant, then it was worth all the sleepless nights and battering anxiety. In a flurry of nervous hands and scattered actions, Rita ran off and snatched her cut-off jeans.

"What are you doing?" I asked.

She pulled the jeans on. "Drug store. Pregnancy test."

"Rita..."

She stopped, looking quickly and intensely at me, with a sudden realization. "That's right. You're a doctor." She charged me, stopping inches from my face. "Should I buy one of those pregnancy tests?"

I was scared. I leaned back against the bedpost and shrugged one shoulder. "...I guess."

"Are they really that accurate? I mean, will we know?"

"Yeah, they're pretty accurate, but they can vary. I mean, the test has to be done right. You've got to check the package and make sure it's not past the expiration date...and you have to repeat the test in a few days, no matter what the results are."

Rita drifted away and found a yellow T-shirt. She struggled into it as she sat down next to me on the edge of the bed, conflicted. "I don't know then, maybe I should wait."

"Maybe... If you use the test too early, you may not have enough pregnancy hormone in your urine to get a positive result."

I saw fear well up in her eyes. "Yeah...right. I took one of those tests about eight years ago. I knew I was pregnant, but it came out negative the first time. I tried again a week later and it was positive. What about medication? Can that affect the results? I'm still taking some medication."

"No, it shouldn't, only if you're taking drugs that have hCG in them... but you're not, right? Well, I mean..." I fumbled, fighting to get the words out. "...I mean, they're used for treating infertility. I mean, I'm taking something, but you're not."

"No. I don't need that. I'm very fertile…used to be anyway." She faced me, worried. "You could give me a test, couldn't you?"

"Well…yes, but I don't have the right stuff with me. I'd have to take it to a lab."

"Would it be more accurate?"

I squirmed. I was too cautious and scared to be excited. "I'm not an OBGYN, Rita."

"But it would be more accurate?"

"…Yes. A blood test can measure the exact amount of hCG in the blood. It can tell if you're pregnant 6 to 8 days after you ovulate."

Rita folded her hands tightly in her lap. "So it becomes a simple yes or no? I am or I'm not."

I nodded. "That's right."

She drew a breath. "Okay, I'll go to the doctor tomorrow morning."

I stroked her hair. "I'll go with you."

Rita brightened. "Really? You won't go back to New York tonight?"

"No. I'll wait for the blood test. I'll ask your doctor to put a rush on it."

Rita shook her head vigorously. "No way, Alan James. I'll ask her. She's pretty. I don't want you two meeting."

She twirled in place, ecstatically happy. "Oh, Alan James, I feel alive again. I feel life growing in me again. I've got to give life again, nurture and protect it. It's my way back, don't you see. It's my way back to life!"

I swallowed. "Yes…"

"Back from the past; back from this town; back from the death I used to feel all around me. That damned depressive cloud."

She danced out of the room, leaving me in a ringing silence, feeling too heavy and clumsy to push out of bed. I didn't feel good. I didn't feel bad. I didn't feel anything.

CHAPTER NINE

Later that morning, I suggested we call Ms. Lyendecker. We needed a good distraction, both being edgy and anxious. Ms. Lyendecker was surprised and delighted to hear from us. She invited us over "for coffee" at three o'clock that day.

We said little while we drove the twenty-five miles along hot shimmering back roads and open land, as the recapitulation of summer was drifting toward the overture of autumn. We drove across a covered bridge and down a low road, nearly lost in shadows. I recalled, with a mounting dread, that the anniversary of Rita's tragedy was only two weeks away. If the pregnancy results were negative, I was deeply concerned that Rita could spin off into a towering depression and I would need to summon a strength I wasn't sure I possessed. We listened to the radio: an oldies station played Seals and Crofts' *Summer Breeze*.

We approached a little town, still and old in the afternoon hush. There was a country store with a sad-looking gas station, both closed, the white spire of a Methodist church, a red-bricked drug store, closed, an old cemetery surrounded with a heavy wrought-iron fence, and a group of two-story homes nestled in a sloping green valley across a six-foot rocky stream. I drove across a rattling wooden bridge, over the rushing water and flat stones, and followed Rita's pointing finger toward the gray shingled three-story house, near an open pasture with fieldstone fences. To the left of Ms. Lyendecker's home, beside a bank of tall trees, stood an old dilapidated and abandoned home. Crows hung out in the trees and on the rusty tin roof, like thick black blots of paint, cawing.

"How did she wind up here?" Rita said. "Didn't she grow up in New York City?"

We turned into the driveway, hearing the tires pop across the gravel, and stopped. Ms. Lyendecker appeared from the screen door, a hunched gray shadow, stepping gingerly down to the porch into sunlight, with the flat of her hand shading her eyes. She was snowy and stiff with age, wearing a blue and white cotton print dress and chunky black shoes. Wire-rimmed glasses were perched on her nose; blue-gray eyes peered at us, lively, bold and curious. We started toward her and she opened her thin arms wide, beaming with pleasure. "Come here, you two. Here's your little old English teacher."

She first hugged Rita and then me, with a trembling strength, smelling like coffee and rose. She escorted us into the house, an old comfortable place, neat, but shadowy, as if natural light were gradually retreating from it.

We sank into a deep cushioned couch, while Ms. Lyendecker insisted on serving coffee and cookies, and doing it independently.

"Not tea, mind you," she said, before she left for the kitchen. "Coffee. I don't drink tea and I don't keep it in the house. I don't even like the sound of tea. Coffee! It's a good strong word that draws a good strong image. You stress the first syllable though… CAW…fee. Tea is weak and flaccid and I don't like the color. I'll be back. You two sit."

Rita and I exchanged grins, as Ms. Lyendecker shambled off to the kitchen. We noticed the glinting green eyes of a black cat stalking us from behind a brown tweed recliner. Rita called to it, but the regal head ignored her.

The room was filled with bookshelves and books, all neatly stacked. The furniture was minimal, an afterthought. The tapestry green and brown couch we sat on was old but in fine shape; the ladder-back chairs near the fireplace were elegant, and the Burberry carpet, sturdy and functional. There were visible plaster cracks on the off-white walls, but the lack of cobwebs in the dim high corners, and the shiny window sills and end tables, all suggested that our teacher was still a good housekeeper. The Tiffany and Victorian lamps were undoubtedly antique, and my mother would have had a field-day examining them. Rita approached them with her newly acquired knowledge, and studied them, hands locked behind her back, head thrust forward in close examination.

"Good stuff," she said, impressed.

Ms. Lyendecker soon returned, shuffling toward

us with a silver tray that supported a silver coffee pot and various assortments of cookies. Rita helped her ease the tray to the coffee table before us. Rita poured coffee into gilded cups, while Ms. Lyendecker tossed treats to the black cat. We chose cookies and sat.

Ms. Lyendecker settled in the recliner opposite us and, as if on cue, her black cat sprang to the arm of the chair and hunkered down next to her, contented, half-hooded eyes glowing. In the country silence, the purring motor was loud.

Ms. Lyendecker adjusted her glasses and looked frankly at Rita. "You're prettier, Rita. You truly are."

Rita looked away, toward the fireplace. "I've got wrinkles, Ms. Lyendecker, and some gray hair. I'm not a girl of 18 anymore."

"No, you're not, Rita, nor am I. I am time grown old. A little ole' granny. I was once an attractive woman—not *very* pretty, like you, but attractive. I had boyfriends and lovers. I was married once, for four years."

Rita leaned forward. "What was he like?"

"Tall and serious. He was a history teacher."

"Did you have children?" Rita continued.

"Yes. One, a boy. He died at 3 years old of pneumonia. We didn't recover from it. We blamed each other. We grew bitter. We did not ascend."

"Ascend?" I asked, setting my cup down on the blue enabled coaster.

"Yes. When I first began teaching, I always required the class to memorize a very simple poem by John Greenleaf Whittier. I thought it set a good tone for the year. I stopped that requirement by the time you two came along. Anyway the poem says, 'I'll lift you and you lift me, and we'll both ascend together.' Howard and I divorced a few months later and we never kept in touch. I heard that he died about 10 years ago."

Her eyes held sadness, as they briefly roamed the room.

"Why did you move here?" Rita asked.

"This is my sister's house. She was sick and I came to take care of her. She died five months ago."

"I'm sorry," Rita said.

Ms. Lyendecker took a drink of coffee. "It was her time. She died peacefully. I have grown to love the place. It's so quiet and comfortable here."

"Do you have friends?"

"A few...A retired math teacher, Russ Horton, lives just a mile or so down the road. He comes by sometimes and flirts a little. He's two years younger than me." She winked at us. "I've always been attracted to younger men."

The room filled with the cat's rhythmic purr and the sound of coffee cups. Ms. Lyendecker's face softened. "Rita...I am truly sorry about what happened. It broke my heart. I sent you a card and a note, but I was sure you were not reading or wanting to receive anything."

Rita stared into her coffee cup. "I didn't read anything, Ms. Lyendecker. I couldn't."

"No one should ever have to go through such

a thing. Truly, no one, and I'm so sorry. But let's not speak about it. Let's delight in being in this wonderful company: my two favorite students." She turned to me. "What are you doing these days, Alan Lincoln? I heard you became a doctor and I was so sure you'd wind up in your father's business."

"No, he sold that about five years ago. It wasn't for me."

"So doctoring is for you."

"Yes."

"Do you like it?"

"Most of the time."

"Why did you become a doctor?"

"I liked the science."

"That's all?"

"I wanted success, security and money."

"Honest. And now?"

"Well I sometimes feel overwhelmed by the instability of it all: the prescription drug culture, the massive number of insurance forms, the ignorance and the politics, the communication or lack thereof..."

"Good. So you're not bored?"

"No ma'am."

"Are you writing?"

"No ma'am."

"I enjoyed your stories, Alan. You were always so intense—so driven to be the best and smartest student, and you were. Did you enjoy my class?"

"Yours and math were my favorites."

"And you, Rita? What are you doing with

yourself?"

Rita shrank a little and her voice dropped. "I'm working at Jack's Diner."

"Don't feel embarrassed by it, dear. When I see you now, so full of life and beauty, I see that you have come through the most difficult challenge of a life. It reminds me of another poem, and you know how I love to quote poets. I was never a gifted one myself, but I was always a gifted reader. Okay, Emily Dickinson:

> 'What I can do—I will—
> Though it be little as a Daffodil—
> That I cannot—must be
> Unknown to possibility—'"

Rita smiled at her gratefully. "...And you always inspired Alan James and me."

"Did you finish your degree, Rita?"

"No...I had to leave in my junior year. I'm hoping to finish it on-line at the Penn State World Campus."

"That's wonderful...What do you want to do?"

"I want to teach."

"You'll be a wonderful teacher, Rita."

"Alan James and I have also discussed turning the house—do you remember the Lincoln's house on Holly Lane?"

"Yes, of course. It was one of the most beautiful homes in the entire area."

"Well, we've talked about turning it into a bed and breakfast."

"A wonderful idea!" Ms. Lyendecker said,

happily, clasping her hands.

"It's just a thought," I said, "but I think my father and sister would love the idea. It would fill the empty rooms and give it new life."

Ms. Lyendecker inclined forward. "I would come and spend some time with you, Rita. Of course, I'd have to bring ten or twenty books. Which reminds me. What about your writing, Rita? Are you writing?"

"Little things here and there. I'm thinking about starting a novel."

"Good, good. You have talent, but then I told you that so many times. But it's hard work and it takes incredible discipline and, of course, a great deal of luck to get published."

We spent the next half hour listening as Ms. Lyendecker told us stories we'd never heard, about our classmates, about the principal's secret affairs and about her last few weeks of teaching, as retirement approached. After retirement, she had struggled over a sense of loss and confusion.

"I've had to learn who I was all over again. I've had to grow in ways I never wanted to," she said.

It was Rita who, after an eager silence, told Ms. Lyendecker that she and I were going to be married and that she was, almost certainly, pregnant. Ms. Lyendecker lit up and applauded us. She rose and kissed us both. I stepped awkwardly out of the room, with the excuse that I needed to use the bathroom. Inside, I stared into the round mirror, quietly cursing my self-doubt and fear.

I prayed again, to whomever—to any ineffable, benevolent being who might have happened by. "Please let Rita be pregnant."

Outside the house, as we stood near the car, Ms. Lyendecker ran her wizened hand across the shiny black hood, oooing and ahhhing. "Dr. Lincoln, I like your snazzy car," she said, with a girlish giggle.

Before we drove away, Ms. Lyendecker leaned into Rita's window. It was clear she wasn't ready to let us go. "Let me tell you about wrinkles, Rita. The other day I had nothing else to do and my damned curiosity grabbed me by the scruff of my skinny neck and dragged me into the bathroom. I counted every line and crease on my face. Is that eccentric, or what, as the kids say today? Guess how many?"

We both shrugged.

"Forty eight. Not bad for an old woman. I expected twice that many."

After we curved onto the main highway, Rita turned to me, smiling, with a relaxed expression. "It was so good to see her again, wasn't it?"

"Yes."

"It's been a good day, Alan James."

I took her hand and gave her a reassuring smile. "And tomorrow will be even better."

CHAPTER TEN

The next two days were blazingly hot and humid. In the mornings, Rita and I worked the gardens, wiping away sweat, longing for a breeze that never came. I squirted her with the garden hose, hoping to lighten our mood, but it only irritated her.

On the second afternoon, I spoke to the office, called a few patients and threw away some old clothes and books. After an uneasy nap, I worked in the cool wine cellar, sorting and noting which wines I'd box up and send to Dad and Judy. Rita worked at Jack's that day until seven. I waited for her on the back porch, sipping iced tea and listening to the katydids, whose presence signaled the end of summer.

On Wednesday, there were still no blood test results. Rita called her doctor, seething, and was assured that we'd have the results by Thursday afternoon at the latest.

Wednesday night I awoke from a fitful sleep to feel the empty bed. I found Rita outside on the porch swing, smoking. She was wrapped in a blue cotton housecoat, her legs tucked beneath her. It was a roasting night, with thick, lifeless air. Breathing was consciously labored. My bare feet stuck to the porch and, even in my briefs, shirtless, I perspired.

"Are you okay?" I asked, lingering 10 feet away.

Rita was in a dark mood. I sensed it more than I could see it.

"I haven't smoked in about 10 years."

"Rita… We'll know tomorrow…"

Her voice turned bitter. "I never smoked when I was pregnant with Darla. I stopped completely when she was four. Didn't drink either, and just in case you were wondering, I never slept around on Dusty. I never cheated on Dusty. Never. Not once. He cheated on me, more than once, but I never did—and I had offers from rich men and younger men, but I didn't. Couldn't. Darla came first. Always! I was a good wife. I wanted that family to work. Goddammit! I was a good mother!"

"I know you were."

"I was the best damned mother you ever saw!"

I watched the orange glow of the cigarette when she drew on it.

"What's the matter, Rita?"

"You should dump me, Alan James. I'm all fucked up."

I went to her. "Rita. Stop it. Don't say things like that!"

"I am!"

My swift pulse pumped waves of heat. "What's happened? Did you get the test results?"

"I don't need the fucking test results!"

"Rita…"

"Why the hell did you come back, anyway?" she said, savagely.

I crouched down in front of her, struggling to keep my voice calm. "Because I love you..."

She flipped the cigarette away, over the shrubs, and shot up. She burned past me. "Leave me alone, Alan James!"

I pushed up and went after her. I grabbed her right shoulder, spinning her around to face me. "Tell me what happened! What is the matter with you?"

Her face tightened with fury. "I took the home pregnancy test! I couldn't wait any longer. Guess what? I'm not pregnant!"

I drew up tall and forceful, more for me than for her. "It's not conclusive, Rita. You can't go by that. It could be completely wrong."

"You said it was ninety seven percent accurate."

"I also said it isn't always accurate. The blood test is more accurate. That's what I said."

"And what if it comes out negative? Then what?"

I fought to keep a clear head. "Rita...listen to me. Let's just wait until tomorrow, and then we'll deal with it. We'll handle it. We'll try again. We can always try again."

She pulled away, shaking her head. "Dammit, I can't stand this anymore! I'm going out of my mind. I hate this goddamn place. I hate this goddamn town and all the rotten memories. I hate everything that's ever happened here! I've got to get out."

I reached for her, drawing her into me, holding her, kissing her hair. "It's going to be all right, Rita.

Hold on just a little while longer. Just a little while longer. We're almost there."

I felt her shiver, yet her body was burning. "…He's back…"

I understood. I froze. "Your father?"

"Yes. He came by Jack's this afternoon."

I wanted to panic. "…What did he say?"

"The usual…insults. Said I looked like a slut. Said I was kidding myself living here with you. He was drunk and high on something. He said you were just using me, like men always have used me because I'm such a stupid fucking woman."

I held her back, gripping her shoulders firmly, staring deeply into her eyes. "He's sick, Rita. Don't even give him a thought. He's sick and you know it."

She was frightened, tears formed. "He threatened you, Alan. He said he was coming for you. He kept saying over and over again how you were using me; how you were going to leave me."

"Look at me, Rita," I said, giving her a little shake. "Look at me."

She did, with effort. "You know that isn't true."

"But he's coming for you."

I pulled a quick nervous breath. "Let him come. I'll handle him."

"He's crazy, Alan James! When he gets drunk, he's completely out of his mind! I've got to get away, Alan James. We've got to get out of here. I can't stand it anymore. I thought we could make a home here, but it's too late. Every damned ghost is here. Darla's here. Dusty's here. I stayed for her, for Darla, but I just can't do it anymore! We've got to get out, Alan James. Promise me. Promise me you'll take me away from here, when we get the test results. I don't want our baby to be born here."

"Sure. We'll move to New York. You'll love New York."

"No…I don't want to live in a big city. Let's go south or west. Any damn place."

I wiped her tears. "Okay…Okay, Rita, we'll leave. Whatever you want. Let's just get through tomorrow and then we'll figure it all out."

I gave Rita a sleeping pill and she was asleep in twenty minutes, lost in a blessed tranquility. I lay beside her until dawn, hands laced behind my back, rehearsing for the moments to come. As sunlight released the shadows of night and revealed the shapes of the room, I punished myself with self-incrimination. I should have taken her away. I should have sold the house and taken her away from all the old memories and pain.

And what if she wasn't pregnant? In my head, I rehearsed every line, expression and tone of voice to cover every possible outcome. I prepared alternatives: fertility specialists we could speak to; adoption agencies I had explored when I'd first learned of my condition; a vacation to Hawaii, the Caribbean or Italy or France. We would move immediately to anywhere in the world she wanted to go, whether she was pregnant or not. "We love each other, Rita, that's the most important thing," I'd say. "The rest we can get through. We will ascend,

Rita. We will."

We ate a late, silent breakfast. Rita's eyes were swollen, her face wan. I had the ragged low energy of the forlorn and defeated. Every time I started a conversation it fell flat. None of my practiced phrases seemed inspirational or intelligent: just the fragments of a selfish, pathetic and desperate man.

In the garden, the heat weakened us further, until we left it, retreating into the air-conditioned house, me again to the basement wine cellar, and Rita to frantic vacuuming.

I didn't hear Rita's cell phone ring, but something urgent took hold of me at about 1:15. It was a disconcerting strangulation of hope. I replaced a bottle of Bordeaux into the rack and hurried upstairs. I searched the rooms and found Rita on her knees in the library, staring deadly out at the pond.

"Rita..."

She didn't move or speak. I crept toward her, pausing three feet away.

"Rita..."

Her voice was lifeless. "Negative... The blood test was negative. I'm not pregnant. I imagined the whole thing."

I shrank in defeat and injury. We didn't move for minutes. We hardly breathed.

Rita finally rose to her feet, still staring at the hot line of sky and trees and the glare of sunlight on the pond. "I've failed you, Alan James. I've failed myself."

"No, no, Rita," I said, quietly. "No, you haven't. You haven't failed anybody."

She began to pace. "God is punishing me. No more kids, Rita Fitzgerald Palmer. You didn't protect your first. You killed your second with resentment and anger at your husband. You refused him your love and your body. You pushed him away when he came for you, needed you and wanted you, because he disgusted you with his weakness and his constant whining about how life had treated him so unfairly.

"'If I hadn't destroyed my knee, Rita, I would have made pro. If Dad hadn't drunk up all the money, Rita, we would have had so much success. If you had just believed in me, Rita, I mean really believed in me, just once, we could have really done something with our lives!'"

Rita stopped pacing and whirled toward me. She was burning with remembered hate. "I despised him, Alan James! I despised him in those last two years and I finally told him so. I told him that he sickened me! I told him how he frightened Darla! I told him he had destroyed us! I told him to get out and leave us alone! And he did! He did!! He left for a while. But he came back that Sunday morning. He came back..."

Her shoulders sagged. Her eyes drifted up, then down to the floor. She drew a long resigned sigh. "So, I've been punished again. Finally, punished. No more children. No more family."

She looked at me with regret. "I'm sorry, Alan...

Ja...." Her voice fell away into despair.

I stood utterly motionless and ruined. "No, Rita. It's not you. We both know that. It's not you. It's my fault."

She turned away.

I continued, shaking. "It isn't. God isn't punishing you. I am. I should have taken you away from here. Right from the beginning. I should have."

My voice was urgent. "We can try again, Rita. We can keep trying. It's only been three months or so. There are so many things we can do. Easy options and solutions. Artificial insemination, in vitro, adoption. We can have kids, Rita. We can have a fami..."

She turned and in her eyes I saw a savage misery. She wilted into deep sorrow. She threw up a strong hand to stop me; shaking her head, entranced by pain. "No... Alan...James..." her voice fell to the floor in quiet defeat. "I know that now. I'm being punished."

I started for her. "No, Rita! It has nothing to do with being punished. We just have to keep trying, that's all. You've got to keep believing in us. It will happen...!"

"Believing in us?!" she yelled, strongly. "Believe!" she shouted. "That's what Dusty said! The same damned thing, Alan James!" Her face tightened in pain. "I was stupid. I trusted again. I trusted us. I trusted you just like I trusted Dusty. 'Just give us more time, Rita, and everything will work out.' I didn't leave Dusty when I should have and look what happened."

I felt a driving panic. "I'm not Dusty, Rita. You know that!"

Rita's face was set in a fire of determination, anxiety edging forward. "I can't do it anymore, Alan James. I've got to get out of here. Out of this town. I should have left after Darla—never moved into this house! Never called you back here."

I blinked fast against her painful words. "...Rita...don't..."

She turned sharply and started for the door. I went after her. She stopped in the doorway and whirled to face me—to stop me. Her eyes were firm, face taut with hurt. "We can't go back, Alan James. We tried our best, but we can't. Let's just face it. Our relationship ended years ago. It died when I went off with Dusty."

"No, Rita. We've just started. You can't say that these last three months haven't meant anything. You can't!" I pleaded. "We have a new life now."

I felt her retreat from me. I saw the fire leave her eyes. I strained for the right words. "Rita, we love each other. We will help each other. We will get through this. We'll move somewhere. Anywhere. We'll start again. We'll do whatever it takes."

Her voice was soft and beseeching. "Let me go, Alan James. Please let me go. I can't stand this place anymore. I can't look at it, remember it... I can't look at you anymore, Alan James. You're the past. The past that died when Darla died. The past that will never let me forget... You've got to let me go."

I shivered. "I can't, Rita. I can't do that."

She came toward me. She lifted her hand, gently brushing my cheek. "Yes. Let me go, Alan James... Please... let me go...If you truly love me... let me go."

The gap between us grew, as she backed away, holding me in her grieving eyes. I kept my eyes on her. She turned and started for the front door. I took two impulsive steps toward her, and then froze with a little jolt. I inhaled, sharply, hearing an inner scream—a rant against the impossibility of the moment.

I heard the front door close; heard the car engine turn over; heard the motor die away in the still afternoon, leaving me in an agony of silence.

CHAPTER ELEVEN

In the wine cellar, I drank a 2003 Cabernet Franc that Dad had brought back from the Jefferson Vineyards on his last trip to Monticello. I was crouched in the corner, knees up to my chest, sipping the fruity wine from an opulent crystal glass. I tasted red berries, spice and flowery aromas. It would go nicely with chicken, pasta or a light beef dish.

I recalled my father once telling me how much Thomas Jefferson loved the wines of Bordeaux. He'd invested in an Italian winemaker, whose name I couldn't recall, and in 1774, this Italian fellow bought 400 acres of Virginia land adjoining Monticello. His sole purpose was to build a house, start a vineyard and make wine. Jefferson had attracted famous investors, including George Washington.

Unfortunately for the Italian fellow, the Revolutionary War ended his efforts to make wine and it wasn't until the early 1980s that the owners of the old property resurrected the vineyards and made the dream come true. I was sipping part of that dream, and the wine was good. I'd ship some off to Dad before Thanksgiving.

At sunset, I was nearly drunk when I piled into my car and drove off in a flair of fishtailing and squealing rubber. I took the back roads, leaning into the curves, dropping low into the hills, skimming the crests, bouncing, yelling and screaming at the sinking sun, like a mortally wounded animal. I drove for hours, losing time, plunging into the darkness with a careless speed, confident that there was no danger in this aggressive driving—assured of my safety because, as the song goes, *"Only the Good Die Young."*

When hunger gnawed, I pulled into Big Joe's Truck Stop, but didn't go in. I stared, blankly, suddenly unable to move. I sat there for a time, watching the great semi's rumble on; watched the drivers wander by with ball cap bills pulled low, working tooth picks or pulling on a cigarette. I watched them swing up into their cabs, start their engines and crank through the singing gears as they jolted heavily toward the interstate highway.

I wanted to go with them, befriend them, talk of travels, trucks, and women who were waiting anxiously in some distant honky-tonk bar. I wanted to listen to country music and drink beer. I wanted to travel to some unknown spot, tug on that airhorn and take the steep hill, yanking through those stubborn gears. I wanted to be anywhere but where I was. I wanted to be a truck driver.

I drove to the Holiday Inn where Rita and I began our final date. It was still there, looking much like it did fifteen years ago. I parked and got out, cursing the stifling heat, leaning back against the car, feeling its fever. There was no motion in the air. I pushed away and fought a mosquito.

Looking up at the green neon sign, I focused on HOLIDAY. I wondered where Rita would go. South to Florida? West to California? Maybe to Canada? I kicked across the parking lot, taking in the still glass-enclosed swimming pool, remembering.

I'd have to change my life, too. I'd sell the house, leave the practice in New York and maybe start a fellowship in cardiology at Harvard. Maybe I'd do something trite, like others do after a breakup, and travel for a while. Where? Maybe I'd leave medicine altogether and find a new career. What?

At first, I was only vaguely aware of the sirens. They were just insinuations, cutting in and out of the counterpoint of thoughts and memories. But they drew near, startlingly close and dominant, finally seizing my full attention. They were wobbling alarms, piercing the night with fear, as a hook-and-ladder truck raced by on the interstate below. I heard others in the distance, echoing an instant emergency.

I fumbled with the car door and, once inside, strapped myself in and shot away. I drove with deliberate speed, following the trail of sweeping red lights and harsh pumping horns, off the Hartsfield exit, onto the two-lane road that led to the house, swerving and passing the leisurely traffic. I was caught by the incarnate horror of a half-recognized thought that I'd suppressed and locked away. I heard the converging cacophony of wailing sirens just up the road and smelled acrid smoke. I shoved the pedal to the floor, tearing across the shoulder of the road, passing slow curious traffic.

When I saw a bright smudge on the horizon, like the slow rising of an orange flickering moon, I knew. I had forgotten to reset the house alarm. Traffic snarled, slowed and stopped. I pulled up on the right shoulder and cut the engine. I bolted from the car, slid down a rocky embankment and raced across the dark wildflower field, heaving in hot dry breath. My chest burned, I felt tears, I sprinted up the hill, stumbling—hit the path that led to the pond—broke through the trees and stopped dead, gasping at the sight.

The house was engulfed in flames. Cobalt smoke columns billowed from the angled bay windows. Ugly red teeth devoured the gabled roofs; licked at the turrets and lively facade. Fire engulfed the porch, the gingerbread trim, the ornate spindles and spandrels. It swarmed the shrubs and the helpless trees.

I charged ahead in a dead run, lengthening my stride, struck dumb by the shock, sure that I could help save the house somehow. Most of the family albums were there; mom's and dad's letters to each other when he was in the Navy. My old yearbooks, short stories; my high school and college diplomas, most of the antiques still not sold! All of the loves, hates and confusion of lifetimes were in that house!

I could at least save a floor, a room—preserve some small part of the past that had given me life, guidance and definition. I could save my mother's memory, my father's old books and wine, rescue those last hopeful nights with Rita, when I'd believed.

But I was blocked and wrestled to the ground by a hard, stocky fireman, who shouted phrases I didn't hear. Heat poured over us in waves, hurting and angering us. The smoke stung my eyes with tears. Two firemen heaved me up and dragged me off toward the pond, dropping me in a defeated heap. I watched helplessly.

Firemen, gray frantic shadows against the spreading blaze, attacked the fire, tugging hoses, stomping through the gardens, hacking through walls, slamming down doors and shattering glass. I watched it on my knees for a time as the hoses, like huge tentacles, crossed and sprayed streams of water, in hopeful, terrible and, finally, fruitless action.

As the roof buckled and plunged and the walls collapsed into great sweeping plumes of fire, and as I heard ringing shouts of fright and warning, I struggled to my feet. I stood firmly, bravely. I stood for a long time. I stood until the house smoldered and died. I stood drenched with sweat, beaten and lost, unable to call down any guidance from the gods, or the ancestors.

I sat by the pond until dawn and finally fell asleep there.

Part Three
Ascension

CHAPTER ONE

During the autumn, I worked five mornings a week at the hospital and five afternoons at the office. I volunteered at a homeless shelter on Saturday and a free clinic in the Bronx on Sunday. I slept only three or four hours a night.

"You look tired," Megan, one of my hospital colleagues said, as we passed in the hallway, on the way to collecting our next patients. She was kind, soft-spoken and lovely. Megan had a child, Tyler, who had just turned two; Nicole and I had spent some time with Megan, her husband, Paul, and Tyler before we split up.

"I'm good," I said, with a syrupy smile.

Megan stared doubtfully, from behind her concerned aqua blue eyes. "Alan…you look terrible. I can barely see your eyes and you've lost weight. Let's not belabor the obvious: you never took time off when you should have and you're working too many hours now. Are you sleeping at all?"

We paused at the door, before entering the reception. I beat back a yawn with my hand. "I think that probably means, no."

Megan laid a gentle hand on my shoulder. "Alan…take some time off. We can cover for you."

"Not now. Maybe later."
"You've got the classic symptoms, you know."
"Of what?"
"Self-punishment. Guilt."
"I deserve them."
"Need I say it: and self-pity."

I fingered the stethoscope that was wrapped about my neck. "You know it's funny, I woke up this morning and I remembered something I wrote in my diary when I was in high school. I wrote it just after a girl named Rita, left me for another guy:

> I want to return to the 'Big Bang' of my life, just before everything exploded, expanded, and scattered in obfuscation and affect. I will accomplish this by starving these damned adolescent emotions and silly orbiting thoughts of desire and guilt."

Megan smiled. "And you're starving yourself, too."

I winked with dark amusement. "I am growing in wisdom, stature, and strength, like a resolute monk, whose reward will be a stupendous enlightenment—an authentic discovery of the simplicity of living and being. I am abnegating the throne of self-aggrandizing obsession and willful egocentric living to become good and wise. And that, Dr. Megan Corcoran, takes sacrifice."

"And you, Dr. Alan Lincoln, are full of bullshit

and I have no idea what you're talking about." She shook a finger at me. "Take some time off and stop thinking so much!"

But I pressed on, until my tenuous outward warmth was eroded by combustible emotions.

I shouted at reception for the least mistake: the wrong chart was pulled; a referral was forgotten; an insurance form was lost. My somber dignity turned to self-righteous indignation. Friends stopped calling and that was just fine with me.

My sister called several times, inviting me to Florida for Thanksgiving. When I finally returned her call, I told her I was too busy.

"Busy doing what?" she asked.

"Does everything I say warrant a cross-examination, Judy?" I said, sharply. "I'm working at a homeless shelter, for God's sake. There are people out there who are starving and scared and poor, okay! Somebody has to help them. Everybody can't just stay locked up in their gated communities and comfortable multimillion dollar condos and pretend that everything is just great! Just grand! Just fucking marvelous! Can they?! Somebody has to…"

I heard the dial tone, loud and final. I slammed down the receiver, fuming.

A week before Thanksgiving, I heard the alarm. I went to reach for it, to turn it off; to rise and start the day. But I was paralyzed. The alarm was in my head, ringing frantically, and I couldn't turn it off. The bedroom was dark, like the darkest cave in deepest earth. I was wet with sweat. I felt as if an elephant were sitting on my chest. Through clenched teeth, I painfully and desperately gasped for air. I was sure that I was having a massive heart attack. The alarm screamed on.

I struggled to move a finger, toes, anything, but I was a frozen block of terror. Death would surely come swiftly, I thought. It would rip me away from my goal, and I had not become perfect. I had failed. I had not passed any of the tests. I had not healed anyone. I had failed them all.

I saw their floating liquid eyes clearly—all the eyes of all the patients I had ever treated, drifting by me, over me, looking at me searchingly, with pity. I tried to find the voice to assure them that there was more time—that I could still find the true efficacious medication, technique or diagnosis that would heal them—save them—but I couldn't speak, and so I watched and listened to them. I listened to their weak, insistent voices pleading for help and begging for a cure.

I saw medical charts blowing past the foot of my bed, like leaves, with boldly written words: HE COULDN'T BARE HIS PAIN, and WHY CAN'T YOU FIND THE CURE, DOCTOR?

Infinite moments pulsed, as faces slid by, like projected slide images on the wall, until a final image appeared, lingered and spoke. It was Rita. She gave me a critical glance from a gorgeous face. She gave a forlorn sigh. "Alan James...Did you really believe? Did you? We don't want to join your unhappy little circus. Your little crusade is just another silly ride on the Ferris wheel of life."

And then she was gone.

At first light, easier breaths cooled some of the fear and lifted the heaviness. I lifted an arm, a leg. Five minutes later, I stood precariously with a racing heart, bracing myself with my hands crabbing along the wall, until I sank into the nearest chair. I leaned back, remembering only vague fragments of Rita's words. I strained to remember, but they fell away into an incoherent echo, and then plunged deep into my subconscious, like a rock in black water. They returned later and I wept.

I couldn't go to work that day, nor the next. I slept and ate little. I missed Thanksgiving altogether and didn't make it to the homeless shelter.

A week later, I arrived in Florida with the intention of staying only a couple of days. From there, I had booked a flight to Barbados, where I was going to spend as many weeks as I needed to recover.

Judy was still livid at me over our previous conversation and over the total destruction of the house. I listened, humbly resigned, as she closed the door to Dad's room and returned to me in the kitchen. She threw me all her unexpressed anger, which she javelined at me for 30 minutes. I'd never given her the chance on the phone. I'd hung up on her twice.

"That was my inheritance, too, Alan. It was so irresponsible to let that woman stay there. She came from a loony family. I mean, God forgive me my rightful anger here, but what in the hell were you thinking about?"

"We'll get more from the insurance than we'd have gotten from the sale, Judy," I said, dimly.

"That's not the point and you know it."

"You didn't want the house, Judy. You wanted the money. Okay, so you'll get money. Plenty of it."

Judy fumed.

The great kitchen was a gleaming canary yellow, with a skylight and generous windows that looked out on a peaceful rolling golf course, where her husband, Greg, was playing golf. He had escaped, knowing good and well that Judy was going to blast me. The kids were with neighbors, and their latest scribbled artwork was magneted to the gleaming yellow refrigerator.

Judy was thin, fit and high strung, with short, tight ash blond hair and a tight thin mouth. She had the friendly assuredness and good-natured smile of a Weather Channel expert and the energy of a sprinter. She was always in motion, as if the clock was running down and the game was nearly lost. Some thought was always spinning—some project hovering—and she balanced them all expertly like a happy juggler, looking over her shoulder for the next challenge. Because of this, the kids were never bored and Greg, a more relaxed and easy-going fellow, often appeared breathless and slightly startled, as if he were waiting for the next inside fast ball from his wife.

Judy stood by the sink, right foot tapping the floor and sparkling blue-gray eyes rolling with irritation. "It has been three months now and I am still in shock. I still wake up from nightmares and anger over this! I just hate it, Alan! I hate it! I'm devastated. And I have to lie to Dad and open his mail so he won't read the cards and newspaper clippings his friends are sending every other day. It would kill him, Alan. It would just kill him if he knew he'd lost his true home and all those things he'd collected and loved. It would just..." she stopped, throwing up her hands in vexation.

She tossed a newspaper clipping down on the table in front of me. "This one came this morning. It's two weeks old, and people we haven't spoken to in years are sending them. God only knows how these people get our address."

It was from a Pittsburg paper. I scanned the article.

> *In a bizarre story of love and revenge, fire engulfed an historic Victorian home in Hartsfield, Pennsylvania...*
>
> *At first, arson was suspected, but police found no evidence to support this suspicion. They only know that the fire started on the first floor. It was learned that the owner of the house, Dr. Alan Lincoln, and his live-in girlfriend, Rita Fitzgerald Palmer,*

had had a bitter argument the day of the fire. The police searched for Rita, but quickly discovered from her mother that Rita had left town the same night, after quarrelling with Frank Fitzgerald, her father, whose whereabouts were unknown.

The FBI was called in and, two days later, Rita was found on Interstate 70, her car broken down by the side of the road near Lawrence, Kansas. She was arrested and taken to the local police station. While she was being questioned, investigators discovered a charred body in the basement of the Lincoln house, near the location of the wine cellar. The identification was made through dental records: it was Frank Fitzgerald.

A stack of unopened wine bottles was found next to a rosebush garden. Most likely, detectives said, Frank was hurriedly stealing the wine from the cellar, when he was either overcome by smoke or trapped by falling debris. How the fire actually started is still a mystery and, according to Fire Chief McCann, "We may never know what really caused the fire."

There was an 8 million dollar insurance policy on the house.
Ms. Fitzgerald Palmer was released and her whereabouts are unknown.
Dr. Alan Lincoln returned to New York City, where he practices medicine as a general practitioner.

I pushed the clipping aside and folded my arms.

"It's so humiliating, Alan. I just despise everybody in the world knowing about this. Knowing about our personal lives and our money."

"Hey, we're providing a nice living for the journalists and bloggers."

"Don't be sarcastic."

"Whatever."

"And don't be flippant about this, Alan. I'm just so disappointed in you. It's just unthinkable that you let this happen. All my friends have been texting me and e-mailing me.... It just...Just...."

I stood, weary of the conversation. "Okay, fine... I'm sorry, Judy, I really am, but there's nothing I can do about it... And I'm leaving."

Judy lifted a perfect eyebrow. "What do you mean, leaving? You're staying for two days."

I shook my head. "No...I need to be alone."

Judy started toward me. "Alan, don't do this. Don't make me feel terrible."

"Judy..." I said dropping my arms to my sides with frustration, "I'm going to go spend some time with Dad and then I'm leaving. I'm tired of hearing about this, talking about it, thinking about it. I'm fed up, okay."

Judy scratched her ear, softening. She reached for a bottle of water and drank. After she'd replaced the cap she faced me. "Alan…has the divorce come through?"

I nodded. "Signed, sealed, and delivered. I'm not her man anymore. Nicole is going to marry the guy she's been with for a while."

Judy's glance traveled the room, finally resting on me again. "Please stay for a day. At least for a day. You haven't seen the kids in so long."

"I don't want to see kids." I snapped.

"Alan. Don't say that."

"Rita…" I heard the name fill the room. I quickly recovered, embarrassed. "…I mean…Judy…" Then more quietly, "Judy…I need to go. It's not the kids or you. I'm just tired. I need to rest and think things over. You know I love the kids. You know that. You know I love you."

Judy drew in a long breath and released the words on the exhale. "All right, Alan. Go visit Dad. He was really looking forward to seeing you."

Dad was in his wheel chair, folded slightly forward, half asleep, his nose making a little whistling sound. He wore navy blue cotton pants, a white cotton shirt and sneakers. He still wore his wedding ring. His moist eyes found me. In them, I thought I recognized borderline worlds: old memories looping; astounding things remembered;

glorious visions soaring in a high noon sky, too well remembered but too painful to let go. His eyes dimmed. The visions fell from lofty flight, through the dark clouds of present bewilderment, and into the quiet low dusk of evening.

The room was a cheery robin egg blue, with a cream-colored carpet, a medical bed, plenty of CDs, some audio books, a wide screen TV and, on his dresser, framed photographs of the family. There was plenty of sunlight from the windows and there were fresh lilies scenting the room. Judy truly was a saint.

The photos showed the four of us seated under the Christmas tree in the living room, wearing red and green sweaters, corduroy pants, and broad smiles; standing by the pond in summer, subdued and casual after a long day in the gardens; and standing tall and gleaming, in formal dress, beside my mother's blossoming roses, after Judy's wedding.

There were two large photos of mom. One captured her wry humor; the other, her refined features, luscious long auburn hair and indulgent lips. She was probably twenty five.

"Hey Dad," I said, softly.

He nodded. "Son..." His voice was thin, eyes vulnerable, his countenance, humble and frightened.

I found a chair and sat opposite him. "Sorry it's been so long."

"...Busy?"

"Yeah."

Dad lifted his left arm, shaking. His right arm was frozen, dead. His hair was cotton white and thinning on top. "Skinny... too... skinny."

"Yeah, I've lost weight. I'll gain it back." I paused. "Judy said you're improving. Said you've been working with a speech pathologist and a physical therapist."

He shrugged his left shoulder. "Wasted... money...time."

I searched for an attitude, and pushed at a smile and a bright tone. "Your color is better. Must be working. Your speech is good... and I think you've gained some weight. Judy's a great cook."

He saw through my bad performance. "Nicole?"

"Fine. Doing fine."

"Divorced?"

"Yes."

"A...shame. Good... kids you know...no kids... there."

"Yeah...it's good we didn't have kids," I clarified.

"Liked her."

"So did I. It happens."

He stared with attentive seriousness. "You... work...you work at it. Got to work... at it."

I kept my voice even. "Yeah...we did, Dad. We worked hard at it. Things just...go a different way sometimes."

He shivered.

"Are you cold?"

His sagging mouth was set in a frown, as he weakly shook his head. Saliva trickled from his mouth. I reached for a tissue, stood and wiped the sticky dribble. "Surgery?" he forced out. "Surgery…" he repeated, straining for words and thoughts.

"Me?"

He nodded.

"Oh, you mean have I started my cardiology fellowship?"

His eyes opened wider in affirmation.

"Haven't given it much thought recently."

"…What…. waiting for?"

I searched for warmth in his eyes, but saw accusation. They were crystal clear, more so than I'd remembered since my last visit. His professional suavity and careful breeding had been stripped away, leaving behind the frankness and entitlement of a patriarch. His eyes burned at me. "Become… something…" he said. "Lincolns become…" his voice fell away and his body shook with frustration because he couldn't find the words to finish the thought. But he saw that I understood his stern meaning.

Dad's articulate and refined communication style had always marshaled carefully chosen words loaded with inference and subtext. I'd learned to understand and obey him that way. This "new" direct style was a little off-putting.

"Yes… Yes, Dad, I will be applying to Harvard soon."

His face pinkened. His left eye watered. "House? Selling….it?"

I gave him a swift glance, and then looked at the

flowers. "House is fine, Dad. No, I'm not selling it. No plans to."

His chest sank a little in relief. "… Good…"

We listened to the silence. I couldn't think of another single thing to say.

"A girl… friend?" he finally asked.

"No, Dad. No girlfriends. Just work."

He lowered himself and his eyes, as if to close the door and end the visit. I stood and leaned, and put a gentle hand on his shoulder. "You sleep now. It was good to see you."

He reawakened and found my eyes. He blinked lethargically. "Son. Glad. It's… good… you came by."

I felt so far away from him and it saddened me. "I'll be back at Christmas."

I left the room, closed the door and leaned back against it, hearing the kids' voices rising excitedly, as they ran into the house.

CHAPTER TWO

Under the baking Caribbean sun, I strolled the blanched beach like a pilgrim, wide-brimmed straw hat tied firmly under my chin. My T-shirt billowed, and my feet cooled as they caught the edge of the tide. Even with sunglasses, my eyes were stunned by the explosion of light, the turquoise glass of the sea and the sugar-white beach. I passed a string of yellow bungalows, with vivid orange shutters. I took a path through palms, which arched high and away from the sea, like tall runway models, pausing, swaying, with feathered hats and too much attitude.

I wandered by couples in embrace, and passed families, kicking at sand, building with sand, rolling in sand, and skittering across the hot skillet of it, dashing from beach umbrellas and candy-colored towels, heading to the beach bar for a drink or snack. I saw glistening bodies turned boldly to the burning day, seeking the tattoo of color to tempt a lover, to change the facade, or perhaps to shed the old skin without exposing the heart.

Skin cancer didn't exist here and never would. It simply wasn't allowed. Life was eternal in this most elegant of islands, where trade winds send enchanting breezes to tempt the skin, heal the mind and stir the heart. And so I mended toward wholeness, trotting away from the beach, toward my hotel.

It took five days to find the near perfect pitch of the place; to match the metronome of my body with the rhythms and themes of spreading peace, rising sun, and curling sea; to be conducted by the downright languid largo of the night music.

Nicole and I had come here for a vacation more than a year before, roaming the beaches, hand in hand, like real lovers, discussing law, medicine, and politics. We sought approbation in the eyes of waiters and affluent guests who were staying at Villa Nova, one of the top new hotels. We were excited to learn that Elton John had just left and were disappointed when told that Madonna would arrive a few days after our departure.

We called friends back home, high from rum and sun, and described the 28-room country house that lay elegantly among fig trees, wrapped in extravagant tropical gardens. We described the view of rippling cane fields and sleepy villages. We described it all to ourselves as we drove to Sam Lord's Castle, and sought exaltation in each other's eyes, as we gave ourselves this exciting, idyllic "presentation."

Alone now, kicking at the sand, reflecting, I clearly perceived that inside, Nicole and I had already begun to create new presentations, with bullet points such as "What Is Happening to Us?" "Is There an Effective Antibiotic for This Dying

Relationship?" and "Who Really is(are) the Guilty Party(ies) Here?"

I did not wish to stay anywhere near Villa Nova this time.

The hotel I had chosen was a series of high and low painted buildings: turquoise, peach and purple. From a distance, they reminded me of tropical fruit drinks. Color simply vibrated. Red, yellow, and ivory flowers cascaded over walls and balconies, spilling onto landscaped paths and gardens, rich with exotic frangipani, bougainvillea and golden apple trees. At night, on the patio terrace where I ate dinner, the candlelight, the smooth rasp of the sea, and the gathering sugary scents all merged in the gentle scattering breeze. A drenching moonlight speckled the sea, making life unbearably romantic.

As I sat in the black leather piano bar, I thought of Rita with a brand new kind of aching love. My eyes took in the hanging Japanese lanterns, and the huddled couples. I listened to the gentle lap of the sea. I listened to a black female pianist/vocalist, spotlighted behind a shiny grand piano, singing, *IF I HAD YOU*. I was slumped over a brandy near an open window, attuned to the breathy alto, as she played low, dejected chords, and caressed each phrase with a heavy longing.

> *I could show the world how to smile.*
> *I could be glad all the while.*
> *I could turn the gray skies to blue,*

If I had you.
I could leave my own day behind,
Leave all my pals and never mind.
There is nothing I couldn't do,
If I had you.

On the sixth day, I began writing to Rita, and continued twice a day for a week. But I didn't finish a single letter. By the middle of the third week, I began a short story. Maybe it would take us back—way back to Jack's diner and our first date. I wrote enthusiastically by the sea under a flapping beach umbrella. By the end of the week, I paced the beach with it, wrestling every word, every verb and noun and, finally, on Monday, I threw the story away.

I stayed another week and began another story, but this one was no better than the first. I ripped it up, just like they do in the movies, tossed it into the waste basket and wandered down to the beach bar.

She wasn't a beauty. Her name was Wendy Ketching. She was bronzed, buxom and from Atlanta, Georgia. Spreading in the hips, with a bit of a tummy, her neon red skimpy bathing suit suggested she was comfortable with her less than classic proportions; her take-it-or-leave-it insouciance was attractive, even if her face was a bit hard, her dyed blond hair damaged, and her husky voice suggestive of vocal nodules. She was no more than twenty-five or twenty-six.

"A doctor? Wow," she said, drinking from a long-stemmed beer bottle. "New York? Wow," she continued, sizing me up, with some interest. Maybe it was my wide-brimmed straw-hat. "Never been there...Big. Loud, I think. But I love watching the ball drop on New Year's Eve."

Her parents owned a bar, where she bartended. She'd gone to college and took a degree in business. "We're going to open another place down in West Palm Beach, and I'm going to run it," Wendy said, with pride.

Two of her girlfriends came over, laughing and fluttering. One was thin and tipsy, the other, heavy, with a bountiful sense of dark humor. I liked the heavy one the most. We talked about beer, about the sea and about nothing.

By late afternoon, Wendy lay next to me on the beach, her glistening buttery breasts loose in those obliging cups. After three beers, her eyes hazed over, and she grew restless with obvious desire. "I can't believe you're alone," she said. "You staying here? We're leaving tomorrow...my last night." She drew a happy face in the sand. "I've been kinda bored. First time here. I'm not sure I'd come back. Maybe Jamaica next time. We heard they have a lot more parties and young people there. ...I'm going to tell all the barflies back home that I've had a hell of time. Parties and booze...well, you know."

Her friends splashed in the sea and left us alone. They had obviously worked a code.

Forty-five minutes later, we were in my room, fitted together, ramping, bodies greased and gritty from sand. She was high and eager, throwing her hips and breasts into the driving sex.

I sensed a near miss had been avoided. She'd paid her money, planned and dreamed the vacation, with all of those romantic days and nights with Mr. Right or Mr. Sexy. But, until now, she had come up empty, feeling shut out and sexually orphaned in this tropical paradise. She had not been plucked, like those exotic flowers and fruits; she had not been smelled or tasted. Not until I'd come along.

Surely I was not in her original, or even in her revised, vacation dreams; surely not the best or the worst, but a doctor after all, and from New York, she'd probably reasoned. It would add stature and appeal to her back-home bar stories, told in little whispers, with waitresses leaning close, but imparted with enough volume for the sexy man with the roving eye to hear, whose roving eye had never before landed on her. I could hear the embellished story—launching quiet, lurid excitement into the smoky air: I was handsome and, perhaps, I owned a 60-foot yacht that, at sunset, we had sailed to Mustique and Basil's Beach Bar, where some famous rock group had just happened to be hanging out.

I sensed that her body's abandoned force was making up for the two-month anticipation and four-day package that hadn't, until now, paid off.

My passion was lonely, angry, and bitter. When it was over, I lay flat—deadened—as if shot through. She kissed my lips, a chilly kiss, and then spoke about a party somewhere down on the beach and did

I want to come. I declined. She dressed and left the room. The next morning Wendy was gone, without a word. I'd sent her a rose and a little note.

> *Wendy:*
> *Thanks. It was a Caribbean delight.*
> *Alan Lincoln*

I sat alone on the beach for another week, trying to write the worthy story that I could send to Rita. It never came to fruition.

I spent Christmas with Judy and returned to work in January. The first weeks were difficult, and my colleagues were supportive and watchful. Insomnia returned but I took sleeping pills. I applied to Harvard and made an extra effort to meet friends for dinner, movies, and the occasional party. I realized that when loneliness and regret procreate, the mind grows new weeds that clog the field and choke the flowers. I was still trying to yank up and burn the old ones.

When I heard that Nicole was married and pregnant, I went to see a therapist.

Dr. Marina Raskoffsky was Russian, and although she'd lived in the United States from the age of 10, she still had a little accent; a little hard-edged and wise-about-everything accent, that pushed most of my buttons. I thought, at the time, that it was probably a good thing.

Now in her forties, tall, dark and assured, in her sharp face and clean lines, and in her very piercing slate-gray eyes, I perceived a placid malevolence that never allowed me to engage in an easy flow of expression. Her short hair and firm mouth suggested a general at work—at work on her war plans that would surely save the world from itself. With this interpretation, I also realized that I could very well be projecting.

"You are intelligent of course, Alan," she said. "But so what? So damned what? Why do you say you're obsessed with this woman? Why? Huh? What does that mean to you?"

"Okay... Let's change the word, obsessed, to love then," I said.

"Are you playing games with yourself and with me, Alan?"

I stood abruptly, glaring down at her, sitting behind her stained oak desk, with the 8 by 12 photograph of her severe looking husband and Adams Family looking children, all staring at me with an aloof challenge.

"Look, doctor, I know all the psychological babble and the tricks..."

She cut me off. "...and I propose, Alan, that you really know nothing. I propose that you really know nothing at all about anything."

I saw through her trick and I grinned. "Okay, fine." I sat down, rigid, feigning defeat, but furiously planning another course of attack. "Okay. I know nothing." I crossed my arms, smugly.

"But we both know, Alan, that you *feel* things very strongly. You feel strongly about nearly everything that I can see. So what do you think about that?"

"Think or feel?" I challenged, glowing.

"Make your choice, but be honest with yourself. Are you playing games?"

"Maybe I am. So what? Look, we know my father was calculating and arrogant. We know he was cold to me, warm to my sister and devoted to my mother. Okay, so I..." I slapped my chest, forcefully, "... feel that. For some reason, for some friggin' reason that I don't know, my father just didn't like me. Okay, that's simple and that's just too bad. Most everybody has a rotten parent or two. But, as a result, I lacked a sure foundation emotionally. I know that! I never knew how to please him and no matter what I did, nothing seemed to work. Okay, I know that and I analyzed it and I thought about it when I took psych courses in medical school."

"You thought about it?" Dr. Raskoffsky asked, with raised eyebrows.

"Yes, dammit, I thought about it and I *felt* about it."

"Your father loved your mother?"

"Yes, deeply. I saw it, felt it. They were in love. When she died, he fell into a deep depression. I'm not sure he ever got over it. He had a stroke some months back, and has lost his will to live."

"And you can relate to that?"

I considered her words. "Yes...I can."

"And how do you feel about this woman you say you love? Rita?"

"That was abrupt."

She shrugged it off. "So?"

I sighed deeply, and thought uncomfortably. "I feel… twisted by her."

"Twisted? That's an interesting choice of a word."

"Yes. Twisted. Twisted around her. Molded to her, rings interlocking, breathing her breaths, wrapped about her like a vine…"

"So very poetic for a scientist."

"But so scientific for a poet. Rings interlocking?"

She sniffed that away. "Perhaps you are clogging up your emotions with too many thoughts and words. What do you think?"

"Yes…clogging… maybe you're right. Maybe I'm all clogged up with her."

"Are you constantly finding some word to separate yourself from just letting yourself FEEL, Alan?"

"I feel, dammit. That's the whole problem. That's why I'm here. I'm here because my dead sperm killed everything."

"So dramatic you are."

I lifted my gaze and fired revulsion at her. "Go to hell."

She didn't blink and we sat in a deadening silence. My time was almost up. I sat back, squeaking the leather in the emerald upholstered chair, staring at the ceiling. I continued. "I believed, at least for a while, that I could get Rita pregnant. I felt it intuitively. I really did feel it."

"Obviously, you have given this a great amount

of thought and you feel deeply about it."

"And I'm here for a give-and-take conversation about it! Not to hear boilerplate psych talk."

"So you couldn't get her pregnant. So what? You're a scientist. What does science say about such notions or feelings or intuitions?"

"I think science has a hard time answering questions like this. This is where science gets stuck or we just don't have enough information to form a rational conclusion. How do you do a mathematical equation to prove intuition? How is that possible? But then it didn't work out anyway, so, so what? Sometimes I just feel punished or shit on by the universe. I mean, despite all of your best efforts, your life just gets all screwed up or something."

"You chose to see Rita again, did you not?"

"Yes…but I was just going back home to sell the house."

"But you could have chosen not to see her again?"

"Yes."

"Then did you choose to see her again?"

"Yes, I chose to see her again, but how did I know that it would lead to where it did and that it would converge in such a devastating way?"

"You can choose right now, can't you?"

I switched around in the chair. "Yes… But."

"So choose."

I edged forward in agitation. "It doesn't change the fact that the infertility destroyed both relationships! I mean, you know… there are some women who just don't give a damn about having children! Why couldn't Nicole and Rita have been one of those?! Why in the hell did Rita's whole life—her entire recovery—depend on me getting her pregnant again!?"

"We choose, we choose, we choose, Alan. You can't always choose the outcome but you can choose to think something else and to choose another course of action. Take charge of the situation and choose. Move the energy—your life energy—your thought energy into a different course of action."

"We're going nowhere, here." I said, angrily.

"You are here, Alan. Now. Not in the past. Now. What are you going to do with all this new, ever-possible energy?"

I shook my head, overwhelmed. "Ah, the hell with it. Sometimes I think everybody just thinks too much about everything. My damned head is spinning." I put my head in my hands.

"We can sit quietly and say nothing, if you want."

I sat quietly for a moment with my eyes closed. When my cell phone rang, I snatched for it and shut it off. Pushing to my feet, I stalked the thick burgundy carpet, enveloped in anger and confusion. Finally, when I heard a siren screaming by outside, I spoke. "I wrote to Rita once, but I didn't send it. I wrote it last winter when I was on the beach in Barbados... It was all about silence. How the quiet of her always healed me somehow—not that she doesn't have a temper—she does, but there is this inexplicable peace I often feel with her; that feeling of coming home."

"What did you write about her? Do you remember?" the doctor asked.

I settled down into the chair. "...Yes, I remember." I closed my eyes, hesitant and diffident. But recalling the words warmed and healed.

"Her silence was loud with fascination. Her greatest magic was her lack of words; the way she positioned her body on a blanket by the lake, or in a restaurant chair or on the bed, when she blew on my hand and it felt like sand trickling through my fingers. Her still eyes were constantly breaking the code of my heart's secrets."

Moments later, my eyes opened. Dr. Raskoffsky sat still. I sensed impatience.

"So are you a poet at odds with the scientist, Alan?" the doctor asked.

"I don't know what that means." My voice cooled and I sat up. "I learned recently, by looking at old medical records, that my grandfather had had an infertility problem. My father was born when grandfather was twenty-two years old. He was unable to have another child. They adopted my father's brother. My mother said my grandfather was a severe man, and very hard on my father, even in his last years. You wouldn't think so, would you? You would think that he would have adored his only begotten son. But he didn't. He favored Raymond, the adopted son. Go figure.

"My mother said that my father basically

despised his father. My mother also said, when she was dying, that my father had an obsessive love for her, right from the very first meeting at that country club dance. He told her that he loved her and that he was going to marry her, and he did."

I stood again. My time was up. "So you see, doctor, it's all just the silly games and play of good old DNA. Even a good or complete understanding of the genome doesn't tell us what it means to be human."

"Meaning?"

"Meaning, we keep killing, stealing, lying..."

"Are we talking about your guilt and your feelings of failure?"

"I'm saying that, even if we were to modify those 30,000 plus genes with which human beings are encoded, and we produced a race with Shakespeare's brain power and Derek Jeter's athletic power, we still couldn't produce a race of angels. So where in the hell are we really going?"

"Alan. Are you talking about your guilt? Your failure to impregnate Rita?"

"I'm saying that it is extremely hard not to feel a victim of one's own software program. That's what I'm saying. I mean, I spend a lot of my time telling patients to be proactive with their health and not to be a victim. That's what I'm saying. I'm saying that we all may be, in fact, victims, after all—victims of some "thing" out there or in here, and yet we've duped ourselves into believing and acting like we're not victims."

Dr. Raskoffsky folded her hands on the desktop and leveled her confident eyes on me. "And I say that is a cop-out. I propose to you this: now that your "house" has burnt down, you have the opportunity to find an original life. Isn't that what you said about your quantum physics a session or two ago, that there are infinite possibilities just ripe for the choosing within the cosmic soup? So what do you feel, Alan? Want do you really want?"

By July, I'd stopped seeing Dr. Raskoffsky. I'd made a decision.

The first week of August, I called information to get Rita's phone number. It wasn't listed. I searched the internet but found nothing. Megan's husband, Paul, a computer programmer, assured me that he could find Rita, and he did. The next morning Megan texted me the information: Rita was living in Sedona, Arizona.

I wrote to her that night.

CHAPTER THREE

Dear Rita:

What would a true hero of the story do? Demand we meet again? Travel to Arizona, unannounced, and demand an audience with you? Does he wait, hoping without hope, that the heroine will call or write or send him another of her wonderful stories? Tell him he's forgiven for failing you? For failing us?

What does a hero do when he doesn't know what a hero really is anymore? When the "white hat guy" has dropped his hat in the mud and only finds mud with which to clean it?

Is the hero just a guy who, stumbling forward into a forest of obstacles, strains to learn some lesson that will make him "better" or "good" or "wise" until that fine day when he drops dead or, accidentally, falls into the pit of illumination?

Does the hero just sit and watch

the movement of his mind, feeling its impulses, its desires, its fantasies, hoping they'll just dissolve away someday, so that his true inner self can break out and shine in all its effulgence? What does he do in the meantime?

What does the hero do with his love, when she lives in his heart, but not in his life? She, the incarnate definition, reflection, and heartbeat of his love; his life's true path and purpose, feeding him, maturing him, marrying his heart and mind and making him complete, like duality joined to eternity.

"Wordy" stuff, my old therapist would say. Too many damned words. Feel it more with an honesty of simplicity.

Okay, Rita. Simple. I love you. I'd hoped that somehow my sickly sperm would come through for us this time, but it didn't. I hoped for so many things.

Rita, I'd love to see you again. I waited nearly a year before contacting you. I miss you, I love you, I want you. Simple.

Can I come and see you? I'll sit in

silence and listen and not talk about the past. We know it all so well anyway, don't we? We don't even have to talk about the future.

I'm a better hero now, Rita. Better because of you. Because of us.

I'd love to hear from you...in any way you wish.

With love,

Alan James

Hero, who is looking for a clear, cool spring, where he can clean his dirty hat.

P.S. I'm taking jazz piano lessons. I can almost play Twinkle, Twinkle Little Star.

I mailed the letter and waited, in agony, for a response. A little over two weeks passed before I received one. I tore open the envelope, drew out a single typed page, and read.

Protection

Sometimes it all comes crashing down.
Roofs, walls, glass, hope, trust
All
Those things that hold things up
Body, Mind, Spirit
Keeping them safe

Crushing
Those solid things of comfort
Slicing, grinding, burying.
It happens too fast to run
No emergency kit
Forget
Preparedness
There is no escape, no hiding
You've just got to die
Breathe
In and out, cry out like a newborn
And let it happen, like a new birth
Dead
Awakening to new breaths
New life to have it all come
Crashing
Down to begin rebuilding
A house with no walls
—Rita

I wrote her the following letter that same night.

Dear Rita:

I loved the poem. When did you start writing poetry? Are you writing other things? I'd love to read them. Did you ever start that novel? Someday, maybe we could discuss chapters, like we used to do at Jack's. I would even try to throw something together; maybe some stories about my patients or about the medical field and its complexities, with a bent on what the word "healing" really means. Who knows, we might even get into some good arguments.

Are you happy living there? What are you doing? Have you met interesting people? Made friends?

I've been doing some <u>pro</u> <u>bono</u> work on Saturday mornings with addictive patients: drugs, alcohol, tobacco, and food. It's really challenging. I try so hard to listen, counsel, understand and advocate. Sometimes I think I'm getting more from them than I'm giving. As I get older, I really do feel the need to try to give something back to the world, besides all my confusion and insecurities. Remember? We talked about all that last year, during the 4th of July fireworks down by Crystal Lake.

Anyway, I do like the people I'm counseling. It's so tempting to blame them—not overtly—but subtly and in weaker moments, and then I realize I'm not really listening or I'm falling back into old patterns of thinking. So damned easy to do.

I was offered a job in Boston a couple

> *of weeks ago. I guess the Boston area is hyper-specialized. A lot of wealthy people there. My colleague says that the disjointed care people get from a multitude of specialists is clearly worse care than the care they get from one primary care physician. I don't know.*
>
> *The whole medical environment is so messed up right now. I'm just trying to do the best I can with it all. I have applied for a fellowship in cardiology at Harvard, but I'm not moving to Boston, at least not right now.*
>
> *Rita, I'd love to hear from you again. A line, poem, story, anything.*
>
> *Love,*
>
> *Alan James*
>
> *P.S. Jazz piano lessons continue. I'm playing a very clumsy Blue Moon.*
>
> *P.S.S. My email address is enclosed. Do you have one?*
>
> *P.S.S.S. My phone number is enclosed. Text me if you want to.*

An e-mail from Rita arrived a week later, while I was at the office. I printed it out and disciplined myself to read only the first paragraph, waiting restlessly until early afternoon when I could read without interruption. I was in the Hungarian Pastry Shop on 111th Street and Amsterdam Avenue, sipping a cappuccino, when, with anxious heart beats, I read.

> *Dear Alan James:*
>
> *Sedona is in northern Arizona (the high desert). Red Rock country. It's hot, dry and stunningly beautiful. I drive along interstate I-17 sometimes, from Phoenix, and gaze out at the Saguaro cacti and take in the red monoliths and shimmering heat and I feel lifted up—free—and dissolved into it all, baptized by the drenching sun, desolate peace and endless sky. During jeep rides through the mountains, red dust gets all over me —even in my ears—but I love it. The seasons are mild and there's plenty of sunshine. I feel an umbilical connection to this place that I can't describe. It invites forgetting and a new "nowness" continually, with all its rust-red color, history, soaring eagles and wonderful 30-foot natural rockslide at Slide Rock State Park. I love watching the kids there.*
>
> *I've started meditating. Okay, I've gone a little "new age"—but this place seems spiritual to me, so naturally*

and easily "religious;" so deeply quiet inside, if you know what I mean. I meditated at the Sinagua Indian ruins recently and I could almost feel the Earth spinning on its axis. It made me so high; so connected to the Earth. Strange? Yes, but it's true.

When I first moved here, I waitressed at a small airport restaurant that you have to get to by dirt road. Red biplanes fly in and out, constantly, with 3-hour flights over the Grand Canyon and other places. I worked there for about five months. From there I went to the Oak Creek Brewery, a fun place to waitress, and then finally, through the help of a new friend, to The Sedona Golf Resort. I'm working at the Grill at Shadow Rock. I'm also working part-time at a gallery in Sedona, that sells Native American jewelry. The shopping area is called Tlaquepaque. The whole area is modeled after a Spanish village and it has many little shops and restaurants. Sometimes I feel so enlivened and "fresh" and full of the dance, that I think I must have been a Spanish senorita in a former life.

It's easy for me to set goals here, Alan

James. I'm taking on-line courses from the University of Phoenix and hope to finish my liberal arts degree in a little over a year. I'll take the necessary teaching courses in Flagstaff, I think, and, hopefully, begin teaching in a little over two years. That's the plan for now. But we both know how things can change…so very suddenly.

Alan James. I have no words to apologize for the destruction of your family's home. Dad and I had a terrible argument when I was packing to leave. He threatened me. He said he was going to kill you. I told him I was leaving town and never coming back. Please forgive me, Alan James, for all that happened. I am so sorry.

My father was sick and, God forgive me, I'm glad he's dead. I feel so much better inside just knowing he's dead. Is that a bad thing to say? I don't care. It's true. I have wanted to write you my apology so many times—I even thought about calling, but I couldn't get up the nerve. So I ran and ran. I disappeared from view and I have not looked back or reflected often. I'm still much too frightened to do that. I know I'll have to someday. Even writing you now takes tremendous effort.

Those two months I spent with you in that house were the best time of my life. A big part of me was "healed." You, Dr. Lincoln, did heal so many of my wounds and I will always thank God for the time we had together. I will always love you for that and for so much, much more.

Now, I feel so removed and somehow protected by these glorious mountains; by the Chapel of the Holy Cross and Courthouse Butte; by Bell Rock and its energy vortex. The desert keeps the devils away. The crisp blue sky covers me and envelops me in gracious protection. The people here are so kind, creative and generous.

Dear Alan James. I cannot ask you to come. Someday, perhaps, when I have the strength, the distance, the grace to face the past again. Then maybe. I cannot right now. I'm sorry, darling.

When I was pregnant with Darla, I thought of myself as walking Earth—a holder of life; a participant in its purpose and glory. I'm learning to just let go a little now. Letting go little by little until I can just freely and naturally and quite probably, finally, let go. I'm praying for that.

How does one become wise, Alan James? How do we understand the things that happen to us? How does one accept this world, so frightening, so treacherous, so very beautiful, and breathe, and say "Okay. Yes. Okay, I accept, I struggle, I see, I don't really see at all."

Sometimes I wonder how people can be so damned calm about living, when we don't really know very much about it. We don't know anything about where we came from or where we're going. No one can tell us where the Earth is really located. We're just spinning around out in the middle of nowhere, in a void, in darkness. Sometimes I think we should all focus our energy, skills and knowledge in seeking to find the true mysteries of life, instead of continually repeating the same damned mistakes over and over again until we fall over dead.

Listen to me go on, Alan James. See what living out here has done to me. Who knows, maybe you'll find out some of the answers someday. You're so smart.

My dear, Alan James. I hope you have

the happiest of lives. I'm so proud of you for what you're doing, for how you're growing as a man and as a doctor. I hope you remain the golden man I have loved since I was eighteen, when you came up to me and asked, with those frightened little eyes, if we could meet and exchange our stories. What was that spark that set me ablaze with comfort and longing for you? I don't know. Mystical. But you know my love for you is an "always" thing. A growing thing. A wonderful, healing thing that will continue to heal me for as long as I live and even, perhaps, beyond.

I may not write again, Alan James. I need to go back into my little safe cave for a while. But we know that life will steer us toward each other again, as it must, because we truly are lovers.

With all my love,

Rita

I folded the page in half and creased it. I sat breathing and staring at nothing.

CHAPTER FOUR

It is an easy day to remember, a Thursday, the third week of October. Trees blazed with color, vibrated spectacles of color, scattered color in bursts of chilly wind, flinging gold, ocher and red like confetti across parks, sidewalks, and crowded streets. Sunlight glinted from towering windows, reached through shadowy streets with crossbeams of light, finding the delicate tremulous leaves of the smallest tree near a firehouse, a library, or a block of 5-story brownstones. New York was art in all that color and, under a sharp blue sky, it was painted anew with every brush of sunlight and every moving cloud.

Yellow cabs, slicing through Central Park, sprayed leaves. Kids kicked at them, talked to them, studied them. Leaves carpeted the carriage path in Riverside Park and, as red double-decker tour buses slid by Riverside Church and its gothic spires, leaves exploded from curbside trees, like crazy birds.

Autumn sang through trees, rippled the gray Hudson River, and reminded students from Columbia, Barnard, and Manhattan School of Music, who persisted in shorts and T-shirts, that winter, mounted and approaching, was, indeed, part of the curriculum.

I had gone to a morning seminar on obesity at the Pierre Hotel, returned to the office at 2 o'clock, saw patients for three hours, and took a walk along Riverside Park at around five, just as the sun was beginning its descent. The temperature was dropping.

My cell phone rang. I stopped and answered.

"Alan. It's Megan."

"Yes...what's up?"

"How was the seminar?" she asked.

"Good. You scooted out early."

"Yeah, Paul called. Tyler had a fever and was calling for me."

"Is he okay?"

"Yeah...weepy and irritable. But okay. I was on the internet and guess what?"

"No idea."

"There's a seminar in Phoenix...right now."

"...And?"

"Alan...come on. You're an intelligent man and a helluva doctor who wants to keep up on all the latest medical trends and techniques, such as alternative treatments and doctor/patient trust and..."

I had been reviewing the facts of the seminar I'd just completed, rewinding, and playing back, in my head, conversations with patients I'd had that afternoon. They were instantly erased from my mind. I cut her off. "...In Phoenix?"

"Yes, Alan. Phoenix. Did you know that my mother lives in Phoenix and that Sedona is about a hundred miles or so from Phoenix?"

My wide eyes jumped from empty benches, to trees, to squirrels, to the rosy sunset.

"Alan?"

"Yes, Megan, I'm here. I could use another seminar...there's so much to learn and so many things to catch up on."

"And surely you remember the mythological Phoenix who crashed to the earth, and was reborn?"

"Yes..."

"We can cover for you, Alan."

I perched on a park bench, my mind alive with anxious possibility. "Megan...I'm leaving tonight. And...thank you."

I called the airlines as I hurried home to pack. This new thought brought an urgency of action, as if all the time wasted and all the mourning and regret had suddenly been defeated by the cheerful blows of expectation and possibility.

There were two flights that evening and both were out of Newark, New Jersey: one was at 7:05, a non-stop that arrived at 9:25 p.m., Phoenix time. Then I'd have to drive the 125 miles to Sedona, another two hours. That plane would be difficult to make since it was already 5:20.

The next left at 8:39, with a change in Las Vegas. I'd arrive at one in the morning. I booked the 7:05, hailed a cab and went directly to Newark.

In heavy, erratic traffic, I called and reserved a rental car in Phoenix. I pounded the seat several times, hollering at the cab driver to hurry. He finally whirled, with broiling eyes, and told me to shut up or get out.

I made the 7:05 flight by minutes. During the endless 5½ hour flight, I tried to sleep; tried to find some relaxation technique that would free me, even for a minute, from the blistering worry of seeing Rita. Was I doing the right thing? Would Rita really want to see me again? I'd tell her I just happened to be in the area and thought I'd stop by and say hello. What was wrong with that? Nothing. Just two old friends saying hello. No, nothing wrong with that at all. What if she was with another man? I pushed the thought out of my head and ordered a scotch on the rocks. I watched a silly romantic movie. I talked politics with the middle-aged woman next to me. I finally tugged out my iPod and listened to Bach's *Well Tempered Clavier Book II*, because it had been a consistent favorite of my father's and I'd recalled it sliding in and out of my consciousness, back in those long-ago high school days, when I was dating Rita.

"This is a mature work of art, Alan," Dad had said that night, before my final date with Rita. "When you hear this music you feel like you can rise up into heaven. What do you think about it? Do you like the music?"

I was distracted by Rita, then, just as I was now. "Yeah, it's okay. It's kind of moody and nervous," I said.

"They're revelations, Alan. Little musical poems of revelation. If you listen with your whole body, not just your ears, but your entire being, you'll feel the power of them."

When we were an hour from Phoenix, I shut my eyes and listened to Bach. I ached for Rita. I wanted Rita.

I drove through a profound darkness along I-17, reproaching myself for not coming sooner. I should have shown up at the restaurant where Rita worked, just as I had at Jack's. I should have written some silly, vacuous story and presented it to her for her comments, just as I had intended to do on the beach in Barbados those many months ago. It would have worked. Rita wouldn't have sent me away. She would have chastised me, perhaps, scolded me with her eyes; maybe even ignored me for a while, before giving me an affectionate glance, but she wouldn't have turned me down. We would have exchanged enigmatic smiles and that would have been the end of it. We could have begun where we'd left off. We could have slapped all our cards onto the table, discussed the complexities, laughed at our past mistakes and adolescent fears; exposed the dinosaur emotions that had driven the wedge between us. I should have come. I should have come a long time ago!

I pulled into the parking lot of a long dark motel, under a yellow neon light that said VACANCY. Weary and jumpy, I hardly noticed the dry desert air. I woke up the owner, a brown sleepy man in his fifties, with a silver pony tail and frank dark eyes. He wore loose shorts and a blue Hawaiian shirt. He swiped my credit card, slid me a key across the counter and grunted a good night.

The room was basic and stuffy, with desert decor. I turned on the air-conditioner, showered, brushed my teeth, and dropped into the double bed. I laced my hands behind my head and stared into thick darkness, hearing only the low hum of the air-conditioner. Rita was close. So very close. As the thought reverberated, like a mantra, I dissolved into a restless sleep.

The next morning, I emerged from my little room into the cool morning air, standing in rapt awe at the desert landscape. I saw the expansive iron-rich reddish soil, blooming desert flowers and infinite blue sky. I stared into the brilliant day, toward the towering distant fiery rock formations, following red airplanes gliding lazily over them. All of it made me want to breathe deeply, and I did.

I ate breakfast at a little red and yellow roadside restaurant. I nudged at the sunny-side eggs, nibbled toast, and drank two cups of black coffee. I noticed patrons wearing cowboy hats and boots, with the occasional tourist like me, looking strangely out of place and time, like we were actors who'd accidentally stumbled in from a different movie.

I drove into Sedona, with a little boy's searching wonder. It was smaller than I'd anticipated. I drifted through heavier traffic than I'd expected, past a variety of shops, and gawked with surprise at the Sedona Public Library, a rather ostentatious A-frame building.

I parked on the street, pushed out, surveying the area, sheepishly, as if I were already under Rita's scrutiny. The lively dry wind whipped at my hair; I fingered it back in place, as I wandered uneasily along the downtown strip. It was touristy and bustling, with quality shops mixed in with the trinket stores. Shuffling through an airy hotel lobby, I saw brochures advertising an early-morning hot-air balloon ride that included a traditional champagne breakfast. There was a brochure for Pink Jeep Tours, hawking a fascinating ride through the desert.

Back in my car, I studied the map and drove across the Oak Creek Bridge toward the Tlaquepaque Arts and Craft Village (pronounced Tla-keh-pah-keh.) My guide book said that it meant the "best of everything." I found it nestled beneath sycamores on the banks of Oak Creek. According to Rita's e-mail, this was where she worked, in a Native American jewelry store.

I parked and sat in the car for a few minutes, screwing up the courage to face the wonderful and dreadful possibilities.

I ambled through several courtyards, with their vine-covered stucco walls, cobble-stoned walkways and impressive arched entryways, viewing ceramics, blown glass creations and contemporary Southwestern art and weavings.

With unsteady and hopeful eyes, I entered art galleries, jewelry stores and restaurants, angling around a stream of probing tourists, looking for Rita, behind counters, in the courtyards, near the splashing fountain.

I saw contemporary jewelry and designer causal wear in leathers and silks. I smelled the sweet and pungent spices of Mexican cuisine. A wedding party exited the little Chapel and mild Chapel bells drew smiles and curious eyes.

I didn't see Rita. I don't think I expected to. It was nearly 11 o'clock. I took a chance and entered a shop that offered Native American jewelry. I shoved my hands deep into my jeans pockets and hunched my shoulders as I perused the sculptures, pottery, and turquoise and gold masks. As I eased by the glass jewelry case, I glanced up into the clear brown eyes of a Native American man, who wore a deep purple silk shirt and a cowboy hat. He smiled warmly, his brown weathered face suggesting a calm strength.

"Very nice," I said, quietly.

He nodded.

I drew a sudden breath. "Does Rita work here?"

He didn't move. He didn't blink.

His voice was a single struck bass string. "Yes."

My pulse quickened. "Is she working today?"

"She'll be here at twelve o'clock."

"…Good. Thank you."

I took a business card before I left.

I sat in the Secret Garden Café, sipping an espresso, overhearing a couple from Wisconsin talking excitedly about Sedona's famous energy vortex.

"The Airport Vortex is supposed to be a weaker vortex, but I really felt more there than at some of the others," the blond, in-her-twenties, said.

"Yeah, me too," her tattooed-on-both-arms boyfriend said. "It was like a little positive sensation or something."

"Yeah, yeah!"

"And like, a little tingly."

"Yeah. I felt that too. And I just felt happy."

"Yeah, it was cool."

"So we've got to go to Rachel's Knoll today," the girl said. "It's supposed to be holy ground."

"Yeah. I should bring my parents there," he said. "It's supposed to be like this great place to help with relationship problems. According to this guy I talked to, it really works. You like just sit up there and it really helps get your head together."

My ears perked up.

"Your parents wouldn't go," she said, gloomily.

"No. No way. They just want to stay home and fight all the time," he agreed.

I glanced at my watch every five minutes and tried not to look solemn or worried that Rita was going to ignore me or tell me to go back home. I kept my eyes low on my empty cup of espresso and waited, opening my hand, and then closing it into a tight fist. Finally, fighting boiling nerves, I stood and stepped to the entrance, away from the gaiety of sunlight.

At ten minutes to twelve, I saw her. There was no mistaking that languid walk, the easy swing of her hips; her long golden hair, tied into a pony tail, swinging jauntily from side to side. I nearly shot out the door as she drifted by—only twenty feet away! She wore jeans, cowboy boots and a loose fitting white cotton blouse, that rippled in the gentle wind. When she turned toward me, but didn't see me, I was startled, breathless. I saw a pastoral quality of peace on her lovely face; I recognized the symptoms of happiness in her eyes.

When she was gone, I went back inside and settled back down into my chair, a mass of nerves. Heat rushed to my face. The Rita Fever had returned.

Ten minutes passed before I reached for the red and white colored business card and my cell phone. I punched in the number and waited, mouth tight, throat dry.

"Red Rock Canyon Selections, this is Rita, can I help you?" Her voice was throaty and sultry.

I croaked out a sound, but no coherent word.

"Hello?" Rita said.

"Ah…yes, it's…ah, Alan."

Dead silence.

"Rita…it's Alan James." I sprinted out the words in case she was going to hang up. "I was at a medical conference in Phoenix and well… you know, I was close, so I thought maybe I'd stop by and say hello or something."

I heard her sigh into the receiver. It made a little whoosh sound. "Are you in Phoenix now?" she asked, cautiously.

"Well, actually, no. I'm in Sedona."

"Where in Sedona?"

"Well… ah… I'm actually sitting in the Secret Garden Café."

More silence. I pictured her standing erect, chewing on her lower lip as she considered her options. "I have to work until five o'clock."

"Okay…Sure. I understand. I just thought that…"

She interrupted. "I'll be right there."

I stared, astonished, and elated, after she'd hung up. I stood, paced the room, and ordered another espresso, just so I'd look relaxed and casual. I sat and waited, foot tapping the floor, mind disturbed, emotions alarmed; heart pumping wary celebration.

It was ten minutes before she arrived—actually twelve minutes. She appeared in the doorway and searched. I swallowed, smiled briefly under her lowering tentative gaze.

She came toward me, slowly. I stood, shaking a little.

She shook her head, pointing at the half drained cup of espresso. "How many of those have you had, Alan James?"

"Oh… not too many. Just this one… well, no, this is the second."

She sat down opposite me. I sat. "Want anything?" I asked, in a thin struggling voice.

"No."

She studied me carefully.

I said, "Nice place…I mean, this whole area…the

whole town. I like it."

"When was your conference?"

"It was… oh, for a couple of days."

"What was it on?"

"The usual things…you know health and medicine. I mean, what else could a medical conference be on?"

She let out a little laugh. "Alan James, you didn't go to a medical conference in Phoenix, did you?"

I folded my arms, looking toward the pastry stand. "…No."

With this confession came a relaxation of tension. I looked directly at her and spoke quietly. "I came to see you."

She folded her arms and crossed her leg. It bounced a little. "And what do you think?"

"I think you look wonderful."

She smiled her appreciation. "Have I changed?"

"You seem calmer."

"I am."

"You're still beautiful."

Her eyes held me. "You always thought so."

"Have you been writing?" I asked.

"No, not really. Just a few poems for a while, and then nothing. I think I'm done with all that. It brings back bad memories. I don't want any more bad memories."

"How's your mother?"

"Good… better. I call her pretty regularly."

"How's your school coming?"

"Coming along."

"Good… real good, Rita."

"And how are you, Alan James? Is the divorce final?"

"Oh, yes. Long ago. Nicole's remarried and, I think, she has had a baby."

The air filled with uncertainty. I could see that Rita was searching for the right words. She played with her pony tail. "That must have been difficult, Alan James. That must have hurt you a lot."

I shrugged. "For a while." I wanted to lift the mood quickly. "It's over and done with. Water under the bridge. So do you like it out here?"

"I love it. I'm so happy."

"… I'm glad, Rita. You deserve it."

I took a beat and then dropped my gaze to the espresso. "Are you seeing anyone?"

"I was… for a while. Not now."

I faced her; her eyes seemed to fill with contrary thoughts as they wandered the room. "You scare me, Alan James."

"I don't mean to. I don't want to."

Her tone struck an accusing note. "It just brings it all up again. You being here. Don't you see? Don't you understand that…" She stopped, lifting a weak hand. "… All the damned ghosts."

"I'm not a ghost, Rita. I never was."

"But they follow you."

"I don't accept that. It's not fair."

Her chin lifted; eyes flickered up. "What's fair, Alan James?"

"I don't know."

She stiffened, putting all her attention on me. "I can't forget her... I can't forget Darla. I will never forget what happened, Alan James."

"Of course not, Rita. And why should you forget Darla?"

I saw the struggle on her face, a dark radiance, straining, even now, for illumination.

"You honor her life by remembering her, Rita. You honor the love you still feel for her. Why should that be forgotten?"

She slackened, eyeing me attentively. "There is a place for lost children, isn't there, Alan James? I mean, there's got to be."

"I'm sure of it, Rita. Yes."

She looked beyond me, as we sat in a long dangling silence. "Well...are you just passing through then?"

I waited a long time. I stared at her. "Only if you want me to just pass through."

When her eyes found me again, they had cleared. They regained their peaceful luminance. She reached for my hand. That's when I saw the ring. She still wore the diamond ring I'd bought her over a year ago! I steadied myself and took her hand, weakly. She squeezed mine.

"I suppose I should at least offer to be a tour guide or something," she said.

I grinned, relieved. "I accept."

She retracted her hand and stood abruptly. I stood.

"I'll meet you here at five o'clock."

And then she was gone.

An ineffable glory filled the shining desert afternoon. It beat with the broad wings of soaring eagles and burnished the Red Rock monoliths that met the dome of a sharpening blue sky.

I walked aimlessly in an effort to shake off the ghosts, appealing to the ancient spirits of the place, and the vortexes, and Rachel of Rachel's Knoll, to banish those old perfidious ghosts from Rita's and my life, forever.

I returned to the café at 4:45 and waited for her.

CHAPTER FIVE

Joined at the elbow, Rita took me to a quaint little Bed and Bakery called The Red Garter. Rita announced, "It used to be an old brothel."

It looked like it.

I registered for the night, dropped off my bags and showered, while Rita went home to shower and change.

We met again at seven for dinner at the Heartline Café. She had herb-crusted trout and I the beef tenderloin. For dessert we shared an apple tort with vanilla ice cream. We talked about authors and movies and threw in some politics, and then moved on to the next day's itinerary.

"I want to do the balloon thing," I said.

"The hot air-balloon? You're kidding?"

"Nope. With the champagne breakfast. I want to do it."

"I never thought of you as being a balloon guy," she said, finishing her coffee.

"Balloon me up, baby." I joked.

"You are going to be scared out of your mind, Alan James."

"I am not." I said, feigning insult. "Have you ever done it?"

"No."

"Well, then..."

"But I went up in one of those little airplanes and I wasn't scared a bit. We flew all around the Grand Canyon. Not even butterflies."

"I don't believe it."

"Well, maybe some moths."

"Do they hand out parachutes in those balloons?" I asked, nervously.

We strolled the streets in the cashmere night, relaxed and a little high from the bottle of California Merlot we'd consumed. I stopped to look at cowboy boots. Rita said I had to have a pair or she wouldn't be seen with me. I don't remember when she left my side. It was out of the corner of my eye that I saw her break from the sidewalk and dash out into the street.

I pivoted. I saw her reach for the child; a sudden stretching of her rescuing arms to scoop her up to safety. But the SUV slid sharply into my view, moving too fast! I opened my mouth to scream out a warning. A man made a move—a frantic search, whirling. His lost child had vanished. He saw Rita. He saw her goal. He saw his child in the street. We saw the charging SUV. The father lurched, made a frightful cry.

The sounds were ugly and harsh. The screeching brakes. A dull thud. Screaming. The sound of my own frantic voice.

Rita and the child were hit—tossed like a bundle. The world shattered into bits of slow motion chaos.

CHAPTER SIX

My self-command took over. That trained emergency room self-possession that shows no alarm and allows no panic. I darted off toward them, pulling my cell phone from my pocket to call 911.

I ignored the sights, the blood, the horrific sight of Rita and the unconscious child, still vice-gripped in Rita's arms. I went to work, shouting out commands, hearing shrieks, scattering footsteps and weeping. I worked with the steadiest hands and the calmest mind of my life.

Rita and the child were taken to the Verde Valley Medical Center. The paramedics would not let me ride in the ambulance, so I sprinted to my car, shot away from the curb and asked for directions when I wasn't sure.

At the hospital, I flashed my credentials and was asked, in spite of them, to wait in the waiting area. I did. I still had Rita's mother's number on my speed dial. I called her and calmed her. Told her to come. Told her everything would be alright.

"Rita's strong," I said, using a positive cliché that was part of my repertoire of phrases. I shook it away, irritated at myself for using it. I yanked something else out of the air, just as inane. "Rita has goals, Mrs. Fitzgerald. That will pull her through."

Mrs. Fitzgerald's weary voice wanted to believe me. "I hope so, Alan... She's all I have left in this world. I can't lose her. God... I can't lose her."

It was 10:25 in the morning the next day, when Mrs. Fitzgerald found me in the waiting lounge. It was an impulse. I hugged her. When she drew back, gently startled, I ignored my own surprise and updated her on Rita's condition.

Then, in a quiet, procedural voice, I told her that Rita was unconscious and critical. She'd lost a lot of blood, had a ruptured spleen, perforated lung, broken ribs, a shattered left leg, some head trauma and internal bleeding.

Mrs. Fitzgerald's lined, haggard face sank.

"The doctors have been working all night. I've talked to them several times. She's going to get through this, Mrs. Fitzgerald. She is."

"How is the little girl she saved?" she asked, twisting her wizened hands.

"A broken arm and some scrapes. But she's fine. Her parents want to pay for everything. They're insisting. Her father claimed he'd just turned away for a minute and then...she was out in the street. The girl driving was talking on her cell phone and didn't see them. She was driving too fast."

Mrs. Fitzgerald wept a little and then recovered.

"Rita saved the little girl's life, Mrs. Fitzgerald. There's no doubt. The child would have been killed.

She's only three and a half years old."

We both fell into a nervous silence.

"Have you talked to Rita?" she asked.

"No...she's been unconscious since it happened."

At eight o'clock that night, Dr. Lowry approached us. He was a small, slight man in his fifties, with kind blue eyes, thin graying hair and a round ruddy face. In a confidential conversation, after an update with Mrs. Fitzgerald, he confided to me that he didn't think Rita would survive another night.

"There's too much hemorrhaging. Too much internal damage," he said.

I wanted to grab his broad shoulders and shake the hell out of him—slap him, kick him in the ass. A malicious anger pummeled me. I said, "Don't ever give up, doctor. Don't. Don't tell me or anyone else that you've given up. Never. Rita is strong. You don't know how strong she is. How determined. She's strong as hell!"

He stepped back, his eyes blinking fast. "Yes...of course. Obviously, she's strong."

He turned from me and walked down the hallway, with rapid foot falls.

We lived in a long, awful silence through the night, while Rita remained in intensive care, closed to visitors. I questioned doctors and nurses, making myself a nuisance while I loafed the corridors, restless and distracted. Mrs. Fitzgerald would not go to her motel room and she could not sleep.

The next afternoon, we learned that Rita had

stabilized.

Dr. Lowry said. "Frankly, I'm surprised she's pulled through, although we're not out of the woods yet."

CHAPTER SEVEN

The next day, in the evening, Mrs. Fitzgerald was allowed to sit with Rita. I waited in a desolate anxiety, too exhausted to pace.

It was the next morning before I finally got to see Rita. Mrs. Fitzgerald called me in, her countenance hopeful.

I entered the room eagerly. Silently. Mrs. Fitzgerald smiled at me—a warm, encouraging smile.

"She was awake a few minutes ago. She just fell back to sleep."

"Can I just sit for a while?"

She nodded.

I sat next to Rita, across from her mother, a pale, near-lifeless being herself, hunched in solitude, praying for her daughter, pleading for her life.

Rita was asleep, the sheet pulled close to her chin. Her face was in peace. There were no marks or cuts. Her head was bandaged. She looked remarkably young again, almost as if being close to death had somehow brought back her youth. I thought of how close she had been to death. I remembered the many deaths I'd witnessed in hospitals: mothers, children, old men, teenagers. Their deaths were never easy to watch, but I'd developed some detachment. It's life, after all, this business of death. All the tubes, million dollar equipment and miracle drugs were worthless when death was imminent. All of our medical technology, our education, seminars, drugs, alternative therapies, positive thinking—all of our ancient and future skills, hopes and experiences were useless in the face of death. Death, that subtle soft-stepping specter, would always, eventually, win the battle against life.

I crossed my legs, unable to feel any detachment from Rita. On the contrary, I felt as though I were breathing along with her, her shallow breaths.

Sunlight filled the room, wonderfully for a time, yellow and golden, and I used all of it to fine-tune my vision on her and to send her my love. I silently sent all my love and gratitude to her. I bowed and thanked her for her love of me.

An hour or so later, her eyes opened, not fully, but with a kind of startled wonder.

I stood. "Rita…?"

She didn't seem to hear me. Her eyes didn't move.

Mrs. Fitzgerald rose, suspended over her. "Rita, baby" she said, realizing new hope. "Rita, honey, it's your Mama. Rita…?"

I struggled to read Rita's face for anything. I longed to pierce that blue fog in her eyes and reach sunlight, for any message, for any hint of recognition. Rita's face softened and yielded itself silent. Then gently, her eyes slid toward me and struggled to focus.

I quivered with joy. "Rita…?"

She blinked, slowly.

"How are you?" I asked, clumsily.

She blinked again, and with effort, slid her eyes toward her mother. Mrs. Fitzgerald beamed. "Hi, baby. You're going to be fine. Just fine."

She looked at me again, with some surprise, and a tornado of emotions swept through me, leaving me silent and wanting. And then, involuntarily it seemed, Rita's eyes closed and she returned to sleep.

Two days later, Dr. Lowery said that Rita was improving, though they were still concerned about potential internal bleeding.

Mrs. Fitzgerald left me alone with Rita several times throughout the day. The three dozen roses I'd sent, and the dozen her mother had sent, were glorious, but the scent was nearly overwhelming. And more flowers had arrived from Hartsfield—from Jack's Diner, from the churches, from the families, from old classmates and teachers. Cards arrived and were opened. Mrs. Fitzgerald had placed many of them on the window sill and on the table beside Rita's bed.

Rita was asleep when I took my seat beside her. I was comforted by the rise and fall of her breathing, but caught in apprehension and uncertainty. The human body—life—healing, is finally a mystery, dependent on so many complex variables. I prayed that Rita would choose to live—that she would, in some conscious or unconscious realm, choose to go for life, regardless of the disappointments, tragedies and pain.

All the collective memories I had of Rita's life—every look, action, and word that I'd felt or experienced—returned, and I relived them. I shuddered when I thought how close to death she'd been. Life and death took on new meanings: life became more precious; death more present.

We seem to pass through the world like gusts of wind, like faceless prints, like shadows moving and groping and filling a busy space, and seldom finding the source of light that gives the shadow life. Love is that light. Rita is my light.

On the evening of the sixth day, as I sat alone, nodding off to sleep, Rita awoke, and her eyes found me. There was clarity in them—a recognition. I stood, frightened that she'd turn away from me, or become angry and ask me to leave. I tried not to show her my fear. I bolstered myself with a nervous smile and fumbled out some words.

"Hi…Feeling better?"

She stared at me, silent. Finally, with a dignity of effort, she spoke. Her voice was weak, broken and wonderful. "Alan…James… here?"

I felt the start of tears. I fought them. "Yep… Can't get rid of me."

She gave me the slightest of smiles, but it was the smile of a lover, and the beauty of it brought tears of relief. "What... took you so... so long to come... Alan James?"

I grinned, shaking my head. "Well... I'm here, now," I said, taking her hand, and caressing it.

She swallowed away obvious discomfort.

"Are you alright? Can I get you something?"

Her adoring eyes lingered on me. "Will you stay?"

"Of course I'll stay. Always. Yes."

Her clear eyes opened in a wide pleasure. "...Then I'll just sleep for a while..."

I kissed her hand. "Yes... you sleep. You sleep all you want, Rita. Sleep and get strong. I'll be here when you wake up."

Her eyelids fluttered, gently. She closed them and sank into peace. As I eased down on the edge of the bed beside her, she opened her eyes again. They held a warmth and contentment I'd never seen. They held a gala of love. "...Alan James..."

"Yes, Rita...?"

"... I won't leave you this time. No... not this time, my love..."

While Rita slept, I went to the window to watch the sunset. It was a flaming "ascentional" sky, with golden flowering clouds and orange and crimson bursts of light shooting, like searchlights, through great porcelain clouds, down to the red mountains and desert.

Ascension, if it comes at all, will be a slow process, a slow progress. I do not believe that it will come in a dramatic illumination, but in suffering stumbles and lengthening strides of patience, compassion, and self-forgiveness. I suppose that is the way of the hero. And what keeps the hero going?

Hidden within a scented breeze, a broken night's sleep or an unexpected gap of pleasure, an essence of Rita will always awaken and arise, and I will reach for her and want her. Of course. That's the way it has been and the way it always will be.

Simple. I will never stop wanting her.

EPILOGUE

In the backyard, Shane Fitzgerald Lincoln tottered along freshly cut grass, in staccato steps, rushing toward Rita, who was coaxing him on. He was giddy and assured, his face full of hope, hers adoring. As Shane struggled to close the distance between them, I watched from the red and yellow swing-set. I held a digital camera, but I wasn't filming. I was just gently swinging. It was Sunday, the day was warm, the sky was blue and there were no emergency calls.

Rita's hair was long again and artfully tangled by the desert wind. She was barefoot, wearing white shorts and a yellow v-neck t-shirt that invited second looks at her full breasts. She thought she was overweight, and was working hard to shed pounds.

"My ass is fat, Alan James! I never lost those pounds after Shane was born."

But the girlishness had returned and a freshness of spirit that I hadn't seen since Jack's Diner.

Rita had recovered swiftly. I moved to Sedona and spent four months taking care of her. With physical therapy and a second operation on her left leg, Rita was beginning to walk without a limp, although she still had some lingering discomfort.

She was student-teaching third graders, three days a week, and though it often fatigued her, she loved it. There was a pride about her I'd never seen—a pride in herself that she'd achieved one of the major goals of her life after so many years of difficulty.

Shane stumbled on, his mother's arms outstretched. "Come on, Shane, you can do it. Come on. Come to Momma, Shane."

Shane was blond, pudgy and, thankfully, he looked more like Rita than me. He was blessed with her wide, wonderful eyes and glowing skin. Unfortunately, he had my stiffness and tendency to brood.

"You can work with him on that, Alan James. You're an expert."

It was Rita who had first believed in the miracle. Before leaving the hospital she'd told me we would have a child.

"...It's a no brainer, Alan James. Don't you see? All the demons have been released; all the bad stories told and tossed away; all the little hurts and wounds are healed. We're together now and we will have a child, Alan James. As soon as I am well...we will have a child. Didn't two doctors tell you it was possible?"

And so it was that, with medication, exercise, timing, and faith, Rita had become pregnant.

We were married in Hartsfield, five months after

her second operation. It was supposed to have been a small wedding, but a lot of old high school friends and family showed up and threw us a big reunion party at Jack's Diner. Old "Big Jack" himself was there and he danced an Irish jig for us. Betty Fitzgerald had a little too much Pinot Grigio and danced along with him, until she nearly passed out on the floor. Rita laughed for minutes, having never seen her mother so free and uninhibited. Rita had told her only that morning that a baby was on the way: "Alan James and I are pregnant, mother."

Ms. Lyendecker brought champagne, chocolates, and a book of poems by Marie Ponsot. She kissed me on the cheek. "Please come see me again when you can, and bring the child. I'll read poetry."

Shane ventured on toward uneven and treacherous ground. I saw the sudden alarm on his face. Rita went to grab for him, but stopped. She dropped to her knees and called him on. "Just a little more, darling. Come on, Shane. You can do it. Don't be afraid."

Shane persisted, though frightened and unsure. His little legs couldn't navigate the rutted earth. He lost his footing and tumbled.

Rita rushed to him and had gathered him up into her arms by the time I arrived.

He cried out only once. But it was a long, high sound, filled with fear and puzzlement.

"Yes, yes. You're okay, Shane," Rita said, gently rubbing his head. "You are doing just fine, baby doll.

Your Mommy and Daddy will never let anything happen to you."

She rocked him. I looked at Rita and winked.

"You know something, Alan James?" Rita asked, batting those long, lazy eyelids.

"... Yes, Rita?"

Rita kissed Shane on the forehead and then snuggled in close to me, resting her head against my shoulder.

"We should have done this a long time ago. What took us so long?"

The End

ABOUT THE AUTHOR

Elyse Douglas

Elyse Douglas is the pen name for the husband and wife writing team of Elyse Parmentier and Douglas Pennington.

Some of Elyse Douglas' novels include: "The Other Side of Summer," "Time Stranger," "The Christmas Eve Series," "The Christmas Diary Book One and Two " and "Time Visitor." They live in New York City.

www.elysedouglas.com

elysedouglass@gmail.com

PRAISE FOR AUTHOR

Elyse Douglas provides her readers with a fast-paced, emotional, and well-written romance novel. The characters she develops are believable and engaging, but their story is one you might never imagine. A light but very enjoyable and face-paced summer read, "The Summer Diary," is well-written, and the characters felt like neighbors living next door.

- PUDDLETOWNREVIEWS

The true genius of "Wanting Rita" is that the problems are true to life. This is a story that could happen to anyone. It tugs at the heart-strings because it is unfailingly honest and brutal in its honesty. You will laugh, cry, swear, yell, and still keep reading because the story will have you in its grip.

- BOOKS, BOOKS, AND MORE BOOKS

"The Christmas Eve Letter" is a wonderful time travel book and one of my favorite books of the year

- THE BOOK RETURN BLOG

BOOKS BY THIS AUTHOR

The Other Side Of Summer

A Secret Affair that Touches the Entire World…

Joanna Halloran, a best-selling writer and astrologer, lives in a beach house overlooking the Atlantic Ocean. While roaming the beach after a storm, she spots a man clinging to a piece of wreckage, fighting for his life. She dives in and pulls him to safety.

The Summer Letters

A beach cottage holds the key to a timeless love story.

Reeling from her recent divorce, writer Vanessa retreats to a beach cottage to work on her novel — and finds a series of secret letters dating back to the 1950s.

The Summer Diary

After her best friend dies in a plane crash, Keri discovers that she had a secret lover — Keri sets out to find him. When Keri finally reaches Ryan, could she unexpectedly find a new chance at happiness?

Printed in Great Britain
by Amazon